Once Upon a Scandal

JULIE LEMENSE
Author of *Once Upon a Wager*

CRIMSON ROMANCE
F+W Media, Inc.

Published by
Crimson Romance
an imprint of F+W Media, Inc.
10151 Carver Road, Suite 200
Blue Ash, OH 45242. U.S.A.
www.crimsonromance.com

ISBN 10: 1-4405-8664-0
ISBN 13: 978-1-4405-8664-4
eISBN 10: 1-4405-8665-9
eISBN 13: 978-1-4405-8665-1

Cover art © 123RF/jovannig; iStockphoto.com/captblack76.

After the debut of my first novel, *Once Upon A Wager*, I was surprised and thrilled to receive letters asking for Jane's story. And Benjamin's story. Or best of all, a story that found the two of them together. So, to everyone who wrote, emailed, sent a note through social media, or left a message on my web page, thank you so much! This book is for you.

Acknowledgments

This is one of those books where you have to suspend your disbelief and hop along for the ride, hopefully an enjoyable one! Thanks to my wonderful editor, Julie Sturgeon, for not laughing out loud when I first proposed the plot. To my husband and family for suffering through late nights, cranky moods, and a complete absence of home cooking as my deadline approached. To my son Benjamin, who wanted to be in my first book but was a bit dismayed to find himself the hero in my second (since kissing was bound to happen). To Sophia Grimsley, for letting Aunt Sophia show up again. To Jessica Oakley, because she liked *Wager* so much, I wanted to put her in *Scandal.* And lastly, to Miss Violet Coates, who doesn't get to read this for another decade at least.

A side note … As with *Once Upon A Wager*, the majority of the secondary characters and settings in *Once Upon A Scandal* are drawn from Regency-era history. The people, of course, have passed, but many of the settings remain.

Next time I'm in England, I'm going to Painshill Park!

Chapter 1

London, England
June 16, 1813

One young lady, going astray, will subject her relations to such discredit and distress as the united good conduct of all her brothers and sisters.
—Fordyce's Sermons to Young Women

It was a miserable day by anyone's measure, unseasonably cold, with rain just beginning to fall and thunder rolling across a darkening sky. As Jane burrowed deeper into her black, woolen cloak, a sigh escaping the tight line of her lips, she decided the weather was well-suited to the occasion. That was her father, after all, boxed up in a casket and being lowered into the ground. At least her veil hid the fact that she wasn't crying.

Not that anyone was there to notice. Despite having passed only two days ago, Lord Reginald Fitzsimmons had been dead to the world these past nine months, an outcast in Society, a scandal. The wages of sin and all of that. When you maligned a war hero and tried to compromise the girl he loved in the process, you were not well-liked. And his passing had made him all the more shameful. He'd died in a pool of his own blood outside London's most hardened gaming hell, either murdered for his winnings or set upon for sport. The Bow Street Runners hadn't even mounted an investigation. As if she'd needed a reminder he would not be missed.

Nor would she be, if some unfortunate accident happened to befall her. She was all but invisible now, just like her father, a pariah in the Society that had once prized her. Such a paragon she'd been, no less than the founding patron of The Ladies Auxiliary to

Improve Manners and Morals. How amusing to remember a time when friends did not cross to the opposite side of a street as she neared.

She shook her head to clear it. She was not only being maudlin, but also unfair. Not all of them crossed the street. Nor was she entirely alone. Sir Aldus Rempley, Father's only remaining friend, was here at the graveyard too, a small act of kindness, even if he was a good distance away. Beside another grave entirely, as a matter of fact. Far enough away that no one would see him offering his last respects to a rogue.

Just yesterday, he'd sent a note promising to call, along with a bank draft to settle the burial's expenses. She should have refused it, of course, but she could no longer afford her pride. The reading of Father's will had made that abundantly clear. He'd gambled away almost everything in the long, final months of his disgrace.

A cough sounded, recalling her attention to the two men waiting with shovels nearby, the grave diggers, clearly restless. Waiting for the minister to finish, so they too could finish, covering Father's casket with the dirt piled beside it. Returning him to the earth, and ultimately to dust.

She wished the cleric would get on with it. What was the point of praying for absolution when there was none to be had? Besides, the rain was starting to come down in earnest now, pooling in the dirt, sending streams of muddy water into the pit where Father lay. She could feel it seeping into her cloak and through the leather of her serviceable boots. How she envied the enclosed carriage that had just stopped at the edge of the graveyard. The walk home would be interminable. Perhaps the loneliest she'd ever undertaken.

With a dull sense of detachment, she watched as a postilion jumped down, umbrella in hand, to open the carriage door. A man with a multi-tiered greatcoat stepped out, though she couldn't make out his features at this distance. He took the umbrella and turned towards her, coming forward with long strides, moving like a shadow through the descending darkness.

Was he here for someone else? She looked behind her, but even Sir Aldus had departed now. Turning back, she lifted her veil, the better to see the stranger's approach, and her breath caught. How quickly he had come upon her. Benjamin Alden, the Viscount Marworth. It made no sense he was here.

"I am sorry I did not arrive for the start, Miss Fitzsimmons," he said, his voice hushed. "Please accept my sympathies for your loss."

For a moment, she didn't know what to say. He had come here, in the pouring rain, to pay his respects when they were only acquaintances. She ought to be touched—moved even—but instead, she was suspicious. Because Marworth was one of those other people, the kind who'd been born under a perfect alignment of the stars. Parties in Society weren't counted a success until his arrival. When he wore a new style of waistcoat, men raced to their tailors for the same. And he was almost painfully handsome—blond, with the bluest of eyes and classically sculpted, symmetrical features. The man moved seamlessly through life, encased in a nimbus of perfection. Even the minister had stopped his droning, struck no doubt by the appearance of a seemingly celestial being.

"Thank you for coming, Lord Marworth, and for the protection of your umbrella. A moment later, and I would have turned my back on this whole sorry affair and swum my way home."

And what incredibly poor taste she had, to jest at a funeral, to disrespect the dead. She felt so far away now from the woman she'd been just nine months ago. Was that why he'd come? For a moment's amusement, to see a lesser being laid low? To marvel at the depths to which mere mortals could plummet? Didn't he have a party to attend or an innocent to seduce? According to rumor, he excelled at that, too.

But he merely gave her a sad smile and said, "I am sure it is the rain that has kept others away."

"I am sure it is not, but how polite you are to say so."

The minister cleared his throat then, apparently freed from his Marworth-induced bemusement. "May he rest in peace," he said, before ducking away and heading for cover. Determined to move quickly, the gravediggers punched their shovels into the dirt—thick mud now—slopping it into the pit, her father's final resting place, where she doubted there was any peace to be had. Marworth clasped her gently by the elbow, perhaps to move her from the sad scene and towards the carriage.

"You needn't witness this."

But she would not move till it was done. She stood firm until he released his hold. Then she reached down and took a fistful of the mud, and then another, throwing them onto the simple pine casket, which was rapidly vanishing beneath the muck. "My father left me alone to clean up the mess he made of things," she said, hearing the bitterness in her voice. "This is as good a place as any to start."

• • •

Much later, Jane was once more in the home that was no longer to be hers. Gerard, her cousin and Father's heir, had sent a note that his family would be moving into the house on Curzon Street by the month's end. Supposedly, little Violet, his daughter, loved the view from Jane's bedroom window, with its small, enclosed garden filled with roses. So, quite simply, she would have it, along with the bedroom Jane had slept in since she was a child. They would tolerate her as a guest, but not for long. It was the way of things. No matter how unfair.

The house felt so empty now. When they'd been consigned here together, Father had at least been company, despite his misery. She was eternally grateful to Thompson, their longstanding butler, for staying on despite the fact that his wages were overdue. And also to his wife, Bess, who served as cook and housekeeper. Jane was struck again by the irony of it. She was gently bred, of course, but as poor now—if not poorer—than the pair of them. If anything, she should be the one cooking and cleaning. But it was not the way of things, so they would not hear of it.

Really, there was so little she was suited for now. She was more than well-enough educated to be a governess, but who in Society would hire her? And while she could probably give a lecture on Britain's parliamentary system, having learned it at her father's knee, she had no other discernible talents. She painted watercolors insipidly, desecrated any tune, and couldn't stitch a straight line, despite her best efforts. She'd never be hired at a dressmaker's, that much was certain. The one thing she excelled at was being a lady in the strictest sense. But that did not feed you. And how she loathed her self-pity, even though she couldn't seem to suppress it.

All of a sudden, however, a solution presented itself. Thompson entered Father's study and announced a visitor. Sir Aldus Rempley.

Willing away the indigestion the announcement prompted, she took several calming breaths. Because there could only be one reason he was here. She'd turned down his previous proposals of marriage, but she no longer had the luxury of choice. And really, she should be thankful for his offer. He'd come to rescue her from a fate unknown—and likely terrifying.

She ran quickly to her bedroom via the backstairs and rinsed her mouth out with a brush and powder. After a glance in her bedside mirror, where she smoothed her hair and pinched her cheeks, she descended the front stairs with as much dignity as she could muster, to find him waiting, hat in hand, in the drawing room. With a smile at Thompson, indicating they would be fine alone, she sat upon Mother's favorite settee and waited for her future to unfold.

"May we speak privately, Miss Fitzsimmons, or if I may call you so, Jane?"

"Of course," she said, even though her smile was forced. Didn't he realize they were already alone? Their union would be truly tedious if he hadn't wits enough to discern that. It was unkind to think it, but he was grey-haired and paunchy, when she'd once hoped for so much more. This would likely be the man to bestow her first kiss. To introduce her to the intimacies of the marriage bed. A remarkably depressing thought.

"You are looking unwell, my dear. Understandably so, given the shock you have suffered, but you owe it to your looks to take better care."

"Burying one's father in a storm does make appearances difficult to maintain. Wouldn't you agree, Sir Aldus?" Dear Lord, had she really voiced it aloud? When had she become so flippant? Surely, he expected better manners in a would-be wife. Even in the face of a comment bordering on the obnoxious.

He flushed an unbecoming shade, embarrassed perhaps. "One does not wish to speak ill of the dead," he continued, "but your father has left you in a vulnerable position. Alone and without the funds to support yourself."

Really, had it been necessary to remind her? Did an intelligent person ever have to state the obvious? According to Father, Sir Aldus was a man entrusted with state secrets, for goodness' sake. A bit of subtlety should come naturally. But she held her tongue. The one that suddenly wanted to run away with her mouth, contravening their longstanding peace. "May I thank you for your help with his funeral and for your attendance? It was an affirmation of the friendship the two of you shared, and I am sincerely grateful."

"It was but a small thing, the first of many I hope to do for you, Jane," he replied, his gaze disconcerting. "Can you guess why I am here?

"I think so," she said, with what she hoped was becoming modesty, even as her stomach roiled. She could do this. She knew she could. She had no other choice.

"I have a very personal question to ask, an offer to make," he said, smiling intently, looking quite old and oily. Old, she'd reconciled herself to, but oily was another matter. She decided to be bold, though, because the quicker this was settled, the better.

"My answer is yes, Sir Aldus."

She'd expected a smile and a small expression of affection. That dreaded kiss, perhaps. Instead, there was only a look that struck her as sly, lascivious even.

"Do you know what you are saying yes to?"

"I was foolish to refuse your proposals of marriage before. I can see that now," she said, as discomfort settled upon her. "However, I know we will deal well together. Our lives intertwined will be happy ones."

"Jane, you do understand I no longer offer marriage? Your reduced circumstances and reputation don't support that possibility."

Over on the mantel, the clock struck, its clang a dull thud echoing in the room. "I'm sorry," she said. "Could you please repeat yourself? I'm afraid I don't understand." Even though she suspected she did.

"If only you'd not spurned my last proposal, when I was still willing to protect you from all this." His eyes were harder now. "But I can offer carte blanche. A small home of your own, a carriage at your disposal, a lady's maid, a butler, and a modest clothing allowance. I'd prefer a bit more color on your person, however, and necklines that showcase your assets."

She was dizzy with mortification, and for the briefest of moments, she wondered what the members of The Ladies Auxiliary to Improve Manners and Morals would do in this situation. Politely decline? Offer tea and a tract on the unfortunate diseases associated with indiscriminate sexual congress? If only she could be Shakespeare's Ophelia in this moment and get herself to a nunnery, sidestepping the need to reply at all. Although, wasn't a nunnery actually a brothel in the Elizabethan era? She'd read that somewhere. Perhaps a brothel was more appropriate after all.

All the while, he sat watching her, that sly smile on his face, hat in hand, oozing expectancy. He had a bulbous lower lip. If she pulled on it hard enough, could it be swept up over his face and secured at the back of his head with a spike? How tempted she was to try. "Is this how you repay my father's friendship to you, Sir Aldus?" she asked, ice in her veins and voice. "By shaming his daughter?"

"I should think you'd be honored by my willingness to see you set up in a house of your own. I understand you won't long be welcomed in this one."

"You do me no honor. When have I led you to believe such an offer would be welcome? I've been raised as a lady, and despite my reduced circumstances, a lady I will remain."

"Always so proud, Jane. On the contrary, I do you a great honor. You have your mother's beauty, which I greatly admired, but none of her zest. It's unfortunate she died so young. She might have loosened you up a bit."

This was all so hideous it couldn't possibly be happening. And how dare he mention her mother, who'd died when she was only twelve.

"I insist that you leave."

"There are things I can show you, Jane, and pleasures to be had. Better me than a stranger on the street."

"You are a disgusting individual." It would serve the man right if she vomited upon him, for she was distinctly nauseous now. He'd donned his hat and eyed her up and down in the most outrageously insulting fashion.

"I will give you a week to understand just how desperate your situation has become, and then I will return. I sincerely hope we can come to the point that very day, so to speak, because it's better for you to know how it will go on between us, don't you think?"

"Nothing will go on between us," she seethed. "Of that, you may rest assured." But dear God, he was right. Her situation was far worse than she'd allowed herself to believe. And he knew it. He'd discarded all pretenses of gentlemanly behavior.

"If you choose the streets over me, Jane, your fine manners and lofty pretensions will hardly protect you." He turned to the door but stopped before opening it, looking back at her. "Then again, it might be exciting to see you brought low and not quite so proud."

And with that, he departed, as her horrified gasp echoed in the room.

• • •

After the frightening encounter with Rempley, Jane returned to the library, her feet unsteady. Everything in the room was several degrees off center, as if distorted in a poorly crafted looking glass. Or was she the one off center? She'd always been so proud of her place in Society, confident her breeding would protect her. She'd just learned otherwise. None of her etiquette books would offer a way out of this fix.

She sat behind Father's desk, withdrawing a piece of parchment and a quill to write out a list of her options. She was very fond of lists, which were so orderly and concise, after all. Once she'd mapped everything out, things would seem far less bleak.

Option One: Submit to Sir Aldus.

Which she refused to do. Better to take up holy orders, even though she wasn't much in charity with the Lord right now. And given her behavior this morning, He'd probably spear her with a lightning bolt if she dared to try.

Option Two: Throw myself upon the mercy of my few remaining friends.

When the scope of Father's misdeeds had become public, Alec and Annabelle, the Earl and Countess of Dorset, had invited her to stay at Arbury Hall in Nuneaton, away from the palpable disaffection that followed her in the City. But, any day now, Annabelle would give birth to their first child. And besides, one could only tolerate so much marital bliss. When she was feeling less than charitable, their love bordered on the nauseating.

There was also Sophia Middleton, the Countess of Marchmain. An eccentric with a spotted reputation of her own, Lady Marchmain was planning a European tour and had claimed she'd be lonely without Jane's accompaniment. A bold lie, of course, though an appreciated one. But the countess was in Nuneaton, as well. Annabelle was her niece, and while it was difficult to imagine her bearing witness to the birth, Lady Marchmain would certainly be the first to toast it with a glass of brandy. Not that she would stop at one.

Option Three:

She chewed on her lower lip, because that small bite of pain sometimes sparked inspiration. So did drumming her fingertips on the surface of the desk. She also stroked the quill against her cheek and moved the inkwell precisely two inches to the left, because it looked better there.

Unfortunately, Option Three was not making itself readily apparent. Perhaps answers lay elsewhere? Her eyes swept the room, falling to the sideboard not far from the fireplace. Upon it sat the last bottle of Father's prized French cognac, a short glass beside it.

She promptly looked away. She'd never indulged in spirits, and now was no time to start. The very idea!

Then again, Father had always claimed it made a bad day brighter. She'd need a vat of the stuff to improve this one. Setting aside her list, she walked over and uncorked the bottle, pouring a small measure and lifting it to her mouth. Its wafting smell was enough to make her eyes sting. Best to get it down all at once then. Offering a silent apology to *A Lady of Distinction's Guide*—which glowered from the bookshelves in condemnation—she closed her eyes and swallowed. The cognac burned, nearly curdling the contents of her stomach, but she'd not let weakness defeat her. She was far too determined.

Luckily, the second glass descended more easily.

And the third? Well, it was very nearly bliss. No wonder Father had liked it so much. Ladies of Distinction did not know what they were missing!

She'd read that the excessive consumption of spirits led to very bad things ... bilious features and fevers, degenerative illness, and atrophied body parts. But none of that seemed consequential at the moment. She was so glad she hadn't saved the cognac for her cousin, Gerard. He was a bit of a bastard and hardly deserved it.

Dear Lord, just a few small tipples and she was swearing like a docker. Not that anyone could hear her. And wasn't that a marvelous thing to realize? She could think all sorts of shocking, scandalous thoughts. She just couldn't say them aloud. The rule to which she'd always adhered—be ladylike in thoughts as well as deeds—had just been shattered by the lovely haze of her insobriety.

She wished she'd discovered cognac sooner. She was close to crying because she hadn't. Why must men keep all the best things for themselves? Like strong spirits, and boxing clubs where one could purge one's frustrations, and ancestral homes. God save the King and all that, but Britain's inheritance laws were horribly unfair. And very possibly, they encouraged insanity. After all, old

King George had been given any number of titles, estates, and countries upon his birth, and he babbled incessantly now, talking to dead people. Or so Father had said.

She wished she could talk to dead people. She'd ask Father why he'd mucked up so many things.

Why she was being forced to leave their home.

If little Violet, too, would sit in the window seat of Jane's bedroom, dreaming of a handsome husband and the blessings of children …

This would not do, this depressing turn in her thoughts. Perhaps another glass—just a tiny one—would return her to the heady state of her initial euphoria. She poured a draught, although the mouth of her glass had shrunk in size, causing some of the cognac to slosh over its sides. Such a loss! But she swallowed its contents nonetheless.

Really, it was marvelous stuff. Perhaps Thompson and Bess would like some? She reached for the bell pull, but they'd be too shocked by her drunkenness to join in. With whom should she share the pleasures of this sin, now that she'd abandoned all propriety? Because one ought to be generous. She'd not forget that dictate.

Someone known for enjoying sin. Someone who'd already proven he had little else worth doing today. Someone well acquainted with the intimacies the wretched Sir Aldus had hinted at.

It took her a moment to find a piece of stationery and yet another to still her hand enough to write the thing. Even if her usually impeccable penmanship had deserted her, she was quite happy with the note when she was done and rang for Thompson. She had an invitation that needed delivering this very instant.

Chapter 2

Like everything else of greatest value,
sobriety's worth is best known by its loss.
—Fordyce's Sermons to Young Women

Benjamin read the note in his hands for the third time, as if that might possibly change the wording of it and make him feel less guilty than he already did. When it had arrived, he'd been preparing for an evening out, making the final adjustments to a new cravat design that Withers, his valet, called The Pinstripe. It had been more than an hour in the making—an absurd waste of time—but people expected perfection from the Viscount Marworth. Not to mention effortless charm and wit. How long had he pretended to be someone he was not? A lifetime, it seemed. And now this note, a reminder that his time was not his own and that his actions were less than honorable.

Lord Marworth,

Thank you for coming to my father's graveside. At first, I suspected your motives. But I've since decided you are my best and most sincere friend. Therefore, I invite you to join me in a bottle of cognac. Although be warned, it is vanishing quickly.

Sincerely,

Jane Fitzsimmons

He rubbed a hand over his eyes to block his vision of the thing, because the woman hardly deserved the situation in which she found herself or the condemnation that had befallen her. Nor, in all honesty, his visit to her father's funeral today.

He was not her best friend. Far from it.

While there were those who suspected otherwise—people who made it their business to be suspicious—he knew her to be an admirable woman. He'd been there, after all, at the occasion of her downfall, the debut of the luminous Annabelle Layton, now married to his friend, Alec Carstairs. Jane's father had planned an elaborate ruse to destroy them. All because Alec had fallen in love with Annabelle while courting Jane.

But Miss Fitzsimmons had uncovered his plan and exposed it, causing her own social suicide in the process. Because, in London society, scandal was a contagion, killing off not just the guilty but their family members, too. It had been a singularly courageous act on her part.

Really, Benjamin had felt like a vulture circling a corpse today. That slight figure, wreathed in mourning, alone in a cemetery in the rain. Her grief had been a palpable thing. Her bitterness, too, well-earned, because Lord Reginald Fitzsimmons had been an ass of the first order. But was he any better? He'd gone to the graveyard not to offer comfort but to sow the first seeds of a connection, to ingratiate himself and gain her trust.

He just hadn't expected to accomplish it so quickly. Good God, best friend indeed. No doubt that had been the cognac speaking, though it was hard to imagine her indulging in spirits, let alone to excess. Jane Fitzsimmons had always been as stiff and starched as any dowager duchess. Even his best attempts to charm her had fallen flat—and he could be very charming when he set his mind to it. In his line of work, it was an imperative.

Still, the deceit of this left a sour taste in his mouth. She was a woman in mourning, vulnerable and possibly drunk in the bargain. Essentially defenseless. This was no time to take advantage. It went against every gentleman's code of conduct.

But he would set aside his guilt, because he was a gentleman in name only, and her invitation was too good an opportunity to pass up. Turning to a cheval mirror, he made a final check of his appearance and paused. So many seemed to envy the reflection staring back. Was he the only one who noticed the stiffness of that ready smile? It had etched faint lines near his mouth and at the corners of his eyes, each of them cracks in his façade. Turning away from the image, he called out to a footman for his carriage to be brought round. It was too late for self-reflection and past time to find out if Miss Fitzsimmons knew any of her father's secrets. Because there was every chance he'd been more than just a man trying to avenge his daughter. There was every chance he'd been a traitor, selling Britain's secrets to her enemies.

• • •

"The Viscount Marworth, to see Miss Fitzsimmons," he said, handing the butler his card. The older man stepped aside, ushering him into a broad hallway with marble floors and pleasing lines. There was very little furniture in the large space, however, and its walls, covered in a faded cream damask, showed the outlines of paintings no longer there. Fitzsimmons's gambling losses had not been exaggerated.

"Right this way, my lord," the butler said, disapproval steeling his voice. No doubt he'd been the one to see her note sent, and they both knew it was not done—inviting a gentleman to visit an unmarried woman alone. Just a short way down the hall and to the left, they stopped. The butler rapped gently on the door, a female voice mumbling something in response. "My mistress is not herself this evening, so I will be right outside this door." And though the man was at least thirty years older than Benjamin and about six inches shorter, he'd obviously intended the words as a warning.

With a faint nod, Benjamin moved into the room, and whatever he'd expected to see, it had not been this. Prim and proper Jane

Fitzsimmons sitting in a puff of black skirts on the floor, tossing books into a fireplace with the zealousness of a religious convert, and sighing in satisfaction as they curled to a crisp.

"I didn't take you for the sort to burn books, Miss Fitzsimmons."

She turned at the sound of his voice, her eyes widening as they settled upon him. "Lord Marworth, you've come. I'm so glad! It has been a challenge to save the cognac for you, but that's what friends do, is it not?"

And if the whole of her statement had been slurred rather than spoken, he would not mention it. "The books, Miss Fitzsimmons? May I ask what they've done to deserve such a tortured end?"

"These books, you mean?" She gestured haphazardly to the pile beside her.

"Indeed." His eyes scanned the shelves behind her. At least she hadn't pulled all of them down. Socrates and Plato were still safe … for the moment.

"Well, they're good for nothing now, you see. They're books on etiquette and manners, and I've decided not to give a damn about them anymore."

Had she really just done that? Sworn out loud? Society's paragon of all things proper?

"I hadn't known there were so many on the subject." At least a dozen remained in the pile, and by the look of things, she'd been at this for quite some time. Her face was flushed from the heat of the fire, and her brown hair had escaped its tight bun to curl in tendrils about her face. She looked … beautiful, actually, if slightly manic. He'd always considered her an attractive woman, with a high forehead, an elegant nose, and striking eyes. They were a rich chocolate in color, flecked with amber. But he'd rarely seen her smile. One always had the sense she had something more important to do than fritter about Society. And his persona was very much that of a fritterer. Right now, though, she was beaming up at him, and it was something to behold, that smile. It seemed to light her from within.

"Oh, the cognac!" she suddenly cried, rising unsteadily on her feet to toddle over to the desk. "I'm afraid there's only the one glass, but you can drink out of the bottle if you want to … no, I forget myself. That is an impolite offer for such a good friend. You may have the glass, and I will take the bottle."

"That won't be necessary, Miss Fitzsimmons," he said, fighting back a wry smile. "I'll request an additional glass." As promised, her butler was still at the door. "An extra glass and a pot of strong tea, if you please," he said in an undertone. "If you can make it resemble cognac, all the better." When he returned his attention to Jane, she was watching him with soulful eyes, like a puppy. Damnation, he'd always had a weakness for strays, and she seemed more lost than most. It would make his task here all the more difficult.

Speaking of difficulty, she was experiencing quite a bit of it as she tried to pour cognac into the waiting glass. With great concentration, however, she managed it without a spill and turned to face him, beaming with pride, her slender body swaying slightly.

In three quick strides, he was taking the glass from her hand and guiding her by the elbow to a wing chair near the fire. He sat down in a matching chair on the opposite side, determined to get this over and done. "Miss Fitzsimmons, you've had quite an upset, what with the sudden passing of your father. It must have been a shock."

"Oh, yes indeed," she said, the glow dimming in those remarkable eyes. "He'd been so desperate of late, what with the scandal and being booted from the Lords, and losing the income on his lands. And, of course, no one liked him anymore. I think that was the hardest thing of all … "

Intoxicated individuals were often moody, but she'd fallen into sadness so quickly, it was like watching a candle be snuffed out. She was staring into the fire, and he fought the instinct to offer comfort, because she'd share more information this way. Grief usually broke through the strongest wall of reserve.

"And the manner of his death," he continued, feeling like a reprobate. "That was most unfortunate, as well."

"Beaten to death outside a gambling hall." She said it without looking up. "A very sad end, indeed."

"Sharpe's ... I was surprised to learn he'd been found there."

"He said he was going to restore our fortunes," she said quietly. "I'd thought he had plans to discuss with Sir Aldus. But he must have gotten waylaid. Damn the man."

"You've every right to be upset. Your father said and did things he ought not." Betraying his country most likely among them.

"I know that," she huffed, her eyes taking on a militant light. "But I'm not damning my father. I'm damning that damned Sir Aldus."

She had an inordinate fondness for the word. Four damns in a single conversation. Astounding. "What did Sir Aldus do?" It was because of Rempley, after all, that Benjamin was here. He'd reported the theft of the dispatches, sent from the frontlines by Wellington himself. If they ended up in the wrong hands …

"He's the reason I must burn all my books," she replied, tossing another one into the flames.

Obviously, Benjamin needed to be more specific. "What did Sir Aldus do to upset you?"

"He was at the funeral, you know," she said, sliding back into her sadness. "And he sent a draft to help cover the costs of it. I was certain he meant to propose when he came to the house today. He's proposed any number of times."

Unease crept along his spine. "What happened instead?"

"He insisted he was doing me quite the honor."

"Go on," he said, as unease flared into something else. Something darker.

She flushed with color. "He expects me to be his mistress."

How repugnant, to take advantage of a woman who'd buried her father this very day. Pushing aside the nagging thought he was doing much the same thing, he focused instead on the man trying to debase a grieving innocent. It went against everything decent.

"Are you sure that was his intention? It sounds out of character."

"I may be drunk, Lord Marworth, but I am not a dullard," she said haughtily, only to ruin the effect by hiccupping. "He is giving me a week to realize I have no other options."

"No matter what he says, you need not submit to him." The bastard.

"Oh, I'd never submit to old Rempley. But perhaps you can help me," she said, brightening briefly. "By reputation, you're familiar with the ladies of the demimonde, and I'm wondering if that's something I should aspire to. Because courtesan sounds so much nicer than whore, don't you think?"

With that bald statement, she burst into tears. Shattering sobs, messy and unattractive, but they tilted something within him, throwing him off balance. Perhaps it was the helplessness of her situation? Life wasn't kind to women without standing or fortune. He'd always known this, but Jane Fitzsimmons was flesh and blood before him, the picture of despair.

His purpose in being here felt absurd now. He'd been foolish not to see it sooner. If she'd suspected her father of betraying the crown, she would have called him out for it. After all, she'd already done so in front of the ton at great personal expense. It didn't mean Fitzsimmons wasn't guilty, but it absolved his daughter of the knowledge of it.

"Don't cry, Miss Fitzsimmons," he said, moving across the room to pat her rather awkwardly on the back, because he had little experience with drunken women in tears. "I will return tomorrow, with a far better choice for you."

He didn't add that he had no idea yet what it would be.

• • •

After seeing her into the care of the butler and his wife, both of whom had swept in moments later with that much needed tea, Benjamin excused himself, returning to his waiting carriage, his driver and postilion at the ready. But inside the carriage, he was alone with his thoughts. And his conscience.

At the start of the evening, he'd planned on paying a visit to Claudette, his mistress of over a year. She was beautiful, charming, and best of all, they didn't have the messy entanglement of sincere affection between them. For the first time, though, he wondered how she'd settled upon her profession. He'd never bothered to ask, because they generally had far more enjoyable matters to attend to. With her skills, it was difficult to believe she'd ever been an innocent, like Miss Fitzsimmons. Still, the thought persisted, making him uneasy. Only a hypocrite would try to protect one woman from a life of prostitution while enjoying the admittedly inventive talents of another.

A better man would offer Miss Fitzsimmons marriage, but that was not a sacrifice he was willing to make. Not when it would cost him the petty but perfect revenge he'd planned against his father. He could always settle money upon her, of course, but she'd still be an outcast. People would assume he'd become her protector. Alec and Annabelle would take her in, but that would be akin to torture, living in the same house as the man you'd once hoped to marry, as Miss Fitzsimmons had.

Surely there was another option. She was courageous. And intelligent, tonight's behavior notwithstanding. When Alec and her father had co-sponsored a soldier's bill in the House of Lords, she'd reportedly offered insights on its crafting that stunned them both. He knew she was fluent in French, courtesy of her native-born mother and the nurse who'd helped raise her. She was well-read, too, and not just on the subject of etiquette. He'd once offered a snippet of obscure verse, and she'd known the author instantly. He'd memorized the stupid thing to impress Annabelle Layton, only to forget it a day later.

And she was beautiful. How odd he'd not really noticed it before.

There was also the problem now of Rempley, a suspicion that could not be ignored. He'd been one of the few members of the ton not to shun Reginald Fitzsimmons; supposedly, they'd been friends of long standing. Yet Rempley had admitted to Whitehall when reporting the theft that Fitzsimmons was the only likely culprit. Days before making a vile proposition to his daughter.

Over the course of the evening, as Benjamin traveled first to a musicale, then on to a ball, and finally to a card game ending just before dawn, an idea percolated. The more he pondered it, the more audacious it seemed. He'd have to speak with the others, of course. As highly placed members of Society, they knew the circumstances behind her disgrace. But he'd have to convince them of his plan. It would keep Jane Fitzsimmons close, so he could dig deeper into the extent of her father's involvement in the theft of the dossiers. And it would allow him to explore Rempley's role in all of this. His attraction to the woman might prove useful.

But would she do it? Should he even ask? Knowing too much information might put her in danger. As if what he meant to propose was not dangerous enough.

• • •

"You can't believe she'll actually agree to this scheme of yours?" Lucien St. Alban, the Duke of Greystoke, all but exclaimed. Which was itself rather shocking. Rigid and forbidding, he rarely showed emotion of any kind. "Miss Fitzsimmons is a sober sort. She'll think you've taken leave of your senses. And I'll agree with her."

"She's not as sober as you think, but I know it's an unorthodox plan." Benjamin watched the faces of the men around the table, trying to gauge their reactions. If Greystoke could be convinced, the other two would likely follow his lead.

"It borders on the absurd." This from Ian Hampden, the Viscount Torrington, who had a reputation for being direct and also merciless.

"Perhaps, but people see what they expect to. And they generally believe what they're told. It's one of the things we count on in our operations."

"This isn't what we planned," Greystoke said dismissively. They were not friends after all, merely a network of associates at the urging of Lord Liverpool, England's prime minister. On this night, they were tucked away together in a secure room in the basement of Whitehall. "You were supposed to insinuate yourself. Gain her confidence. Find out what she knew of her father's dealings."

"As I said earlier, she'd have come forward with anything suspicious. She's already proven that."

"It's one thing to expose your father's schemes to right an injustice," said Nicholas Borneman, the Marquis of Winchester. "It's quite another to offer up information that will see him charged with treason and hung by the neck."

"Granted, but the man is dead now and thus safe from repercussions. If she'd discovered the dispatches among his papers, she'd have informed the authorities."

"I'm willing to acquit her of any complicity," Greystoke said. "But we know Fitzsimmons was a desperate man. And we know he was at Rempley's the night the dispatches were taken, less than twenty-four hours before his death. I still believe they're hidden somewhere in his house."

"Doesn't this make you at all suspicious about Rempley? His behavior towards Miss Fitzsimmons proves he's not the man he'd like others to believe."

"Neither are we," Torrington said. "I can find him guilty of extremely poor taste but little else."

"What about a marked absence of good judgment?" Benjamin asked, frustrated by their inability to recognize what he saw so clearly. "Why were the dispatches at his home to begin with? They should never have been taken from the committee's files at Whitehall."

"Regardless," said Winchester, "that's his prerogative as chairman. I sit on the same committee, you'll recall. And Rempley has always been aboveboard."

"Well, I find it bloody suspicious. Why did Rempley need to study them in the privacy of his own home, before you and the other committee members had seen them? What are the chances he was in collusion with Fitzsimmons? That with Fitzsimmons's sudden death, he had a convenient scapegoat to disguise his own involvement?"

"I find it highly unlikely," Winchester replied. "While I might be disappointed in his behavior towards Miss Fitzsimmons, I've never had cause to doubt Rempley's patriotism. He was the person, after all, to bring the case to Lord Liverpool. He knows the prime minister has a network that will investigate his accusations, even if he doesn't know our identities."

"Still, Marworth makes a good point," Greystoke said. "Several, in fact."

"If Miss Fitzsimmons agrees to my plan, we'll not only have access to the documents she may unwittingly have in her possession, we'll also have the means to tempt her father's accomplices—if there are any—out into the open. And if Rempley is involved, all the more reason to act quickly. The man is privy to our nation's most guarded secrets, and, I might add, he only succeeded to his post after Fitzsimmons's downfall."

"I realize her present circumstances are perilous, but I can't believe Miss Fitzsimmons will want to play a part," Torrington said. "Why would she be willing to sacrifice so much, when this will likely end with her father being exposed as a traitor?"

"We don't know that for certain," he replied, willing away an uncomfortable flush of guilt. "And I think it's best she not know he's a suspect. We've a better chance of securing her involvement that way."

Perhaps it was unfair. A manipulation of sorts. But then again, little in life was fair. He knew it from personal experience. And she'd be compensated in the end, after all, even if her father proved to be the culprit. She'd have the means to secure a new future for herself, away from Sir Aldus Rempley. That was more than enough, wasn't it?

A low whistle sounded in the room, drawing his eyes to Winchester. "You're a cold one, Marworth."

How well he knew it.

Chapter 3

Nature appears to have formed the faculties of your sex with less vigor than those of ours.
—Fordyce's Sermons to Young Women

Jane awoke the next morning to the sound of someone groaning piteously, only to realize she was the one doing the groaning. Surely she was near death. If only her heart would stop beating already, so the pain cleaving her head could cease.

She'd once read even a broken heart would beat, however, and after a few more minutes of intense misery while she lay still as a corpse, waiting for the Reaper to strike, she realized her heart meant to keep at it. Thump, thump, thump, in a steady and torturous drumbeat so loud, surely even Bess and Thompson below stairs could hear it.

During the night, someone had replaced her brain with rocks that ground against each other whenever she tried to lift her head. She couldn't bear to open her eyes either. But she must do both, because very soon now, the contents of her stomach would empty themselves in a highly unpleasant way. If she didn't reach her chamber pot in time, they'd be scattered all over her counterpane.

Somehow she managed it, and as she retched, she was almost grateful for the privacy of her disgrace. Were her life its formerly well-ordered self, she'd have been forced to go on morning calls today, all while on the verge of expiring from nausea. Then again, in her former life, she'd not have gotten riotously drunk. The shame of it was almost as bad as the nausea.

Dear God, had she really invited Marworth to join her in a bottle of cognac? Or offered that the word courtesan sounded nicer than whore? Not to mention all the swearing. How appalling.

Best to pretend it had never happened. No doubt Marworth must be eager to do so. Despite a vaguely remembered promise of assistance, she doubted he'd ever again acknowledge her. In similar circumstances, she'd respond the same way. As she stood hesitantly, wiping her mouth with a nearby cloth, Bess entered the room, chattering about a restorative brew specially ordered by Lord Marworth last evening. "He said it would set you to rights, my lady," Bess declared, even as she flushed with what was likely mortification.

Unable to meet Bess's eyes, Jane took the brew and a small sip. She'd become quite good last evening at swallowing past an initial burst of pain, but this was something else entirely. "What in the world is this horror?" she wheezed, eyes watering.

"A bit of this and that. Perhaps it's best if I'm not overly specific."

"If you told me an eye of the newt and the toe of a frog, I'd not be surprised," she said, morbidly pleased she could remember Macbeth in a moment such as this. "I've never tasted anything more revolting."

"Still, my lady. Lord Marworth insisted you'd feel better afterwards. He said it'd help with your … ah … recent indisposition."

She would never recover from this embarrassment. To have fallen so far into her self-pity that others had been forced to take care of her. Thompson had practically carried her up the stairs last night. "I do thank you, Bess, for your concern. And … for staying with me, the both of you, when you've far better opportunities."

Bess's brows shot to her hairline in surprise. "Why, Miss Jane," she sputtered. "Don't you realize you mean the world to us? We've been with you since you were a wee one. We'll not abandon you now."

She wanted to hug the woman, but it would be quite out of character, and she'd done enough of that already, with appropriately disastrous consequences. So instead, with a grateful smile, she swallowed down the rest of the concoction. At first, it threatened to follow the cognac right into the chamber pot. Moments later, though, it settled in her stomach, establishing an uneasy truce with her digestive tract. Minutes after that, her headache eased slightly, enough that she could begin to contemplate more important things. Like her future.

As Bess bustled out of the room, Jane decided it was not as dire as she'd first believed. She was not the first woman, after all, to find herself in reduced circumstances. She could move far away from London, perhaps finding employment as a governess in a remote village. Perhaps she could even author a primer on how to fall from grace with aplomb. Surely, with time, she could find a place for herself and some way to be useful. And if she'd once dreamed of something more, dreams were not reality. She'd learned that well enough.

How she despised last night's weakness. It was the sort her father had indulged in, and look where it had landed him. She might have lost almost everything, but she still had her dignity. At least most of it.

• • •

"Are you at home to visitors, Miss Jane?" Thompson asked after she'd settled herself in the family parlor with a stack of Father's legal papers and personal correspondence. The task of sorting it was better suited to the library, but she wasn't ready to face the scene of her shame.

If a caller was here, there was even more shame to come. She was dressed in a light blue gown, which violated every rule of mourning. One should wear black for at least a year following the death of a family member. However, there'd only been time and money for one mourning outfit, and it was a wrinkled mess now, the smell of cognac clinging to it.

"I suppose it depends on who that visitor is," she replied cautiously. "It's not Sir Aldus, is it?"

"No, my lady. Lord Marworth has requested a moment."

Her still fragile stomach sank. He'd said he would return today, but she'd hoped he would save her the embarrassment. Apparently not.

"Thank you, Thompson. I will join him in the drawing room shortly." As he departed, she stood, sighing as she caught a glimpse of herself in the wall mirror. Whether it was vain or no, she generally approved of her appearance. She had pretty hair, a straight nose, and a chin that did not offend. But to say she was not in her best looks was redundant. How could her eyes be both puffy and sunken at the same time? And she was unnaturally pale. Not that it mattered. If one thing was certain in her upended world, it was that Marworth was not here to pay court. She'd be lucky to get through this encounter without collapsing into a humiliating heap upon the floor.

Smoothing her hair, she made her way to the drawing room, moving past the door to find him leaning against the fireplace mantle. And she could not help it. For a moment, she marveled at the sight of him. The good Lord advocated moderation in all things, but he'd not been the least bit moderate with Marworth. He looked like a sculptor's model, his skin kissed by an adoring sun, his golden hair curled artfully around that shockingly handsome face, despite a second day of inclement weather. And his clothes were equally impeccable—a deep blue cutaway coat over an immaculate linen shirt and buckskin trousers, not a wrinkle in sight. Even his cravat was a marvel of beauty. She was an utter frump by comparison.

"Miss Fitzsimmons," he said, straightening to offer a bow. "I hope you are on the mend following your recent illness."

She could feel herself blush. "The illness has passed, Lord Marworth, but the mortification remains. I hope you will forgive my behavior."

"There is nothing to forgive. Rempley's proposal would drive anyone to drink."

With a weak smile, she motioned him to a settee striped in green silk and sat down in the small Queen Anne chair beside it. "I appreciate the convenient excuse, but I behaved disgracefully all the same."

"Think nothing of it. I have done far more disgraceful things on any number of occasions, and not in the privacy of my own home either."

Speaking of things that must be conducted in private, was he here to discuss the demimonde? "I was not myself last night, Lord Marworth." Her heart was galloping in her chest. "I think it best we forget our shared conversation."

He cocked his head, staring at her intently, and she saw something like sympathy in those blue, blue eyes of his. "My dear Miss Fitzsimmons, ignoring one's circumstances does not change them. You are in a difficult position. But you have natural assets in abundance."

Dear God. Natural assets? She could feel a bead of perspiration trickle down between her shoulder blades, eager to make its escape, like a sailor abandoning ship. It would be better to expire here, right on this spot, rather than listen to what he was about to say.

"Rempley made you a scandalous offer. I believe I have a better alternative."

He'd said the word scandalous. Hopefully, that was a good sign. Because life in the demimonde would be that and much more. She forced herself to take a slow, calming breath. "What do you mean, if I might ask?"

"This may come as a surprise, given his reputation, but Rempley is a man under some suspicion. Some important dispatches have gone missing, and I think you may be uniquely qualified to help find them."

"What sort of dispatches?" Did Rempley hold some kind of sway over him? It was hard to imagine anyone having an advantage over Marworth.

"Suffice it to say that in the wrong hands, their contents could change the course of the war."

She pondered his statement for a long moment, replaying the words, hoping she'd misunderstood. But only one conclusion was logical. A dark one. "You are obviously having a bit of fun at my expense, although I fail to see the humor in it."

"I'm quite serious, Miss Fitzsimmons." He was staring at her intently now. "It is absolutely vital they be found."

"And you are ... what?" she mocked. "Some sort of agent for the crown, I suppose? Sent here to enlist me for service?"

"You could say that."

A burst of anger, hot and devastating, surged through her. "It is one thing, Lord Marworth, to amuse yourself by imagining international intrigue," she said, her voice rising. "But it is quite another to involve someone else in your fantasy. I'm afraid I haven't the time for it. If you will excuse me … "

She stood, intent on rushing from the room.

"This is no fantasy, Miss Fitzsimmons."

She spun to face him, as both head and stomach protested the sudden movement. "You'll forgive me, of course, for not believing you. Given your busy schedule of idle amusements and seductions, it's hard to imagine you've the time for anything substantive. Like saving the country from Napoleon. That sort of thing."

"Appearances are not always what they seem," he replied, his expression guarded.

"If you are some sort of spy, Lord Marworth, prove it. If it is your job to know everyone's secrets, tell me mine."

He fell silent then, as she'd known he would. After all, it was never fun to be caught out in a lie. And, obviously, self-amusement was of paramount importance to him. It would be bitterly amusing watching him try to justify his delusions.

"Very well," he said at last. "You are twenty-two years old, with no family left in England to speak of. A generous dowry was once set aside for you, but little of it remains. Your father gambled it away after the incident involving Carstairs."

"Let me guess," she scoffed. "You were the one to win it from him."

"No, I was not," he said, and she hated him in that moment for the gentleness in his voice. The feigned sympathy. "Your mother fled France during the Revolution, along with her family. She met your father in London at a ball hosted by the late Lord Donovan and his wife, Matilda. They married less than a month later."

"It was a love match, obviously. You've told me nothing not widely known."

"But it was not a love match, was it?" he said softly, those blue eyes of his fixed upon her once more. "Not one that lasted, anyway."

"I think it's rare they do." She'd not cede anything, even as the memories came rushing back. The slamming doors and the tears. The way she'd been a weapon between them, when she'd only wanted to be loved.

"Your mother's family returned to France when Napoleon seized power, leaving her alone with a husband quickly distracted by political aspirations and in a Society that suspected her allegiances."

"My mother was not alone. I was with her." And this was becoming far too personal. Not to mention exhausting.

"It didn't help when your mother's twin brother became one of Napoleon's most trusted aides, just as the emperor was starting to threaten Britain's interests."

"That's enough, I think."

"She died in childbirth when you were twelve, along with a stillborn son who in no way resembled your father."

"Enough!" she cried. "Must you utterly humiliate me? How do you know these things?"

"It's my business to know them," he said, running a hand through those carefully disordered curls. "Your father, before his downfall, was an important member of the House of Lords. He wielded significant power. The Crown has extensive files on such men. It needs to know who can be trusted ... and who cannot."

Dear God, if her father had been under some kind of suspicion, she didn't think she could bear it. "Reginald Fitzsimmons had personal failings, but he loved our country. He would never have done anything to compromise its standing. You know that, don't you?"

"There was nothing in his file to indicate otherwise." Marworth looked almost uncomfortable now. "And I did not say those things to hurt you."

"No. I all but begged you to strip away the last shreds of my dignity." She sank back into her chair. "It's odd, isn't it? The pain we unwittingly call upon ourselves?"

"You have faced a number of challenges in your lifetime," he said. "But you've risen above them. You can do so again, in the pursuit of a noble cause."

Whatever she'd expected from his visit today, it had not been this. "This is all so difficult to believe. That you are a spy. In the Crown's service."

"I don't sneak through the streets of Paris in a mask and cape, if that's what you're imagining."

She didn't know what to imagine, given the bizarre nature of this conversation. If this was all a dream, it was past time to wake up. "Would you enlighten me then?"

He seemed to be trying to gauge just what to say. "Do you remember that scandal several years ago, the one involving the Duke of York and his mistress?"

She nodded. "Mrs. Clarke used her influence to secure army commissions in exchange for money, all while the duke was commander in chief."

"Afterwards, the prime minister realized he needed eyes and ears, not only abroad, but also here at home and in Society," he replied. "So I find out who is on the verge of insolvency. Which wife is willing to betray her husband's secrets. Who, in a position of power, might speak indiscreetly for a price. All are possible threats to our security in a time of war."

She couldn't resist a disdainful shake of her head. "You seem an unlikely choice for the job, given your reputation." Not to mention his beauty. Weren't spies supposed to slip about unnoticed? Marworth was not a man who could be missed.

"Is it that you think me incapable of being discreet?" he asked. "Or that you think I'm above deception?"

"I think you are above very little, actually," she replied, only to cringe immediately. "I'm sorry. That was uncalled for."

"No offense taken. I've worked hard to become the charming and urbane Lord Marworth, with an ear for gossip but a reputation for keeping secrets."

"Which, as it turns out, you don't keep at all."

He was still smiling, but his lips had thinned. Had she stumbled upon an unsettling truth? Perhaps maintaining his façade was no easy task.

"Again, I am sorry. I seem more than willing to lash out at others, instead of focusing on my own, rather pathetic, state."

"But that is why I am here, Jane, if I may call you so. I believe you have much to offer. That you can help your country in a unique and unexpected way. Although my plan is not without cost."

"I haven't much to lose, have I?" For any number of reasons, she'd always lived a quiet life, one constrained by convention. But a small part of her had dreamed of adventure. Of doing something special. Meaningful, even. Had the time come to indulge in those dreams? So very few of them were possible now, after all. And she could not help but be tempted by the chance to see Rempley laid low. If he was guilty of a crime, she would love to be the one to catch him in it. She took a deep breath, trying to bolster her resolve.

"I will do whatever's needed. But have you forgotten I'm no longer welcome in Society? I can't listen for rumor and innuendo if I'm not invited to the parties at which they're spread."

"Well, it's true your reputation must be rehabilitated for this to work." He hesitated then and blushed. Benjamin Alden, the unflappable, untouchable Lord Marworth, actually blushed. "It will likely require your imminent demise," he said. "In name only, of course."

"I beg your pardon?" Obviously, she'd misunderstood. Her wits were addled, even if she could no longer blame the cognac.

"When we're done, everyone will remember you fondly. Now tell me, Miss Fitzsimmons. How well do you swim?"

Chapter 4

That men are sometimes dreadfully successful
in corrupting the woman cannot be denied.
But do the women on the other side never corrupt the man?
—Fordyce's Sermons to Young Women

And so, here she was, one week later, on the cusp of her demise. She'd hoped it would be decades hence, but after learning the specifics of Marworth's plan, the possibility of redemption had proved all too seductive. To be reborn, in a sense, as someone else entirely. And if she felt the faintest needling of unease, given that she was about to perpetrate a hoax on the whole of Society, she'd dismiss it. Because there was no going back at this late moment. She'd asked Marworth for a spectacular death—verging on the legendary—and she was about to be obliged.

She'd done her best to prepare. She'd taken all of Father's correspondence—at least all she could find—and reserved a box at the Bank of England on Threadneedle Street. There was another there, the one containing her mother's personal effects, packed away upon her death for her only living child. Evidently, Father had found them too painful to keep close. Either that, or he'd hoped she would forget Jeannette Martine Fitzsimmons altogether. The two boxes were to be opened either at her own direction or at that of Madame Lillianne Martine Fauchon, soon to arrive from France to mourn the passing of her cousin Jane. Not that she told the bank officer that.

When she'd left home this morning, having secreted out a small valise with only the most necessary essentials—things no one else would miss—she'd hugged both Thompson and Bess. "To thank you for standing by me, despite my disgrace," she said, trying her best not to cry and give away the whole of it. "I didn't want to let another day pass without telling you how much you have meant to me." They'd been utterly befuddled by her behavior, because she was not, by nature, demonstrative. But she'd been unable to stop herself. She was about to sever all ties to her former life. Hopefully, her family name would be redeemed in the process.

"So you know your part. You are sure of it?" Marworth asked as they stood, shaded by a cluster of trees, along the banks of the river.

"I'm to jump into the water, rescue the child, and drown in the Thames. Trust me when I say I've thought of little else since you proposed it."

"You seem almost bloodthirsty in the anticipation of your passing," he said, his expression curious.

"No, Lord Marworth. I wish quite desperately none of this was necessary. And on principle, I can't like the deception involved. However, if this is the only way I can be of some use going forward, so be it."

"You are brave, Miss Fitzsimmons. Never believe otherwise."

"The word you are looking for is foolish."

"I know it is not," he said. "Now, once again, the Gardens will open at five o'clock. Prinny will be arriving on the Royal Barge just before seven o'clock. I'll be with him, as will several members of the Carlton House set."

"I'll make sure I'm seen prior to the accident. You are certain this is safe for Jackson?"

"My stable boy is older than he looks."

"This really is the most absurd plan." How could she have allowed herself to be talked into it? It wasn't as if she knew Marworth well. Given what she'd heard, this might very well be a grand lark, cooked up to ease his ennui. She'd pull herself out of the river downstream, and he'd be there with his cronies, laughing uproariously.

But she didn't think so. Not really. In the past week, he'd shown himself to be a capable planner and a master of intrigue, with a serious bent she'd never guessed at. She was merely apprehensive. That was all. God willing.

"I specialize in absurd plans," he said, flashing that blinding smile of his, probably because he wasn't the one getting dunked in the river. And she wished he would stop looking at her that way. Being the focus of his undivided attention was too heady, almost dizzying. She needed her wits about her.

"Remember, you cannot be seen after the cloak is released. It's only a short distance, but you must stay underwater. I will do my part to keep the attention focused on the scene of the rescue, so that your exit will go unnoticed. A carriage will be waiting in the alley that abuts the Vauxhall Garden wall."

"Well," she said on a deep breath. "I'm not sure there is anything left to discuss, although I'll admit to a strong case of nerves." Restless as she was, she could sprint all the way to Nuneaton. Surely she'd be better off if she did.

"Actually," he said, head cocked to one side, "I'm starting to believe you're as fearless as Jackson."

"He has the excuse of his young age for it. I've only a rather pathetic case of desperation."

"Never pathetic. And going forward, never desperate. Not if we do this right."

Chapter 5

What honor can be enjoyed by your sex, equal to that of showing yourself every way worthy of virtuous tenderness from us?
—Fordyce's Sermons to Young Women

It was a temperate evening, dusk just beginning to fall as the royal barge approached Vauxhall's water gate, the river lapping against its brightly painted sides, a light breeze stirring the colorful pennants strung from stern to bow. A trio of violin players, perched on tiny wood stools, played Handel as the boat swayed gently, because on the opening night of the Vauxhall Gardens season, no other composer was appropriate.

"We are glad you convinced us to come, Marworth," said George Augustus Frederick, the Prince Regent of England, known as Prinny to his intimates and as "the worst sort of voluptuary" to almost everyone else. "After the unfortunate Grand Masquerade here last season, we have been hesitant to return."

"I thought it inspired to honor Britain's victories on the Peninsula," said William, Lord Alvanley, in an obvious effort to soothe the prince, who was notoriously thin-skinned. The Masquerade had been widely derided as outrageously extravagant, not to mention poorly planned.

"Getting anything to eat or drink that night proved its own kind of battle," sniffed George Brummel. "I feared a riot, so many people were crushed together, the haute ton pressed against the lowest sorts in their rank woolens. Nothing holds the odor of perspiration quite like wool."

"Any tailor's son will tell you that," said Alvanley, in a wicked slight against Brummel's upbringing. They were friends, but

Brummel was on the outs with the prince. The withering glare he'd just been given confirmed it.

"Petunia gets nervous in crowds," said the Honorable Frederick Byng, clutching his miniature poodle as they neared the shore. People were already lining the waterfront in anticipation of the barge's arrival, jostling for a good view of the prince.

"I hear Vauxhall's Tyers is staging a sea battle enactment tonight, complete with canons and burning ships," Benjamin said. "That's sure to calm the dog."

"Should have left Petunia at home, eh, Poodle?" The prince chuckled at his own joke, his good mood restored. They all knew Byng never went anywhere without his dog. "Jolly good fun, Marworth. You always know what will amuse us."

During the short trip from Whitehall, Benjamin had smiled at all the right moments, pretending sincere interest in the ongoing conversation, while his mind was on the events ahead. He was more than a bit nervous. Surely, only a fool mythologized a drowning, especially given his personal history.

He scanned the waterline. The Vauxhall stairs led directly to the main entrance of the Vauxhall Gardens, London's greatest playground. Jane, though, would be found along the slim walkway bordering the Garden wall, an area usually populated by ferrymen and unfortunates begging for coins. Benjamin saw her just as Brummel stiffened beside him.

"Could that be Miss Fitzsimmons?" Brummel raised his quizzing glass. "Dressed not in mourning, mind you, but in a gown the color of ditchwater and a blood-red cape?"

Jane had just passed by the stairs. He could not help but admire her single-minded focus, one foot in front of the other and head down. The fading sunlight played on her hair, picking out strands of caramel color.

"Disgraceful," Brummel continued. "A lady always wears a hat out of doors. And to be seen, frolicking at Vauxhall, so soon after her father's death ... "

"A shocking lapse," Byng huffed, and Benjamin had to stifle the urge to defend her. After all, they'd planned said lapse. Red attracted attention in a way that black did not.

He cleared his throat. "I understand she hasn't the means to purchase suitable mourning attire."

"Goodness, has the girl not heard of credit?" Brummel's lips curled with derision. "One needn't pay tradesmen in the end. Not if one is a member of Society. Although perhaps"—he chuckled here—"Miss Fitzsimmons no longer claims that."

How easily Brummel dismissed her when he hadn't the means to support his own vanity. His personal debts were staggering.

"Credit isn't extended to women who are alone in the world," Benjamin said, tempted to make an equally cutting remark, with Brummel as his victim. But he must remember to temper his words.

"Marworth," said Prinny, "it's good of you to worry about the unfortunates like Miss Fitzsimmons. But we shouldn't wish those observations to ruin our enjoyment." He slid a brief look at Jane before turning away. "One need not notice something unpleasant."

Had she heard their exchange from the shore? Voices carried in from the water, after all. It must hurt to be so ignored.

But Jane had moved on to her appointed place, stiff with resolve. She really was a remarkable creature to have willingly taken this on, despite its cost to her. Not to mention its inherent dangers. If their plan failed, it would not be her fault.

It would be his.

• • •

As the barge was secured at the gate and its gangplank lowered, Prinny was smiling widely. The gathered crowd was bowing; they were not always so solicitous towards the unpopular regent. Then again, the king's guards were lining the walkway, a colorful if imposing presence. Two sets of footmen rushed up with a small oriental carpet to ease his passage onto the walkway, but just as he stepped forward, his corset creaking, a woman in the Gardens high above them screamed. "Look there! A boy! He's fallen into the river!"

The crowd turned towards the water, where Benjamin's stable boy, Jackson, was doing his best to draw everyone's attention. His arms were flailing dramatically as he bobbed up and down in the currents a few feet from shore, looking helpless.

Benjamin knew nothing was further from the truth.

"How sad," Alvanley said, pulling on one of his cuffs to straighten a crease. "Someone should rescue the urchin. He doesn't seem to know how to swim."

While Benjamin pondered that statement, a splash sounded nearby, and new voices rose around them. "Look there! A girl is willing to try," said one. "Good luck, dearie, and watch the currents!" yelled another. "Such a waste of a pretty cloak," observed a third, faceless in the throng watching from above.

"Sink me," Brummel exclaimed. "It's Miss Fitzsimmons!"

Sure enough, there she was, seeming to struggle at first in the choppy waters of the Thames. She'd dipped beneath the surface right at the edge of the wall.

"The silly gel will drown if she's not careful," Byng said.

Benjamin knew, though, that she was latching onto a tether, which looped around a band that would guide her along the wall. Within moments, her head bobbed back up, and she started swimming with firm and steady strokes towards Jackson, her red cloak trailing behind her. It was a beautiful sight really, her swift movement through the water.

"Save me! Please save me!" Jackson wailed, no doubt to heighten the drama. Surely the whole of the Gardens could hear him. But everyone was fixed on the proceedings, content to let Jane see to the messy business of it. A rather sad commentary Benjamin had counted upon.

"She's being uncommonly brave," Prinny said as he rushed back onto the barge to get a better view from its railings. Rush being a relative term, since his size prevented any real burst of speed. "We wouldn't wish to swim here. The water is quite filthy. Look, though! She's got him now."

And so she had, meaning the real drama was about to unfold. Jane would have to get the boy back to shore and then falter convincingly, so that the currents would seem to carry her off. Then again, perhaps no real acting was needed. Jackson was still flailing as she pulled him towards land. It could not be an easy go of it, keeping both of them afloat.

They got close enough for Jackson to grab a foothold on the wall, cantilevering himself up as the crowd cheered. But in the excitement of the moment, Prinny inadvertently knocked into Byng, and the terrified dog leapt from his arms. Another, smaller splash sounded in the water.

"Petunia," Byng cried. "My darling, Petunia!" Tiny thing that she was, no more than a fluff of elaborately coiffed fur, the poodle was no match for the currents.

Benjamin turned his eyes back to the river where Jane was already swimming towards the dog. And for the first time during the whole of this, he felt a spike of fear. Her arms must be tired now. She was struggling to catch up to Petunia, fighting against the sodden weight of her garments. The cloak must be heavy, as well. Why hadn't he told her to leave off her petticoats? This, they'd not planned.

"Oh, please, Miss Fitzsimmons! Please catch her!" Byng cried piteously. Obviously, the thought of jumping into the water to rescue his own pet had not occurred. But Jane had reached the dog, which latched onto her with all its strength, scratching at her face and hair in desperation. Fighting to secure it beneath one arm, she was swimming on her side now, kicking with her legs, which kept getting wrapped up in her skirts. The crowd was nearly silent, transfixed as she pushed closer to the wall, each stroke slower than the last.

He could not stand here, helpless. He had to jump in after her, even if it meant the ruination of all their plotting. Any moment now, she could become entangled, either in her clothes or her tether, and be dragged below the surface. He'd seen firsthand the power of water, seen how a life could be lost in an instant. He'd understood the risks, damn it, known them, and proceeded anyway with a surfeit of confidence.

He stripped off his jacket, cursing the fashion that required clothes to be molded like a second skin. For an infinite moment, his hands were trapped in the damned thing, but then he tore free, pushing past Alvanley to the railing. He climbed over, just as Brummel called out, "Don't do it, Marworth. Think of your cravat!"

With a spare moment, he'd have punched the man for his idiocy, but he was already leaping towards the river and splashing down, shocked by the sudden assault of its cold, murky depths. Clawing towards the surface, he broke through, water streaming into his eyes, a heavy lock of hair obscuring his vision. Scraping it back, he frantically scanned the river. Thank God. There she was by the wall, holding the bedraggled dog up with both hands, as a man leaned down to grab Petunia, excitement and applause rippling through the crowd. Behind him, he could hear the prince. "Jolly good show, Miss Fitzsimmons! Three cheers of hussah!"

In a rare moment of comradery, ferrymen, indigent children, and members of the haute ton chanted happily in unison, not seeming to notice that Jane had fallen back into the river. Now this, they'd planned, but what if her exhaustion was real? Her head was lolling, as if the effort of keeping it above the water was too much. The tide pushing against the wall was rolling back into her, moving her inexorably towards the currents. And then she was dipping beneath the surface, rising above it with barely enough time for breath, and he was swimming towards her as fast as his limbs would allow, heart pounding.

Twenty feet away now. Her body had turned over and was bobbing helplessly, her red cape spread wide and floating on the water, trails of auburn hair catching the dim light. His heart sped with horror. Faster! Ten feet now. The crowd had gone silent again, at last recognizing the terrible danger she was in. His arms and legs were burning, just as they had on that darkest of days, the current fighting him with every stroke. Five feet. Stretching out, he just caught the edges of her cloak, determined to pull her limp body against him. But there was only the fabric of it and a patch of river grass gone brown, slowly falling into the depths.

For a moment, panic claimed him, throbbing and twisting. But then he remembered this day was not that one. She'd done just as they'd planned, and his relief was stunning. Had he been on land, his knees would have buckled.

Taking several deep breaths to calm himself, he turned, his face a mask of grief as he lifted up the sodden cloak for all to see. "I am too late. The river has gotten her," he cried out. "Miss Fitzsimmons is gone."

Chapter 6

Nature seems to say to us men, pointing to her yet uncorrupted daughters, "Behold these smiling innocents ... they are timid and want to be defended. They are frail ... "
—Fordyce's Sermons to Young Women

She took in great gasps of air as she pulled herself onto the shore, utterly spent, branches catching in her hair and clawing at her dress. Summers with her grandparents on Scotland's coast had taught her about frigid waters and strong currents, but the Thames had been something else entirely. The muck of it had filled her mouth. And she'd seen things floating she hadn't wanted to recognize. It had all been rather frightening, even if she pulsed with exhilaration now.

She'd done it, which seemed impossible. She didn't yet know if anyone believed the ruse, but the sounds in the near distance weren't generally heard at Vauxhall. An almost deathly silence was broken only by occasional sobbing. She felt a bit guilty about that, truth be told. But the dog? Why, she'd actually saved it. The poor thing had been terrified, and she'd seen it safely back to shore. She'd done something good. She'd made a tangible difference and was irrationally happy for it.

Irrational, because she'd just killed herself off from every experience and friendship she'd ever known.

But she needed to stop thinking and start moving. Breaking free of the debris, she edged along the west side of the Garden's wall. A black carriage, free of markings, was stopped at the foot of Coombe's Alley, its horses pawing restlessly. As she approached, the carriage door opened, a fresh-faced maid peeking out, motioning with her hands to hurry. Moving as fast as she could, Jane climbed up and inside. Once the door was secured behind her, they were off, clip-clopping down the street to a destination unknown. Marworth had promised a safe haven, where she could get on to the difficult business of becoming Lillianne Fauchon.

"My lady, begging your pardon, I'm Jessica, Oakley if you prefer. Lord Marworth said to make certain you get out of those wet things."

"But I couldn't possibly change in a carriage." Jane glanced at the small windows on either side of her. "Someone might see me." She could swim in the Thames and perpetrate a lie in front of the prince regent himself, but somehow, the idea of undressing in a moving conveyance went too far beyond the pale.

"I won't look, if that's what you're thinking," the maid replied, pulling dark curtains down over the windows. "We've several hours in this carriage. If you want to spend them chilled to the bone, that's your choice."

It was hard to argue with the logic of her statement. Still, Jane stiffened out of habit. "You can't have been long in service, Oakley. You're too impertinent." She was also very pretty, though, with blond ringlets beneath her mob cap, bright eyes, and a trim figure. She would never be hired in a married woman's house. That was certain. But given Marworth's reputation …

Coloring, the girl pressed her mouth into a thin line. "I've been in service long enough to know foolishness when I see it." She pushed a dress towards Jane. "It's nothing fancy, mind you. Just something comfortable to wear on the journey. And there's toweling, too. No mirror, though. I wouldn't want you to frighten yourself."

"No doubt I'd faint with mortification," she said wryly. "But I do appreciate the dress. Truth be told, I'm exhausted and uncomfortable. Both things make me snappish."

"We'll agree on that, then," Oakley said, although not unkindly.

Changing out of her wet clothes was among the more challenging things Jane had done. Her limbs resisted every movement, the coach swaying as they picked up speed. Her undergarments finally gave way with a sucking sound as she peeled them off, embarrassed even for a moment to be naked in front of a stranger. Oakley kept her eyes adverted, though, packing the discarded ensemble into a coarse cloth bag and tying it tightly with a length of rope. "Hopefully, that will contain the stink," she said as Jane did her best to dry off before slipping into the modest dress, its linen soft and pliable, and a pair of worn slippers.

"Thank you, Oakley," she said once she was buttoned back up. "This makes me feel much better." It was only marginally true, though. Never a particularly good traveler, Jane found that the jostling carriage was upsetting her stomach. She was also prone to megrims—was the dull ache settling in her head the prelude to an attack?

Nearly two hours later, she knew it was not a megrim but instead a strange disease that would likely end in her second death of the day. Her dress was sweat-soaked, and the carriage had stopped three times en route so she could retch, obviously a disgusting new habit.

When they arrived at their final destination—in the dark it appeared to be a sizable estate—she made every effort to smile weakly at the young boy, illuminated by torchlight, running towards the carriage in welcome. But even that smile set her off kilter, and moments later, everything faded to black.

• • •

As Jane stirred, the disturbing figures in her dream slipped away like a receding wave. The images still haunted, though, and she cracked open her eyes to be free of them, only to see an angel standing above her, limned in light. Blinking to clear her vision, she discovered what she'd already begun to suspect. This was no angel, after all.

"Lord Marworth." Her voice was scratchy, a neglected hinge protesting its use. And she was in a bed, dressed in a linen rail not her own, in a room she did not recognize. "May I ask what you are doing here?" she asked, squinting up at him. "And also where I might be?" Glancing about, she saw a pretty room with blue damask wallpaper, silk-tufted furnishings, and a soft-hued Aubusson carpet. But even that cursory observation was exhausting. She felt like she'd been thrown from a horse and dragged behind it until there was nothing but the heap of her, a broken mass.

"We are at Painshill Park, a small estate I own in Surrey. You are safe here, and I am so glad to see you are feeling better. My housekeeper, Miss Banning, has just gone down to have a tray made up." He offered her a tall glass of water, and in that moment, nothing had ever looked so delicious.

Sitting up slowly, careful to keep the counterpane wrapped tightly about her, she took it, swallowing the contents in a long draught. "I fell ill in the carriage. I remember a burning sensation, hot like cinders in a fire, and a terrible thirst."

"You've been delirious for five days."

"Five days!" she exclaimed, her thoughts still tangled. It seemed impossible. Every limb screamed it, though. And it would explain her reaction to his presence. The world had tilted a bit at the sight of him. Instead of embarrassment, she'd felt something quite close to relief.

He refilled the glass, and she drank the contents down once more, the water soothing her parched throat.

"I believe the Thames is to blame. Did you swallow a great deal of it?"

"Far more than I would have wished. It was filthy."

"I'm sorry not to have considered that danger," he said, a tiny furrow forming between his brows. She noticed he was dressed in a black coat and trousers, and her heart stilled.

"Jackson is all right, isn't he?"

"He is more than fine and inordinately proud of his performance."

"Thank goodness. But what of you? I saw you jump from the barge. Why ever did you do that?"

"To be honest, I thought you were drowning."

"I must be a better actress than I thought," she said with a weak smile. "But I will admit to a few moments of fear. The currents were quite strong."

"I know. I once lost someone close to me in a similar situation. A boating accident."

The tone of his voice made her uncomfortable, because for a moment, there had been real grief behind those words. She hadn't thought him capable of it. With his many blessings, what in life did he have to regret? Evidently, more than she'd realized. "I am so sorry."

"It was a lifetime ago in any case," he replied briskly. "But you were brave to go back for Byng's poodle. In fact, in a society that cossets its pets more than its children, you are now a heroine of the highest order. However, please do try not to scare me like that again."

He'd been worried for her. It was a warming notion. Either that, or she was not quite recovered. The curious fluttering sensation in her stomach could just as easily be indigestion. Or more likely ravenous hunger.

As if sensing her thoughts, Marworth held out another hand, this one bearing a napkin and a biscuit glazed with butter. "I snuck it when the morning cook wasn't watching. She will not be pleased with me, but I thought you might be hungry." She snatched it with unladylike urgency. "It's a good thing I pulled my fingers away," he observed wryly. "You might try to eat them, too."

"You're quite right," she said after she gobbled down the biscuit. But he merely laughed in response, and the sound of it surprised her. She wasn't used to making people laugh. She'd certainly never realized impertinence might be amusing. And she suddenly wanted more than anything, even more than another biscuit, to make him laugh again.

Before she could try, however, a beautiful woman walked through the open door, dressed in the sensible grey uniform of a housekeeper, bearing a footed tray topped with food. She made a careful approach towards them, her face angled away. Was this Miss Banning? For some reason, Jane no longer felt like laughing. Surely, any decent housekeeper should be married. She disliked the woman on sight.

"Be careful, Banning," Marworth said. "You risk life and limb approaching our patient with so much food. She's likely to pounce upon you."

"Nonsense, my lord," the woman replied, her voice crisp as she rested the tray upon the counterpane. "Should you like me to sit with you, Miss Fitzsimmons, while you eat?"

No. She wasn't interested in having this glorious creature watch her fall upon her food like a ravenous animal, incapable of asserting any self-control in the face of coddled eggs, a rasher of bacon, three extra biscuits, and a pot of steaming tea.

She looked vaguely familiar, though, this Banning. Images from Jane's dream trickled back. A woman pouring a strangely sticky liquid down her throat and running a cool cloth across her brow. An ancient man, dressed as a butler, standing close by. A footman in the shadows, one sleeve of his livery pinned and empty. Which made no sense. What good was a footman with one arm?

"Did you tend to me while I was sick, Miss Banning?" She was sorry now to have judged her so quickly. "I think you must have, and it was surely an unpleasant business."

"It was no trouble, my lady. I've been through far worse." She turned then, and it was all Jane could do not to gasp in shock. The right side of the housekeeper's face bore a long scar, puckered and disfiguring. It ran down the side of her forehead, slicing towards the edge of her nose before curling back across her cheek to end in a point near her chin. Someone had cut her deliberately, and Jane swallowed past the urge to look away. Instead, she said, "Thank you, Miss Banning. For all that you have done, and for this delicious assortment of food. Lord Marworth is right. Guard your fingers."

And so she ate, thanking them both for the wonderful meal, exclaiming between bites that each new thing was the most delicious she'd ever had. In truth, though, it tasted like dust in her mouth, because the haunting nature of Banning's disfigurement hovered. Not the look of it but the how and why. Once the housekeeper had withdrawn with the remnants of the tray, Jane turned immediately to Lord Marworth.

"If you know who did that to Miss Banning, I hope you submitted him to the authorities at the worst or gutted him at best."

"Are you a defender of innocents, then?" he asked, head tilted to one side.

"I should hope so. I'm appalled by what she suffered."

"I met her four years ago. She was a barmaid at a tavern near my ancestral estate. As you might imagine, it was the most popular one in the village. She's beautiful and kind, as well."

"Why would any human being inflict that kind of pain on another person?"

"She rebuffed the advances of a longstanding patron, and he retaliated. He tried to flee the village afterwards, but the others set upon him. They broke every limb. Still, it was not a pleasant business. She lost her job and had nowhere else to go."

"So you hired her here?" Jane asked, something stirring deep within her. "A tavern wench for a housekeeper?"

"Why not? She's a bright woman with a tremendous capacity. She's learned the job quickly."

"As the patroness of a society for indigent women and children, I applaud you."

"You sound surprised. Do you think me incapable of a kindness?"

How could she say this without giving offense? "I've never heard you express an interest in the less fortunate."

"You never took me for a spy either. I'm not all I seem, Miss Fitzsimmons." But then his face broke into another smile. "In any case, I have lots of news about you to report."

"News … about me?"

"Yes, indeed. I'm just back from London. I will send Oakley up to set you to rights. If you are feeling well enough, have her send word. I will meet you downstairs in the library whenever you might be ready."

A memory beckoned. "Does Oakley have a child? A small boy with dark curls?" The one who had raced towards the carriage upon their arrival.

"She does. Arthur is quite the charmer."

"Is she a widow then?" Housemaids were not allowed to be married, let alone have children, and she didn't want to ponder the likely alternative.

"Oakley is much like Miss Banning. A victim of something no one should have to endure."

He turned then from the room, leaving Jane ashamed of the conclusions to which she'd leapt. And wondering if her heart had just melted a little.

Chapter 7

The world, I know not how, overlooks in [my] sex
a thousand irregularities, when it never forgives yours.
—Fordyce's Sermons to Young Women

When Oakley ushered Jane into the library much later, Benjamin was glad to see she'd lost her unnatural pallor. She'd looked tiny in the large guest bed, swathed in yards of white linen, her hair matted. And her eyes had been shadowed, a testament to the long days of her illness. Now, she seemed a different person entirely.

Then again, he'd never known the real Jane Fitzsimmons. Never suspected the depth to her. Behind the reserved façade she'd always shown to the world, there was humor, wit, and a fierce compassion. She was utterly unique. And he wished to God he'd never discovered it. She suddenly felt like a nettle beneath his skin, a prickling preoccupation.

"You look much restored," he said, standing at her approach to offer a seat opposite the desk. Hair freshly washed and dressed, she was wearing one of the gowns hastily made up in the village from a sample she'd given him. Its soft lilac color was very becoming, though it was far less fitted than it should be. Her face was noticeably thinner after her ordeal, making her eyes seem especially large and bright. Bewitching, really.

"Thank you, Lord Marworth. I feel like a broken teacup pieced back together, but even that is an improvement."

"You may call me Benjamin, you know." But she only smiled hesitantly and settled herself into the ebonized Adams chair, her eyes falling to the stacks of papers covering his desk. There were broadsheets from all over London, several copies of *The Times*, a number of illustrated flyers from the penny presses, and a delicate book, bound with red silk, hand-painted gilt lettering on the cover.

"How beautiful," she said, staring. "May I see it?"

"Of course." A smile twitched at the corners of his mouth. "I think you'll find it interesting."

Leaning forward, she rubbed her fingers along the smooth silk before reading the title, a soft exclamation showing her surprise. "Who did this?"

"The prince regent himself oversaw the design. There were those who thought the color a bit audacious for a funeral program. But Prinny insisted, and he does argue from a position of authority."

"Lady Jane Martine Fitzsimmons," she read. "Born October 29, 1791. Died June 26, 1813, in an act of great heroism, a testament to all that is best about Britain's spirit." She leafed through several of the pages. "I was buried in Westminster Abbey yesterday?" she asked, seemingly wonderstruck. "The prince regent himself gave the oratory?"

"Indeed he did. I was there myself as witness. It was very touching but occasionally difficult to understand because Prinny was weeping throughout."

"I … I find I'm nearly speechless. And you're in black, with an armband. I appreciate the tribute, but surely it's overdone?"

This would come as a shock. Indeed, he was quite curious about what her reaction might be. "I'm in mourning, of course. Society is abuzz with the secret attachment you and I shared before your demise."

"Attachment?" Her bewilderment was obvious. "I don't understand."

"Why else would I willingly ruin a cravat in my attempt to rescue you?"

Her eyes rounded, and a pretty flush of color swept across her cheeks. "What nonsense. What a lie we have perpetrated. I am feeling quite guilty now."

"You shouldn't. I daresay everyone was entertained by my suitably lovelorn display. And really, your funeral was like a theater performance. The haute ton elbowing each other for a better view. Crowds of commoners waiting outside. Petunia, the dog, in the front row with Byng, dressed in a miniature red cape."

"Oh no." She brought a hand to her mouth, perhaps to stifle a gasp. "That is going too far. It borders on the ridiculous."

"You don't know the half of it, my dear. There hasn't been a more beloved woman since Boudicca, who saved Britain from the Roman legions. Some are calling you Jane of Arc, because we like to take things from the French whenever we can."

At that, she burst out laughing, the sound of it untamed. And he couldn't hold back his answering smile. He'd never seen her like this. Yet another surprise. She laughed until she was nearly weak with it. "Oh my," she finally gasped, a hand fluttering to her waist. "Much more of this, and I shall suffer another upset."

"You requested a legendary death," he said with a courtly bow, absurdly pleased. "I'm happy to have obliged."

"Well, it was a preferable one to poor Joan's, I must say." She laid the book back down. "What of these other papers? They're not all about the Thames incident, are they?"

"I merely brought my favorites. Here, let me share some." He picked up one of the penny sheets, which featured an illustration of Jane in tempestuous waters, swimming towards a boat filled with orphaned children, as a half dozen dogs bobbed helplessly in the water.

"Gracious, don't they realize there was only Jackson and little Petunia?"

"Stories tend to be embellished upon the retelling. This time next week, you'll have single-handedly destroyed an enemy ship in the English Channel."

Her answering smile nearly sparkled. "Gerard must be appalled."

"On the contrary. Montford seems to be reveling in the attention. He and his wife were seated next to the prince at your funeral."

"Did he levitate with delight? He has always craved position." But then she blushed again and knotted her hands in her lap. "I shouldn't say such things. We are not close, but we are cousins, after all. I wish Gerard well. Charlotte, too. Her head is filled with bows and fripperies, but she's very sweet. And given that she was Sir Aldus's ward, she has always had my sympathies."

"They are more than well." Already, they'd moved into Jane's townhouse, hampering his investigations. "You've restored the Fitzsimmons name in spades, and, of course, Montford has your father's title now."

He regretted his careless words, because the spark that had so enlivened her dimmed, then flickered out entirely. Silly to imagine it, but the room grew darker as she sat silent for a long moment, caught up in thought. "I am glad, then," she said at last. "It was well worth the sacrifice."

Sacrifice indeed. In his amusement over the lurid press coverage of her passing, he'd nearly forgotten. For him, this was a means to an end, satisfying a number of needs, not all of them implicitly fair. He had not been entirely honest with her, after all. But Jane had trusted him. She'd played her role, but really, it had not been playacting. She'd set aside her former life at his suggestion, with no hope of retrieving it. The weight of it was suddenly uncomfortable, and he grasped the back of his neck, kneading it to ease the sudden tension there.

"Are you ready to move forward?" He searched her face for any lingering doubts, wondering if he'd been foolish, cruel even, to expect so much from her. "Assuming an identity involves more than putting on a new suit of clothes. It is quite easy to lose yourself in the process."

Those large, brown eyes watched him speculatively, and he had the prickling sensation that she saw straight through him. That she was looking for the real Lord Marworth, when he'd been lost long ago. "It's far too late to turn back now, Benjamin."

"You are right, of course." The time had come to focus on the task ahead, not on the guilty spurt of pleasure he'd felt at hearing his name upon her lips.

• • •

Sipping slowly at his glass of wine before dinner, Benjamin waited by the fireplace in the hall for Jane. She would come down soon, Banning having sent word she was well enough to do so. He did not want to overtax her, after all. The weeks ahead would be challenging ones, and if he was apprehensive about them, what must she be feeling? It was not as if he'd be here to smooth her way. He needed to return to London to see the last of his preparations put into place.

Essentially, they'd created a person from whole cloth. The real Lillianne Martine no longer existed. According to Jane, the two had exchanged regular letters when they were young—belabored exercises designed to polish their French and English skills respectively—but Lillianne had died in a smallpox outbreak shortly after her fourteenth birthday. There had thus been no marriage at the age of eighteen to Pasqual Fauchon, an obscure but wealthy nobleman from the north. No Pasqual Fauchon either. He was yet another fabrication.

However, even a suspicious individual would be hard-pressed to discover the deceptions. If there was one thing Benjamin did well, it was seamlessly weave lies with reality. He'd created a convincing new personal history. Forged identification and travel papers. Established lines of credit all over London. And tomorrow, a woman who was no stranger to reinvention would arrive at Painshill to bring Lillianne back to life.

In less than a month's time, the mysterious Madame Fauchon would arrive from Paris. She would bear a remarkable resemblance to Jane, because they'd been blood relatives after all, the daughters of twins. But there would also be differences both significant and subtle. She would take up residence in a suite of rooms at Grillion's Hotel and present herself to thc Bank of England, taking possession of the personal effects bequeathed to her.

Armed with a new wardrobe from the most exclusive modiste in France—a neat trick, that—Lillianne would insinuate herself into Society. It should be an easy task, given Jane's notoriety. As a widow from the Continent, Lillianne would not be constrained by the strictures governing a debutante's behavior. And that was crucial. There was every likelihood she'd find herself in places no lady should be.

This being a time of war, people would wonder what she knew of the goings on in Paris. What was rumored in its streets. And if anyone else was involved in the missing dispatches, they would be curious indeed about the contents of those Bank of England boxes. While Lillianne mingled in Society, listening for rumor and innuendo, Benjamin would have a firsthand opportunity to study the boxes privately.

A stirring from above drew his attention. Jane was moving slowly down the stairs, wearing another hastily made up dress, this one a rose-hued evening gown with a modest scooped neckline. It flattered her coloring, but the cut did little to accentuate her figure. Which was a good thing. He didn't understand how it had happened, this new awareness of her, this ... he didn't even know what to call it. Admiration? It was a distraction he could ill afford. But she was under his protection now, like everyone else who lived here.

"You look lovely, Jane." Setting aside his wine glass, he met her at the landing, bowing over her outstretched hand, just as he would at any Society party. But they were essentially alone, and she smelled of fresh lavender, and he lingered, perhaps longer than he should, to breathe in an underlying note of verbena. Clearing his throat, he straightened. "May I escort you into the dining room?"

"Don't you find this strange?" she said, laying her hand on his forearm. "Here we are, observing all the formalities of a ton function, and yet I am quite soon to impersonate another person entirely, and you are a spy."

A smile tugged at his lips. "I thought you might appreciate a return to normalcy after recent events."

She looked up with her own, rather curious smile. "I am not sure normalcy exists for me anymore. I've slid from one scandal into an even more brazen one. And I am about to dine alone with a man for the first time in my life. What would *A Lady of Distinction's Guide* say to that?"

So she too had noticed the intimacy of the setting. "One of your pesky books on manners, I presume?" They'd reached the dining room, colorful with its bright Chinoiserie wallpaper, gleaming woodwork, and French doors opening onto a stone patio beyond.

"It was my favorite," she replied, sinking gracefully into the chair he'd pulled aside for her. "A primer on the strictest morality and decorum. But it's lost now in a heap of ashes with the others."

"No doubt a well-deserved fate." He took a seat across from hers. "I tend not to trust people who flaunt their morality. In my experience, they're the ones hiding the most shocking secrets."

And just when he wondered if he should not have said it, if she would take offense, she giggled unexpectedly. "You are likely right. I'm an authority on the strictest social behaviors, and look at me now."

Actually, he was finding it difficult to look away. Oakley had gathered Jane's hair loosely about her face, and the softness of it gave her an unexpectedly winsome quality. "There are degrees of scandal, Jane. I don't fear for your soul just yet." His soul was another thing entirely.

As the first course was ushered in, he motioned to Maybanks, his butler, who came up behind Jane with a decanter of red wine. "No, thank you," she said. But of course, the old servant ignored her, pouring a generous portion into her glass anyway. The habit of a lifetime.

"Don't mind Maybanks," he said when she looked up at him, eyes questioning. "He can't hear a thing. Besides, wine is a great restorative. Or so I tell myself. He will give it to me regardless."

"A deaf butler? How does he hear the door when you have callers?" Maybanks bowed regally and moved on to Benjamin's own glass. "How does he answer bell pulls?"

"He hasn't always been deaf. In any case, he has been in service here all his life. He knows nothing else. And he has worked out a clever system with the others, who all help out. He's quite good at understanding what people say if he has the chance to read their lips."

"He's obviously a valued member of your household," she said, her voice gentle. "I'm just not certain I can swallow the wine down, given my last experience with spirits."

"But wine is quite different from cognac, Jane." He was happy for a topic that reminded him of their true purpose here, which he should not forget. "Very soon, you will be a French woman raised on wine since birth. Going forward, it will seem odd for you to refuse it."

"One glass only then," she said with a grimace. "But I will count it as a sacrifice in the name of my country."

"Hardly that." He chuckled. "It's an excellent vintage."

So why was he having so much trouble swallowing his?

Chapter 8

You yourselves will allow that war, commerce, politics, exercises of strength and dexterity, abstract philosophy, and all the abstruser sciences, are most properly the province of man.
—Fordyce's Sermons to Young Women

In the end, she had two glasses because Marworth was right. There were many things she could fault the French for, but their wines weren't among them. Precisely how such a delightful beverage had reached the table when there was a wartime embargo, she didn't know, but it was a reminder he occupied two worlds, one familiar, the other dark with secrets. And as they moved into his study following dinner, she fought back a needling apprehension. Their lovely dinner was now finished, and that dark world was about to present itself.

"I must offer my compliments to your chef on a delicious meal," she said, taking the seat beside his desk once more. It had been swept clean of the papers relating to her demise, and instead, a leather-bound portfolio lay neatly upon it, bathed in the bright glow of an oil lamp.

"Pierre will be most pleased to hear it." He was sitting in a chair he'd pulled beside her. "He once cooked for Bonaparte himself, you know. But the emperor has a violent temper, and when Pierre dared to scramble his breakfast eggs instead of coddling them, he needed a quick route out of the country."

There it was again. That ridiculous warming sensation in her chest. "Has every person in your employ been rescued from some sort of indignity? Some kind of danger?"

He tilted his head. "Rescued? I certainly hadn't thought of it that way. I only know they're an intensely loyal lot, and given the work done here, that's an imperative."

Could he not see that his kindness had earned their loyalty? Hers as well. She had the sudden suspicion that she could be talked into doing anything for him. That she could trust him. And it was frightening, because even her own father had abused her trust. She didn't think she could survive the pain of another betrayal.

"Do you work with others in Society?" she asked, willing away a thickness that made it difficult to swallow. It was past time to focus on the task at hand, past time to remember Marworth was no knight in shining armor.

He nodded. "One of them is arriving tomorrow. She'll help prepare you for your role in all of this."

"I know the basics of it, of course. But how can I find the dispatches if I don't know what I'm looking for?"

Benjamin grew serious then. More serious than she'd ever seen him. "You understand that once I share this information with you, there will be no going back. You'll be as immersed in this as I am, which is a dangerous thing."

She took a deep breath. "Of course. Go on."

"There are two fronts to this war. The first is measured in battles won and lost, the second in terms of intelligence uncovered and utilized. Recently, we gained a decisive advantage in the latter. One of Wellington's most trusted aides was able to deconstruct Napoleon's version of *Le Grande Chiffre*."

"The Great Cipher? What is that?

"An incredibly complex diplomatic code with roots in the seventeenth century. It has flummoxed our best codebreakers. Until now."

"Thus giving Wellington the ability to decipher enemy dispatches," she said, the consequences of it just dawning. "Is that why the tide seems to have turned in Spain?"

"Exactly," he said with an approving smile. "Just a few days ago, a key battle at Vitoria was won because we intercepted a letter meant for Napoleon. In it, his brother, King Joseph of Spain, revealed his troops would be joining the French forces there. Wellington learned how many soldiers were coming and, more importantly, when. He routed the French before the reinforcements arrived."

"And King Joseph's forces?"

"They, too, were overcome, their guns either captured or destroyed. Even the king's baggage train was taken, more than 100 wagons piled high with the wealth of Spain. Not to mention Joseph's diplomatic pouches, his ceremonial sword, even his solid-silver chamber pot."

"I'd have left the chamber pot behind," she replied, willing away an inappropriate smile. "But in all, a tremendous victory."

"Yes, it was. Unfortunately, the news of it sent to Whitehall also included the identity of Wellington's codebreaker, along with his position on the staff, even his current location. And that is precisely the information that has gone missing."

A frisson of dread swept through her. "The man will be in grave danger if it falls into French hands."

"Undoubtedly. If and when Napoleon learns the cipher has been compromised, he'll demand a new *chiffre*. He'll not want Wellington's man alive to decode it."

"And you think Rempley is somehow involved?"

"It's quite possible. After all, the dispatches were in his care when they went missing. He's the chairman of a select committee in the Lords that receives such information."

"I wonder if it's the same one Father chaired. It was the first to be informed of battle movements and reported directly to the prime minister himself."

"Did your father ever discuss the information he was privy to, or bring any of the dispatches home?" There was none of Society's indolent Lord Marworth in the way Benjamin held himself, the steady focus of his gaze. It was almost unnerving.

"Not at all. I acted as his secretary in most parliamentary matters, but he didn't believe women should be exposed to the brutal realities of war."

"Most likely he did not want to put you in harm's way. As it stands, only a handful of men even knew about the dispatches … "

"Meaning each of them must be viewed with suspicion."

"I knew you'd be good at this," he said as he reached for the leather-bound folio. "This contains brief dossiers on the four men, including Rempley, who sit on that committee. As Lillianne, you're bound to attract their interest."

"Merely because of my relationship to the erstwhile Jane? That seems a rather bold assumption."

"As Lillianne—newly arrived from France—you'll have ties both to Napoleon's own government and to Lord Reginald Fitzsimmons, once one of the most powerful men at Whitehall. They'll want to know which side of this war you support. And if our thief is among them, he'll want to know if you're a French emissary interested in Britain's secrets."

She opened the folio and quickly scanned the list within. "Henry Brougham, the first Baron of Brougham and Vaux. Father considered him a radical, but I admire his interest in educational and legal reforms."

"The prime minister doesn't share your admiration," Benjamin replied. "They're regularly at odds with one another. Which casts him in a suspicious light."

"I agree." She continued down the list. "William Lamb, the Viscount Melbourne. A strong voice in the Lords, despite the scandal surrounding his wife."

"An unstable woman given to histrionics. She once had her sights set on me, but thankfully, she's moved on to Lord Byron."

"Nicholas Borneman, the Marquis of Winchester," Jane said, dismissing the odious Caroline Lamb, whom she'd never liked anyway. "He's a bit of a mystery to me. Very handsome, of course, but taciturn."

"Handsome, is he? I must tell him you think so."

When she looked up in horror, there was a smile playing along his lips. "Winchester will be working closely with us in this. He's an associate and our eyes and ears on the committee."

She looked to the last name listed. "Rempley," she said, not bothering to keep the disdain from her voice. "How nice it would be if he were our thief."

"He'll be the first committee member to seek you out."

"Why is that?"

"There's no denying he's attracted to you. I think he'll be equally attracted to your French cousin."

The thought of enduring Rempley's leering, sidelong glances made her feel faintly sick. But she would need to draw him out, engage him in conversation, and find out what, if anything, he was hiding. "Regardless of who our thief might be, I think he's motivated by money."

Benjamin tilted his head, his gaze assessing. "What makes you say that?"

She closed the folio, the magnitude of what she'd taken on suddenly inescapable. "If he were a French sympathizer, the dispatches would already be in enemy hands."

• • •

As Benjamin escorted Jane down the darkened hallway towards her room, he listened to the gentle swish of her skirts upon the floor, thankful for the distracting sound. He usually made every effort to avoid this wing of Painshill and the bedrooms at its end. As a little boy, he'd had the last one on the left, while Aiden, his brother, had occupied the one on the right. If he closed his eyes, he could still hear the ghost of their laughter.

He'd adored his brother, who had faced his many physical challenges with such courage. A gentle soul, there was no doubt he'd have grown into a far better man than Benjamin was. Had he lived, he might even have courted a woman like the one walking beside him. Aiden would never have lured her into serving his interests with half-truths, no matter the goal. God in heaven, please let Reginald Fitzsimmons prove to be innocent of the crimes they suspected.

"May I ask you an inappropriate question?"

"Inappropriate? Jane Fitzsimmons?" he asked, forcing a lightness into his voice that he did not feel. "Will I survive the shock of it, do you think?"

She laughed softly. "I thought we'd established earlier that I've freed myself from convention. I'm dancing my way towards perdition as we speak."

"By all means, then. Ask away."

"Why did you become a spy?"

Ah. A complicated question, that. He was tempted to tell her the truth, to share the burden of it, because he had a feeling she would understand. But that was an intimacy he could ill afford. If he gave up even one piece of himself to her, others would surely follow, until he crumbled like a house of cards.

So he replied with studied nonchalance. "To stave off boredom."

She stopped at that, her eyes shaded with something like disappointment. "I expected a different answer."

"Really? And what would that be?"

"To right a wrong," she said, as if it was the most obvious thing in the world. "To make something good out of something bad."

Dangerous. Yet another new word to describe her. If he weren't careful, she would discover all of his secrets.

"Is that why I'm here? Enjoying your delightful company during a time of war, while others fight in my place?" He hoped she'd missed the bitterness in his voice. There had been wrongs in abundance to atone for, but Father had not wanted to risk his heir. His golden child.

"I think you are here because you have responsibilities you must bear." She was looking up at him, her face limned in the glow of the candle he carried. "And people who rely on you. I would never have guessed it before."

"Guessed what?" he asked casually, though his body had stiffened.

"That you were such an ardent defender of the dispossessed. That there was so much more substance to you. You're a very good man, Benjamin Alden."

He forced a chuckle as something cracked inside him. "You give me far too much credit, my dear. And we have a busy morning ahead of us. We should both get some rest." They were just outside her door, and the two of them were alone, mere inches apart. Such an innocent she was, not to realize the danger that threatened. A darkness was yawning within him, and it would be so easy to lean down and press his lips to hers, to discover if they were as soft and delicious as they looked. If they could banish the darkness. Did she even have a sense of how tempted he was to try?

But she merely smiled and uttered a soft good night, opening her door and shutting it fast behind her. Leaving him alone in the hall, wishing she hadn't imbued him with false honor. Because he planned to retire to his study downstairs with a bottle of port, where he would chase away his demons by imagining her body, naked to his touch.

Chapter 9

What words can express the impertinence of a female tongue, let loose into boundless loquacity?
—Fordyce's Sermons to Young Women

The next afternoon, Jane slipped down the stairs to the empty hall. It was a long, wide room with a stone floor and an enormous fireplace, intricately carved wainscoting, and a coffered ceiling. What should have been a cold and forbidding space, however, had been warmed with thick carpets, striped silk-covered walls, and bowls of fresh flowers set atop the mahogany tables bracketing the fireplace.

She'd been promised a home of her own after this was done, a modest property of her choosing, where she could begin anew with enough funds to settle her peaceably. A fresh start and hopefully a happy one, a payment for services rendered to the crown. But on this bright day, she was glad to be here. Banning had given her a brief tour of the estate after breakfast, and unsettled as she was, caught between her past and her future, this house felt like a refuge, despite its secretive purpose.

Was it the same for Benjamin? She'd learned he'd spent his summers here as a child, but that later, the house had been closed up by the last viscount, its staff relocated to other family properties. Benjamin must have fond memories then, to return here. And no wonder. They were not far from the sea. The salty tang of it scented the air. And according to Banning, Painshill Park was a masterpiece of landscape design. There was a large serpentine lake to swim in, vast parklands to roam, and hillsides scattered with Roman follies. She hadn't yet had the chance to explore them. That was not her purpose here, after all. But she could see the lake from her bedroom window. If the weather grew much warmer, she would sneak a swim. No doubt Benjamin must have done the same on more than one occasion.

What had he been like as a little boy? Mischievous, certainly. Most of the witty people she knew had started out that way. And charming, too, able to flatter and cajole. He would have learned early on that he could make people do and say the things he wished. What must it have been like, to hold everyone's hearts in his little hands? What must it be like now, to have so much influence over the thoughts and opinions of others?

In these few short weeks, she'd learned he was not the person he presented to the world. And she did not mean his profession. There was a generosity of spirit she'd never suspected. A creativity. An innate goodness. And oddly enough, an incongruous vulnerability. Did other people see it?

He made her feel her opinions mattered. That he valued her intelligence. Last night at dinner, he'd been amused by their conversation. He even seemed to find her quite pretty, though she hesitated to think it. Certainly, she'd caught him looking at her when he had no need to. And there had been that moment, last night in the hall, when she'd thought he would kiss her. Her heart had nearly stopped in anticipation. But of course, nothing had happened.

A stirring behind her caused Jane to turn. Jonas, the footman, was struggling with a heavy trunk as he made his way down the stairs, and she fought back the instinct to offer help. He'd lost an arm during the war, according to Banning, but a proud solider would not suffer the assistance of a woman, especially when two able-bodied footmen followed behind him, carrying traveling cases with ease. They were handsome leather cases embossed with Benjamin's initials.

He was leaving, then. She'd not known he would be going so soon, and the realization made her inexplicably sad. Perhaps that was why, even when the clang of a door knocker sounded twice, she stood rooted to her spot. As Maybanks ambled towards the front door, urged on by a housemaid, she simply watched, only distantly curious about who had come to call.

Had she been a gambler, like her father, she would have bet a fortune against the arrival of the person who next appeared. And she'd have lost it. What was Lady Sophia Middleton, Countess of Marchmain, doing here? Not that Jane had time to ponder the fact. She was supposed to be dead, after all. She turned to make a quick escape, but already she'd been spotted. "My darling Jane. How lovely to see you again."

Dear God, what to do? The countess was a Society fixture, albeit a faintly notorious one. If she answered as Jane, all of Benjamin's carefully wrought plans would be finished before they'd even begun. "*Je m'excuse, madame*," she said, trying to think quickly, shrinking in upon herself in an effort to look shorter. Anything to seem different. "*Je ne suis pas* … I am not who you think. *Je m'appelle Madame Fauchon.*"

If the countess's expression was anything to go by, it had been a terrible bit of acting.

"You speak French beautifully," she said, waving a dismissive hand. "But there's no need for pretense. At least not yet."

Pretense? Could Lady Marchmain possibly know the reason Jane was here? She couldn't take that risk. "Have we met, *madame*?" she asked, pushing her voice an octave higher.

"Didn't Marworth tell you to expect me?" She offered Maybanks a dazzling smile. In her middle age, the countess was still strikingly beautiful, and the old butler blushed. "Hasn't that wretched man told you anything?"

"Wretched? How you wound me, Sophia." Benjamin emerged from his study, dressed in a fitted, bottle-green riding coat, a snowy linen shirt, fawn buckskin trousers, and gleaming Hessian boots. "Not only do I find you flirting with my butler when you know how jealous I am, I also find you poisoning Miss Fitzsimmons's good opinion of me when I've worked so hard to earn it."

"Pay him no mind, Jane," Lady Marchmain said with a sly smile as he bent over her hand. "Marworth doesn't have to work hard at anything. It all comes effortlessly. We're the ones tasked with putting his preposterous plan into place."

"Do you remember the associate whom we spoke of last evening?" he asked Jane, eyes twinkling.

Annabelle's Aunt Sophia? The woman who'd buried three husbands and drank brandy like a sailor? The woman who'd caused a scandal on nearly every continent? She, too, was a spy? Was anyone in Society the person they seemed? Jane opened her mouth to speak, but nothing came out. Nothing made sense any more.

"Try to hide your surprise, my dear. The ability to mask your emotions is an important skill."

"Does Annabelle know?" she asked when she'd regained her voice.

"There's no need. I was at this long before she and I found each other. I do regret the years we missed, but what an adventure it has been. You're in for a treat."

"Sophia worked on the continent for us," Benjamin continued. "And she leapt at the opportunity to help you."

"I admire you, my dear. And I am so happy you've found a calling for your many talents. While Marworth is away, we're going to turn you into the darling of London Society."

This was moving too quickly. She'd known in the abstract what the next weeks would hold, but she suddenly felt lost, grasping for tethers along the shore. Perhaps noticing her distress, Benjamin came forward to take her hands. "There are leads to be followed in the city," he replied. "Besides, I'll be better able to judge your readiness if I'm not watching the process on a daily basis."

It made sense, but when he withdrew his hands, a fleeting touch, she felt the loss of their warmth. Because he would not be returning for her. He'd be coming back to Painshill for Lillianne Fauchon.

How foolish she'd been to imagine even for a moment that a closeness had been building between them. They were united in a common purpose and nothing more.

"You look a little pale, my dear," Lady Marchmain said, eyeing them both candidly. "I know just the thing for it." Turning to Maybanks, she formed one hand into something resembling a glass and made a drinking motion. With an adoring smile, the butler nodded and turned away. "He's off for the brandy then."

• • •

Leaning against the window frame, Benjamin watched as Jane nursed her brandy, seemingly lost in thought. They were once more in his study, a reprieve from the bustle of the hall, and he could not miss the faint look of worry she wore. He wished he could reassure her, tell her all would be well. He had the utmost faith in her abilities. But he could not, in truth, predict how any of this would end. And he needed to return to London. Already, the final weeks of the Season were upon them. Society would thin out as families left the heat of the city, and he needed to spread the news of Lillianne's impending arrival. Bait for a hook, as it were. Or, in this case, bait for a traitor.

"We shall miss you quite desperately, Benjamin," Sophia said as she poured herself a second measure of brandy. "Rest assured, though, we'll be hard at work. I've no doubt Jane will be a quick study."

"I share your confidence, of course," he said as Jane looked up, offering him a brave smile she seemed far from feeling. "But I'd like to emphasize several things before I depart." He moved from the window to take the seat beside her. "As we've discussed, Lady Marchmain will oversee some changes to your appearance. There will be a new hairstyle, of course … "

"And very discreet cosmetics," Sophia added between sips.

"A new wardrobe is already on its way from Paris," he continued. "And while I expect alterations will need to be made, Oakley is remarkably talented with a needle. She'll make quick work of any changes."

"A Parisian wardrobe?" Jane asked, setting aside her brandy. "However did you manage that?"

"We have a relationship with the leading modiste there." He had little doubt that in LeRoy's designs, she would look very French and very beautiful. He would have to be on guard against the effect.

"Come now, Benjamin," Sophia admonished. She'd taken his place at the window. "Tell Jane how you managed it."

"The contact was made through my chef, Pierre," he said. "Monsieur LeRoy has a famous shop on the Rue Richelieu, and by all accounts, he's an unpleasant man and a terrible snob. He is also a close confidante of the Empress Josephine, however, and once told Napoleon he didn't spend enough money on his wife's clothes."

Jane chuckled beside him, her eyes bright with amusement. "That seems foolish, given what you've told me about the emperor."

"Undoubtedly, but LeRoy is apparently a genius. He dresses the entire French court, where no one is allowed to wear the same ensemble twice. His seamstresses work around the clock."

"And one of them has secreted out an entire wardrobe?" Jane asked, clearly impressed.

"Packed up with Monsieur LeRoy's blessing. He's never forgiven Napoleon for divorcing Josephine in order to marry Marie-Louise of Austria. So he sent word, though our channels, that a particularly large order had been placed by someone in the new empress's inner circle. As long as he's paid for his work, he's happy to claim it's gone missing."

"Leaving Marie-Louise short of one of her ladies in waiting," Sophia interrupted, smiling broadly. "A rather delicious revenge, don't you think? And according to LeRoy, your sizes match up perfectly."

"You've thought of everything, it seems." Jane was looking down at her hands, knotted in her lap. "And you've gone to such expense. I hope I can carry off my part in all this."

She was far more mercurial than he would ever have guessed, emotions flitting across a face he'd once considered impassive. Why had she hidden so much of herself from the world? "Here is the important part to remember," he said, resisting the urge to pull her hands into his own. "People will still think of Jane Fitzsimmons whenever they see you as Lillianne. We can't change that. Therefore, the way you act will be the thing that sells the ruse. From your personality to your mannerisms to the way you carry yourself—all must be demonstrably different."

"I think I can manage it." But she looked overwhelmed. And it suddenly seemed a crime to change anything about her when he admired her far too much the way she was. Not that he could ever act upon it or tell her why, if it ever came to that.

"Even the smallest things will help," he said gently. "Smiling more often and letting people hear you laugh. Drawing attention to yourself. Being inappropriate on occasion."

"Did I really have such a dour reputation?"

"Perhaps I am overstating things. I only know that while in Society, you rarely laughed or smiled around me." It had frustrated him to no end.

"That's because in our previous interactions, you always did your best to annoy me. You were an outrageous flirt."

"Never that, Jane," he said with a quick smile. "But you were always so serious and, thus, a temptation I could not resist. I wanted to unbend you a little."

"Really?" She looked genuinely surprised. "I've never considered myself a tempting sort."

If only she knew. "So says the most dangerous kind of woman. No doubt Eve told Adam the same thing before he fell." A light cough sounded, reminding him that the countess was still in the room.

"Well," Sophia said after a long moment spent watching them carefully. "Quite a friendship seems to have grown up between you. I'm happy to see it."

Friendship. He could better live with himself if that was the right word. But would a friend spend hours thinking about the way she pulled her lower lip into her mouth when she was nervous? The sway of her hips as she moved? The curve of her cheek when she smiled? Those were just a few of the many reasons he needed to return to London. And quickly.

Chapter 10

Dress with decency and moderation. Never aspire above your state, so as to hinder or preclude works of mercy.
—Fordyce's Sermons to Young Women

"Such a handsome one, that Marworth," Lady Marchmain declared later, as they stood in the cobbled courtyard outside of Painshill's manor house, watching Benjamin and his horse fade into the distance. He'd elected to ride ahead of his carriage, obviously eager to depart. "The journey here from Nuneaton was unspeakably tedious. But the chance to admire him has brightened my day considerably."

Nuneaton. Caught up in all that had transpired over the past few weeks, Jane had nearly forgotten. "How are Alec and Annabelle?" she asked as they turned towards the house. "Has the baby been born safely?" How could she not have asked sooner?

"Baby Gareth is nearly a month old, a beautiful creature, as one would expect, given his parents. And a great comfort to them at this difficult time."

"Is anything wrong?" Childbirth was fraught with complications, yet surely a month was enough time to see Annabelle past any danger?

"They are mourning your loss, of course. Heroic though it was, the news of it has left both of them quite distraught. They don't know you are more than fine, safely ensconced in an estate in Surrey."

Nor could she tell them, Jane realized with numbing finality as they ascended the broad stairs leading to the manor and crossed through the doorway. "I'm afraid I didn't consider I might be missed, that I might hurt those I care for."

Sophia stopped. "Marworth hasn't told me the whole of this, and truthfully, it is better that way. I only know you've agreed to help recover critically important information. And that you made a very difficult decision in order to do so."

"At the time, I didn't think I had another choice, but I was wrong." She would not give in to this urge to sag under the enormity of what she'd done. "I was blinded by my desire for a new start. The chance, if you will, to escape from myself."

"We are not so different, you and I," the countess said gently. "When my first husband, the Marques de Vallado, died prematurely, I found myself alone in Spain, with no one to turn to. I'd alienated my family when I married him."

"But surely they'd have welcomed you back to England?"

"Perhaps, but I had no interest in being bound up once more by the strictures of Society. Like you, there was no going back, only forward."

"If only I had a clearer sense of what lies ahead and where it might lead me."

"Therein lies the adventure, my dear. My way forward led me to Capri, to my darling Stephano. And when he died, it led me to Paris just before Bonaparte took control in the coup of 18 Brumaire. Already, tensions were mounting with Britain, and I saw an opportunity to be useful."

"With a coup underway, I'd have been on the first boat back to England."

"I doubt that, Jane. You, too, would have recognized the chance to work for a greater cause. I'd already drawn the eyes of several men in the new consulate, you see. Bonaparte himself had made overtures. And it would have been a shame not to use that interest to my country's advantage."

Her mind stumbled over the implications as she gasped. "You had a liaison with Napoleon Bonaparte?" How naïve she must sound.

But Lady Marchmain merely laughed. "No, my dear, I did not. He's an odious little toad, no higher than my shoulder. But he's susceptible to flattery, like most men in positions of power. They welcome the chance to talk about themselves and the things they do. The trick is knowing what to listen for. And that is one of the things I'm here to help teach you."

"Benjamin believes my notoriety as Jane's cousin will help me attract the interest of a possible traitor. But I've never been very good at holding a man's attention." She had five Seasons behind her to prove it.

"Lucky then, that you have an expert to show you how."

• • •

Becoming someone else was harder than she'd expected, because for all her breezy airs, Sophia Middleton was a demanding taskmaster. At least an hour each morning was spent studying French customs and culture. Another hour was spent speaking the language with Pierre, Marworth's talented chef, because while Jane was fluent, she'd needed to brush up on colloquialisms to make her speech more natural. Somehow, several recent copies of *Le Moniteur*, the most popular news-sheet in Paris, had made their way to Painshill, and she scanned them for the city's political and social intrigues. She studied maps and landmarks, not to mention the most popular shops and meeting places. No detail was too small to overlook.

It helped she'd had an early foundation in the culture. Mother had been inordinately proud of her French heritage and had spent many long hours teaching Jane the history of her native land. Father, in turn, had responded by inundating her with information about all things British—from the nation's history to the intricacies of its legislative system, in which he'd gloried. Because there'd been no such thing as a common ground between her parents. The war in her home had been as real as the one being fought across the Channel.

But she would not think of it now. Better to be thankful she'd always been a quick study. Both sets of lessons had come easily, and they were serving her well in her work with Sophia. Far more challenging were the lessons focusing on her behavior, the ways she moved and spoke. As both Benjamin and Sophia had stressed, these changes would make the most difference. Hundreds of people—from paupers to the prince—had witnessed her death in the murky waters of the Thames. She must do nothing to make them doubt their own eyes.

"Try again, my dear," Sophia urged from the settee in the drawing room. "Remember, every movement must be made more languid. You are a sophisticated woman of the continent."

For the tenth time, she walked from the doorway to the chair beside Sophia's, focusing on the slow sway of her hips, which she matched to the flutter of the fan she carried. She allowed her eyes to carelessly sweep the room before settling on the countess and then inclined her head, as she'd been taught to do, using her fan to hide her frown.

She would never master this.

"Don't look so grim. Let humor dance in your eyes. It will make the men wonder what you are thinking."

"I am thinking I look ridiculous," she replied, flopping into a silk-tufted chair.

"Not at all. You've improved immeasurably since the start. But be more aware of your charms. Have confidence in them! Nothing is more attractive in a room full of simpering Society misses. And we are trying to attract attention, after all."

"I'm sure I've never simpered." The very idea bordered on the offensive.

"No, you're more likely to have argued politics, which is just as bad."

"But I understand politics," Jane said, not a little stung. It had been her father's great passion, after all. "Can't women offer their opinions on matters of national importance?"

"Of course, but a little subtlety is required in the way we present them. You must first appeal to a man's masculinity. You must slip beneath his defenses if you want to learn his secrets. It's what the art of flirtation is all about."

"An art I've never understood." She sighed. "It feels unnatural."

"Nonsense, my dear. There's nothing more natural in all the world. Our feminine attributes are God-given, and they are a source of tremendous power. You just haven't been shown how to use them properly."

"So the secret to capturing a man's interest lies in the sway of my hips? That's rather deflating."

"There might be more to it than that," Sophia said with a laugh. "But it's not a bad place to start. Men are fascinated by the female body. Even the glimpse of an ankle can send them into raptures. Did you know Prince Talleyrand once wrote an ode to the arch of my left foot?"

Such an odd look of contentment had settled on Sophia's face that Jane had to ask the question. "Had he ever seen your left foot?" Women hardly walked about in public without their slippers on.

"But of course! I'd balanced a cluster of grapes on its arch so he could nibble on the fruit."

To that, Jane had no response. At least none to disguise how shocked she was. Sophia had said it so casually, as if such actions were as commonplace as leaves on the trees. Fruit and feet. Who could have guessed?

"Flirtation is a game, my dear. The trick to it is finding which action will draw a man to you. It might be the tilt of your chin. The way you hold your head. How you laugh. Even your eyelashes batting, although that is dreadfully overdone."

"I can't see Marworth being taken in by such tricks." The words had spilled out before she could stop them.

"Marworth is a man like any other, Jane. But he steers clear of entanglement, for reasons entirely his own."

"If one believes the rumors, he's had liaisons with half of the ladies in London." She hoped she sounded nonchalant rather than morbidly curious.

"Half of them have probably tried. However, he doesn't poach on other men's wives, and he certainly doesn't go after innocents."

Which she was. Emphatically. But that didn't mean that during five Seasons, she hadn't wondered what it would feel like to have her lips claimed by a man, their bodies so close, their breaths intermingled.

She took her place once more by the doorway, trying to remember this was a new beginning and that she could be anyone she dared to be. Biting on her lower lip, she straightened her shoulders, lifting her chin and fan.

This time, she imagined he sat before her, his eyes alight with interest as they fell on the swell of her bodice. The nape of her neck. Even her ankles, if not the arches of her feet. Lowering her fan, she brushed the top of it across her lips, imagining it was Benjamin's mouth touching hers.

A sharp clatter interrupted her reverie. The sound of clapping. "That was marvelous, my dear!" Sophia exclaimed. "Every movement, every glance was a flirtation. Tell me, what were you thinking of as you performed? We must make it your near constant focus."

How mortifying. At least she was saved from an immediate reply by Maybanks, who'd just entered the room, approaching Sophia with a note. After reading it, the countess smiled broadly, her earlier question seemingly forgotten. "No more lessons for today. Your new wardrobe has arrived. I suspect men won't be able to keep their eyes off you. And that includes Marworth," she said with a wink. "Just in case you were wondering."

• • •

"Oh my," Banning said.

Jane could only nod in silent agreement, more than a little awed by the reflection staring back at her in the mirror. She'd never worn anything like this glorious dress in emerald green, the precise shade of it shifting in the play of light from the window.

Of course, she'd worn very lovely things in the past, but nothing so extravagantly fashionable. So shockingly daring. The bodice was far lower than she was accustomed to, despite its raised lace collar, and the waist was higher, tucked practically beneath her breasts. The skirt was shorter than English fashion, revealing an almost scandalous flash of ankle beneath the trim of an ivory silk slip. But it was the exquisite embroidery dancing across the dress that rendered her speechless. Silver threads, twisted with gold, had been stitched with the delicacy of an artist's brush, fashioned into woodland creatures and forest sprites, set amidst a profusion of vines and flowers.

"You look like Diana, goddess of the hunt," Sophia said from her chair across the room. "Which strikes me as appropriate."

"The needlework alone is a marvel," Oakley said, lifting yet another exquisite creation out of its packing. "It's a good thing the woman these were made for might have been your twin. It would be a crime to alter a single stitch."

"Not quite my twin," Jane said, looking down at her bodice. "Are you certain this isn't too revealing? Perhaps a fichu, strategically placed?"

"Absolutely not," Sophia replied. "Remember when we spoke of natural assets? You have them in abundance. Indeed, how you've disguised them to this point, I have no idea."

They'd been at this for more than two hours, unwrapping dozens of dresses for every occasion, from morning rides to the grandest of balls. There were also feathered and beribboned hats. Hand-painted silk and ivory fans. Gloves for both day and evening. Cashmere shawls and scarves. Embroidered and beaded purses. Delicate silk slippers and undergarments. They covered every surface in Jane's bedroom, with more boxes waiting out in the hall.

"Really, this is too much," she said, turning away from her reflection. "I'm certain I can hear that poor woman crying all the way from Paris. This was outright thievery."

"Nonsense, my dear," Sophia said as she inspected a particularly fetching hat. "If the theft was anyone's, it was LeRoy's. His prices are exorbitant."

There was no gainsaying his genius, however. Smoothing her fingers over the silk of her gown, marveling at its softness, she'd never felt prettier. Even if her transformation was only a temporary one. "I needed to voice at least a token note of regret." She turned to Banning, who was refolding a lavender cashmere wrap, lined with silk and trimmed with a wide cream ribbon. "That would be beautiful with your coloring. I wish you would take it. Spread the guilt around, as it were."

"I'm afraid I have little use for such an extravagance," Banning said quietly. But it was easy to see the longing in her eyes.

"Please do take it. Each of us should find something among this to remember the occasion. Perhaps years hence, we can meet up, like a secret society, and discuss the day we unpacked a wardrobe fit for a princess. I can't quite digest it all by myself."

"Look at this one," Oakley said, her voice soft with something like reverence, and when they all turned as one, she understood why.

"That is the one you must wear when you first appear in Society," Sophia declared. "Given the color, people will think you had it fashioned to honor Jane Fitzsimmons. It will cause a sensation."

"But there's nothing to it," she exclaimed. "I can't wear that out in public."

"It's made for warm weather, Jane. It's light, airy, evanescent . . ."

"Not to mention transparent."

"Only the top layer. See how the gauze plays with the color of the dress itself?"

"It's unlike anything I'd ever allow myself to be seen in."

Sophia winked at her. "Precisely."

• • •

"I can't thank you enough for my beautiful shawl," Banning said later that evening as they sat together on the flat roof of Painshill Park, an odd habit they'd taken up on balmy evenings. It was a vast expanse, easily accessed by a door from the attic, with a magnificent view stretching all the way to the sea.

"And thank you for my hat," Oakley added. "My son, Arthur, says it makes me look like a peacock, although how he knows anything about peacocks, I can't say."

"I overheard Lord Marworth telling him about the ones that stroll the grounds of the Brighton Royal Pavilion," Banning replied. "He made quite an act of it, flapping his arms about, jutting his head back and forth with every step. Arthur was roaring with laughter."

Of course Benjamin would take the time to amuse the son of a housemaid. He had opened his home to an assortment of outcasts, herself included, when she would not have done the same. And that realization was an uncomfortable one. For all of her so-called charitable work among the lower orders, she had always held firmly to the distinctions of class, to the misguided belief that people had a preordained place in the social order. And yet here she was, enjoying the company of a housekeeper and a housemaid on a starlit night. How many times had she been tempted to join Thompson and Bess below stairs, because she could hear their laughter and was lonely? And yet she hadn't joined them. Not once.

"I'm the one who should be thanking you both. For rescuing me that day at Vauxhall and for tending to me when I was so sick."

"I'm just glad you're not as starchy as you first seemed," Oakley said. "I couldn't possibly change in a carriage!" she mimicked. "You can't have been long in service. You're too impertinent!"

"Well, you are impertinent," Jane admitted, "but that is part of what makes you an enjoyable companion. Still, I am sorry if I gave offense."

"Think nothing of it. The honest truth is I haven't been long in service. It's not … " Oakley paused, looking down at her hands, flat against the roof. "It's not the life I thought I would live."

"Is it something you wish to speak about?" Jane asked as Banning put an arm around the housemaid's shoulder.

"I grew up among the gentry not far from here," Oakley said. "I was expected to make a good marriage, perhaps even to marry into the aristocracy. But I was an independent sort, headstrong if you will, and I was drawn to someone who was completely inappropriate. We were discovered in an indiscretion. A painfully public one. And I was cast off."

It was easy enough to sketch in the rest. "I am sorry," Jane said, careful to keep the pity from her voice. She supposed she ought to be shocked, but Oakley's tale was not an unfamiliar one. "At least you have the gift of your son."

"Arthur came later," Oakley replied, her voice leaden now. "After I went into service and learned that a housemaid is considered fair game."

"And that many men are beasts." This from Banning, staring out into the darkness.

Dear God. What both women had suffered. She couldn't begin to comprehend it.

"But my son is a beautiful boy. And Lord Marworth took us in when no one would. For that, I'm grateful."

"Me too," Banning said. "He brought me here when everyone else believed me damaged beyond repair."

"Why do you think he does it?" Jane asked. "With his looks and position, why should he exert himself?"

She couldn't miss the glance that passed between the other two, hesitant and questioning.

"He's a very good man," Banning said after a long pause. "But I think there is guilt there, as well."

"Guilt because his blessings are so munificent?" If she had the same, she'd revel in them.

"Guilt over his brother, I think," Oakley said. "I heard stories about it in the village when I was a child. The boy was born with some kind of disease—he suffered from terrible spasms and seizures—and was all but housebound at a young age."

She'd not known he had any siblings. And that fact could mean only one thing. She, too, had lost a brother. She'd held his tiny, unmoving body in her arms, weeping for his loss and for their mother's death. All while Father refused to spare him a second glance. Such a pale infant with an unlikely thatch of red hair. What would it have been like to know him as a child and then lose him?

"How tragic," she said, her voice barely above a whisper.

"Rumor has it he wanted to get his brother some fresh air," Oakley continued. "Against his father's wishes, he snuck them both out of the house, to a little punt kept near the shore of the lake here at Painshill. But he was only twelve, his brother ten. They were in the middle of the lake when something happened, and the boat overturned. Their father saw them from his study and raced with Maybanks towards the shore." Oakley's voice faltered here. "But only Lord Marworth could be saved."

Jane's throat closed up, making it difficult to breathe. He'd said he'd lost someone close to him in a boating accident. She'd not known how close. And she'd assumed he had fond memories at Painshill. That he'd reopened the house years after his family had left for just that reason. That he'd enjoyed swimming in the lake she could see from her bedroom window, the lake she could see now, glistening in the moonlight, seductively calm. Why would he subject himself to the sight of it? Why would he choose to return time and again?

She was not accustomed to crying. Other than that miserable incident when she'd gotten drunk on Father's cognac, she kept a tight rein on her emotions. Things were neater that way. But as tears started to trail down her cheeks, she did not bother to fight them. Because she suddenly understood. Acting as both judge and jury, he'd sentenced himself to this. Surrounded himself with people who were as imperfect and damaged as his brother had apparently been.

Benjamin was doing penance for the little boy who'd died in his stead.

Chapter 11

There are a thousand tracks leading to sin and woe, besides that infamous road to which the hand of public censure is pointed.
—Fordyce's Sermons to Young Women

Benjamin removed his topcoat and hat, each of them dripping with the late afternoon rain, and handed them to a steward waiting just inside the door. At White's Gentleman's Club on St. James Street in London, one could always rely upon two things: a satisfying lunch and the latest news in gambling and gossip. Hopefully on this day, he'd have the opportunity to indulge in the first before engaging in the second. He'd been up since dawn, meeting with Greystoke and the others.

As he made his way towards the private dining rooms, however, he saw an opportunity he could not miss. Gerard Montford, puffed up in one of the club's capacious chairs. With his unruly shock of brown hair, eyes that bulged faintly, and a weak chin, Montford was not an impressive specimen. He'd hovered on the fringes of Society for years, tolerated for his connections, first to Fitzsimmons and then to Rempley upon his marriage. But now, of course, he'd inherited a title, and he was clearly enjoying the perks of his newly acquired membership, despite the black band of mourning he wore.

"Fitzsimmons," Benjamin called out. "Glad to see you under happier circumstances." They'd last met at Jane's "funeral," after all.

"Lord Marworth!" Montford smiled fatuously as he jumped to his feet, seemingly surprised to be addressed at all. "Still getting used to the new moniker, I'm afraid."

"That's understandable." Jane's father was less than three weeks gone. "How is Lady Fitzsimmons faring?"

"Charlotte's over the moon. Has been since her new cards arrived. Once this mourning business is done with, she'll be paying calls all over town."

"It can be difficult on the women in particular, can't it?" Benjamin asked, trying to infuse his voice with sympathy instead of annoyance. "No socializing, no amusements of any kind for months on end."

"Oh, it's not as bad as that. Charlotte says only a week is expected for a distant cousin. She'll be dipping her toes into Society in no time."

Only a week grieving for the woman who'd restored their fortunes and their name. And Old Fitzsimmons, not to be mourned at all. "Will you be taking up your seat in the House of Lords then?"

"Not right away," Montford replied. "I've too many things to figure out with the running of my properties. They've been reinstated, you know." Not that Montford had done anything of note to earn them.

"I'm sure Miss Fitzsimmons would have been pleased to hear it."

"What could have possessed her, jumping into the Thames like that?" Montford asked with a shake of his head. "Even though it did me a world of good. Didn't think I'd have much to inherit, once Lord Reginald kicked off."

Instinctively, his hands fisted at his sides because Montford, whom he did not know well, was obviously an ass. But Benjamin Marworth did not brawl. He did not lose his temper, no matter how great the temptation.

Something must have shown, though, in the stern set of his jaw, because Montford suddenly flushed. "Oh dear, I am sorry, Marworth. I'd forgotten you jumped in after her. Who'd have thought my prissy little cousin would draw your eye?"

"Nothing had been formalized, of course," he said, perpetrating the myth of his devotion. "But Miss Fitzsimmons was a remarkable woman. Her father should have seen her better provided for."

"Shocking, wasn't it? Do you know he had the audacity to ask me for money? Just days before he died. Can you imagine? The titleholder gone begging to his heir?"

It *was* highly irregular, and Benjamin forced back the anger distracting him. Why would Fitzsimmons have approached Montford for money if he had the dispatches safely in hand? Or had he simply been covering a shortfall before the information could be sold? "Perhaps you'll find something among his papers that will offer an insight into his difficulties."

"I thought of that. Problem is they've all gone missing. No correspondence. No tradesmen's bills or receipts. Seems Jane took them off somewhere after he died. But of course, we can't expect women to understand the importance of such things."

"I'm sure you'll persevere. If there's anything I can to do help, don't hesitate to send a note round."

"Why thank you, Marworth. Thank you!" He seemed overcome with gratitude. They hardly ran in the same circles, after all. But Benjamin needed to ingratiate himself with Montford. No matter how unpleasant the notion, it was a sacrifice he'd make. Just this morning, he and the others had discussed stealing into the man's home to see if the dispatches were still there. There was no need for that when you were welcomed through the front door.

• • •

When Montford sent a note the next day, asking for advice on an urgent matter, Benjamin cleared his afternoon and made his way on horseback to Jane's former home on Curzon Street. Black crepe cloth had been draped over the limestone window cornice and the front door lintel as well—all appropriate signs of mourning—so it was a surprise when Jane's former butler, looking disgruntled indeed, ushered him into the main hall. The faded damask walls he'd spied on his last visit had been reupholstered in crimson silk, and the previously empty room was now stuffed with oversized furniture. There was an enormous marquetry credenza beside the stairs, topped with an elaborate, bronze garniture clock set. A matching mirror hung above the pairing, reflecting the high-backed gilt chairs that now flanked the hall and the large Romanesque urns spaced between them, potted with palms. Also new were the gold velvet curtains framing the doorways to the adjacent rooms. They were fringed with fat tassels that puddled on the marble floor.

"Obviously, mourning hasn't kept Lady Fitzsimmons from redecorating," he murmured as Thompson took his hat and gloves.

"Indeed not, Lord Marworth. She's eager for the house to look fresh and new when she casts off her blacks. She's expecting any number of visitors." The butler nodded discreetly towards a side table and the elaborately wrought salver settled upon it. Every home in Society kept a tray near the door for calling cards, but that was no ordinary tray. It was a veritable sea of silver.

"A single card would look quite adrift. Rather than subjecting mine to feelings of inadequacy, may I ask you to tell Lord Fitzsimmons I've arrived? I'm here at his request."

"Of course, my lord. But if I may be so bold … " The butler paused, collecting himself, and when he spoke again, his voice was tight with emotion. "My wife and I thank you for your efforts to rescue Miss Fitzsimmons. Her loss has been a terrible blow."

"Yes, it has. She is missed by many, myself included." And it was true. He'd missed her since his return to London. And thought of her far more than he should. But unlike Thompson, he would see her again. The butler's grief was a reminder this deceit had a tangible cost. God willing, it would be justified in the end.

With a mute nod, the butler went off in search of the new Lord Fitzsimmons as a sound from above drew Benjamin's attention. Charlotte Montford was descending the stairs, her face wreathed in a happy smile. Plump and petite, she was an attractive woman, perhaps twenty-five, with childlike features, bright, blue eyes, and blond ringlets. In that fluffy, pink dress, with its bows and rosettes along the bodice and skirt, she looked like a bonbon at the confectioner's. Sweet and insubstantial.

"Lord Marworth," she exclaimed. "What a lovely surprise! Gerard mentioned we should expect you, but of course, we could not be certain you'd find the time, given how many requests you must have on your person. You are so very sociable, after all. To think you are our very first visitor to Fitzsimmons House, other than dear Uncle Aldus, of course. I'm quite flattered. I certainly am!"

On the few occasions when they'd had cause to exchange words, she'd been happy to speak enough for the both of them. Apparently, today would be much the same.

"It's my honor, Lady Fitzsimmons," he said, bowing over the hand she'd extended. "Although I am sorry to interrupt you at this difficult time."

Her smile was still wide, but her eyes had glazed over, apparently with confusion. "Oh, but it's no difficulty at all. We're very well and good. Gerard feels the weight of his new title, of course, but little Violet is ever so happy here. She just adores her new room, and I myself am settling into my new chambers quite nicely. I'll need to have them redone, of course. I've ever been one for cheerful colors, and this house has a touch of the dreary."

"I was referring to the unfortunate passing of Miss Fitzsimmons." He stared pointedly at her pink dress.

"Oh, of course. Darling Jane, such a tragedy. I miss her so! Did I mention Violet has been crying herself to sleep? It's so difficult for a small one to understand the very permanent nature of death.

Just this morning, she said, 'Mommy, I'm so tired of black. It makes me sad.' So I asked Nurse to dress her up in her happiest dress, and I've done the same, as you see. One needs color to chase away the doldrums, don't you think?"

"Don't badger Lord Marworth, my dear," Montford called out as Thompson escorted him into the hall. "He's here to help with a pressing concern."

"We've been enjoying a delightful conversation," he said. "But of course, business matters will not wait, no matter how we might wish them to."

"Is there anything I can do, Gerard?" Lady Fitzsimmons asked. Turning to Benjamin, she blushed prettily. "He's been locked away in his study all morning, and while I don't understand most of what my husband does, I'm actually quite good with facts and figures."

"Of course you are, dear," Montford replied, his head shaking in silent denial as he peered over his wife's shoulder. "But these are things better left to a man's attention."

Jane would bristle at such a suggestion, but Lady Fitzsimmons didn't seem the least bit bothered. "Of course, you know best then, my dear," she said, smiling brightly. "Violet and I are planning a tea party for her dolls this afternoon, and I must speak with Cook about the menu. She makes the most delicious little treats and petit fours. If I don't limit myself to just a small plate, all of my clothes will need to be let out at the waistline. Which would never do. Should you like me to have some made up for you both to enjoy? I can bring them into the study while you're working, along with a pot of tea or something stronger, if you prefer."

"That sounds lovely," Montford said affectionately, even if he was clearly eager to move her along. "But have Thompson bring it in, won't you? We've no wish to be disturbed."

• • •

"I can't thank you enough for answering my note," Montford said, running a hand through unruly hair as he settled behind the desk in Lord Reginald's office. "I'm at sixes and sevens and don't really know to whom I can turn."

The man was short of friends if he'd turned to him on so limited an acquaintance. He and Jane had planned her demise in this very room. And it was jarring that Gerard Montford was now settled here; the shelves behind him still held Lord Reginald's books and travel ephemera. All of which Benjamin needed to inspect. "I'm happy to help. I run several estates myself and understand their challenges."

"This doesn't have to do with estates," Montford replied, waving him into a seat. "It has to do with Lord Reginald's final days. If news of this gets out, I'll be ruined."

"I understand he had significant gambling debts. Perhaps you can negotiate their repayment."

"It's far worse than gambling debts, I'm afraid."

Just what had he uncovered? The missing dispatches? "Perhaps if you explain … "

"Sir Aldus paid me a visit this morning. With all that has happened of late, we hadn't previously had a moment to speak at length. And he shared some disturbing news."

"Go on."

"I'd mentioned to you before that Lord Reginald tried to borrow money from me. It seems he also approached Sir Aldus for money but was, of course, refused. They were friends, but Sir Aldus knew any funds would go to a roll of the dice."

Any true friend, to Benjamin's mind, would have tried to help Fitzsimmons conquer his addiction. And he certainly wouldn't have importuned his daughter. "How did Lord Reginald respond?"

"In short, he threatened Sir Aldus with scandal. He claimed he'd ruin his standing in the House of Lords."

"More easily said than done, of course. Rempley is well respected, while Fitzsimmons was a social outcast. The threat was an empty one."

"It should have been, but the next morning, Sir Aldus discovered that several documents important to our war efforts had been stolen from his desk. Documents normally kept under lock and key at Whitehall."

"And he thinks Fitzsimmons took them in order to embarrass Rempley before the Lords. Is that correct?" If only the motive had been so juvenile.

"Far worse. Sir Aldus believes Fitzsimmons intended to sell them for money and accuse him of the crime."

Benjamin pretended to surprise. "You'd known the former Lord Fitzsimmons the whole of your life. Surely he wouldn't have compromised the security of his country for a bit of coin and a dose of revenge?"

"He was desperate. What if those documents end up in enemy hands? No one will receive us. Charlotte will be brokenhearted."

Obviously, the potential ramifications to his country were not a paramount concern. But it was an opening gambit all the same. "What are the chances Fitzsimmons died before anything could be done with the documents?"

"Sir Aldus believes they might be hidden among his private correspondence. He wanted to sort through it, but, of course, Jane bundled it all up. Supposedly she opened a box at the Bank of England shortly before her death, but I'm not authorized to gain access to it, if you can imagine the gall. By rights, it should all be mine anyway. The chit left everything to a cousin in France I've never even heard of. A Mrs. Lillianne Fauchon."

"The name sounds familiar," he said, with a great show of rubbing his chin thoughtfully. "Ah yes. I saw it in the social notes of the *London Times* just this morning. She's traveling here from Paris at the end of the month to honor Jane's memory. The trip must have been cleared at the highest levels. No doubt she'll be welcomed with great enthusiasm."

"That's good news, then," Montford said, looking relieved. "She's certain to give me that bank box, don't you think?"

"Now as to that, I can't say. But isn't there a chance Lord Reginald hid the documents here, in this very house? He'd not have left them out in plain sight, after all." Unlike Rempley.

"Why, you're right, of course." Montford was wide-eyed. "I don't know why I didn't think of that before."

"I'd be happy to assist in your search, if it would be a help." In fact, more than happy. He'd all but counted on it. "You can trust me to tell no one."

"I know you're a top-of-the-trees sort. Everyone says so. And with the two of us at it, we've a better chance of staying one step ahead of Charlotte."

"I beg your pardon?"

"She's been so busy renovating the rooms here, there's every chance she'll throw anything important out with the garbage."

They were in a race, it seemed, against Lady Fitzsimmons and her questionable taste in décor.

• • •

"You are certain?" Greystoke asked, his face dark as he fisted his hands on the table, a prelude perhaps to pounding them in frustration. Torrington had been delayed, but Winchester sat with them in their private room at Whitehall, where the mood was tense and the evening late.

"Trust me when I say I've spent far too much time in the company of Montford these past few weeks. Together, we went over every crevice of Fitzsimmons's house. The dispatches are not there. At least not in any form I might recognize."

"What about Lord Reginald's personal effects, his jackets and waistcoats?" This from Winchester. "Could he have hidden them in the linings?"

"If he did, they are already gone. Montford's wife starting packing up his belongings the day they moved in. Most, I believe, have either been sold off to the ragman or donated to the church."

"Because the faster they can distance themselves from the man's legacy, the better." Greystoke's fingers were working absently on the latch of his snuff box. "What about the possibility Fitzsimmons hid the dispatches among Jane's things?"

"I think it's unlikely. He'd have risked her finding them."

"But are her possessions still in the house?" Winchester asked. "Her clothing?"

"They've been moved into a separate room and laid out like relics. But given my tragic status as the suitor Jane left behind, Montford's wife invited me to go through them in private. To say my goodbyes, as it were."

And so he had, like the worst sort of voyeur, running his hands along the muslins, velvets, and silks, some still carrying her verbena scent. Caressing the filmy cotton underthings that had lain against her skin. Touching her pantalets, edged with soft Brussels lace, imagining her body bare beneath them. The whole of it had been intensely erotic.

"There was nothing there," he said, shifting in his seat.

"Are you blushing, Marworth?" Greystoke asked. "You are looking distinctly uncomfortable." The man missed nothing. Damn him.

Blessedly, Torrington chose that opportune moment to burst into the room, smelling—perhaps stinking was the better word—of gin and cigar smoke. "I've news," he said as he pulled aside a chair and sat down.

"Good God, Torrington." Benjamin pulled out a handkerchief and retreated behind it. "What the hell have you been doing? Rolling in the gutters of St. Giles?"

"I know I'm ripe, but in that place, one can't help but absorb the stench. I came straight from Sharpe's."

The gaming hell. They all leaned in.

"What did you find out?" Winchester asked.

"The staff there is a suspicious lot, hesitant to admit anything, but I fell in with one of the regulars. Plied him with some of the vilest swill I've ever encountered and waited to find out what he might say. Turns out he knew Fitzsimmons well."

Winchester straightened. "Was he there the night Fitzsimmons died?"

"He was. Saw him dead on the curb. Watched his pockets get picked, the shoes stolen off his feet."

"Had he gotten in some sort of fight, then?" Winchester asked. "Angered one of the other patrons? Or was it a robbery, plain and simple?"

"Apparently, it was neither," Torrington replied. "Seems that Fitzsimmons and this gent made a regular pair at the card tables. Won and lost a pile of money to each other."

"Go on." Greystoke's impatience was obvious.

"My mark claimed he never made it into the hell that night."

"Then it was a robbery," Winchester interrupted. "Footpads figured he'd have more money going into Sharpe's than he would on the way out."

"Let me finish. He said a man came in late, complaining a body had been tossed onto the curb by a passing carriage. He'd had to step over it to get inside. Our gent said the barkeep offered him a free drink to help move the carcass into an adjoining alley. Turned out it was Fitzsimmons."

"He was certain of this?" Greystoke asked. "The course of events and the carriage?"

"He described the scene in detail. Apparently, Fitzsimmons was already several hours gone and stiff as a pike."

Whomever had murdered the man had wanted to make it look like Fitzsimmons had been out gambling, that he'd fallen victim to the cutthroats Sharpe's attracted. When in truth, he'd been murdered preemptively and thrown away like trash. An ignominious and humiliating end. But why?

"Perhaps he'd been too late in paying a debt," Winchester offered. "Gullgropers are hardly patient people."

"But they'd not have killed him." Benjamin knew it for a certainty. "They'd only get their money back while he lived. Someone else wanted Lord Reginald Fitzsimmons dead."

"I'll make inquiries," Torrington said. "See what I can uncover about the man's habits and his final days."

"When will you return to Painshill, Marworth?" Greystoke's eyes were fixed on him.

"I'm leaving in the morning. If all goes well, I'll return by the week's end. Jane, as Lillianne, will go directly to Grillion's."

"We'll meet next Saturday then," Greystoke said with a curt nod, the meeting over and done. But as Benjamin rose to take his leave, Greystoke stayed him with a hand on his shoulder. "A moment." He paused until the others had departed. "Miss Fitzsimmons is obviously coming into a dangerous situation. Given what we've learned tonight, it's important your interest in her remains a strictly professional one."

"Of course. I have the utmost respect for Jane. She is under my care."

But Greystoke was clearly unconvinced. "She unsettles you. That's easy enough to see. And I can only think of one explanation for that."

"You overstep your bounds," he bristled. "You are wrong on that count."

Greystoke merely turned, speaking over his shoulder as he moved towards the door. "I doubt it."

Chapter 12

Men, I presume, are in general better judges than women, of the deportment of women.
—Fordyce's Sermons to Young Women

Sophia Middleton, who was more prone to mischief than anyone he'd ever encountered, practically purred at the sight of him walking through the front door of Painshill.

"I'm so happy to see you returned, Marworth," she said, her eyes dancing, their bright blue a perfect match for the dress she wore. "I've been terribly busy in your absence."

"I hope you're referring to your progress with Jane." She could just as easily be speaking about another conquest. Men—both highborn and low—had a tendency to cluster around Sophia Middleton like puppies. Just look at the beatific expression Maybanks was wearing.

"Jane? I'm afraid she left here weeks ago, disconsolate over your departure. There's every chance she's tossed herself back into the Thames."

For a brief moment, his heart stopped. But it was quickly resuscitated by a suspicion. He shot a glance at the hall clock. "Have you been drinking, Sophia?" Surely it was too early for brandy. He'd left London at first light.

"What a lovely idea! But sadly, no. We must save it for later, when I suspect you'll need something bracing."

"Where is she?" He scanned the hall. "Charming as you are, I am here on a matter of some importance. You will remember, of course, our plans. The task at hand."

"Oh, I never forget a task, Marworth. And I never fail to exceed expectations. Let's adjourn to the sitting room, shall we?

We received your note two days ago, so we've been expecting you. She'll be down shortly."

Trying to brush aside his impatience, he followed the countess into the small chamber, with its delicate gilded furnishings and floral paper. He'd always felt like an oaf in this room, but his mother had decorated it during a far more innocent and happy time, and that was something to be preserved. He lowered his long frame onto a ridiculously petite settee. "We are waiting on Jane, then?"

"Of course not," she said with a sly glance. "We're waiting on Lillianne."

He stole a peek at the doorway, nervous for no good reason. And then Maybanks announced her, and she moved into the room. As he stood, he could do little more than stare. It was only sheer dint of will that kept his jaw from dropping open. Her gown, a sapphire confection, emphasized the curves of her body with tiny pintuck pleats edged in cream, making her legs seem especially long and her waist seem absurdly small and her chest … Dear God, he had not expected that bodice, almost dazzlingly full, trimmed with a fringe of diaphanous lace that swept up, licking along her porcelain shoulders. Her dark hair fell in glossy ringlets that flirted along her jawline, teasing at her full lips. When her pink tongue darted out to moisten them, he shifted in his seat.

This was not good. Not in any way, because when her tongue retreated back into the warmth of her mouth, he had to fight the sudden urge to follow it with his own.

Had the room grown disconcertingly close? He dragged his gaze from her mouth, lifting his eyes to hers. Her brows had been reshaped to slant up at their tips, like birds' wings in flight, and her eyes, always bright, fairly sparkled as she watched him.

Something was pounding violently in his chest. Something that felt quite close to panic.

"Enchanted to meet you, *monsieur*," she breathed, her voice sounding deeper, husky even, as she sank into a low curtsey, watching him through the thick fringe of her lashes.

He blinked to clear his vision. This was Jane Fitzsimmons, and yet she was not. Jane moved with efficient purpose, but this woman had swayed into the room like a seductress, every movement hypnotic. Her features were the same, even if her cheekbones were more pronounced, and her eyes seemed larger, the faintest hint of kohl at their corners. The short bob of her new hairstyle, threaded through with a sapphire silk ribbon, framed her face beautifully and was playful, teasing even. Two words he'd never associated with Jane. But that body. He'd never guessed, and he was a connoisseur of the female form. How had she kept it hidden from the world?

"You look … very nice," he said, his famed wit deserting him.

"You, as well, *monsieur le vicomte*," she replied, gliding towards him. There was an artful lilt to her speech, hinting at French shores and exquisite schooling. "But of course, the *comtesse* told me to expect a handsome man, and I have learned during our short acquaintance she is not given to exaggeration."

He swallowed reflexively. Surely she wasn't flirting with him? Why would Jane flirt with him? He needed to collect himself, fall back upon his manners and an instinctive persona. That would set things back to rights. Very soon now, she would extend her hand so that he could bend over it and break this strange spell.

But instead, she stopped just in front of him, mere inches away. Reaching up, she placed a tentative hand on his shoulder and then leaned in, standing on her toes to place a light kiss first on one cheek and then the other, while he stood utterly still, breathing her in, unable to deny he was lanced with desire.

She pulled back, her hand falling gently to her waist. "That is how I greet my friends in Paris, *monsieur*, and I'm told we are to be great friends."

"If that is how the French greet their friends," he said, fighting to keep his voice light, "I am renouncing my British citizenship."

She laughed, an unexpectedly throaty sound. "Let me be the first, then, to welcome my new countryman."

"Isn't she brilliant, Marworth?" the countess asked, a sudden distraction. "She should be on the stage, trading scenes on Drury Lane with Mrs. Siddons."

"*Alors, madame*," Jane said as she floated towards a chair opposite Sophia, her skirts rustling faintly. "You do me too great the honor."

But Sophia was right. Jane, as Lillianne, was perfect. "The changes are subtle." He cleared his throat. "But the overall effect is a masterstroke. I find I'm nearly speechless. And are you taller, as well? You seem … taller."

Jane smiled provocatively at that. At least it looked damned well provocative to him. Everything about her was a whispered temptation. A seduction. "How kind you are to say so," she said, fingering the ribbon of the silk fan she carried, each movement a caress. "*Maman* urged me from a very young age to walk with my shoulders pressed back. She said it would lengthen my spine, and enhance my ... ah … " She paused, looking adorably confused. "*C'est domage*, I have forgotten the right word." With a flick of her wrist, she opened her fan, her cheeks coloring faintly as she drew it up with agonizing slowness over her bodice. "Do you know the English word for *décolletage, monsieur*?"

"The word you are looking for is breasts, *madame*. And may I say yours are exquisite?"

God in heaven, surely he'd not voiced that aloud? But of course he had. He didn't need Sophia's delighted chuckle to confirm it. Jane's eyes told him all he needed to know. They'd gone wide as saucers, and a flush was burning up her neck, past her chin and cheeks to her hairline. She was clearly horrified.

"I am so sorry," he said, taking a step towards her as she took a reflexive step back. "No gentleman should say such things to a lady."

"Really, Marworth," Sophia interrupted. "You know as well as I that men are more indiscrete around widows. She knows to expect such comments."

"I forgot my role for the briefest of moments," Jane said, trying gamely to dismiss the incident with a weak smile at them both. "It will not happen again."

But the countess was watching her now with a kind of dawning comprehension. "If you would, my lord," she said, not even bothering to turn towards him, "we need a few moments alone."

• • •

"Whatever is the matter, my dear?" Sophia asked after Benjamin offered a final apology and left the room, closing the door behind him. "You are practically purple."

Surely, the room was warmer by a dozen degrees. How could she explain this without further embarrassment? "I know we discussed the things men might say and how I should respond. But I did not expect them from Marworth. It was the shock of it, I suppose."

And she was lying. When she'd first entered the room, his admiration had been obvious, even to a novice. And she could not deny it had been thrilling to watch his eyes turn smoky at her approach. When she'd impulsively kissed each cheek, feeling the hard lines of his face and the faintest whisper of stubble beneath her lips, she'd sensed something barely restrained in him. And it had emboldened her. She'd intentionally drawn his eyes to her breasts. Those so-called natural assets. And he'd responded as any man would to a blatant invitation. The shame of it was humiliating.

"The fact of the matter is you attracted and held his attention," Sophia said gently. "Which means our lessons have been successful in many ways. But I have overlooked something crucial, and for that I am sorry."

"I don't understand."

"You've worked so hard these last several weeks to become Lillianne, a woman of experience. But your response to Marworth's statement made your innocence quite obvious. Tell me, Jane. Do you have any sense of what goes on between the sexes?"

"Well, I know about the kissing, of course. And the tracts we distributed at the Ladies Society hinted at the rest." This was mortifying. She was a grown woman, twenty-two years of age.

"But have you ever been kissed by a man?"

"I'm afraid no one has ever tried."

"With you as Lillianne, they will try. And we must prepare for that eventuality. We can't have you blushing at the first hint of intimacy."

"It's a force of habit. I will work hard to overcome it."

"I'm afraid it won't be enough, my dear. We haven't the time before you go to London. You need a rudimentary understanding of the mechanics, and a man to introduce you to them. It's vitally important to your disguise."

It took her a moment to comprehend the statement, only the fraction of another to be horrified. She was hardly the sort to fling herself at the nearest footman, after all. And she could admit to herself, but no one else, that there was only one man she wanted to kiss. Foolish girl.

"I understand your point, but honestly, I can't." Her voice was a desperate whisper. "There must be another way."

"Jane, you've nothing at all to fear. Tell me, did you ever take dance instruction?"

She nodded mutely. She'd excelled at those lessons. She loved to dance.

"Well, this will be very much like learning the opening movements of a quadrille. You step together and then apart. But of course in this case, your lips, instead of your feet, are doing the dancing."

"That is a ridiculous image," she said, unable to will away a small smile. "And a scandalous one."

Sophia chuckled. "A further example of your innocence, my dear. A kiss is an exploration. And if one is lucky, it can be the prelude to a wonderful adventure."

"Shouldn't it also mean something? I never dreamed I'd have to sacrifice my first kiss for the sake of a cause. To bolster a disguise."

"We all have to make sacrifices for our country." Sophia walked towards the bell pull. "And from the look of things, Marworth will be happy to oblige."

• • •

"You want me to do what?" Benjamin exclaimed. And it humiliated Jane, the vehemence of his response. His eyes swept hers, as if he couldn't believe she'd agreed to such a scheme, before flashing back at Sophia.

"It's a simple enough request," the countess replied. "Jane has never been kissed. She will need to know how it's done. Where the hands might go. The angle of the chin … "

"Can you not be more euphemistic?" Jane asked, cringing. "If only to save me some measure of embarrassment?" Her toes had curled in her slippers, trying to find purchase on the floor beneath her. She'd once read of wood-eating bugs, native to tropical areas. She'd have welcomed them now, in a circle chewing beneath her feet, if only to hasten her escape. Especially with Benjamin clearly struggling for his response.

"It is the dream, of course … of any man. To … ah … have that honor. To find such a woman … Lord, I'm making a mess of this." His eyes were beseeching. "Surely, this should not be forced upon you. You've been waiting, no doubt, for the right man." Obviously, he was trying to refuse her gently.

To think she'd believed, that night in the hall, that he'd wanted to kiss her. And today. Smoky eyes indeed! If she had a stick, she'd likely hit him with it, because she felt like lashing out. It was immeasurably preferable to running from the room in tears.

But instead, she took a deep breath, falling back on her instinct for rigid self-control. "It's all right, Lord Marworth. I understand. Lady Marchmain merely thought it would be a good idea. I honestly don't think such a situation will arise. I'm quite good at deflecting a man's attentions." Which, of course, was a lie. There'd never been the need.

"Really, Benjamin," Sophia said. "I hadn't expected you to act like a child just off his leading strings. Can you not see the wisdom of this? Unless Lillianne endured a loveless marriage to an elderly and impotent man, she would have had some experience at kissing."

"Pasqual wasn't elderly," Jane cut in defensively. "He was in the prime of his life, only thirty years old, when he was thrown from his horse and trampled." And she'd just been reduced to blurring the lines between fiction and reality. "I'm sorry," she finished lamely.

"No, Jane," Benjamin said, taking a step towards her. "In the middle of an awkward conversation, you remembered your role. It's what I need you to do. It was marvelous."

When she flushed with unexpected pleasure at his praise, she wanted to scream at herself. This really was the most untenable situation. "I'll ask Jonas. Or perhaps Pierre, because I assume the French have a different technique than the English, and if any of our targets tries to steal a kiss, that's what they'll be expecting."

"No," he blurted out, just as she was turning to leave. "Please don't do that. It's a dreadful idea."

"Actually, Benjamin," Sophia observed, "it's a sound theory. I wish I'd thought of it beforehand. We wouldn't have needed to bother you."

"It's not a bother," he said, a muscle twitching in his jaw. "And I do see the logic in all of this. I just don't want you, Jane, to feel pressured in any way. A first kiss is something special. It should not be a lesson."

"Isn't it always something of a lesson?" she asked before she could stop herself. "It's a new experience, after all."

"I suppose when you put it in that light ... " His eyes locked on to hers, forcing the air in her lungs from her body. "If you really think it will help ... "

"Very good, then," Sophia said, clapping her hands together. "I'm so glad this problem will be addressed. I'll leave the two of you alone for a short while, and then we'll all enjoy a spot of brandy." She smiled at Benjamin. "I warned you might need it."

God help her. This would likely be the most embarrassing moment of her life. But also the most exciting.

Chapter 13

Curst be the impious hand that would dare to violate the unblemished form of Chastity!
—Fordyce's Sermons to Young Women

It had been so easy to tell himself the countess was right. Jane needed a lesson in seduction to be convincing in her role. She was an utter innocent after all, and there was no such thing as a virginal widow. A lingering embrace—nothing more—would give her an air of experience, yet another layer for her disguise. And couched in those terms, a kiss between them was practically noble.

But he was fooling himself, because he wanted her. He'd wanted her from the moment he'd found her in that study, tossing books into the fire. He'd tried to deny it, but slowly, insidiously, that want had become a craving.

How was he to demonstrate the mechanics of a kiss and not give in to his desire to do so much more? Jane was staring at him expectantly, even if there was more than a little shyness there. She didn't understand a kiss between them would change everything. She didn't know his hands were clenched at his sides, his heartbeats skipping over themselves. So he simply stood there, saying nothing. Hoping the moment would pass, and they'd both come to their senses. Hoping with equal fervor they would not.

"This is rather awkward."

"Not at all," he said, praying humor would mask his turmoil. "I'm approached for this sort of thing all the time. My reputed expertise, you see."

"I don't doubt it." And there was something in her voice. If he didn't know better, he might have called it jealousy.

"I am joking, you know." Her eyes grew wider with each step he took toward her. Did she realize how expressive they were? She was undoubtedly nervous, but curious too. When they were mere inches apart, close enough that her face was almost nestled against his chest, he stopped. "You will need to do one thing for this to work."

"What's that?" she asked, speaking into the folds of his jacket.

"You will need to look up."

She did, and something hot uncoiled inside him. Because her face was flushed, and her breathing had quickened, and those magnificent breasts were pressed against him.

"There are several types of kisses, Jane," he said, his voice raspy now. "A light peck on the cheek. A quick meeting of lips. Both are expressions of affection or friendship. For the sake of our task, I will show you one quite a bit different."

The eagerness with which she nodded was almost funny, but he didn't feel like laughing. He felt like driving her back against a wall and losing himself in her. But he could not. He would not. "Put your hands on my shoulders," he ordered. And up they went, her touch light as butterfly wings, landing far short of his shoulders.

"You're too tall."

"I'm afraid it can't be helped." He put his hands then at her waist and nearly groaned, because her gown was a filmy thing, and she wore no stays, and it was almost like touching skin to skin. She was so delicate. The weight of his desire alone could crush her. "Perhaps it is you who is too short," he said, because he needed the distraction of sound. Something to calm the blood rushing to his loins at an alarming rate.

"I'm afraid that can't be helped either," she said with a soft smile.

It was that smile that stilled him. Shy but willing. And he knew it instinctively. She would give, and he would take. Lesson be damned. A better man would step away and end all of this before it began.

Something must have shown in his face, because she lowered her hands, and those expressive eyes looked down. "It's all right if you'd rather not do this," she said. "You weren't really given a choice."

She'd mistaken his hesitation for disinterest. So even though this was a terrible idea, one he would no doubt regret profoundly, he put a hand beneath her chin and gently lifted her head to face him once more. "Never doubt you are desirable," he said, cupping her cheeks with both hands. "I want to kiss you more than you can possibly imagine." And then he brought his mouth to hers.

When their lips touched, she tensed, understandably skittish. The nervous exhalation of her breath fanned his cheek. So he slipped his hands to the nape of her neck, caressing the soft skin there, kneading gently as he drew her closer, angling his head to take more of her mouth.

So soft and ripe. He focused on her full lower lip, sucking gently to coax her to relax. "Open your mouth," he whispered. And when she did, her warmth nearly overwhelmed him. His tongue swept in to taste her, and after the slightest hesitancy, she swayed into him, arching her back as he leaned over her, matching his kiss with a natural passion.

He knew himself very well when it came to matters of the body. He had kissed scores of women. Had perfected an ability to enjoy the pleasures they offered while remaining separate and apart. But this was something different. He was spellbound by the feel of her, the softness of her skin, the way her flesh seemed to leap at his touch. He smoothed his hands over her shoulders, down her arms, curving to her waist, memorizing her contours. And then his arms encircled her, pulling her flush against him, and he nearly shuddered, because it was an exquisite torture to be nestled so close to the heat of her beneath her dress.

When she gasped, he knew he'd frightened her. No doubt she was shocked by the evidence of his arousal. So he forced himself to loosen his hold, only to be awed when she lifted her arms and pulled his lips back to hers. This time, it was her tongue that stole into his mouth, all hesitancy gone, drugging him with her eagerness. A low moan of longing slipped from his throat. He wanted nothing more than to pull her dress off her shoulders, to kiss down the contours of her neck until he reached her breasts. He wanted to take them into his mouth, drawing in their tips, suckling until she cried out with the same desperation he was feeling. He wanted every inch of her body.

Madness. That's what it was. A sickness that would turn him into a ravening beast if he weren't careful. It was a surrender he could not afford. Not with this woman. With a restraint he hadn't known he possessed, he eased away, rubbing the pad of one thumb over her mouth as every instinct railed against the distance between them. "Those are the mechanics of a kiss," he said, taking a first step back, and then two more, until he nearly tripped over a small side table blocking his retreat.

"So that's what all the fuss is about," she said, her eyes still bright with passion, her lips swollen. She would never know the temptation she presented.

But she must have sensed it, because in the next moment, she sped from the room, brushing past Sophia Middleton as she crossed over the threshold.

• • •

She ran as quickly as she could down the hallway, up the backstairs, and through the servants' quarters to the attic. With a push against the door leading to the roof, she burst into the bright afternoon, her breath coming in pants. Not that she was tired. If she'd been a bird, she could have flown across an ocean. She was teeming with a strange new energy, nearly drunk on it.

Over the course of her life, she'd spent any number of hours—days really—imagining what a proper kiss would feel like. She'd closed her eyes, pressing her fingers to her mouth, pretending they were a man's lips meeting hers. And if in those daydreams, the lips had belonged to Benjamin Alden, she didn't feel guilty. It had only made sense to kiss the most handsome man in London.

She knew now her fingers had been a sad substitute, and bony ones at that. Because the reality of his lips on hers had been magic. So gentle at first, nearly reverent, easing past her awkward innocence. But then his tongue had slipped into her mouth, an unexpected intimacy, sparking so many sensations at once. His body had pressed into hers as he wrapped her up in his arms. She'd felt the pounding of his heart and the desire strumming through him, barely leashed. An answering desire, roiling up inside of her, simmered through her veins, urging her to press still closer, to climb inside him if she could. To discover all the mysteries his eyes and his hands hinted at.

It had been rather silly to exit the room as she had, but it had either been that or surrender to a wicked impulse. One that would have asked him to strip her bare so she could feel his mouth trail along her body.

No wonder girls had chaperones with them wherever they went. No wonder men and women could not be trusted alone in the dark. If she'd contemplated such a rash act mere moments into her first kiss, imagine what might have happened if she'd not heard the footfall of Sophia Middleton's approach.

Just imagine.

Heat swept through her. She was certain now that parts of her body had been made specifically for his touch. The nape of her neck. The tips of her breasts. That secret place at the apex of her legs, which she'd studiously avoided her entire life, because she suspected it had a power she couldn't define. Each had throbbed with anticipation when she was flush against him, as if they'd been waiting for him forever.

Perhaps it was a sin, this newfound awareness of her physical desires. A niggling corner of her conscience said so, and no doubt a minister would agree. But she refused to feel guilty. Something that felt so wonderful could not be sinful. And even if it was a convenient excuse, one which had certainly led more than one woman down Mr. Shakespeare's primrose path, she didn't care. She was sitting on a rooftop in Surrey, a breeze threading her hair, wonderstruck by an undeniable fact. Benjamin Alden had wanted to kiss her. She'd dared before to pretend it, but her body understood now.

And the knowledge that she could make his eyes darken with desire, make his body harden, and turn his breath shallow was a powerful thing. She would never recover from the surprise of it. If she gained nothing else from this mad decision she'd made, she would always have that kiss.

Perhaps if she asked nicely, she'd have more than one.

• • •

"What did you do, Marworth?" Sophia asked idly as she approached a sideboard laden with an assortment of liqueurs.

"No more than you asked me to," he bit out, retreating behind a settee. "It was a damned bad idea."

"Such language," she said, smiling as she surveyed the offerings. "You are rarely so impolite. If I didn't suspect an underlying turmoil, I might even be offended."

"I should never have kissed her. We are linked together because of this scheme and for no other reason."

"Be honest with yourself," she replied, turning towards him, arching a single brow. "You were nearly begging for the opportunity."

"I'm a man, like any other. And Jane is beautiful." How easily he made excuses. Both things were true, but he was beginning to realize neither scratched the surface of his motivations. Not that he would tell Sophia that. "As Lillianne," he admitted, "she's a marvel. You've done wonders."

"Now you disappoint me. She was a marvel long before her latest incarnation. How you didn't see it, I don't know."

"Of course I saw it." A punishing tension was building at his temples. "My regrettable attraction has been brewing for some time."

"Why regrettable?" she asked, breaking into another smile, one that grated.

"This is no fairy tale, Sophia. Jane and I will say our goodbyes when this is done. Her future will be secure, and I will go back to flirting with talkative wives and listening at keyholes." It was an honest enough assessment of his talents. Spy indeed. Imposter was far more appropriate. No matter how hard he tried to honor Aiden's memory, the better Alden son was dead in the ground. And here at Painshill, Benjamin could not escape that awful reminder. He could not allow any woman to make him forget the promise he'd made to himself.

"How is Jane's future secure?" Sophia asked, interrupting his thoughts. "Certainly, she'll be financially compensated, but what then? She can hardly return to her house on Curzon Street. She can hardly return to herself."

"She will have a new life," he replied, ignoring a now familiar guilt. "She can resettle where she wishes, safe from the attentions of bastards like Rempley."

"Sir Aldus Rempley? What does he have to do with any of this?

"Suffice it to say he made her a disgraceful offer the day of her father's funeral. And there's a chance he's involved in the information stolen just before Fitzsimmons's death."

"I had little enough love for Lord Fitzsimmons," Sophia replied, pouring herself a glass of brandy. "His pride nearly cost my niece her reputation, and in the end, he practically abandoned Jane. But Rempley … Now there is a man I thoroughly dislike."

"So do I, but at Whitehall, his reputation is impeccable. And I've yet to hear anything disparaging in Society."

"That's because there are some things women only speak of among themselves."

His pulse quickened with suspicion. "Pretend I'm a woman, then."

"Rempley was on the town when I made my debut. Quite handsome actually, with a full head of bright hair, no obvious physical flaws, and a sizable fortune. But he was a man to be avoided." Sophia paused for a long moment, swirling the brandy in her glass. "Back then, you see, behavior was far less constrained. We were occasionally indiscreet, but we all knew which lines could not be crossed. We counted on the men to respect them. Rempley was not one to stop when he was asked."

A predator then. As if Benjamin had needed another reason to despise him.

Chapter 14

Be not afraid of the bitterness of reproach, or the bluntness of incivility. If anything should appear harsh, be assured it proceeds from real regard.
—Fordyce's Sermons to Young Women

Benjamin had not joined them last night for dinner, nor had he been in evidence thus far today. According to Sophia, he was locked away in his study, preparing for their journey to London in the morning. And if Jane worried he was purposefully avoiding her, in truth, the entire household was busy. Under Banning's supervision, several housemaids were repacking Lillianne's enormous wardrobe, pairing hats, gloves, and shoes with each ensemble. Meanwhile, Oakley was packing her own personal items and saying her goodbyes to Arthur. For as long as this took, she would serve as Lillianne's lady's maid in London, with the excuse that Madame Fauchon's had fallen ill on the journey across the Channel.

Really, there was little left for Jane to do. She was as ready as she would ever be. But she was restless. And given the alternative—that of worrying holes in her skirts with nervous energy—she decided to explore the grounds surrounding Painshill Park. It was perhaps the last chance she'd have to do so, and the afternoon was a beautiful one, a southerly wind slipping through the trees.

And so she walked. Along pathways lined with carefully cultivated blooms. Past a ruined abbey and a temple dedicated to Bacchus, if the statue inside was anything to go by. There was also a gothic tower, artistically crumbling to give it an air of authenticity, and some sort of Turkish-style pavilion. According to Banning, Benjamin's father had overseen the design of the park, inspired by his travels during a grand tour of Europe and beyond.

Glimpsing a white structure through a copse of yew and birch trees, she followed the path towards it, only to find herself at the edge of Painshill's lake, at the base of a footbridge. The manor house looked down from a hill in the distance.

Up close, the lake was larger than she'd realized—perhaps two hundred feet at its widest point, although the bridge before her spanned a narrow inlet. Set amidst flowering shrubs and fringed by cedar trees, it was beautiful, with sunlight dancing on its surface. Which somehow did not seem fair, given what had happened here. By rights, it should be a dark and frightening place, with a perpetual thundercloud fixed overhead.

She crossed onto the bridge. It was a pretty thing, with arched supports below and pillars linking open fretwork panels, but two people could not walk along it side by side. As her footsteps echoed on the wooden beams, a family of geese swam past, and she paused, peering over the railing to watch their progress. How clear the lake was, almost crystalline. Her own reflection stared back at her, soft around the edges, the sky all around.

She was almost tempted to linger here, drinking in the quiet. Certainly, there was little enough of it ahead of her, when she, as an imposter, would rejoin the Society into which she'd been born. But even the rushes in the water and the gulls above could not mask what had once been a scene of immense pain.

Two small boys had been drawn here on a hot summer's day. And how frightened they must have been as their boat sank beneath them, and they struggled to keep their heads above the water. She felt sick at the thought of it, at the anguish Benjamin must have endured. Even now, one could see glimpses of it during unguarded moments, in the set of his jaw, and in the faint creases at the corners of his eyes. If she could, she would spare him the burden of it. She would take it upon her shoulders.

Which was a sure sign she'd come to care for him far more than was prudent. Because any future she might imagine between them was nothing short of fantasy. If she was not careful, he would steal her heart, along with her senses.

But then again, maybe her future was here and now. After all, she no longer had a reputation to protect or even a position in Society to maintain. What else was temptation, if not the chance at a memory to warm the soul when one was old and grey?

Turning away from the water, she hurried across the remainder of the bridge, relieved when her slippers were once more on solid ground. With just a few more steps, her view of the large, limestone manor house was unobscured. Long wings on either side met in a curved center bay, framed by an expansive portico with Doric columns and circular steps that led down to the lawn. Her eyes swept to the tall casement window of Benjamin's study. It lay just to the right of the portico, and if she'd looked just a moment later, she'd have missed it. A figure stepping back into the shadows, vanishing behind a swiftly drawn curtain.

How very curious.

There was every chance, of course, that it had been Maybanks closing the drapes against the afternoon sun. But she didn't think so. Had Benjamin been watching her steady approach from the lake? Had he been embarrassed to be caught spying? Before she could second-guess herself, she decided to find out.

• • •

Caught in the act, peering at her from behind the curtain like a randy schoolboy. He turned from the window in disgust, wishing he had simply waved and looked away. As if that were such an easy proposition. His cravat suddenly felt too tight, and he pulled it off with a vicious tug. He was alone in a darkened room, after all. No one was here to witness the lapse.

He had been avoiding her, of course, and would continue to do so, keeping their interactions as limited as possible. It had proved a successful technique in the past whenever he'd been tempted to explore anything beyond a sexual attraction to a woman. Emotional entanglements were to be avoided at all costs. He could no longer allow this untenable preoccupation to continue.

But when he'd caught a glimpse of her from his study, he'd been unable to resist the pleasure of watching her unawares. She'd chosen an old gown, one better suited to a walk than anything in Lillianne's wardrobe. Not that it had done anything to diminish her beauty. If anything, it had enhanced it, the skirts sweeping about her long legs as she came up the hill, outlining their shape and the smooth movement of her hips.

What was it about her? He'd known women who were prettier. Certainly, he'd known many who were far more sophisticated. One kiss did not make her any less of an innocent, after all. And her starchy demeanor had put off many a man in Society. What fools they all were, himself the biggest of all, not to have seen it. She wore a mask just as he did, hiding a passionate nature, an unconscious sensuality, and a body to tempt the saints. Potent lures, made all the more dangerous because she was fiercely loyal and brave and honest. Hardly for the likes of him.

He returned to his desk, settling into the tufted leather chair that had once been his father's. Was it his imagination that the scent clung to it still? Bay leaf and spice and cigar smoke. Once so familiar and comforting, instead of rank with anger and regret. A reminder that his focus must be unchanged and that wants were not needs, no matter how acute the temptation.

If only this could get underway so it could be done. His eyes fell to the files on his desk. Had he planned for every contingency? They would leave separately in the morning, Jane and Oakley taking the longer journey by linking up with the Dover road and traveling into London from the east. Meanwhile, he and the countess would approach the city from the southwest, traveling directly to Grillion's. They would be the first on hand to greet

Lillianne Fauchon, having noted her impending arrival in the social papers.

No longer would she be under his roof or under his direct protection. And it was safer that way, because of the distance it would put between them. Maybe then he wouldn't spend another night like the one that had just passed, when he'd lain awake, stiff with desire, wondering if she, too, was remembering their kiss.

He put his hands to his temples, rubbing them to the point of pain in order to distract his thoughts. Obviously, he'd gone too long without a visit to his mistress, Claudette. She'd sent several notes over the last few weeks, begging him to call, wondering what she'd done wrong. The fault lay with him, because he'd been worried for the first time that he would call out the wrong name in the throes of passion. And wouldn't that shred his reputation to pieces. Not to mention the embarrassment it would cause Claudette.

A soft knock sounded at the door, probably one of the footmen because it was nearly time for afternoon tea. He bore an invitation, no doubt, from the countess and Jane to join them. Benjamin would refuse politely. One must begin as one meant to go on. Or, in his case, begin again. "You may come in," he called out.

The door creaked open, and he knew in that instant it was not a footman. The scent of lemon verbena was unmistakable. He shot to his feet and braced his hands on the desk.

"I saw you in the window," Jane said as she entered the room. The color in her cheeks was probably due to the walk she'd just finished, rather than any embarrassment she might have about the awkward new tenor of their relationship.

"I saw you as well," he replied, gesturing towards the curtains. "That bridge is sturdy, but the lake is deeper than it looks. And the geese can be rather fearsome. I wanted to make sure you returned to the house safely."

"Fearsome geese, you say?" An impish smile implied she didn't quite believe his excuse. "I'm afraid they need elbows to be truly intimidating."

"Elbows?" Had he missed something?

"If you've ever seen Lady Tremayne in line at a midnight supper, you'll understand what I mean."

"Point scored," he acknowledged, resisting the urge to grin. "Perhaps they're less frightening than I led on. So you were touring the grounds? Were you on the abbey path?"

"I must have been. At least, I saw an abbey along the way. Your property is remarkable."

"Painshill Park, artful contrivance that it is, was my father's pride and joy. All I've done is maintain it." He kept his tone light and impersonal. "It's quite famous among the horticultural set. Both Mr. Jefferson and Mr. Adams came from America to see it when Father was alive."

"The presidents?" She looked not a little awestruck.

"Indeed. We've had all sorts of important personages grace the gardens. Following her visit here, Catherine the Great of Russia commissioned an entire dinner service painted with scenes from Painshill. She particularly liked the hermitage."

"The hermitage?"

"You did not see it? I suppose it is rather tucked away, so as to be more authentic. When I was child, a 'hermit' was hired to live there, but he soon grew bored with playacting, and the head gardener dismissed him for absenteeism."

She laughed, as he'd expected she would, because while true, the story was an absurdity. "Father was very good at creating illusions, you see. Everything here was meticulously plotted and placed."

"So he remade nature to look more natural?" Her expression was a quizzical one. "The results are to be appreciated, but it must have been a tremendous undertaking. Perhaps even a preposterous one."

His sentiments exactly. "Father was a perfectionist." The tension behind his smile had started a slow ache in his jaw. "And as beautiful as this place is, he wasn't convinced God had gotten it right the first time. Even the lake is manmade. Eighty thousand tons of earth and pine forest were moved to create it."

He'd expected her to laugh once more, suitably impressed, but instead, a shadow fell across her face. And despite his decision to remain aloof from her, he could not help but ask the question. "I'm sorry. Was it something I said?" He would take it back, whatever had made her sad, if only to have her smiling again. A thought that should set alarm bells ringing, if nothing else.

"It must have been quite a sight to see," she said after a long moment. "The construction of that lake."

"I suppose it was." He and Aiden had spent many long days watching the workmen with their saws and shovels, attacking the earth and throwing its dirt over their shoulders. "A battle of man versus nature."

"And nature versus nature."

"I think you misunderstand. Nature had no hand in that lake. It was a folly of my father's." His greatest folly.

"Perhaps, but now I know why your geese are hostile," she said, her eyes brightening.

"Really? Please, do enlighten me."

"The lake and its geese displaced many of your woodland creatures. I expect they've been waging war ever since, just like England and France. Goose versus grouse, that sort of thing. Although I shudder to think of their weapons of choice."

He gave a bark of surprised laughter. "You must be right."

She tilted her head then, looking up at him. "It's awfully dark in this study on such a pretty day. Won't you join me for tea in the drawing room?"

When she asked him directly, it was difficult to refuse. "I would like that," he said, walking around his desk to offer her his hand.

But then he remembered the woeful state of his cravat, which could not be retied without Withers's assistance. "I will join you once I'm made presentable."

"I've never seen you with as much as a hair out of place." But she looked intrigued rather than shocked by the state of his disarray. Indeed, for a moment, her eyes lingered on the small vee of skin the open collar exposed, shooting a shaft of desire through him. "I think it suits you," she said, tucking her arm in his. "I like you unbuttoned."

How difficult it was to ignore the lure of her humor and her beauty. To remind himself she was, essentially, a pawn in all of this. But he must. As soon as tea was done. Far better to push for a distance between them than to see the hurt in her eyes at the end, when she discovered he was no better than Rempley.

Chapter 15

Men are so made. They refuse their admiration where it is courted;
where it seems rather shunned, they love to bestow it.
—Fordyce's Sermons to Young Women

"You are more than ready, my dear," Sophia declared as they retired to the drawing room after dinner that evening, Benjamin having left them for a few moments, with the promise of a swift return. "I'm terribly proud."

"I'm rather proud myself," Jane said, beaming. They'd agreed over tea she should practice her disguise once more, to ensure her readiness. And thus at dinner, she'd again been Lillianne. When the conversation turned to life in Paris, she discussed the latest fashion trends and spoke of the wonderful new draper's shop on the *Rue de Buci*. She complained about carriage traffic along the Champs-Élysées, which was more snarled than ever, given the enormous triumphal arch under construction there. And when Benjamin asked about political rumors in the city, she told him Prince Tallyerand, Napoleon's one-time foreign minister, was thought to be in league with the exiled King Louis.

The same Talleyrand who was apparently so fond of grapes.

But one thing still prodded uncomfortably, like a splinter. "Is it wrong to be happy I've mastered a lie?" she asked. "Lillianne is the opposite of me in every way."

"I disagree," Sophia said. "You couldn't have fallen so easily into portraying her were that true. In fact, do you know what I think?"

"I'm almost afraid to hear it." Unless it was a compliment, of course.

"She's the person you've never allowed yourself to be."

"You jest," Jane said with a light laugh. "Had I been sitting beside Lillianne at dinner, saucy baggage that she is, I'd have given her the cut direct."

"I'm being quite serious, my dear." And given the almost apologetic expression the countess was wearing, Jane doubted a compliment was forthcoming. "For far too long, you've let other people's expectations dictate who you are."

Her smile faded, because the observation made her uncomfortable. Even indignant.

"I placed those expectations upon myself," she said, stiffening in her chair. "Why shouldn't I be a model of proper behavior?"

"Because it's unspeakably tedious? And paragons intimidate more than they attract?"

She clenched her jaw, caught up in a well-deserved snit now. "I'll have you know I was universally admired in Society, both for my manners and my temperament."

"Yes, you were," Sophia agreed, her eyes sympathetic. "Until suddenly, you were not. Through no fault of your own."

And how that point stung. It was one she could not argue. Though she would try.

"So instead, I should have traipsed about as if such things didn't matter? Behaving indiscriminately, shaming my father and threatening his aspirations?"

"No, though it might have been fun to return the favor. He certainly deserved it." Sophia leaned forward at that. "Without your mother's guidance, you became the person you thought your father wanted you to be."

Her words hung in the air, a galling indictment. Because Sophia was right. Jane had done everything she could to keep his love, because she'd already seen how easily it could be lost. So she'd mastered her carefully constructed role, only to watch him make a mockery of it in the end.

"I don't say these things to hurt you," the countess said gently. "You've made an incredibly brave decision to reinvent who you are. And after your part in this is done, you will have the rest of your life to live. Make sure it is the one you want. Be bold. And remember, life is more fun when it is unpredictable and a bit off-color."

How easy Sophia made it sound, when Jane didn't yet know what she wanted. She would have said as much if she hadn't heard a door opening behind her.

"I thought you might both like to join me on a tour of the conservatory," Benjamin said, coming to a stop beside her chair. "Hundreds of flowers are in bloom, and Jonas has lit the gaslights so we won't trip over ourselves."

"The two of you enjoy them without me," Sophia said, her hand floating towards her brow like a leaf on the wind. "I'm certain I've a headache coming on."

In fact, Sophia was the very picture of good health, not that Jane would contradict her. Not when the opportunity to spend a few minutes alone with Benjamin had presented itself.

That wonderful, fantastical kiss they'd shared had hinted at so much more. And she could think of at least one thing she wanted ... To know what else she'd been missing.

• • •

Had Benjamin known Lady Marchmain would fob him off with a sorry excuse, all but forcing him to escort Jane to the conservatory alone, he'd never have suggested this tour. Because it was highly inadvisable. He and Jane together. In this darkened place redolent of flowers. No one else in sight. When he longed to touch her.

So, instead, he kept his attention fixed on the room itself, an arched space of iron and plate glass. Or on the long rows of elevated boxes, filled with showy roses, exotic orchids, and a hundred other varietals. On the citrus trees, laden with fruit and planted in large earthenware pots.

"You seem preoccupied," Jane said beside him. "Are you regretting your invitation already?"

"Of course not," he lied. "I'm merely in a contemplative mood." His hands were stiff at his sides, because he knew she'd expected him to take her by the elbow, to guide her through the aisles, as any gentleman would. "Did I mention this was my father's favorite place at Painshill? He considered it one of his greatest accomplishments."

"It's easy to see why."

They continued their slow progress, his right hand reaching out to touch on a petal here, a leaf there, none of them as soft as he knew her skin to be. He cleared his throat, if only to distract his thoughts. "Did you enjoy dinner this evening?" He was determined to keep their conversation mundane.

"I did. I was quite pleased with my performance."

"You did very well," he said, nearly choking on the faint praise. In truth, she'd astonished him. By the end of the meal, even he could believe she'd just arrived from France.

"And it was so kind of Lady Marchmain to lend me this necklace, when it goes so well with my dress. Don't you think?" She'd stopped, her voice expectant.

"Absolutely. Both are beautiful."

"But you didn't even look … "

"I admired them at dinner," he said, sliding her the briefest glance before returning his attention to a trailing clematis vine.

"Oh, no you don't," she said, turning her back to him in a whirl of skirts. "You can't cheat now, not when I've already found you out. Close your eyes."

Gladly. The temptation was less acute that way.

"Describe the dress. And the necklace."

"Something white, I think, with a pretty bauble."

"You were supposed to be judging my readiness for London," she said. Was that hurt in her voice? He'd not meant to hurt her. "You didn't even bother to take notice of what I am wearing."

Oh, he'd noticed. His eyes had slid over every inch of her. "Very well. Your gown is deceptively innocent, in white muslin, with short puffed sleeves." He really should keep his mouth shut and leave it at that. "But the sleeves have thin slits that expose the bare skin of your shoulders. And the thin ribbon of cream silk tied beneath the bodice makes you look like a present waiting to be revealed." Maybe he should open his eyes after all. All too easily, he could imagine unwrapping her.

"Go on." She sounded somewhat mollified.

"The neckline of the dress is not at all innocent. It's daringly low and edged with a pleated tuft of tissue-thin silk. It waves against your skin with each movement you make, like a caress. Or an invitation."

"I'm afraid the neckline couldn't be helped, though I did consider a lace fichu … "

He allowed himself a small smile. "If you had, I'd have removed it and burned it for insubordination on LeRoy's behalf."

She giggled softly. "Very well, you've proved quite observant after all." He could hear her turning back to face him, but still, he kept his eyes closed. Because the image of her had gotten its claws into him, desire trumping determination.

"The necklace … A large teardrop emerald, suspended from a string of rose-cut diamonds ringed with seed pearls. The stone nestles between the swell of your breasts." He could say the word, couldn't he? He'd already shocked her with it once before. "The stones catch in the gaslight, seemingly alive with the heat of you. But they are nothing compared to the glow of your skin." He stopped then, because his voice had gone husky with need, proving he'd already revealed too much. His eyes blinked open to find her watching him, her skin flushed.

"You've a gift for flattery, I think."

"It's not flattery, Jane." His face searched hers. "If you haven't already guessed it, I want you badly. And it's a curse, this desire. Because I can't give in to it."

His breath caught when she looked up and said, "Whyever not?"

"Because of a promise that demands I not take more than I can give." God, how he wanted to pull her against him.

"Surely another kiss would do no harm? I … I need more practice for my disguise."

The words—so innocently bold—were nearly his undoing, but he could no longer use lessons as an excuse. "You don't understand, Jane. Even now, every instinct wants to seduce you. The next time I touch you—if either of us is foolish enough to allow it—I'll not be able to stop at a kiss. I won't stop until you're utterly defenseless."

And with that, he bade her good night, slipping quietly back into the house.

Chapter 16

Daughters of Britain, where is your love for your native country? How long will you be ambitious of flaunting French attire, of fluttering about with the levity of that fantastic people?
—Fordyce's Sermons to Young Women

Over the past several hours, as she and Oakley swayed along in a carriage on the Dover Road, Jane had fought a rising tide of panic. No doubt her performance as Lillianne last night had impressed her audience, but how would it ever be enough? They'd both given her every assurance of success, but Sophia had the brass to pull off any subterfuge, and Benjamin? Well, he was Benjamin. Society might suspect him of divine powers but little else.

She'd barely slept for thinking of their conversation in the conservatory. He'd been trying to warn her away. To tell her his interest was a physical one and nothing more. He'd couched his rejection in the most flattering terms, but he'd obviously honed that skill. Legions of women had fallen under his spell.

But why rebuff her and then all but promise to seduce her?

Because that's what rakes did. Whatever feelings for him she had—and yes, desire was one of them—she'd do well to remember it. Especially given the task ahead.

Because surely, in the history of the British Empire, no one had ever been as silly as she. She would drown in the sweeping currents of her own folly, in the misguided assumption she could fool former friends and family, and indeed everyone she'd ever known, with this ill-conceived plan.

"You're not going to be sick, are you?" Oakley asked. "I've seen that look on your face before, and it did not end well."

God bless Oakley for her utter lack of sympathy. They'd been over this any number of times on the journey into London, and Oakley had offered the same, refreshingly direct reply: "What's done is done. And you'd best not drag me down with you."

How right she was to be concerned. After all, if Jane's deception was discovered, her father's scandal would pale by comparison. So as the carriage pulled up in front of Number 7 Albemarle Street, Jane straightened her shoulders, smoothed the sleeves of her pelisse, and prepared to greet the world—or at least the footmen waiting at the curb of Grillion's Hotel—with a confidence she was far from feeling. The small door swung open as a liveried young man rushed forward with carriage steps.

She'd almost forgotten it, how London assaulted the senses. The clatter of horses on cobblestone and the cries of street vendors. The coal and peat smoke permeating everything. The soot hanging in the air. In all, a filthy and ill-mannered place, making her sudden nostalgia all the more ridiculous.

"Madame Fauchon?" A small, well-dressed man was standing beside the entrance of the hotel, and when she acknowledged him with a slight nod, he offered a deep bow, stepping forward. "I am so proud to welcome you. I am Alexander Grillion, the proprietor of this hotel and a fellow countryman. May I say our entire staff has been eagerly awaiting your arrival?"

The greeting had been spoken in French, so she responded in kind. "Thank you, monsieur. Friends in Paris recommended your establishment, for it has a reputation on both sides of the Channel as a place where a lady will be offered a gentle respite."

He puffed up at her praise. "How pleased I am to know it. Several personages await you inside, eager to make your acquaintance. May I escort you personally?"

"Too kind you are, monsieur. I am desperately in need of a friendly face after my journey. You must know how it is, to travel into a country as the enemy."

"Emperor Bonaparte is the enemy," he replied with a warm smile. "You, madame, are the flower of French womanhood and will surely be welcomed as such."

"And you've a talent for hyperbole," she said with a throaty chuckle as he ushered her into the hotel's lobby, warm with paneled walls and checkerboard marble floors. It reminded one of a luxurious private estate, surely the effect Grillion had sought.

"Are you, too, from Paris?" he asked, guiding her to a door, slightly ajar, off the main lobby.

"I was born there, but I've only just returned after many years along the Côte d'Azur."

"I thought I detected a bit of the south in your voice."

As they passed into a side parlor, she kept her face impassive. She must remember that, as Lillianne, she didn't know these people. Not yet.

"May I present the Countess of Marchmain, Lady Sophia Middleton, and the Viscount Marworth," Grillion said. "Both are eager to welcome you to London, so I will see to refreshments and ensure your trunks are delivered to your suite. Please don't hesitate to ring for me." With that and a short bow, he departed.

She almost breathed a sigh of relief. Grillion, as a Frenchman, had seemed to accept her disguise without question. Still, every word and action must play its part, and because the door was still ajar, she offered a bright smile as they came forward. Sophia was dressed in a beautiful day gown of dove-grey silk, while Benjamin wore a deep blue jacket over buckskin trousers. Both were molded to him in typically disconcerting fashion. Especially disconcerting after last night.

"How kind you are to welcome a stranger. And may I thank you, *monsieur le vicomte*, for sending the carriage to ease my way here? You were a friend to my cousin, I think?"

"Miss Fitzsimmons was a woman I held in very high esteem," he replied, looking appropriately downcast at the mention of her name. How good he was at this. The lying. One would think he'd cared deeply. "And of course, the countess was close to her, as well."

Sophia's attention had already shifted to the doorway. "It seems we're not the only ones eager to make your acquaintance, Madame Fauchon." And while Lady Marchmain's face revealed nothing, her voice held a note of warning. Another test, it seemed, was waiting behind Jane.

"Goodness, you are so like her!" It was Charlotte Montford, rushing into the room to wrap her up in a puff of lilac taffeta, hugging her so tightly the air was nearly forced from her lungs. "Forgive me for being so forward," she said as she pulled away. "Jane was such a dear to me, and we've all missed her terribly. But what a lovely reminder you are of what we've lost. Oh dear, didn't that sound dreadful? I am nervous, even though I shouldn't be. We are nearly family after all."

"Such an enthusiastic greeting, *madame*," she replied, her pulse racing because both Gerard and Sir Aldus had followed Charlotte into the room, eyes assessing. They were the two people most likely to doubt her identity. "My countrymen think the English a stern and dour lot, but you offer ample evidence to the contrary. And we are nearly family, you say? I am Madame Lillianne Fauchon, here in London on behalf of my late cousin, Miss Jane Fitzsimmons."

Gerard stepped forward at that. "I am Montford, now Lord Fitzsimmons, and this is my wife, Lady Charlotte. We saw the announcement of your arrival in the papers and knew we must be here. May I also present Sir Aldus Rempley, Lady Charlotte's former guardian?"

Sir Aldus bowed over her hand, grasping it tightly as he looked up into her face, his eyes speculative. "I was a close friend of the former Lord Fitzsimmons, and of Miss Fitzsimmons as well."

An egregious lie, not that he looked the least bit ashamed. Masking her revulsion, she forced a bright smile. "I am pleased to meet all of you."

"Did you travel here with your husband, Madame Fauchon?" This from Gerard.

"*Mais, non*. I'm afraid I lost him in an accident nearly two years ago."

"How curious that neither Lord Fitzsimmons nor his daughter ever mentioned you in conversation," Sir Aldus said. He'd moved to stand beside her, close enough that she could smell the cologne with which he'd doused himself, a strong scent reminiscent of cloves. He'd also dressed his hair with an oily pomade, to darken it perhaps.

"I'm afraid, *monsieur le baron*, that Lord Fitzsimmons discouraged any communication with our side of the family, especially after the wars began. Jane's letters were a secret between us, full of thoughts we shared with no one else."

"Oh, please do tell," Charlotte said. "Jane was always so terrifyingly proper. How delicious to think she had hopes and dreams, just like the rest of us. Did she tell you a particular man had caught her fancy?" She grinned knowingly at Benjamin.

Well, this they'd not practiced. How to smile when an insult was heaped upon one's former self. Somehow, she managed it. "Jane didn't mention any names," she said, her voice conspiratorial as Sir Aldus stiffened beside her. Every instinct railed against engaging him. "But she did say he was very handsome."

"I hope no one was trying to take advantage at a difficult time," Sir Aldus replied, glaring at Benjamin. "Miss Fitzsimmons was terribly naïve."

Such a hypocrite he was! It was nearly overwhelming, the urge to make an indignant reply and stomp on his foot in outrage. So she pretended instead to a fit of coughing, reaching into her reticule for a handkerchief to complete the deception.

"Are you all right, *madame*?" Benjamin asked solicitously, though his eyes gleamed with amusement.

"It is just … I have been so sad. I only learned of her admirer in that last letter. To think she lost her chance at happiness." She shuddered with what she thought was a rather nice show of delicacy.

"She's in a better place now," Charlotte said. "You must believe it. Things had gotten quite uncomfortable for her in London. But now she is celebrated as a heroine. And as her close cousin, looking so much like her, why, you're bound to be celebrated, as well. It will all be quite good fun."

"Perhaps we shouldn't overwhelm Madame Fauchon," Gerard said. Tact had never been one of Charlotte's strong points.

"You must stay with us at Fitzsimmons House," Charlotte continued, undeterred. "There's no need to rent rooms at Grillion's when you've family here in the city."

How dreadful that would be, to have not a moment's rest from her façade. "It is so generous an offer, but I should never wish to intrude. My stay here is an extended one, as I've several matters to attend to on Jane's behalf."

"But surely we can be of some help? Extra hands will always make a task go faster. I vow I've said it hundreds of times. And once we're done, you'll be free to enjoy London. I can show you all the shops. The best ones are on Bond Street. Really, you must say you'll stay with us."

"Again, you are all that is kind, but it would make me too sad, I think, to be among my cousin's things, when she is no longer here to share them with me."

"Not to worry," Charlotte offered brightly. "I myself have seen to the packing of them. Everything has been labeled and sorted and placed well out of sight."

"Charlotte, that's enough," Sir Aldus cut in, his voice unnecessarily sharp, much as she appreciated his intervention. "You shouldn't be handling Miss Fitzsimmons's personal effects. There are others better suited to the task. And Madame Fauchon deserves some time to acclimate herself to her new surroundings." He returned his gaze to her, and she could not miss the way his eyes swept her body. "Did you travel with a lady's maid, *madame*?" His smile was unctuous. "My niece would be happy to loan you hers, if need be."

"*Merci, monsieur*, but I engaged the services of a young lady in Dover. She is already upstairs, seeing to my trunks."

"You must come to Fitzsimmons House for dinner then, just as soon as you possibly can," Charlotte said. "We want to lay claim to you before the social whirl sweeps you up. Would tomorrow suit?" She turned to Sophia and Benjamin. "You must join us, as well. Shall we say eight o'clock? It will be such fun to learn about Jane's lovely French cousin and about all the goings on in Paris."

"I'd be pleased to escort both ladies," Benjamin replied with a curt nod. "Providing that Madame Fauchon is up to socializing so soon after her arrival."

"*Merci, monsieur le vicomte.* I will look forward to enjoying a meal tomorrow with so many new friends and to visiting Fitzsimmons House once more."

Too late, she realized her mistake. All eyes were suddenly on her; Sophia and Benjamin looked cautious. Montford's head was tilted, and Charlotte was seemingly confused. Sir Aldus regarded her with something very like suspicion.

"If the previous Lord Fitzsimmons wanted nothing to do with the French side of your family," Sir Aldus said, "how is it you were invited to his home?"

"*Alors*, did I misspeak?" How to bluff her way out of this? She couldn't fail when she'd only just begun.

"Have you been to London before, Madame Fauchon?" Montford asked.

"Only in my dreams, *monsieur*. For me, Jane painted both the city and her home in such vivid terms. The famous Bond Street, with the fashionable ladies in their cashmere shawls." She tried for an appropriately wistful expression. "And Fitzsimmons House. How she'd skipped across its floors as a little girl and played among the roses in her *jardin*. The English word is garden, yes?"

"Little Violet plays in that very same garden," Charlotte enthused. "She'll be pleased to show it to you, if you like."

"That would be so kind," she replied. "I have imagined just how it will look."

If Charlotte's answering smile was anything to go by, at least she'd been convinced. Sir Aldus and Montford also looked satisfied … for now.

"We've met you so close upon the heels of your long journey, Madame Fauchon." She could read nothing in Benjamin's expression. "You must be feeling overwhelmed."

"I will admit I am most fatigued, if I may excuse myself. Until tomorrow, then?"

With a final smile, she turned and departed, eager to make her escape.

Chapter 17

[An] ignoble disposition to scandal [is] by many deemed one of the characteristic blemishes of [the female] sex.
—Fordyce's Sermons to Young Women

"Well, that was nearly disastrous," Jane said, sitting upon a richly upholstered sofa in her suite.

"But you recovered beautifully," Sophia said, sitting beside Jane. Oakley had dismissed the last of the hotel maids sent to help with the unpacking, and a fully laden tea cart had been delivered. Jane's hands seemed unsteady, though, as she poured each of them a cup.

For his part, Benjamin was too anxious to sit and too restless for tea. He'd noticed a nearby sideboard with an array of crystal decanters and had set aside his gloves. Already, he had a glass of port in hand.

Jane's one small slip had been a reminder of how tenuous this ruse was. A mistake in such circumstances was hardly surprising. But in her case, the consequences could be disastrous. To be unmasked before the whole of the ton. Or worse.

Swallowing down the port, past a spike of fear, he willed his heart to slow down, even as his mind imagined one hideous outcome after another. "Given Madame Fauchon's native tongue, people will allow for verbal missteps," he said. At least they would at first …

"I think it was Sir Aldus who unnerved me," Jane said. "I hadn't seen him since that dreadful day, when he came to the house after the funeral."

"Benjamin told me he'd made you an outrageous offer." Sophia's expression was one of disgust. "I've already guessed what it was."

Jane nodded. "He said my only other option was the streets, but it might be exciting to see me brought low and not quite so proud."

That, she'd not told him. Was it why he could suddenly imagine the man's neck caught in the grip of his hands? What a pleasure it would be to see Rempley gasping for breath, turning a distinctly unhealthy shade of purple.

"Benjamin, did you not hear me?" Sophia asked, interrupting his reverie.

"I'm sorry. I was daydreaming about the man's demise."

"A sufficiently bloody one, I hope. But as I've just told Jane, it might be wise to subject Madame Fauchon to another unnerving situation before our trip to Fitzsimmons House. One in which she might be tempted to forget her disguise."

"What would you suggest?" To his mind, just sitting alone with Jane in a room could be unsettling.

"Given the way he was eyeing her downstairs, Rempley will likely make a suggestive overture, whether verbal or otherwise. I suggest you do the same, pretending to be Rempley. Let's see if we can find out, in advance, what might fluster Madame Fauchon. It will help her practice a ready response and bolster her defenses."

"But Benjamin is not Sir Aldus," Jane broke in. "How am I to pretend he's … distasteful?"

The way she'd said that last word, as if he was the very opposite of it. As if he were something to be savored. He cleared his throat, forcing himself to loosen his grip on the port glass. "This sounds like another of your terrible ideas, Lady Marchmain."

"Not at all." Her voice nearly purred. "I once tried the same exercise on the Marquis of Vallado, with excellent results."

Vallado … as in her first husband? Had Sophia suggested this to give Jane's confidence a boost, to remind her she had more than enough wit to handle Rempley? Or had she devised it as a special form of torture, to plumb the depths of his attraction to Jane?

It was too late to find out. After tossing a bright smile of encouragement, she said, "Come along, Oakley. Let's leave them to it." Both were already gone from the room.

• • •

The important thing was not to take this too seriously. To treat it as an outrageous exercise in flirtation and nothing more. So when Jane looked up at him, a determined set to her jaw, he waggled his eyebrows, picturing the Marquis of Queensbury, a notorious roué, in order to effect an appropriately lecherous expression. But she did not falter, nor offer even the hint of a smile.

"Would you like a glass of brandy, Madame Fauchon?" he asked. He'd thought to speak in a voice closer to Rempley's distinctively nasal one, but decided it was beneath him.

"*Mais non, monsieur le baron.* I do not indulge in spirits."

"No?" he asked, pouring himself another glass of port. "Then what do you indulge in? Life has so many temptations. Surely you have a weakness for one?"

"But of course," she replied primly. "There's nothing like a good sermon on Sunday at Notre Dame."

A comment designed to cool anyone's ardor. "Sermons are all about sin, *madame.* Could that be why you like them?"

He thought he detected the faintest blush, though her expression had chilled appropriately. When he sat down beside her, she edged away.

"Sir Aldus, I understand you are much engaged in politics. Why does it draw your interest so?"

A clever tactic, to refocus the conversation. Men like Rempley rarely missed the opportunity to trumpet their accomplishments. But Benjamin was not so easily diverted.

"Why, the challenge, of course." He rested a hand on his knee. It was only inches from her own. "In politics, as in sin, a person's passions are engaged. If I play upon those passions in just the right way, they further my own … ambitions."

"I'm quite passionate about politics, as well," she said, regarding his hand with suspicion. "Particularly the advancement of a feminist agenda and the election of women to parliament."

He nearly spilled his port. Rempley would be apoplectic at the thought, any attempt at seduction forgotten. And if the light in her eyes was anything to go by, Jane knew it.

"Have you heard of Mrs. Wollstonecraft, Sir Aldus?" she continued, arranging her skirts fastidiously. "Her works are quite popular in France."

Why did he get the feeling she was addressing the question directly to him and not to his impersonation of Rempley? "Doesn't Mrs. Wollstonecraft argue that a woman should not be influenced by her feelings?" he asked. "When we men so value a woman's sensibilities?"

"You've read *A Vindication of the Rights of Women*?" Her surprise was obvious. "Wollstonecraft believes men exploit our feelings to feed their own desires. Only by reining in those sensibilities can we protect ourselves from domination."

"So women should not feel desire?" His hand had settled gently upon her knee, if only to see her reaction. So far, he could read nothing in her expression. He only knew his own heartbeat was cantering.

"If we do not transcend our 'fleshly desires,' we women will be hostage to our bodies." She swallowed, staring at his hand. "We will only be interested in satisfying … our lusts."

God, to hear her say the word aloud. "Women are forced to make so many sacrifices for men," he said, sliding towards her on the settee, until their sides were pressed together. "Surely desires should be indulged and not denied?"

"That depends," she said in that soft lilting voice she'd perfected for Lillianne, "on whether or not a man plans on exploiting those desires."

It was an invitation he hadn't the power to deny. Not when she was so close. The scents of lemon verbena and lavender, so distinctly her own, so seductive. Lips parting, his lashes swept down as he leaned in towards her mouth.

Maybe that's why he didn't see the slap coming. He certainly felt it, though. A sharp sting, with enough force behind it to turn his head.

"Shame on you, *monsieur*! To importune a poor widow like myself." She was sputtering with indignation, though her eyes sparked with something like mischief. "To speak of desire when I am loyal alone to my poor, lost Pasqual."

Confused, he slid back to the other side of the settee. Had she missed the subtext of their conversation? Or had he imagined it? Was his own desire so uncontrolled that he'd seen invitation where there was none? Or had she been teasing him all along?

"I think that was well done, don't you, Benjamin?" she asked, smiling happily, obviously pleased with herself. "I feel quite energized by the whole episode and far more confident in my ability to deal with Sir Aldus."

He tested his jaw, rubbing the point of impact. "You've a powerful backhand."

"I am sorry. It's just you were doing such a wonderful job of imitating him, I felt as if I were slapping Sir Aldus instead."

"It stings," he said, feeling rather ridiculous.

She glanced towards the doorway and then leaned in with a whisper. "If Lady Marchmain weren't standing right there, I would kiss it to make you feel better."

The minx. It had been mischief all along.

• • •

"She is settled in, then?" Greystoke asked. They were ensconced once more in the basement room he was coming to hate.

"She is," Benjamin replied.

"And she is ready? She is convincing?"

"She had the merest misstep with Rempley, but she quickly recovered." He didn't bother to hide his admiration. "She might fool Napoleon himself."

Greystoke glanced at the others before answering. "She may have to fool our own Prince George, so let's hope so. Tell me, was anyone else at Grillion's to greet her?"

"Shortly after her arrival, Rempley came with Montford and his wife in tow."

"Rempley needs to find those documents as much as we do," Winchester said. He was sitting directly across the table. "Lord Liverpool is furious about the way things were mishandled."

"Is his position on the committee threatened?" Torrington asked.

"I suppose it depends on how much of this gets out. It would prove a major embarrassment, not only to him, but also to the prime minister."

"At least there's still no evidence the documents have reached enemy hands," Greystoke said. "Napoleon's communiques continue to use the *Chiffre*."

"Meaning it's all the more likely they're hidden among Fitzsimmons's things," Benjamin admitted, unable to escape the most logical conclusion.

Winchester leaned in. "When will you collect them?"

"I'll escort her to the Bank of England when it opens Monday morning."

"The sooner, the better," Torrington said. "Depending on what you find among them, they may also contain clues leading to his killer."

"Have you asked Miss Fitzsimmons if she has any suspicions?"

"I haven't told her about how he died." He pushed a hand through his hair, hating the thought of putting her through such a discussion. Better for her to think it had been a random and senseless crime instead of a premeditated one.

No one said anything in response. The three others were watching him, their expressions curious.

"That's very unlike you," Torrington said.

"What is?" Did they really believe he would willingly hurt her?

"I agree," Winchester observed. "This time next week, there will be scuffs on his boots."

"And wrinkles in his jacket, perish the thought."

"Clearly, you've all gone mad," he said. "I'm trying to solve a crime, while you're prosing on about my grooming habits."

"We're trying to say you're dangerously out of character." Greystoke's voice held a warning note. "Benjamin Marworth does not muss his hair, no matter the provocation. Nor do you fail to explore every opportunity for information. Regardless of your feelings for Miss Fitzsimmons, you cannot allow them to cloud your judgment. This is an investigation. Treat it like one."

Greystoke was right, of course. He'd been trying to protect her from further pain. But sometimes the truth required it. "I will speak with her after dinner this evening. We've been invited to Fitzsimmons House."

"That should prove interesting," Torrington replied.

"It will give me the opportunity to study Rempley's behavior more closely."

"And when will she be formally introduced to the rest of the ton?" Greystoke asked.

"Lady Marchmain will be hosting a ball in her honor, and the cards have already gone out. In addition to the cream of English society, each of the committee members have been invited, to gauge their interest."

"It's an excellent idea," Winchester replied. "I'll be eager to see whom the mysterious Madame Fauchon attracts."

Not nearly as eager as Benjamin was.

Chapter 18

It is not to be denied that from the head to the heart,
the distance, in moral reckoning, is often immense.
—Fordyce's Sermons to Young Women

The familiarity of it almost overwhelmed her. The shadows the fast-fading sun cast on the limestone stairs. The sound of the door's bell pull. Even the shuffling of feet in the hallway beyond, as she waited, breath bated, to enter. And when the door swung open, it was all Jane could do not to give herself away. There was Thompson, in a strange new beribboned livery. As they crossed over the threshold, stopping in the hall so a footman could take their cloaks, he bowed first to Sophia, as the highest ranking member of their party, then to Benjamin, with an impressive show of deference. Finally, his eyes fell upon her, tumbling over her person. Rushing back up to observe her face one more, touching carefully on each feature. "*Madame*," he said quietly. "I am already your most devoted servant. How you remind me of someone lost, and very dear."

And even though, in France, one barely acknowledged servants in another person's home, she said, her voice slightly husky, "What is your name, *monsieur*?" How it stung. The grief she saw in his face.

"Thompson, *madame*."

"I thank you for your very kind welcome to my person, Thompson. I have been told by several of my new friends I greatly resemble *ma chère* Jane. I hold it as an honor."

"Thank you, my lady." He cleared his throat, offering a deep bow. "If I may escort you to the drawing room, Lord and Lady Fitzsimmons are eagerly awaiting your arrival."

She noticed, then, that nothing else in the hall was the same as it had been. It was completely redone in a style she could not admire, and she snuck a wide-eyed glance at Benjamin, who merely shook his head. The drawing room, when they crossed into it, was another surprise. The walls had been repapered with alternating emerald and burgundy stripes, the furniture replaced with items that might have been liberated from Versailles. All gilt and discomfort. Nothing soft-looking in sight. And in a way, it was a relief. It served as a reminder this was no longer her home.

"How happy we are that you're here," Charlotte trilled as she came forward in a flattering robin's-egg-blue gown, Gerard on her arm in black evening attire. "Welcome to Fitzsimmons House, Lady Marchmain, Lord Marworth, and of course, our dear Madame Fauchon. Was the journey here at all troublesome? The city should have thinned by now, so late in the Season as it is. But I think the ton is waiting to meet you, our newest treasure from across the Channel."

"Surely, you flatter," Jane said with a demure smile.

"You underestimate your appeal," Sir Aldus said. "You have very notable charms." She'd not noticed him standing beside a tall casement window overlooking the gardens. Again, he wore an excess of pomade, and the snug fit of his jacket hinted at an uncomfortably corseted waist. She could not like the way he watched her, his eyes filled with undisguised interest. Or was it suspicion?

"*Monsieur le baron,* how nice again to see you," she lied, resisting the urge to back away as he came towards her and offered a bow.

"Tell me, do you like your suite?" he asked with an obsequious smile. "Is everything to your satisfaction?"

"It is very charming, with a lovely view of the city." Best of all, she couldn't see the gutter Sir Aldus had likely crawled out of.

"Speaking of charming things," Charlotte said, "we have someone very special to introduce." She motioned towards the door. "Come in, dearest, don't be shy."

Violet, their daughter, was standing in the doorway, dressed in a white linen dress with a blue sash and a matching hair bow. At nine years old, she was a pretty thing, with pert features and masses of strawberry-blond hair, but Jane knew from experience she was nervous in company. Even as her nurse pushed her forward, her eyes darted between each of the adults, one hand working at a strand of hair, twisting it.

"Come now, dumpling," her mother urged. "Madame Fauchon, Lady Marchmain, and Lord Marworth are eager to make your acquaintance. And of course, Uncle Aldus is here, too, and he loves you very much. Can you show everyone your best curtsey?"

But Violet had fixed her attention on Jane, eyes unwavering, her confusion obvious, her lower lip trembling. Clearly, the girl was close to tears, so Jane approached her and leaned down, smiling. "*Bonsoir, my petite fille.* What a lovely child you are."

"Say hello, Violet," Gerard said.

But the girl merely reached a hand up, pulling on her sleeve to urge her closer, until she was almost kneeling upon the floor. "Are you my cousin, Jane?" she whispered.

And she could not help it. Her eyes welled with tears. Never had the weight of her deception been more acute. She hated lying to an innocent. "*Non, ma pauvre chère.* My poor little one. But just for you, on this one night, I wish I was."

"Me too," she replied, although a faint smile had started.

"Can you not take the girl away, Nurse?" Sir Aldus cut in. "It's nearly time to go in to dinner." He hadn't even acknowledged Violet. How could anyone be so disinterested in a child, so casually cruel? He was studying his pocket watch as if it were the most intricate instrument in all the world.

"Come now, Sir Aldus," Gerard said. "You know how Violet treasures your visits. Give your great uncle a hug, my dear."

But the girl stood rooted to her spot, no doubt quelled by Sir Aldus's exasperated sigh.

Jane turned back to Violet. "Do you like dolls, my little one?" When the little girl nodded carefully, Jane said, "Then I shall start looking for the perfect doll tomorrow. I will know it when I see it, and I shall send it, wrapped up in a box and bow for you."

Her smile now fixed firmly back in place, Violet reached for her nurse's outstretched hand and left as Jane returned her attention to the others.

"How good of you, Madame Fauchon," Benjamin said, all charm and good humor, perhaps because he sensed her anger and wanted to distract it. "You've a way with children and a generosity of spirit, I think."

"Yes, you do," Charlotte added with a wide smile, seemingly oblivious to her former guardian's rude behavior. But not Gerard. He was glaring at Sir Aldus when he said, "Let's go in then, shall we?"

So he had some spine after all. Jane was glad to see it.

The table gleamed, each place set with a dozen or more pieces of sterling cutlery. Undoubtedly new, since the Fitzsimmons family silver had been sold off long ago. But Jane could not fault Gerard and Charlotte for setting aside a tarnished past. Whether it was redecorating in a style that didn't suit conventional tastes, or putting aside a traditional period of mourning for her father, the disgraced titleholder, she found she could no longer judge harshly. Life was too precious and short.

The dining room, however, had not yet been redone. The chairs they sat upon were upholstered in a fabric Jane herself had chosen, the linens embroidered with her family's coat of arms. Unbidden, a lump rose in her throat, and as they settled at the table, she struggled to find a distraction, seizing on one Pierre had spoken of. "If you will pardon me," she said, glancing up at Charlotte and Gerard before returning her attention to the table, carefully turning each fork face down, so its prongs rested against the cloth below.

"Is that a French custom?" Charlotte asked, quickly doing the same with her own place setting.

How gifted she'd become at pretense. "In France, people of a certain status have avoided prongs since the Revolution. They look too much like the pitch forks of the *sans-culottes*."

Her hostess looked completely befuddled. Even Benjamin seemed surprised, so she quickly followed up on her reply. "*Je m'excuse. Sans-culottes* ... it is a term referring to the peasants who stormed the Bastille. You know of the famous prison, yes?"

"Indeed," Benjamin replied, as both Sophia and Sir Aldus nodded in agreement.

"The peasants did not wear culottes, you see," she said, addressing her remarks to the table. "The silk knee breeches worn by the nobility and the bourgeoisie. They wore pantaloons instead ... trousers, you call them."

"Are you such a great student of trousers then?" Benjamin asked smoothly. He excelled in this world. One in which banter was infused with innuendo.

"Only when they are worn by a very handsome man," she replied, watching him carefully over the edge of her wineglass. "It makes the study of them far more appealing."

His eyes flared as Charlotte giggled. "Oh, *madame*, you mustn't say such things. You'll embarrass Lord Marworth."

"I have been reminded by friends in Paris that the English are more circumspect," she replied. "I will do my best to remember it. I shouldn't wish to seem forward."

"You're welcome to be as forward as you like," Sir Aldus cut in, his smile obsequious.

"Tell us about Paris, Madame Fauchon," Gerard said, seemingly eager to change the subject. "Is it as beautiful as they say?"

"It is no longer the city of my childhood, of course. It is larger, louder. And the army is everywhere."

"Don't you wish the men would be done with it?" Sophia asked, joining in. "How long now have our countries been at war?"

"For far too long," she agreed. "And though *Le Moniteur* extols the brilliance of Napoleon and trumpets a string victories on the continent, the populace understands it is propaganda from the regime. I've heard it rumored *la Grande Armee* met with a devastating defeat in Russia and that your General Wellington is close to controlling Spain. The emperor claims victory will come with perseverance. But I believe he is straining the loyalty of France."

"Those are bold opinions to voice, *madame*," Sir Aldus said. "Would you say the same thing on the streets of Paris?"

"But of course not, *monsieur*," she said, forcing a smile. "In France, I flirt with Napoleon's commanders and profess my utter devotion to the cause. One does what one must in such situations, *n'est ce pas*?"

"If I recall," Sir Aldus continued, "Lord Fitzsimmons once told me his wife's family was closely connected to the regime."

"My father knows the emperor well. It would be a lie to say otherwise. At one point, all of France was caught up in his vision of glory. But that is changing. The people are weary of the costs of war, both in money and in men. Every family has offered up a son. We want peace."

"From your mouth to Bonaparte's ears," Gerard said.

"I would appreciate the chance to speak with you further about the situation in France," Sir Aldus said. "Perhaps a carriage ride in Hyde Park? I know I'd be the envy of every gentleman there."

"But of course. I'd like nothing more." It was her boldest lie yet.

"Would tomorrow suit, then?"

"*Bien sur*. The following day, I must see to business at the Bank of England."

"Should you like me to escort you there, as well?" he asked, leaning forward. "I'd be most pleased to be of assistance."

"I've already offered to help Madame Fauchon, Sir Aldus," Benjamin cut in smoothly. "She has the use of my carriage for as long as she might need it. It is an unfamiliar city to her, after all."

Sir Aldus stiffened, clearly annoyed. "Once again, you have the advantage over me when it comes to a beautiful woman, Marworth." His eyes slid back and forth between them. "First, it seems, with Miss Fitzsimmons, and now with her cousin."

She pretended surprise. "Were you an admirer of Jane, as well as a friend? I did not know it."

"For many long years," Sir Aldus admitted. "Marworth's interest was a sudden and unwelcome surprise."

"I can't deny *monsieur le vicomte* is all that is charming, But I also appreciate a man of dignity and distinction, such as yourself," she said, infusing her voice with false enthusiasm. How hard it was to encourage him. "I will look forward to our ride in the park."

His slow, appreciative smile unsettled her stomach. "As will I."

• • •

"He is reprehensible," Jane said as the carriage ambled its way back after dinner. Outrage had painted bright spots of color high on her cheeks, and in the gaslight, her eyes flashed indignantly.

"You remind me of one of the mythological furies, my dear," Sophia said as she settled back against the leather squabs. "A modern-day Tisiphone, ready to wreak vengeance on the damned. Or in this case, Aldus Rempley."

"Didn't Tisiphone have black bat wings and a head of hair entwined with serpents?" Jane asked. "Both might be worth it if they spared me his company. As the meal progressed, he could not have been more encroaching."

"He finds you attractive, Jane," Benjamin said. "As we suspected he would." And how could anyone not? She was luminous in a green evening gown, its elaborate embroidery mirrored on the cashmere shawl slipping from her shoulders. "At the same time, I don't think he quite believes his eyes. Your knowledge about current-day Paris may have alleviated many of his suspicions, but Rempley didn't rise to his position of authority without being a skeptic."

"I think the better word is misogynist. He was abominable to poor Violet and seemed embarrassed by Charlotte. What a miserable upbringing she must have endured as his ward."

"If rumor serves correctly," Sophia said, "her parents died when she was close to Violet's age. Why anyone thought he'd make an appropriate guardian, I can't say. She was shuttled off to his country estate, neither seen nor heard of until her marriage was arranged with Montford."

"They seem quite happy together, though," Jane said.

"Given that Montford was your father's heir, I'm sure a minimum of effort was needed to secure the deal. Rempley married her off at the first opportunity, when she was not even seventeen, to rid himself of the responsibility."

"Speaking of Montford." He turned to Jane. "I saw him pull you aside as we were leaving. Was there something he wanted?"

"It seems several important documents related to my father's estate are missing, and he thinks they're among the papers at the bank. He asked to review them first, because of their sensitive nature. But I said they'd been entrusted to me for a reason, and I would pass along anything that seemed relevant. He was not pleased."

"He's not used to being contradicted by a woman," Sophia said. "Charlotte's not the sort to stand up to anyone."

"I've done her a disservice all these years," Jane said, her face thoughtful. "It's easy now to see why she talks as much as she does. Sir Aldus obviously ignored her growing up, and children will go to almost any lengths for attention and love. We're rather desperate for it."

• • •

After they took Sophia back to Marchmain House, the carriage, with just the two of them inside it, felt all too intimate. Benjamin's fingers itched to slip that shawl from Jane's shoulders. "I don't like to think of you being lonely as a child," he said, in an effort to distract his thoughts.

She merely smiled, her head slightly tilted. "We all have our moments of loneliness, don't you think? But my upbringing was not overly so. My parents may not have always loved each other, but they loved me. It is what I try to remember when I look back over their lives and think about the choices they made."

Her words were a terrible reminder of the grim task facing him. "This is not an easy thing for me to ask you, Jane." His palms were sweaty in his gloves. She sat there, a quizzical look on her face, a last moment of blissful ignorance before he destroyed it. "Did your father have many enemies?"

"It might be difficult to point to only one," she replied. "You'll recall he was not well liked."

"No, at the end, I suppose he was not. But can you think of anyone who would intentionally do him harm? His death, we've learned, was not the result of a chance encounter. It was premeditated."

Her eyes widened, as he'd known they would. "How can you be certain?"

"There were witnesses at Sharpe's. Without recounting the details, suffice it to say he did not die there."

Her lower lip had started the slightest tremble, and her eyes were suspiciously bright. "I'd reconciled myself to a random act of violence. London can be a dangerous place. But something preplanned? How can he have fallen so far, that someone would do such a thing?"

"Can you recall any details about that night? Anything you might not have mentioned before?"

"He was agitated," she said, her voice wavering. "But then he often was before a night at the tables. I should have guessed it then, that he wasn't meeting up with Sir Aldus. He'd already been to see him the day before."

The day the dossiers had gone missing. "Did he mention the purpose of that prior meeting?"

"He'd been trying to find ways to bring in money, and I think he'd stumbled upon something. He'd just returned from a trip out of London, although he wouldn't say where he'd gone or why. I assumed he wanted to discuss it with Sir Aldus. He went to see Gerard, as well."

"What was his mood upon returning from those visits?" According to Montford, it was the day he'd begged both men for money, so his trip had failed to net anything substantive, at least in terms of funds.

"Resigned, perhaps? He retreated into his study with a bottle of cognac and did not emerge for the rest of the evening. Before I went up to bed, I peeked in on him. He was sitting in his chair, staring at the fire, an empty glass in his hands."

Was it the behavior of a man who'd just stolen state secrets? It was difficult to say. "Do you recall any other correspondence that night or the next day?" Surely, Fitzsimmons had begun to explore avenues of sale if he'd had the documents in hand.

"None that Father sent out, but he did receive two other notes in the afternoon. After reading them in his study, he told me he needed to see to a personal affair. That once it was settled, everything would take a turn for the better. When he left, the sun had not yet set. It was the last time I saw him alive."

"How did you discover what had happened?"

"Father's pockets, of course, had been emptied, but the thieves had little use for his calling cards. They'd been dumped beside him, and someone had the decency to track down a night watchman. When I received word in the very early morning, Thompson kindly delivered a note to Gerard. And Gerard informed Sir Aldus."

"Why wasn't an investigation launched, the runners involved?"

"Neither of them thought it would help. Father was dead, and in a most mortifying way. The scandal would have grown exponentially if the press got word of it. And by all appearances, it was a random act of violence. It was horrible."

"I'd have tried to see you through it, had I known." He might have found a way to keep Fitzsimmons home that night. Home even from Rempley's and what must have proven a terrible temptation to a desperate man.

"We hardly knew each other well, Benjamin," Jane said, a single tear finally breaking free, tracing a glistening path down her cheek. "And yet you came to Father's funeral. It was such a kindness, when no one else would."

He swallowed, something like bile in his throat. "I was … awed … that you would risk so much to save Alec and Annabelle." And he had been. But it was hardly the reason he'd joined her in the rain that day.

"It's ironic, isn't it, that such a great price had to be paid for telling the truth?" She'd turned towards the carriage window, clearly struggling to mask her emotions. "No wonder it is so much easier to lie."

"No, Jane. The cost of lies may not always be readily apparent, but you lose a little piece of yourself every time." Until nothing was left of you but a shell all too easily broken.

Chapter 19

Bashfulness, the flower of female chastity, is of a nature so delicate and tender, as always to thrive best in places the least frequented.
—Fordyce's Sermons to Young Women

"It's a lovely day for a ride in the park," Sir Aldus said as he greeted her in the hotel's lobby. "And I am blessed to share it with an even lovelier companion." He'd obviously taken great care with his attire. His hair wore its customary pomade, but his dark green jacket and fawn trousers fit better than any clothes she'd seen on him previously. Probably because they were a size larger.

"Such compliments, *monsieur le baron*," she replied, already regretting the excursion. "You will turn my head."

"That's my sincere hope, *madame*," he said, eyes gleaming until he noticed Oakley standing behind her. "There's no need for your maid, surely? I've brought my barouche, which is open to the sun, so there can be no question of impropriety."

"Of course not. But as you say, the day is such a pleasant one. And she, too, is eager to see this Hyde Park. It is very fashionable, no?"

He pasted on a smile. "Indeed. Especially at this time of day," he said, walking them towards his carriage. It was an expensive vehicle, led by two beautifully matched greys and a liveried driver. Once Oakley had climbed up onto the perch, Sir Aldus joined Jane on the squabs, and they set off.

"We have many such parks in Paris," she began. "But my favorite is the Jardin des Tuileries, near the Place de la Concorde. Such beautiful sculptures and fountains, with small tents set around the perimeter, offering petit cafes and the most wonderful treats."

"It has been many years since I've been to the city, of course," Sir Aldus said. "That brief peace at the end of the First Coalition War. You'd have been a young girl then. But there was a wonderful restaurant not far from the Place de la Concorde, just off the Champs-Élysées. It had a two-story pavilion with terraced gardens. Do you know it?"

She swallowed, suddenly ill at ease. Was he testing her? She'd studied countless news-sheets and journals. She and Pierre had even discussed the most popular restaurants, but in that moment, she couldn't name a single one. "So many wonderful places ... " she said, with a breezy wave of her hand, hoping that would end it.

"I'm certain it was the oldest establishment in Paris. And very popular. I can't believe you'd not know it."

"Perhaps the street name would help?" Something. Anything.

"Come now, *madame*," he said, stiffening beside her. "I don't like to admit my memory occasionally fails me. Save me from the embarrassment of it."

She'd wager his memory was perfect. And any true Parisian would know the name. Pierre was certain to have mentioned it. Think! Sir Aldus was watching her carefully, his eyes dark.

"Ah yes, but of course!" Thank God. "You are speaking of Ledoyen, on the Avenue Dutuit. How could I not have known it the instant you mentioned the gardens?"

"It is still there then?"

"Yes, indeed. Supposedly, Napoleon first laid eyes on his Josephine there."

"I didn't know that," he said, relaxing once more beside her. "I recall they served a delicious breakfast."

Let him doubt her now. "You must have been there with all the duelists then," she said, laughing gaily, nearly giddy. "After shooting at each other in the Bois de Boulogne, they reconcile over breakfast at Ledoyen."

"I'd fight a duel for you, *madame*," he said, not bothering to mask his sudden interest in her bosom, even though she'd worn the most modest dress in Lillianne Fauchon's wardrobe. She pulled her shawl more tightly around her shoulders.

"La, *monsieur*," she said, with what she hoped was an appropriately flirtatious smile. "You'd not be the first one."

The park was thronged with carriages, their progress slow as the driver navigated between a seemingly endless stream of pedestrians and men and women on horseback. Rotten Row was always a spectacle, young bucks eyeing the Season's debutantes, while matrons looked on, stiff with disapproval. Gossip thrived here, too, and already, dozens of people had watched them pass, openly curious as Sir Aldus nodded to each of them, smiling broadly. "You'll be the talk of the city by nightfall, *madame*."

"Oh, I hope so," she said. "One does like to be noticed, as long as it is for the right reasons. Before my trip, I worried a French citizen would not be readily welcomed." A rather clumsy attempt to sway the conversation, but she needed to get a better sense of where his sympathies lay.

"There is much about your country an Englishman will admire," Sir Aldus said. "The wines are a marvel, and the food is vastly better. Even the prince regent employs a French chef."

"He doesn't worry about spies beneath his roof?"

He shot her a quizzical look. "What do you know of spies?"

She hoped she hadn't overplayed her hand. "Only that they are rife in Paris. Napoleon's ministers are suspicious of everyone, and the emperor insists a soldier taste every dish before he will eat it."

"He's a wise man, then," Sir Aldus said, an edge to his voice. "There are many who'd like to see him dead, myself included. But let's not speak of politics when I can learn more about you."

"I am no great mystery." Indeed, he might be surprised by how little substance Lillianne Fauchon had.

"I disagree, and I plan to discover all your secrets. But know this," he said with a leering smile, "I'd trust you to put anything into my mouth. In fact, I'd welcome it."

"How you tease, *monsieur*!" she said, rapping him playfully with her fan when she'd rather break it over his head. Even when he'd been her father's friend, she'd never been comfortable with the way he watched her. It was one of the many reasons she'd refused his repeated proposals of marriage. But she'd never suspected the depths of his lechery. Benjamin had saved her from a fate she couldn't imagine without nausea.

"Rempley, won't you introduce us?" asked a voice nearby. Welcoming the reprieve, she turned to find Nicholas Bourneman, the Marquis of Winchester, staring down at them from a massive black stallion. With equally dark hair, blade-sharp features, and an imposing physicality, he was very handsome, so intimidating in his riding attire she didn't immediately see Henry Brougham, the Baron of Brougham and Vaux, beside him. A small, middle-aged man, he had a kind smile and lively brown eyes. Both, she knew, masked a fiery temperament. He was also a staunch supporter of Queen Caroline, the regent's estranged wife. But did either fact make him a likely suspect in the theft of the dossiers? It was hard to imagine it.

Rempley hastily performed the introductions, obviously wishing them on their way, but neither seemed so inclined. "It is an honor, Madame Fauchon," Winchester said. "Lord Marworth has spoken at length about your beauty and poise."

"I didn't realize the two of you were so close, Winchester," Sir Aldus said, apparently miffed. "I'm surprised he'd share such thoughts."

"You know how it is with Marworth. We all like to think he's a good friend. It puffs up our sense of importance."

"I understand you're newly arrived from Paris, *madame*," Brougham said. "I hope you will find your stay here hospitable, despite the sad tidings precipitating it."

"Thank you, *monsieur le baron*. The purpose does indeed pain me, but everyone has been so kind."

"I understand you're staying at Grillion's?" Winchester asked. "I hope you'll allow me to pay a call. I did not know your cousin well, but hers is an inspiring story, one about which I'd like to hear more."

How sincere he sounded. One would never know he was a partner to their duplicity. "I would so enjoy the telling of it. Please do."

"Rempley, surely you know the prime minister is eager for your attention on at least one matter," Brougham said, his manner gone stiff. "I'm surprised you have time for a leisurely ride in the park."

Was he referring to the missing dossiers? Would Brougham mention them aloud if he was in any way culpable?

"I am doing what I can to get to the root of the matter," Sir Aldus sniffed, clearly annoyed.

"Good. Because we need its resolution. *Madame*, it has been a pleasure."

Both gentlemen tipped their hats and moved along. Unfortunately, Sir Aldus remained. They were in his carriage, after all. "I hesitate to cut our afternoon short, but I'm reminded of pressing political concerns."

"*C'est domage*." She sighed. "I was so enjoying myself." On the inside, she was dancing.

• • •

Benjamin had been pacing far longer than he should have been in Grillion's lobby. Indeed, the fact that he was pacing at all had drawn more than one surprised stare. But surely Jane should already have returned from her ride in Hyde Park? Or had Rempley ordered his driver to take a protracted route back to the hotel? He'd not attempt something inappropriate with Oakley close by. Would he?

Perhaps Benjamin was being overprotective. To ensure he'd not miss her, he'd cancelled his weekly sparring session with Gentleman Jack, heretofore sacrosanct. He'd also fobbed off the prince regent's request for advice on renovations at Carlton House. And he'd sidestepped another invitation from his mistress, Claudette, to call.

Nor could he offer himself a convenient excuse for his actions, other than to admit that his focus was on Jane and the dossiers right now.

It was only logical he spend as much time in her company as possible.

When at last, however, Jane swept into the lobby, he ignored his many justifications and simply admired her. Dressed in a walking dress of cerulean blue, with an emerald green pelisse and a matching hat adorned with plumes, she looked happy and possibly relieved. The ride must have gone well. Or perhaps she was merely glad it was done. Oakley was just a step behind.

"*Monsieur le Vicomte*," she said as he approached. "Such a lovely surprise. Did we have an appointment I'd forgotten?"

"Not at all, Madame Fauchon," he replied, bowing over her hand. "I was merely wondering if you'd had need of your impressive backhand today."

"Sir Aldus was suggestive," she said in a low whisper, to make sure they were not heard. "But he kept his hands on his own knees."

Evidently, Rempley had more restraint than he did in close quarters. Thank God. "Would you care to accompany me to Gunter's for an ice?" It was perhaps the last thing he'd come here to do, but it was a warm summer day. And he had a regrettable weakness for ices. And for Jane Fitzsimmons. "I understand they've just introduced a new flavor."

In less than a half hour, they were settled beneath one of Berkeley Square's large maple trees, having just received their order from a waiter dashing between traffic with his tray. Caught up in the antics of a group of small boys playing on the manicured lawn, Oakley was sitting with her ice on a bench in the square, Benjamin's driver beside her. Meanwhile, Benjamin and Jane sat together in his barouche as he watched her slip her spoon between her lips.

"Elderflower ice," he said, rolling the word on his tongue. "I should have thought you'd prefer lemon."

Jane, too, had been watching the young boys, but her head turned at that, her expression amused. "Because it's so tart?"

He grinned. "I was thinking of the word sharp."

"This from the gentleman who ordered a parmesan ice … " Her head gave a small little shake before turning back to the boys, who were laughing with delight as they chased a flock of pigeons up into the air. There was something like longing in the way she watched them. Perhaps for the brother she'd never known. Or the playmates she'd never had. No doubt, she'd have been a reserved child, with a spotless white dress and crisply curled hair done up in bows.

He looked around the square to be certain no one was listening before leaning closer. "Chasing pigeons is not as fun as it looks."

"I'll have you know I was a very active little girl," she said archly, as if she'd been insulted. "I've seen my share of scrapes and bruises. And pigeons."

He lifted a hand in mock surrender. "I meant no offense," he said. "But you hardly seem the type."

"If you are referring to my always stately reserve, that came after mother died." Her eyes swept the park, and then she, too, lowered her voice. "But when I was a young girl, most of my summers were spent in Scotland with my grandparents. I ran wild, traipsing all over the estate."

"Is that where you learned to swim like a water sprite?"

"Indeed. It's also where I learned not to climb rocks after I'd been swimming." She'd withdrawn her gloves, holding out her left palm so he could inspect the long, white scar that bisected it.

Unthinking, he traced it with his finger, the stiff ridge of it so at odds with the softness of her hand. "How far did you fall?"

"Far enough," she said, slowly pulling her hand away. "But I had the respect of the village doctor who bandaged me. I didn't cry, not once."

"Brave girl," he said, something twisting inside him. "Though I've said it too many times, in shockingly redundant fashion."

She merely smiled. "What were you like as a child, then?"

"Oh, I could do no wrong. I was handsome, and strong, and above all, healthy." The last word had tumbled out before he could stop it. "I was the perfect heir, not only to my father's noble bloodline, but also to everything else he'd built. The ideal choice to one day populate the whole of England with his progeny."

"No one is perfect," she said, head tilted with something like sympathy.

"My brother came very close," he said. But he didn't like to talk about Aiden. His memory was something to be kept private, his own intimate form of torture. "He died when he was only ten."

"Such a loss never quite leaves you, does it? I am sorry."

And looking into her eyes, he could see she was. There was none of the morbid curiosity he'd seen in others, who'd guessed at the details of his involvement on that hideous day. Just sorrow and pain for the brother he'd lost, as the breeze ruffled her hair.

It suddenly seemed important she know something.

"I wish you could have met him." Surprisingly, he meant it. "Aiden was everything good and innocent, and he was far brighter than I could ever be." Aiden had been able to grasp the most difficult concepts, while Benjamin stood by, dumbfounded. "We all marveled at his abilities. But he had physical challenges.

"You see, he was born healthy enough, but when he started to crawl, my mother noticed a weakness in his left leg. By the time he was four, that entire side was affected." The story had not been shared in so long, it somehow felt dark and secret. In the end, it had been. "He struggled to walk, even with crutches. And he suffered from horrible seizures and spasms."

"I can't imagine how difficult it must have been for your family, to see a loved one so burdened."

It had torn them apart. "But he was remarkably resilient. Aside from his physical difficulties, he was like any other boy." Even if his father hadn't been able to see it. "We laughed, and we fought. We played at war. His favorite role was that of Lord Nelson, ordering me to report from the front lines, to spot the enemy's weaknesses." He could still picture the hat they'd fashioned from old news-sheets, a paper version of the admiral's own. "Had he lived, I'm certain he'd have been a statesman or a great general. Someone who made a difference."

"Is that why you are a spy, then?" she asked. "Because he was the first person to make you one?"

He could feel his pulse at the base of his neck, beating like a battlefield drum. "Well, that, and because it's the last thing my father wanted for me before he died," he said, flashing a weak smile. Hopefully, the comment had been just flippant enough to distract her. Those soulful eyes saw too much.

She watched him for several long moments, as he resisted the urge to loosen his collar. "What was the first thing your father wanted?"

She'd not been distracted after all. "For me to populate the whole of England with his progeny, of course," he said, keeping his voice light. "Haven't you been listening?"

As Oakley and his driver rejoined them, they set out for the hotel. Their ices were done, but it was just as well. All he could taste now was regret.

Chapter 20

I should be afraid of learned ladies of any kind . . .
lest the pursuit of such elevations should interfere with the plain duties and humble virtues of life.
—Fordyce's Sermon to Young Women

At the bank the next morning, Benjamin watched Jane charm the head clerk, looking adorably confused as he explained the papers requiring her signature. "It must be why you are winning the war," she said. "The British are so very thorough." And he'd almost laughed when she waxed on about how large the bank was. Such an impressive testament to its sober management. Clerks at the Bank of France were terribly rude to poor widows like herself, when he'd been so kind, so patient. By the end of the performance, Benjamin had little doubt the man would have given Jane anything for which she'd asked, even bank boxes that weren't her own.

They'd stumbled upon Winchester there, although Benjamin was certain it had been no accident. Jane had mentioned the interlude at the park yesterday, and the marquis had obviously wanted another opportunity to judge her readiness. By the look of things, he'd been more than impressed. In fact, he'd not needed to make his admiration quite so obvious.

However, as they made their way back to Grillion's in Benjamin's carriage, she was unusually subdued, staring at the two cases beside her with apparent trepidation. And there were faint shadows beneath her eyes. He'd not noticed earlier. "Is something wrong, Jane?"

"I didn't sleep well last night." Her attention was still fixed on the cases. "I haven't been able to stop thinking about the way in which Father died. It made me wonder if his papers might hold any clues."

"And you're afraid of what you might discover?" Just as he was.

She nodded. "He wasn't himself at the end. What if he was engaged in something truly nefarious? Why else would anyone plan his murder?"

"I can't answer that. I wish I could." Was it too late to bargain with the devil? To argue Rempley alone deserved the hellfire reserved for traitors? Perhaps he could find a way to look at Fitzsimmons's files before she did. If he were lucky enough to find the dossiers among them, Jane need never know. Surely, the deceit would be a just one, to spare her? "I can review them first, if you'd like. I might have a better sense of the things to look for."

"Would you?" The relief in her eyes clawed at him. "I find I'm hesitant to discover the truth, cowardly though it might be. And it would offer me the chance to go through my mother's mementoes. It's been a long time since I've had anything tangible to remember her by."

"Do you favor her?" It was hard to see traces of Fitzsimmons in the elegant line of her features.

"Both in looks and temperament, according to Father. In those early years after her death, he found it upsetting."

Was that why she'd hidden her vibrancy behind so many stiff layers? In order to strip herself of the characteristics Fitzsimmons had once adored, then despised? It was not a question he could ask as they rolled through the streets of London on a stifling summer day.

• • •

After an hour spent reviewing the papers from his home near Berkeley Square, he was no closer to learning the fate of the dossiers. Nor was there much in the way of clues to unmask a killer.

There were documents splayed over his desk—newspaper clippings, tradesmen's bills, and assorted personal correspondence—but nothing more. Not yet.

He'd organized everything by type and date. Fitzsimmons had saved copies of articles quoting his speeches. Every laudatory statement made about him by the editors of *The Times*. Every notable legislative achievement. Apparently he'd enjoyed reveling in past glories. Conspicuously missing was any mention of the scandal leading to his downfall.

Other clippings, yellowed with age, were more sentimental. Fitzsimmons had kept his wedding banns and the announcement of Jane's birth. He'd saved the news of Nelson's death at the Battle of Trafalgar, as well as other key victories in the war thus far. There was also the announcement of Charlotte's marriage and the subsequent notice of Violet's birth.

The earl's unpaid debts went back more than a year, but while numerous, they weren't out of the ordinary. There was a disgruntled tailor intent on getting his due. Meat and fishmongers who were refusing an extension of credit. The chandler, too. But there was nothing to indicate Fitzsimmons had been to the moneylenders. Instead, there were bills of sale—stacks of them—for carriages and horseflesh, paintings and jewelry, a property in Shropshire, yet another in Dorset. Despite the money raised, only one recent entry in the accounts had been marked paid, and that just a few days before the earl's death. Fifty pounds, a not insignificant sum for a man deeply in debt, had been sent to a Madame La Farge of Whitecross Street in Clerkenwell. It was an area of London rife with prostitution and thievery.

Had Fitzsimmons kept a mistress then? Despite the French name, it was unlikely she'd been a conduit for the dossiers. Else, he'd have been receiving funds instead of spending them. But there was also a chance he'd been buying a contact. One who could notify the right people about the information he had for sale. It would bear investigating.

Most of Fitzsimmons's personal correspondence was made up of letters from former friends, saying loans would not be forthcoming and they'd not be at home should he insist on a personal call. One was from Winchester himself, who'd served with him in the Lords. Had he mentioned the earl's entreaty during any of their meetings? Benjamin didn't think so. There were also several letters from Montford, complaining about his dwindling inheritance, and notes from Rempley, all of them evasive when it came to requests for assistance. And dated the day he'd died, a missive from Montford, saying he was considering his proposal but that he would need proof; another from Rempley, claiming he was outraged and offended. Both had insisted he pay them a visit by evening's end. Visits which apparently had never transpired.

There were, however, a few pieces of correspondence not yet opened, letters that had arrived either just before or perhaps after the earl's death. Most were additional bills, but two were not. One was from the mysterious Madame La Farge, a simple letter folded but not sealed. The lettering was crude, the message direct.

> I'll not swear to nothing. I've said what I know.

Swear, as in a court of law? Why would a man likely engaged in treason want to open himself up to the scrutiny of the English courts? It made no sense. Nor did Madame La Farge sound like an *émigré*. More likely, she was London born and bred, and not from Mayfair, either.

The second letter had also been sent by a woman, an Althea Mortimer from Luton in Bedfordshire, not thirty miles from London.

> It is good you found us. My mother, ill as she is, has long been burdened with her knowledge. She hopes, at last, to make peace with her Maker.

Some sort of sin then in Luton, revealed to Fitzsimmons, but why? Was that where he'd gone in the days before his death?

He tucked the papers back into their box and locked them away in a secret compartment hidden in his desk. No sooner had he stepped away than there was a knock on the door. "You've a visitor, Lord Marworth," his butler announced. But the visitor had hardly waited in the hall, as was customary.

"I'll not be put off any longer," a feminine voice trilled as Claudette pushed past the butler into the room. His beautiful, erstwhile mistress, with a temper to match the hue of hair.

• • •

Jane sat alone in the bedroom of her suite. How thankful she was for Benjamin's offer, because in this moment of weakness, it was easier to ignore certain truths. That her father had obviously been caught up in something he should not have been. That the price he'd paid for his transgression was the highest one could pay. It would all come out in the end. She had no desire to speed the process when there was a good chance it would crush her.

She'd rather give in to breathless anticipation. Setting the case with Mother's things upon a delicate lady's desk placed near the fireplace, she undid the leather straps and peered inside.

Even now, years later, Mother's things still held the faintest hint of her perfume, a lavender scent reminiscent of childhood summers in Provence. There, tucked in one corner of the case, was the small oval portrait Father had commissioned after their wedding day. So pretty, she'd been, with glossy, brown hair, and bright, brown eyes, her generous lips curved in a smile as she stared off into an unseen distance. Had Mother ever again been as happy as she'd been that day, when the likeness was painted?

A similar but larger portrait had once graced the main hall on Curzon Street, but of course, it had been taken down long ago.

Father had destroyed quite a few things in the weeks following her death, but Jane's nanny—once Mother's own—had saved what she could, hiding the mementoes away in a box beneath her bed.

Such a generous gesture. One that would no doubt have seen her sacked had it been discovered. But Nanny had been loyal to the end. For it had not been Father who'd opened the Bank of England box in her name. It had been the wise, gentle woman who'd helped to raise her, gone now for ten years or more.

There, in the opposite corner of the box, lay the linen cap Mother had embroidered for Jane's baptism, edged with silver fleur-de-lys. And just beneath it, a drawing Mother had once done for her, depicting the house in Paris where she'd been raised, a generous dwelling behind iron gates, set amidst a profusion of summer blooms. And tucked beneath the first layer of items, the small doll—cherub-faced and blue-eyed—that she'd played with as a child, still dressed in the white pinafore she and mother had sewn together.

So many wonderful things, long forgotten. One by one, Jane removed each precious thing. Amethyst earrings set in gold filigree, Mother's favorites, sent by her parents one Christmas. Several jeweled bracelets, which Jane had often worn as a child, pretending she, too, was dressed for a fancy evening ball. When it had been just the two of them together, mother and daughter, there had been joy and often laughter. Each new item recalled a memory. How could she have forgotten so many of them?

Nanny had also saved some of Mother's correspondence. A beribboned stack of letters from Father, love notes, apparently. It would be too sad to read them now, knowing how little love her parents had shared at the end. There were also letters from Mother's family, written in French. While they'd lived, her French grandparents had sent her beautiful gifts for birthdays and holidays, but she'd never met them. As far as she now knew, Mother's brother was the only remaining member of her immediate family. A member of Napoleon's inner circle. Lillianne's father.

On this day, though, she was not Lillianne. She was merely a daughter playing dress up in someone else's clothes. A daughter missing her mother.

With a husky sigh, she peeked back inside the box. Only one small stack of letters remained, addressed in a hand she did not recognize. They were creased, a haphazard pile, as if hastily folded and hidden beneath the rest. She wondered, with a kind of morbid fascination, if they were from Mother's lover. The one Father had spent subsequent years reviling, all too often in the presence of his daughter. The man who surely must have mourned Mother's loss, as well as the loss of the son they'd created. Or had he even known? Perhaps Mother had been as promiscuous as Father had insisted. Jane didn't like to think so, but she had a better appreciation now of the temptation a man's touch presented.

Why had Nanny saved them? Had she simply swept things from Mother's bedside in the aftermath of that terrible evening? She'd been grief-stricken, too, after all. No doubt everything that had touched the hand of a person she'd loved had seemed precious.

Jane fingered the letters, waging a debate within herself. It would be the worst sort of intrusion. Like turning back the shroud of a woman long dead. But she'd seen her mother taken far too soon, in circumstances that had torn her own life apart. And so she opened each one and read them. Notes scribbled in haste, only one or two lines each, with no signature.

I live for your smile. I am utterly in your thrall.

I cannot be sorry for wanting you. I will not be sorry.

How can you be so cruel? To not even acknowledge me when you know how I feel?

It fills me with unspeakable joy. That the babe might be mine.

Tears slipped down her cheeks as she collected the letters. It was a crime, really, this hot summer's day. Else, the fireplace behind her would be lit and burning brightly. With a flick of her wrist, the horrible things might have been consigned to dust, never to return.

Instead, she refolded and packed them away once more, the evidence of transgressions past. Different, of course, from the ones she'd earlier tried to ignore. But just as painful.

• • •

Despite the oppressive weather, she decided to venture out. Or was "needed" the better word choice? Oakley wanted to accompany her, but Jane was suddenly desperate to purchase the doll she'd promised Violet. And she preferred to do it alone. She was a widow, wasn't she? She hadn't the need for the fuss and bother of a maid. That watchful, mindful presence. All too aware of moods and likely to comment upon them.

So she dismissed Oakley for the day and walked out into the heat of a humid afternoon. She hardly cared. There was a doll to buy, and pain to escape, and the whole of London before her. She knew the city well. Grillion's was at the heart of Mayfair, only slightly removed from Bond Street and the shops that beckoned. It hardly mattered that within minutes, her walking gown was damp with perspiration. No doubt her coiffure was wilting in similar fashion.

She glared at any man bold enough to make eyes at her. And the women, too, always in pairs, with their condescending expressions. She wasn't dressed in widow's weeds, after all, which made her status suspect. How freeing it was to ignore them. All that was needed was one shoe in front of the other, a purpose and a path to lead her away from things preferably forgotten.

She'd just turned from a side street onto Bond when an odd premonition halted her progress. The famous thoroughfare was thronged with customers, but her gaze was immediately drawn to a figure standing outside a shop near the far corner.

Benjamin, Lord Marworth, surrounded by several men, all of them dandies by the cut of their coats.

She quickly retreated behind a nearby bow window, the movement born purely of feminine vanity. After all, she didn't want him to see her like this, upset and undoubtedly bedraggled, like poor Petunia in the Thames.

But what a marvelous opportunity to study him through the glass. Because this was the Marworth who was slavishly admired in Society. Though his pose was relaxed, almost careless, he radiated an intensity that captivated. And while the men around him were laughing, he looked faintly bored. That, too, was part of his magic.

If a man made Marworth laugh, he was considered a wit of the highest order. If a woman caught his eye, she was suddenly a prize beyond compare.

Quite simply, people were drawn to him. It was how he learned all their secrets.

But what was he doing here? When he'd left her this morning, he'd said he was returning home to study Father's papers. Had he already found something among them? Something to lead him here?

Evidently not.

Despite the heat of the day, a chill ran through her as a stunning redhead, dressed in the height of fashion, emerged from the shop, and Benjamin straightened, raising a negligent hand to call for a glossy barouche. The one emblazoned with his coat of arms and parked nearby. The one they'd had ices in yesterday.

He lifted the woman up into his carriage, as she smiled down at him in delight. And then he settled beside her on the squabs, far closer than he'd sat beside Jane. No doubt he needed to make room for all the beribboned packages belching forth from the shop, carried by a steady stream of liveried staff. One after another, they were stacked upon every available surface.

Finally, the carriage pulled away from the curb, heading in her direction as whistles and catcalls sounded from sycophants on the street. Not that Benjamin noticed. He was too busy whispering into the ear of his beautiful companion.

Jane spun on her heel and ran back down the side street, weaving between surprised shoppers until she burst onto Piccadilly. Still, she kept running, all the way to Haymarket Street, as the sky turned ominous. Just like her mood.

And then suddenly, like horses balking at a jump, her legs simply stopped. Having spent the last several minutes demanding relief, united in protest with her lungs and her heart, they'd decided enough was enough. As her breath sawed in and out of her throat, she wrapped her arms around her sides, her body cracking at the waist, forcing her eyes to the stone pavement below.

His words in the conservatory rang in her ears ...

If you haven't already guessed it, I want you badly. And it's a curse, this desire. Because I can't give in to it.

Not with her, anyway. Obviously, the redhead was another matter entirely.

Perhaps women were like flavors of ice cream when it came to desire. You might crave chocolate, but if strawberry was readily available, it tasted just as sweet.

Really, she had no right to be angry. He didn't owe her anything. He'd offered her the chance to catch Sir Aldus in a crime, and nothing more. Sophia had warned her he steered clear of entanglements. She'd simply chosen not to listen. Miss Strawberry was likely his mistress, and he'd spent the morning far more pleasurably engaged than she.

But all the same, she was hurt. Painfully so. He'd made her feel wanted, in a way no one else ever had. She'd confused desire with something else entirely.

Thus, when the first raindrops started to fall, she was not surprised. Like Sophia, the sky had offered her every warning. And while a small, peevish part of her hoped that Miss Strawberry's lovely presents were also getting soaked, no doubt Benjamin's driver had noted the signs and closed up the barouche.

Her legs already spent, Jane went to the closest shop, grimacing when she read the hand-painted letters on the sign above its door. Fribourg & Treyer, Royal Tobacconists. She could hardly go in there, but at least its awning offered some protection. She flattened herself against the shop window, resigned to the fact her derriere, likely outlined by her wet skirts, was pressed up against the glass, framed like a picture for the clerks inside.

It was why she did not hesitate when a large carriage stopped in front of the shop, its door opening, a hand beckoning her within.

• • •

"How lucky I spotted you, Madame Fauchon," Lord Winchester said as he handed her a dry blanket from beneath the squabs. "The storm came without much warning."

She regarded him balefully. "There was ample warning," she said, wrapping the blanket about her. She was soaked to the skin, hair clinging in wet tendrils to her cheeks and brow. "But still, I thank you for stopping." The carriage reverberated with the sound of rain beating against its roof, its interior a gloomy reflection of the tumult outside.

"Is the area where you live in France prone to quick storms, *madame*?" he asked solicitously as he lit a pair of sconces.

She hadn't the energy or the patience for this. "I know your role in this as well as you know mine. In the relative quiet of your carriage, can we not abandon pretense and simply mourn the sorry state of my attire?"

He gave a bark of laugher. "But of course. Consider my carriage your sanctuary. May I ask what it was? The great urgency that made you taunt the weather gods?"

"I'd wanted to escape the indoors." She would not mention the scene with Benjamin. She didn't wish to remember it. "And what of you? At the bank, you mentioned affairs needing your attention at home. What brought you back out, just in time to rescue me?"

"The opportunity to catch you unawares and in my debt, of course." When he smiled, it softened his features. "Why else would I subject my carriage to the elements? It will have to be polished now with a special oil my stable master swears by. The stuff smells awful."

She looked down at the smooth leather seats, caramel in color, save for the dark ring seeping from where she sat. "I'm afraid he'll need a cure for water stains, as well."

"Think nothing of it, Miss Fitzsimmons."

Odd, how her name no longer seemed to suit. "You've made me wistful," she said, pulling the blanket about her more tightly. "I didn't think I'd ever be called that again."

"Are you having regrets?"

"None I can't survive. And it's good to have a purpose." She must remember it was why she was here, why she'd made such a sacrifice. Benjamin Marworth could do what he wanted and with whom. Surely, if she kept telling herself that, she'd be convinced of it.

"I must say it's difficult to reconcile the woman I see before me with the one I knew in Society."

"Come now, Lord Winchester. You did not know me. Before today, we've not exchanged more than pleasantries. I was too busy trying to avoid you."

His eyes widened. "Why is that?"

"You're quite an imposing man. Very tall and very dark."

He arched a black brow, a half smile playing at the corner of his mouth. "You're not tempted to add the word handsome?"

"There's no need for me to," she replied, before she could think the better of it. "You seem quite capable of flattering yourself."

But he only laughed again, leaning forward to brush a damp tendril away from her cheek, making her breath catch at the unexpected contact. "It's easy to see why Marworth is so taken with you."

Obviously, Marworth was not so taken. But Winchester was studying her as if she were an unusual new species and all the more interesting for it. What had possessed her, climbing into the carriage of a man she hardly knew? She didn't feel threatened, but she wasn't comfortable either. And she didn't quite know how to reply. The sheer size of him felt overwhelming in the confined space.

"I was sorry to learn of your father's death," he said at last. "I'd worked closely with him in the House of Lords."

"Thank you, I know he respected both your legislative acumen and your ability to persuade others to a cause." Even if he'd considered him too ambitious by half. Winchester, according to rumor, meant to be prime minister one day.

"You bruise my ego one moment only to stroke it in the next." He wore that strange half smile once more. "I could see you becoming quite addictive."

Was he flirting with her? He'd leaned closer again, his handkerchief in hand, his eyes touching on each of her features. "We're almost at Grillion's," he said, drying her face with the cloth, still warm from his breast pocket. The intimacy of it was shocking.

She was tempted to snatch the handkerchief away, but then she remembered Benjamin and that woman. How he'd whispered in her ear. How interchangeable desire seemed to be. Winchester *was* terribly handsome. And his hand was gentle, a caress really. Sophia had urged her to be bold, to try to find out what it was she wanted. So Jane closed her eyes, softening her mouth as the air in the carriage grew thick.

Odd, how time slowed in the dark. She could feel his breath warm against her cheek, his mouth not far from hers. "You're very beautiful." His voice was an octave lower. And she could not deny she felt the stirring of something.

Unfortunately, it was a sneeze.

Thankfully, she turned away just in time, brushing her damp hair against his lips as a deep chuckle rumbled in her ear.

"A most creative diversion," he said. He offered her a fresh handkerchief before settling back. "I shall have to make note of it in the little book I keep about such things."

"Really?" she asked, tilting her head to one side. "And what will you say beside my name? 'Given to sneezing?'"

"No, I will say, 'bruise, stroke, and then back to a bruise.'"

"I wonder if Lord Marworth keeps such a book?" She'd asked the question aloud, though she'd not meant to.

"More likely, he keeps a library. That's why you should fix your interest on a simpler man." The carriage had rolled to a stop beneath the porte cochère of the hotel. "Someone like myself."

He was joking, obviously, given that wicked smile. So when a footman opened the carriage door, she looked over her shoulder before stepping out. "I hesitate to correct you, *monsieur*," she said, Lillianne once more. "But the word simple? I think you misunderstand it."

The door closed behind her, but she could still hear his laughter.

Chapter 21

Wit is commonly looked upon with a suspicious eye.
It is especially, I think, dreaded in women.
—Fordyce's Sermons to Young Women

Giving Claudette her congé had proven an expensive prospect. Benjamin doubted there was anything left for purchase at Phillips jewelry store on Bond Street. But he'd been happy to buy her whatever she wanted. It wasn't her fault, after all. Such relationships always reached their natural conclusion, didn't they? And she had gotten the send-off she'd wanted, a very public manifestation of his respect. No doubt she already had a new protector.

A strange term, protector. What exactly had he kept her safe from? In exchange for her favors, he'd given her a home, a staff, and a generous allowance. A convenient arrangement that had not required the investment of sincere emotion. But she'd cried in the end all the same.

And the entire time, he'd thought only of Jane, whose favors he wanted so desperately. But their price was not one he could pay. A depressing thought. Almost as depressing and bleak as the location in which he now found himself. Outside the Clerkenwell shop of the mysterious Madame La Farge.

In an area rife with cutthroats and light-skirts, La Farge's House of Fashionable Delights still managed to look unusually disreputable. Refuse littered the curb in front, and the shop's bay window was rotting in its sash. What business could Fitzsimmons have had here?

Thankful for the silver-tipped walking stick in his hand, the one with a sharp blade hidden in the shaft beneath its collar, he rapped on the shop door and waited several long moments. Finally, a peephole opened beside the knocker. Dark, flat eyes stared out, sparking with interest as they took in his attire, widening as they settled on his face. The hole closed again, locks were unbolted, and the door swung wide to reveal a tall woman in a garish gown, her hair an improbable shade, a wide white streak flaring away from one temple. She might have been pretty once, but her features were hard, with deep lines bracketing her mouth and brow.

"Be you buying for your lady, *monsieur*?" she asked. "I can stitch up anything you fancy, and I've lots for show." She stepped away from the door, drawing him into a dimly lit room. There were a number of dress forms inside, flaunting an assortment of costumes to shock even the most dedicated debaucher. Apparently, the shop catered to a very certain sort of clientele.

"You are Madame La Farge?" When she nodded, he continued. "I understand you offer a variety of services." An assumption, but unless Fitzsimmons had made a habit of dressing up in salacious women's clothing, the House of Fashionable Delights was a front for another purpose, likely criminal.

"You want to spread my legs, then?" she asked. "A bang-up cove, looking like you do, needed to come all the way to Clerkenwell for that?"

"Tempting though you are, I'll admit it's not the purpose of my visit. I was wondering what fifty pounds might buy."

"Fifty quid?" Her mouth, a slash of red, had widened into an uneven smile. "You can have most anything for that, guv'nor."

"I'm an associate of Lord Reginald Fitzsimmons." If she was a go-between for those with information to buy and sell, the name would be of interest.

"Never knowed the man. Ain't even heard his name."

And yet she'd referred to him in the past tense. Benjamin withdrew the pound notes from his pocket. "Did I misspeak? I meant 100 pounds."

"Cor," she breathed. "Why so much? I don't make that all year."

"I know Lord Fitzsimmons paid you half that not six weeks ago. I'd like to know why."

She hesitated, biting at the edge of those blood-colored lips. "I told him I'd not swear to anything. I'm not risking my neck. I just go about my business. I provide a service. It's not like I force the girls into it."

Did she run a flash house? "Go on."

"Every so often, one of your fine Mayfair ladies gets herself in trouble, don't she? And when she does, she has to come down off her pretty little pedestal and make her way to me shop on Whitecross."

Realization dawned. "You make her trouble go away."

"If she's lucky. Been at this a long time, but it don't always work out so well. I prefer the powders and potions myself."

"And Fitzsimmons needed your brand of help?" Why and for whom?

"He wanted a name from way back. I keep books, you see. A bit of protection."

Understandable, since the crime could see her hanged. "Did he find the name he was looking for?"

"He did. A Mrs. Venetia Mortimer. Came all the way from Luton for apiol oil and some Queen Anne's Lace."

• • •

Despite what he'd learned at the House of Fashionable Delights, he was no closer to finding the dossiers. All he'd discovered was that an indiscretion, committed years before, had resulted in unwanted consequences. Had Fitzsimmons been carrying on an affair while his wife engaged in hers? It was hardly unheard of in Society, despite the irony.

Should he tell Jane? Was it something she would even want to know? What if the name was familiar to her? He would need to travel to Luton, of course. Fitzsimmons had been there shortly before his death, after all, and there was a chance he'd hidden the dossiers there, perhaps even without Mrs. Mortimer's knowledge. Her daughter's letter had said she was ill. While Mrs. Mortimer was confessing her past sins, not to mention an abortion, had Fitzsimmons seen an ideal opportunity?

He'd planned on returning home, but instead, after calling out a new direction to his driver, they headed towards Albemarle Street and Grillion's Hotel. He'd do his best to protect Jane from her father's actions, but perhaps there were clues among Jeannette Fitzsimmons's things, ones that might reveal something about Venetia Mortimer and the man he suspected they'd shared.

Traffic, however, was unbearably slow. Any type of weather snarled London's streets, and more than an hour passed before he finally arrived, only to see the Countess of Marchmain's carriage beneath the porte cochère, being loaded with trunks. The trunks procured for Lillianne Fauchon, complete with her gilt-stenciled initials.

Something had happened.

Banging his walking stick against the roof of his carriage to alert the driver, he swung open the door, leaping out before the carriage had rolled to its stop, and raced into the lobby, making for the stairs, taking them two at a time until he reached the door of her suite. It was open wide and bustling with activity, a half dozen footmen lifting portmanteaus into their arms. He could not see Jane. Pushing past the men, he made for her bedroom, its door slightly ajar, only to find her sitting on her bed, dazed by her surroundings. The case holding her mother's mementoes had been broken open and upended, its contents strewn all over the floor, letters torn open and trinkets crushed underfoot. The glass covering a small portrait had been cracked in two.

"Are you all right?" he asked, holding her gently by the shoulders to look for any signs of injury. But she would not meet his eyes.

"Someone stole into Madame Fauchon's rooms when she was out shopping." Sophia was standing in the doorway, reminding him others could hear them. "Thankfully, she wasn't here when the thief was."

"You'd gone out?" he asked Jane.

She nodded, still looking away. "I promised a doll to Violet Fitzsimmons. I did not wish to forget it."

"Did you tell anyone about your plans? Anyone on the hotel staff?"

"*Mais non*, only my lady's maid." It was an effort, he sensed, to maintain her disguise. She was clearly shaken. And hurt by what had happened. "The letters in the case … some were upsetting, and I wanted to clear my head out of doors. I told Oakley to enjoy the rest of the afternoon."

He stood, taking in the room. A pair of jeweled bracelets sparkled from beneath a mahogany bedside table. Picking them off the floor, he tucked them carefully into her hands. "He wasn't a very efficient thief, to leave those behind." Then again, he might have been searching for something quite specific. Perhaps the dossiers? Any number of people had known she'd gone to the Bank of England this morning. And the person who'd done this must have expected to find Fitzsimmons's papers here, too. Somehow, he had eyes either inside this hotel or watching it from outside. He'd known when she'd left and had seized his opportunity. "Is anything missing?"

"I'm not certain. As soon as I saw what had happened, I asked to have a note delivered to Lady Marchmain. So new to the city, I did not know what else to do."

Why hadn't she sent a note to him? He turned to Sophia. "You're moving her things to Marchmain House?"

"I think it best. There are those who prey on visitors to the city, especially foreign ones. It's obvious she's caught someone's attention. *Madame* will be safer with me."

He nodded. "I couldn't agree more."

"This is all quite overwhelming," Jane breathed, directing her comments to Sophia but not to him. "There were only small things, personal and of little value."

"But our thief didn't know that." Hearing the dismay in her voice, though, he knew one thing. He'd catch whoever had done this. And he'd make him regret the grief he'd caused her.

• • •

"I'm relieved Miss Fitzsimmons was not harmed during this unsettling development," Greystoke said later, just as evening was starting to fall.

"But I'm afraid it's yet another confirmation of her father's suspected role." Torrington removed his hat and gloves, taking his seat at the table at Whitehall. "The robbery was obviously a targeted one. You say only one thing appears to be missing? A letter from Lady Fitzsimmons's lover?"

"Apparently, it was a note expressing his joy that her babe might be his," Benjamin replied.

"Any indication who the man was?" Winchester asked. "Or that Fitzsimmons had any suspicions about his identity?"

"Not thus far, and not in his papers, either. It seems he was too busy engaging in his own affair, not only in the months before Lady Fitzsimmons's death, but also after, if the timeline I gleaned from Madame La Farge is correct."

"The letter was unsigned?" Torrington asked. "Stolen from a packet of other letters relating to the indiscretion?"

Benjamin nodded.

"Perhaps it was a crime of opportunity, then. Having lost out on the dossiers, the thief decided to try his hand at blackmail."

"But what value could the letter have? Even if he'd recognized the handwriting, both mother and child are dead. There's no one left to embarrass with the revelation."

"What if this isn't related to the dossiers at all?" Winchester asked, his expression dark. "What if her former lover was desperate for a bit of sentimentality? A confirmation that Lady Fitzsimmons had cared enough to keep his letters?"

"How could he have known Madame Fauchon would have them?" Torrington asked.

"The papers said she was arriving from France to settle Miss Fitzsimmons's affairs. It noted the date of her arrival and the hotel at which she was staying."

"Hard to imagine an obsession with a woman lingering for so many years. She's been gone for nearly a decade." But, in truth, it wasn't so difficult after all. There was the small portrait of Jane's mother they'd found, its glass cracked. She'd been remarkably beautiful. Just like her daughter. Who looked so much like Lillianne Fauchon.

Benjamin's jaw clenched, every muscle stiffening. "Rempley."

"You can't think he was involved in this, too?" Winchester asked. "He's been far too busy trying to smooth things over. Word is Lord Liverpool wants him off the committee as soon as tomorrow."

"Rempley certainly wasted no time in coming to meet Madame Fauchon, though." He could hear the anger in his voice, the utter certainty. "Just weeks before, he'd been trying to force Jane to become his mistress, after she'd repeatedly refused his marriage proposals. He'd been friends with her father for years and, thus, undoubtedly knew Lady Fitzsimmons."

"If any of this is true, why would he have remained friends with Fitzsimmons following her death?" Greystoke interrupted. "Surely, he'd have despised his lover's husband."

"Because all this time, he's been waiting for Jane. If he couldn't have the mother of his child, he would have her daughter."

The room fell silent, as the men no doubt pondered the implication of his statement. The very idea of it was sickening.

"No matter how sordid, this is purely conjecture," Winchester said at last. "I think we have to keep our focus on the dossiers."

"Tell me, Winchester," Benjamin said, a suspicion sparking, "if Rempley steps down from the committee, who will take over?"

"Why, myself, I'd assume," Winchester replied, suddenly wary. "I'm next in line in terms of seniority."

His anger needed a vent. "How convenient. We all know how ambitious you are. And you've also been remarkably interested in the whereabouts of Madame Fauchon. You tracked her in Hyde Park. You were at the bank when she retrieved the papers. You just happened to come upon her in the rain when she was shopping, rescuing her from the downpour."

"Will you fault me, then, for a providential sense of timing?" Winchester's voice was mocking. "And what's not to admire about Jane Fitzsimmons? I couldn't help but enjoy the way that wet dress clung to her body."

He didn't think, just acted, leaping across the table to strike, the impact knocking Winchester from his chair as they both fell to the floor, his fists pounding, their bodies slamming into the adjacent wall.

"Marworth!" Greystoke shouted. "If you can't get a hold of yourself, Rempley won't be the only one gone from Whitehall. You'll no longer have a role in this case."

That stilled his hands, embarrassment swamping him. He'd lost control over his emotions, his actions motivated by something like jealousy and nothing else. When Winchester had mentioned her body … Benjamin had not been so enraged since his brother's death. He stood, struggling to breathe evenly, brushing the wrinkles from his jacket, straightening his sleeves and his cravat.

"Gentlemen … Winchester. You've my sincere apologies." And with that, he turned from the room, striding down the long basement hall and up the stairs. Nodding to the door guards as he departed, he hurried to his waiting carriage, a shudder running through his body as he ordered his driver on to Marchmain House.

He only wanted to make sure Jane had recovered from the theft. Even though he'd seen her safely into Sophia's carriage, she'd been terribly pale and quiet, her shoulders trembling. The merest assurance would be enough. Then he could return home and indulge in far more brandy than was wise. With any luck, it would erase the memory of his disgraceful behavior at Whitehall.

"Canby," he said with a nod when Sophia's butler answered his knock. "Is the countess at home? Is her guest, Madame Fauchon, well settled?"

"They are in the drawing room, Lord Marworth. Should you like me to escort you there?"

Another nod and they were on their way, down the wide hall, the floor echoing their footsteps. But when they entered the drawing room, it was obvious Jane was not at all settled. She was lying on a pinstriped settee, a hand covering her eyes, even though Sophia had dimmed the candles. He rushed forward, seeing her wince at the sound of the sudden movement.

"I wasn't sure what to do," Sophia whispered. "It washed over her at dinner, like a fog. She could hardly stand."

"Please … " Jane's voice was nearly inaudible. "It is only a megrim. It will pass."

But he knew just how debilitating those could be. She might be in agony for hours. "We need to move her. The room is too close to the street. The clatter of the carriage wheels will be torture."

"Canby, would you show Lord Marworth to *madame*'s room? I'm sure we can prevail upon him to carry her there."

"I can walk … " Jane tried to sit but swayed with the effort, wilting back against the settee. "I only need a few moments to collect myself."

He'd already lifted her body into his arms, savoring the feel of her—a private, sinful pleasure. Every curve nestled against him, her warm breath at his neck, her head tucked carefully against it. He followed the butler up the stairs, Sophia close behind. But her bedroom came too quickly. If he could, he would slow their pace, for just a few more moments spent holding her. And how ignoble that was. To prolong what was undoubtedly awkward for her.

Oakley had seen their approach and pulled back the covers on Jane's bed, so he laid her down gently upon it, tucking the blankets around her. When he turned back to the others, varying degrees of curiosity were writ large on their faces. "You'd make a good nursemaid, Marworth," Sophia said. "Or do you make a habit of putting ladies into their beds?"

He didn't answer, only ushered them towards the door. "I've experience with megrims," he said, despite Oakley's protests. "I will sit with her."

"It's all right, Oakley," Sophia said, her eyes never leaving his face. "Marworth will care for her. I doubt a single breath will escape his notice."

Chapter 22

Your business, chiefly, is to … make yourselves agreeable and useful.
—Fordyce's Sermons to Young Women

"Do you often get such headaches?" Benjamin asked, his voice soft through the haze of her pain.

"Since my mother died," she whispered, her eyes closed against the violent light. At least it felt violent, although only a handful of candles lit the room. How embarrassing to have him witness one of her great weaknesses. She must look dreadful, pale, with perspiration slick across her brow. Nothing at all like the luminous Miss Strawberry.

"It's disconcerting to see you so helpless, when you are the least helpless person I know."

She'd have laughed had she the energy to do so. "My current state gives lie to that, I think." It was odd, that she should find his voice soothing, when normally any sound would have been all but paralyzing. Perhaps it was the cadence of it, measured and low.

"My brother used to suffer from megrims. Crippling ones."

"I'm sorry. I'd not wish them on anyone," she said weakly. "Well, Rempley perhaps …"

"Aiden used to find a cool cloth soothing. Shall I get you one?"

"That would help, I think." She heard him moving carefully about the room. And in mere moments, it was there, laid across her eyes with infinite care, a rustle sounding in the chair beside her. Surely he didn't mean to stay? "Please … don't sit with me." It would be mortifying. And no doubt, he was eager to be engaged elsewhere. With someone else. The realization of it felt like a sharp, driving pain in the area near her heart.

"Shhh," he whispered. "I'm not going anywhere." He took hold of her hand, and to her surprise, he continued to hold it, which should have been off-putting. When she suffered through an attack, even the clothes on her body felt heavy, like chains tethering her to a bed. But he'd removed his gloves, and the feel of his skin against hers was startling. She focused on the warmth of it. How he unclenched her hand, laying it flat against her waist, tracing concentric circles on her palm, smaller and smaller, until they ended with a dot, before he began again.

How did he know what would settle her? His brother, perhaps. What a gentle child Benjamin must have been, to have harnessed all the impatience of youth—the restless energy of it—to sit, quiet and still, with a boy who was suffering. A boy so different than he must have been. Facing every challenge when Benjamin had been gifted with every advantage and had every reason to be absorbed in himself, instead of his brother.

In that moment, perhaps because her mind and body were weak, she was very afraid she was falling in love with him. And she wanted to cry because of it. It was surely the most irresponsible and awful thing she could do to herself, when he'd never indicated he had any interest in a future with her. Not hours ago, she'd seen him with a woman who could offer the things she should not.

"Don't cry," he said softly. "I know it's painful, but you will be right soon enough."

She would never be right again. The enormity of it was pounding in her heart, equal to the pounding in her head. She just wasn't strong enough to face it now. In this moment, she would relish his presence beside her, offering comfort when there was so little to be had. And ridiculous creature that she was, she felt grateful. She ached, every limb filled with lead, but if she focused on the feel of his hand in hers, she would get through this, even if everything ahead seemed unsustainable. For this one night, she would lie supine on her bed in a darkened room, with Benjamin giving comfort. Just this once.

His hand brushed gently across her brow, easing back her hair, damp against her head. And she felt rather than saw him lean down, his breath a rush of air against her cheek. He touched his lips, first to hers, and then to her cheek, before settling back. "I will be here if and when you need me," he said.

How she wished it could be true.

• • •

Sometime in the night—she could not have guessed when—she stirred. How she'd slept, when it was always so elusive during such attacks, she couldn't say. But there was peace in the room, a certain calmness. And she could hear him beside her in the chair, his breathing steady and regular. She lifted the cloth from her eyes and turned to watch him, cloaked in shadow. What a luxury, to study him unawares, with only a shaft of light seeping in from the window.

The moonlight sculpted his lips and gilded a heavy lock of hair fallen across his brow, making him look surprisingly young. She'd once told him she liked him unbuttoned, and it was true. He was mussed and creased, his jacket and cravat long since abandoned in favor of comfort, his shirt open at the neck. Her eyes caressed the sharp lines of his face and jaw. How she wished she could trace them, edging her fingers along warm flesh and bone and sinew.

He was far too dear to her. And she knew now with a certainty how this would end. She would take her earnings and move far away, so far she'd not run the risk of being found out. She would be neither Jane nor Lillianne, but someone new all over again. After this fascinating escapade with Benjamin Alden, a society darling, a rake and a spy, she'd have her memories but little else. Which was why her feelings for him were such a terrible indulgence. They would leave behind a scar. Of that, she had no doubt.

Maybe she would find a man to love her back one day. A good, decent man who would understand the things she'd done and forgive the lies she'd told. Perhaps they'd even have a family together, with several children. It was not impossible, even if it was altogether unlikely.

But she wanted this man. Wanted him so fiercely she should be frightened, because she longed to abandon things like common sense and take whatever he might be willing to give, consequences be damned. If the greatest pleasure she'd ever felt had been in his arms, with his lips on hers, imagine how great the pain would be when he was gone and she was once more alone. He'd said he would not offer more than he could give. What if she demanded nothing more than the pleasure of his touch?

Gingerly, she sat up, slowly swinging her legs over the opposite edge of the bed. She was desperate to get out of these clothes, still sticky against her. Her mouth felt as if it had been stuffed with wool, her limbs unsteady as the day-old kittens she'd once seen at her grandparents' estate. There was a basin of water and a changing screen not far, and she used the last of the candlelight, burned low now, to make her way, hands clasped upon each piece of furniture she passed. Reaching behind her, she found the buttons securing her gown and undid them, the neck and sleeves slowly easing off. Such a relief, to feel a rush of cooler air.

Quietly, so as not to wake him, she edged behind the silk panels, stepping out of her underthings, naked to the moonlight as she reached for the nightgown hanging there. Slipping it on, she crept back around the screen and splashed water from the basin against her face, closing her eyes against the rush of it. Rivulets streamed down her neck, seeping into her white linen night rail. Blinking against the water on her lashes, she reached blindly about for a nearby cloth, until quite suddenly, it was tucked into her hands.

Benjamin stood mere inches away, very much awake, the air gone heavy all around him. "Are you feeling better?" His eyes, usually so blue, were smoky now, almost a slate in the shadowy room.

"I am," she said, as heat crept up her cheeks. He had seen her undo her gown. She was certain of it.

"May I?" She could only nod mutely, spellbound by the intensity of his gaze as he slipped the cloth from her fingers. "Close your eyes," he ordered, and she did, plunging into darkness. Across the sweep of her lashes, along the edge of her brow, his touch gentle, almost reverent. Soft linen, a caress down the slope of her nose, the curve of her cheek, before dipping lower, past the tip of her chin, to the lace of her nightgown, several buttons still undone at the neck. A sudden hesitation and the sound of breathing gone raspy. The sound of him stepping away.

Her eyes fluttered open. He was an arm's length from her, the cloth clenched in his hand, his eyes fixed on the skin exposed at the base of her neck, his expression caught between awe and anguish. Had he seen the beads of water slipping beneath her gown, forging a path between her breasts?

Heat pooled in her veins while he stood there, seemingly transfixed. And she swallowed, because she knew why he'd stopped. He understood what would happen if he touched her there, while she did not. But how she longed for the knowledge. She wanted to know where a kiss and a touch could lead. If the combination of them could feed this desperate hunger. Nothing else mattered. Not when he was here, alone with her.

Hands trembling, she reached up to undo first one button, then another, until the valley between her breasts was exposed to his gaze. How far she was from any version of herself she understood.

"There's a spot still wet, Benjamin."

• • •

"God, Jane." His voice was raw with emotion. "You don't know how you tempt me."

"I only know we are alone in this room and no one is watching. I want you to kiss me. I won't hold you to anything but the memory of it."

The cloth fell to the floor, and he leaned closer, as if sharing a secret. "Do you know I often regret that I ever came to know you?" Even as her heart dropped, something in his eyes kept her from looking away. "You make me feel things I've told myself not to feel, make me want things I can't have. But I can't fight my own longing anymore. I just can't."

With agonizing slowness, he lifted his hand, touching a finger to the pulse point at the base of her neck. Could he feel it? The desperate pounding of her heart? He traced the path of the water droplet, down to the valley between her breasts, catching it there. Lingering, before he tucked his hand beneath the neck of her gown, easing it off her shoulder to expose the globe of one breast as she willed herself to breathe.

When he smoothed his wet finger across the tip of it, she gasped.

"Any man would kill for the sight of you like this." His eyes were nearly black, his voice strained as the finger traced slow circles, his touch feather-light, sending bolts of sensation through her. She wanted to moan with the pleasure of it.

Instead, Benjamin moaned, as he swept her up, carrying her to the bed. Laying her across it, he settled his body on top of her body, one leg between hers, the other to the side, his arms bearing the brunt of his weight. "Just for a short while … please let me adore you."

His mouth claimed hers, coaxing her lips apart with the heat of his tongue, invading her mouth with devastating sweetness.

So many sensations all at once. His taste, his warmth. The feel of his hand cupping her breast, his fingers gently probing. The pad of his thumb, brushing across its tip, back and forth, stoking the heat flooding her limbs. His mouth, so supple, kissing along her jawline, nuzzling the lobe of her ear, the long line of her neck. His tongue sliding down, raising goose bumps wherever it touched.

Never had she imagined this, his mouth at her breast now, pulling the tip into its heady, slick heat. Suckling until she was panting with a strange, new need. Somehow, he'd opened her gown to her waist, and he was trailing his tongue up the slope of the other breast, circling the tip as his finger had, every nerve in her body flaring.

So restless. Her fingers could not be still. She pushed them into his hair, reveling in the soft strands of it. She coursed them along his back, corded with muscle beneath his linen shirt. If she could pull him into her, melding skin with skin, she would. And it suddenly seemed a hideous crime that so little of him was exposed. She was nearly ravenous with the need to touch more. To feel more.

"Please," she whispered, hardly recognizing her own voice. When he lifted his head, she reached for the buttons of his shirt, fumbling with them in haste, until finally, they gave way, and she stilled, drawing a deep breath. She'd seen sculptures of men in the British Museum, captured for posterity. But they'd been marble, cold and white, while Benjamin was honey-toned flesh, hard ridges and indentations. Captivating. She trailed her hands along his shoulders, smoothing them down over his chest, fascinated by his hiss when her fingers touched the beaded nubs there. Could they be as sensitive as her own? With his eyes on her, seemingly spellbound, was she bold enough to find out?

She warmed two fingers in her mouth and then traced them over each nub, as he'd done, marveling when he shuddered. Everything about him was tense and hard, his breath sawing in and out of his throat. The veins in his arms raised, as if he were straining against something, though he was utterly still. She could feel his heart beneath her hands, every pulsing beat, as she continued her slow exploration. Flesh and bone and sinew. All so different from her own. She wanted to touch every inch of him, though it wouldn't be enough. When her fingers dipped inside the waistband of his trousers, drawn to the intense warmth there, he groaned, catching her hands in a tight grip.

"That is not a safe path for you, Jane."

"Then kiss me again."

And he did, letting her feel the weight of him now, flush against her body. His mouth against her lips, driving into her with his tongue. His chest against hers, teasing her breasts, skin on skin. His legs nestled between hers, something heavy and hot against the apex of her thighs, that place cloaked in mystery, separated only by her filmy gown and his own clothes. She reacted instinctively, urging her hips against his, shocked by the sensation they sparked, moaning with the pleasure of it. Suddenly desperate to feel more of the same, she moved her hips again, pushing herself against the hard length of him.

"God, Jane. The feel of you … " He tried to lift himself off her, but she was lost in a haze of desire. She opened her legs, sensing the movement would bring him still closer, holding his hips with her hands so he could not pull back. Could he feel it, this thing so powerful between them? Surely he must. Something melted inside her when she saw the strain on his shadowed face. The tension along his brow. Eyes hooded, he was staring down between them, to the point where their bodies pressed against each other through their clothes. "This is what I was so afraid of," he said, his voice pained.

But then he arched his hips, rubbing against her, driving the fabric of her gown against her core. Friction, sensation, a sudden clawing need centered there. He pushed against her again and again, the rhythmic movement making her writhe as he captured her mouth with his, his kiss fanning her need. Her body pulsed, the place between her legs now swollen and mysteriously wet. She felt as if she were running towards something. Did he feel the same way? His skin was slick now, his movements increasingly unsteady, his breath coming in pants, just like hers. The heat and the awareness all around them was almost too much, like the air before a summer storm. And then suddenly, an incredible cresting of sensation sped through her limbs, making her tremble with the power of it. Nothing had ever felt so exquisite.

Had he felt the same? She didn't think so. He was staring down at her, his mouth still etched with need, his eyes glossy. But she didn't know what to do. She would give anything to have him feel that same, intense pleasure. Already, though, he'd pulled away, as if desperate to put distance between their bodies, his hands unsteady as they buttoned his shirt and yanked on his jacket.

"Benjamin?" She didn't understand this unexpected change in him, this haste.

"I didn't come here to do this," he said, grabbing his cravat from the chair, tying it so tightly against his neck it must be hard to breathe. "I only meant to give comfort."

"I know." Sudden and unbidden, the guilt, the knowledge she'd all but begged him to seduce her. How many times had he tried to push away? None of this was new to him. Even today, she'd seen him whispering into the ear of another woman. Was it wrong to want to hunt that woman down, to make her swear on her life she would stay far away, so Jane alone could be his temptation?

Because he wanted her, that she knew. But it didn't mean he loved her.

She'd promised not to hold him to any expectations, only pleasure given and received, with no demands. But would she be able to say goodbye when the time came? Or was it already here? Because he'd quietly slipped from the room, leaving only the memory of his touch.

Chapter 23

One thing is certain, that witty men for the most part
have few friends, though many admirers.
—Fordyce's Sermons to Young Women

Benjamin stabbed his hands into his pockets, nearly groaning at his throbbing discomfort, disgusted by his lack of self-control as he sped through the darkened stairwell of Marchmain House. He was far over his head in this. How had he so forgotten his sense of self-preservation?

She would be the death of him. He'd awoken just as she slipped behind the dressing screen. Was he dreaming, caught up in yet another erotic fantasy? Her figure outlined by the moonlight, a gloriously curved shadow, bending and twisting, the outline of her breasts pressing against the screen when she'd reached for her robe. If only she hadn't needed that cloth, he might have stayed firmly rooted in his chair, as his mouth went dry and blood rushed to his loins.

But she'd clearly been struggling to find it, hands reaching about blindly. He could hardly have ignored that. When she'd opened her eyes to find him standing there, he'd sensed her surprise. But there had also been curiosity and innocent invitation. Or so it had seemed to a man desperate to believe it.

He'd never had a problem in the past keeping his focus on the job to be done. But she was dear to him. She had the unique ability to tempt him out of the darkness, the place where his regrets and remorse held sway. How had he believed he could put himself into such a situation, the two of them alone, when his thoughts could not help but turn to how very much he wanted to kiss her? So many long weeks had passed since he'd last touched his lips to hers.

He'd meant it when he said he wanted to adore her. To give her any pleasure he could, while taking none for himself. How far he'd fallen from that goal. She'd been caught up in something she did not understand, but he'd willingly stoked it, driving her to the point of culmination. It had taken every bit of his willpower not to lift her skirts and drive into her. To revel in her warmth, when she'd been so ready.

At least he'd not gone that far, though God knew, he'd gone far enough. So far that he wondered if he'd ever find his way back to his true purpose. How it melted away when she was in his arms!

When the morning dawned, she'd no doubt be horrified.

Grabbing his coat, hat, and walking stick, he slipped out the main door, closing it behind him, crossing out into the warm night air.

He sensed rather than saw the danger lurking. It was never safe, after all, to be alone on the streets of London at night, even here in Mayfair. But he welcomed it. He was almost desperate to hit something, to lash out and punish, even if he, too, was punished and bloodied. It was no less than he deserved.

Hand tightening on the tip of his walking stick, he took note of the narrow gaps between the mansions fronting the street, the tight passageways leading to back entrances for staff. They were perfect hiding places for anyone lying in wait. He looked across at the manicured gardens centering the square. Like many in London, they were only open to the surrounding residents, each holding a key to unlock the high iron fence surrounding it.

There, at the farthest corner, a figure quickly slunk back out of sight. Benjamin set off at a sprint, heading directly for the corner, but when he rounded it, the man was gone. Obscured at first glance by shrubbery, there was a small gap in the fence railings, but not one he'd ever fit through. Damn it, he could hear the stranger's footsteps trailing through the brush on the other side. Quietly as he could, he followed the sounds until they stopped completely. The stranger was hiding behind a copse of trees just visible through the growth. Which meant he had no other means of escape. Unless the man had a key, which was unlikely, he'd need to come back out the way he'd gone in.

And Benjamin, blood surging, would be there when he did. He had all the time in the world.

An hour, perhaps two, passed before there was a rustling once more, the man slipping back through the fence, only to be collared and forced to the ground, held fast by Benjamin's forearm. For several moments, the stranger fought the hold, flailing his arms and fists ineffectually. Not a cutthroat, then, who would never have ventured out without a knife in hand. Nor did he have the size of a street fighter, sent in ambush to exact revenge.

"I didn't mean no harm. Out for walk, 'tis all," he gasped. "Let go of me neck. You're like to snap it!" Slight, with dark eyes and pale skin, he was dressed in black, his clothes far from the first stare of fashion. Or even the tenth, though his chin jutted out in defiance.

Benjamin slackened his pressure but only just. "Rather far from home, aren't you?"

"What of it? Air's not so rank on this end 'o town."

"Is that why you were standing here, eyes fixed on a very specific house?"

"It's no crime to dream. Me and the missus be moving up in the world."

"Are you now? What's your profession, then, and your name?"

"Dobbins. And me business is me own. No need to answer to a toff like you."

"Who paid you to watch that house tonight?"

"Nobody. I don't know nothing." And yet his eyes had gone wary at the accusation. Caught out. Benjamin redoubled his pressure on the man's neck.

"I'm in no mood for lies, Dobbins. It has been a trying day, one's that left me bereft of patience. And you wouldn't be the first man I've left to die on a street corner." If it weren't precisely true, Dobbins needn't know it. Not when he was being starved of air.

"Enough," he wheezed at last. "I done nothing wrong!"

Benjamin pinned the man's arms beneath him, waiting for a violent fit of coughing to abate. "Who paid you to watch that house? What does he look like?"

"Another toff like yourself," he panted. "Covered up, though. Didn't give 'is name."

"Why that house?"

"'E wants to know the doings of that pretty French piece wots there. Gave me five quid to keep me peepers on 'er. Been at it for days, too. Seen you plenty … " His lips curled into a sneer. Quite a bit of pride he had, this Dobbins.

"How did he find you?"

"Come now, me fine lord. There always be men about, available for a price. I be at Sharpe's mostly."

"How do you get your information to him?"

"I bring it to that fancy spot on St. James. The place without a color." White's Gentleman's Club. "Leave it at the servant's door, folded. No marks. Someone always gets it straight away."

Not a bad place, in truth, to leave information. The servants at White's were remarkably circumspect. If they'd been paid to pass a note to someone, they'd not give up any names. Lord knows he'd tried in the past.

"I'd like you to send a message to your employer for me."

"Wot's that?"

"Tell him I will find him out. And soon."

• • •

Hailing the first available hackney as the sun crested over the rooftops of Mayfair, Benjamin returned home to clean up as best he could. Withers, his valet, nearly fainted at the sight of him—grass stains on his trousers, scuff marks on his jacket, his cravat in complete disarray. But he had time only for the most cursory ablutions and a quick change of clothes. He meant to be at White's the moment it opened.

Leaving Withers bemoaning the loss of his reputation, Benjamin called on his footman to bring the carriage and set out for the men's club on St. James. Stepping out in front of its Portland stone façade, with its tall, ionic pilasters and scrollwork balcony, he made short work of the stairs, the door sweeping open as he was welcomed inside by the head butler.

"I'm sorry to be uncertain of your breakfast preferences, Lord Marworth. Should you like to enjoy a full repast in the dining area or something lighter served in the morning room?"

"Nothing for now, Bates. Has anyone else yet arrived?"

"We're very quiet at the moment. Most of our members prefer an afternoon respite." And that was a good thing. Benjamin wanted to see everyone's comings and goings. Dobbins would deliver his note at the first opportunity, if it wasn't here already. "Though both Sir Aldus and Lord Winchester are engaged in the morning room."

What could the two of them be discussing at this early hour? "I'll make my way there. No need to escort me."

"As you wish," Bates said, bowing before he slipped back into his windowed closet, tucked behind the paneling, where he kept watch for members approaching on the street.

The door to the morning room lay at the end of the hall, on the left-hand side. With it shut tight, their conversation was obviously meant to be a private one. Not that he had any qualms about eavesdropping.

"I'm afraid there's nothing I can do to help your cause." It was Winchester, his voice muted through the door. "Lord Liverpool's decision has already been finalized."

"But I've done nothing wrong!" Sir Aldus was clearly agitated. "I've told you all along it was Fitzsimmons, stealing them to embarrass me or worse."

"Perhaps. But now, it is also an embarrassment to Lord Liverpool. Someone has been leaking information to the press. He's been asked about the mishandling of war communiques."

"It must be Brougham. We both know he's in Queen Caroline's pocket. Liverpool wasn't the regent's first choice for prime minister, but he still serves at the request of the crown. She'd be eager to shame him. It's meddling and nothing more."

"Either way, you can see a scapegoat is needed."

Behind him, the butler's closet was reopening. Another early riser at the club's door, when it wouldn't do to be found lingering in the hall. With a quick rap of his knuckles, Benjamin entered the room. "Winchester. Sir Aldus. Good morning to you both."

They were seated opposite each other beside the fireplace and looked up in surprise. "Shocked to see you here, Marworth," Sir Aldus said, nodding towards the wide bay window overlooking the street. "Brummel and the rest of your set won't be here for hours."

"I'm not one to sit and ogle unsuspecting ladies going about their daily tasks," he said. "I'd rather engage a willing one in a mutually pleasurable afternoon."

Winchester knew his rakish behavior was for show, but Sir Aldus, bristling, did not. "We all know you've plenty to choose from," he said, his expression resentful. "But you're not the only one planning pleasures. During our recent outing in Hyde Park, Madame Fauchon was more than amenable to my attentions."

How unfortunate that he'd left his walking stick with Withers. The stiletto blade in its shaft would have slipped quite nicely between the man's ribs. A threat teased on his tongue, but Montford's sudden arrival at the door forestalled it.

"Sir Aldus." Montford's breath was coming in winded pants. "I'd hoped to catch you at the house but was told you were here. I've brought the morning paper. I'm afraid it's bad news." He held *The Times* out to Rempley, who snatched it, scanning it quickly, his expression dismayed and then outraged.

"He's gone and done it," he said, his face a violent color. "I'm to be made a laughingstock. I won't have it, I tell you." He stood quickly, calling for his coat. "There must be something I can say to reverse this course. Come, Montford. We're bound for Whitehall."

"I can only imagine how this will upset my Charlotte." Montford was wringing his hands. "She loves you so. Just as you love her, don't you, Sir Aldus? We'll be able to stop the word of this, don't you think?"

"It's too late for that," Winchester observed, glancing at the news-sheet discarded on the floor. "Unless you mean to track down every subscriber, this will be all over London by mid-morning."

• • •

"This will end badly for him," Winchester said, once the two other men had departed. "You can't wield power you no longer have."

"A power that is now yours, I presume," Benjamin said, taking the seat Sir Aldus had vacated.

Winchester shrugged. "I could not have planned it better myself, although I had nothing to do with the leaks. Someone else has Rempley between the crosshairs."

"Odd, isn't it? How committee members are toppling one by one."

"Fitzsimmons brought about his own downfall, his unfortunate end notwithstanding," Winchester replied. "And Rempley can rail all he likes, but it will change nothing."

Bates had returned to the morning room. "May I have some tea sent in, your lordships? I could offer a platter of breads and pastries, as well."

"I'm amenable if you are, Marworth."

He nodded. He'd not eaten since luncheon the day before, having come straight from Whitehall to learn of Jane's incapacity. And then he'd stayed at Lady Marchmain's, which had led to things he'd had no business doing or discussing.

"I must say, you're not yourself, Marworth. You're not quite so ... complete. I find it surprising."

"I rushed here, following a discovery I made last night." But now was not the moment to discuss Dobbins, Bates having just returned with the tea cart. Instead, Benjamin reached for a plate and a pastry as the butler poured them each a cup. Winchester, meanwhile, had turned his attention to a note set beside him.

A note.

When Winchester looked up, his lips curved at the corners, Benjamin knew. And it was all he could do to keep from throwing aside the tea cart and smashing that smile through his teeth.

"Bates, Lord Marworth and I need a few minutes in private. Can you see that we're not disturbed?"

No sooner had the butler left the room than Winchester turned back to him, perfectly at ease, as if all of this were quite amusing. What game was he playing at?

"I understand you were at Lady Marchmain's home very early this morning. I find I'm inordinately curious about the reason why."

"Why the hell are you having her watched, ordering reports on her every movement?"

The bastard took a long sip of tea, watching him over the brim of his cup. "Perhaps the better question is why you've not thought to do the same?"

He would not be distracted. "Dobbins told you when she left the hotel to go shopping. You followed in your carriage while he stole into her room and tore things apart."

"Believe what you will." Winchester brushed an errant pastry crumb from his sleeve. "I had nothing to do with the theft. And as for Dobbins, I've used him before, even if I'm careful to disguise my identity. He's close enough to London's underbelly to hear rumors where we can't. He has a keen eye for anything out of the ordinary."

"Obviously, not keen enough," he bit out. He and the others hadn't agreed to these measures.

"There were too many people going in and out of the hotel. He didn't have a clear view of the door."

How convenient. An answer for everything. If he'd put Jane in harm's way …

"If you can separate your feelings for her in this," Winchester said, leaning forward, "you'll see this needed to be done. You can't be with her every hour of the day. We need a record of what goes on around her. Who, if anyone, is trying to make contact with Madame Fauchon."

Much as he longed to smear that cloyingly sympathetic expression off Winchester's face, the man was right.

"Just as you have your suspicions, Marworth, I have mine. So I will ask you once more. What were you doing at Lady Marchmain's house so early this morning?"

"Jane was ill with a megrim. I stayed to help see to her care." Even though it was the truth, something must have shown in his face, something telling. Self-loathing, perhaps.

"Does our dear Madame Fauchon know about your brother? About your determined bachelor status?"

"She knows pieces of the story. The whole of it has not been important to the task."

"If you choose to make your life an unhappy one, the decision is yours. But you owe her an explanation for what will happen when this is done."

"I'd not intended on getting so involved," he admitted. Not that he had any interest in sharing confidences with Winchester.

"One never does. But at least I can offer this comfort. When you are done, there are others who will admire her, no matter who she decides to be."

He looked up sharply. It was no comfort at all. Instead, it felt like he'd been gutted.

Chapter 24

[If you do not] avoid Dangerous Connections,
what is there on earth or in Heaven that can save you?
—Fordyce's Sermons to Young Women

Sophia was seated in the breakfast room when Jane entered, a sure sign noon had already slipped past morning. But after last night—she'd not slept at all once Benjamin left—it had been especially difficult to put on her disguise and pretend to a gaiety she was far from feeling.

"*Bonjour, la comtesse*," she said, smiling weakly as she acknowledged a lone footman hovering near the sideboard. "I apologize for my tardiness."

"The hour is still far too early for my tastes," Sophia insisted as she waved for another cup of tea. "But I wanted to see how you were feeling. Though you are pale, I must say, you seem much restored. Have we Lord Marworth to thank for that?"

Hopefully, nothing showed in her face, even if she suddenly felt faint. She needed a distraction before the countess questioned her further. There, by the window, dozens of beribboned boxes sat on a table, when the ball Sophia was holding in Lillianne Fauchon's honor was just days away. "You've been inundated by gifts, *madame*."

"Actually ... " Sophia was smiling as she spread preserves on a sweet roll. "They're for you. And if you'd like some privacy while you open them, I am sorry, but I'm far too nosy to oblige. They've come from Hamley Brothers on Regent Street."

The very shop for which she'd set out yesterday, it had made the dolls she'd played with as a little girl. She picked up the note laid carefully beside the packages, Marworth's signature upon it.

> I worried you might go shopping for Violet today, when you should be resting, so I've taken the liberty of bringing Hamley Brothers to you. Any dolls you like will be delivered to Miss Montford, and the rest will be donated to the Foundling Hospital near Great Ormond Street, in memory of Miss Jane Fitzsimmons. I will pay a call later. I hope you will receive me. I have much to apologize for.

Unbidden, the image of the woman in his carriage came to mind. She, too, had been surrounded by opulent gifts. Payment for services rendered, perhaps? Dear God. Jane was weak at the knees.

She needed to consider this rationally. There was every chance the dolls had been meant as a thoughtful gesture. But she was quite certain an emptied shop was overdone. That when judging Benjamin's motives in the face of it, the scales tipped towards guilt instead of generosity. And there had been that word at the end of his note. *Apologize.*

"Aren't you going to open the boxes, my dear?" Sophia asked.

Jane nodded, took a fortifying sip of tea, and started untying bows. So many pretty little dolls, with hair and eyes in every shade, gowns fashioned from all the colors in a rainbow. Wax dolls. Wooden dolls. Each face with a Cupid's-bow mouth. One blending into the other. After an hour, even Sophia lost interest and wandered away.

But Jane stood fixed to her spot. Because the dolls no longer looked like children's playthings to her. They looked like every woman Benjamin was rumored to have dallied with. Or at least a fraction of them. A scientific sampling.

As if she'd needed a reminder.

She turned her back on the boxes, focusing instead on the books Hamley Brothers had also sent. Bedtime stories and beautifully illustrated fables. There were also folios, the kind newly popular, with stiff paper figures that could be dressed in paper outfits and hats, transformed in mere moments. All one needed was a pair of scissors and a steady hand.

Or in her case, Monsieur LeRoy, of the Rue Richelieu in Paris.

Like the paper dolls, she too was a milliner's mannequin, dressed up in someone else's image, to be packed away when her usefulness was done.

Last night, she'd conveniently forgotten it.

The tea on the sideboard had gone cold, but she drank it down anyway. Then she carefully boxed everything back up and retied the bows, asking Canby to call for the footmen at Hamley Brothers. Each and every doll was to be delivered to the Ormond Street hospital.

She would give Violet the doll that had been tucked among her mother's things. It had seen Jane through some of the most painful days of her childhood. With any luck, it would offer comfort to Violet, as well.

She then spent the rest of the day waiting for Benjamin to call. Though Lord Winchester, Sir Aldus, and a number of others had paid visits, Sophia had met them alone, saying *madame* needed her rest, for which Jane was grateful. At last, nearing four o'clock, Canby rapped on the door of her suite. "Lord Marworth has arrived. Would you be willing to meet him in the family parlor?"

A private meeting then, if it was not in the drawing room. "*Merci*, I will be but a moment." She dreaded this. Call it a premonition. She looked in the mirror hanging above her escritoire, refusing to glance over at the dressing screen in the corner or at the bed close by it. It was neatly made, no signs of mischief now, despite the odd look Oakley had given her this morning. Her color was high, flushed by a rapid pulse and a nervous stomach. If she did not look her best, she looked as well as she could under the circumstances. Past time, then, to see what Benjamin wanted to apologize for.

• • •

He was standing beside the window, seemingly lost in thought, but when he turned at the sound of her footsteps, her heart stilled. How could they be one and the same? The man who'd kissed her so passionately last night and the one standing before her, wary and unapproachable? He looked … tired. Perhaps he'd slept as little as she. A small, bitter part of her was glad for it.

"Are you feeling better? I hope the effects of the megrim have passed." His voice was all solicitousness, despite the tension she sensed in the room.

"I am as well as can be expected, considering the circumstances." She should set his mind at ease. Reassure him he had nothing for which to apologize, because she'd welcomed every touch between them. But she was not always the person she should be.

"I was sorry to learn none of the dolls would suit," he said, his shoulders squared and stiff. "I only thought to save you the fatigue a shopping trip might cause."

"I'd already found a doll among my mother's things," she said. "And the orphans will love their gifts."

"That is good to know." He'd assumed one of his easy smiles, the kind he so often hid behind. "I worried you might have taken offense."

"Because gifts are not exchanged between unmarried men and women?" she asked. "Because they might be construed as payment for favors of a sensual nature?" She should clap a hand over her mouth, or sew the thing the shut. She had no right to feel betrayed. But at least his smile was gone.

"You are offended," he said, taking a step towards her. "I am sorry."

"No, truly, I'm not," she replied. "Now if the gifts had come from Bond Street, I might have been offended. But they came from Regent Street, after all."

His jaw tensed, which told her all she needed to know. She settled herself into a nearby chair, her feet unsteady.

"You saw me with Claudette yesterday," he said, taking the seat opposite.

Jane had always admired honesty, so she swallowed past her pride. "She is very beautiful. You have excellent taste."

"I had just broken off things between us, Jane," he said, his expression still guarded. "I have not ... been with her in some time."

"Whyever not?" What a glutton she was, to ask him to explain a relationship that tore at her innards.

"It seems her hair and eyes are suddenly the wrong color." He'd looked away at that and rightly so. How could anyone be that shallow? Benjamin had encouraged this thing she felt, this ... weakness. He'd laughed, and flirted, and cajoled, and teased. Just as he had with that redhead, and all the others.

"That is hardly Claudette's fault, is it?" she asked, indignant on the woman's behalf. "I hope you've left her well provided for. Gifts alone will not do it. She needs a roof over her head. What if she is already with child?"

"She is not pregnant," he ground out, his own voice indignant now.

"Can you be so certain? Such things are not always immediately evident. I learned that much from the Ladies Society."

"I take every precaution." A twitch was working in his jaw. "I've no wish for children."

"Surely you don't want to be a disappointment to your father?" Such hurtful words her mouth could utter. "You're meant to populate the whole of England with his progeny, remember?"

His eyes swung back to hers, and the emotion in them made her suddenly uneasy.

"There will be no progeny." He was rigid with anger. "That is my father's punishment. Not to mention my penance."

Just like that, she was swimming in waters far too deep. "I don't understand," she said. They didn't seem to be talking about gifts, or Claudette, or even her own feelings any more.

"Everything comes back to Aiden and his death, don't you see?

She didn't see anything. "I only know it was a terrible tragedy."

"It was far worse than that," he said, studying the floor intently.

Surely, he didn't blame himself for his brother's death? "It was not your fault. It was no one's fault."

"How I wish that were true," he said, his words bitter. "Father and I share it, but he had the temerity to up and die. And I still live, when I've done nothing at all to deserve my reprieve."

"You can't believe that." How could he have such a tortured view of his role?

"It was a beautiful day, too beautiful to be cooped up inside, as Aiden so often was." He was staring past her now, his voice dull. "We could see the lake through the windows, and he wanted to play at being Lord Nelson again. It was all I needed to know."

Her heart ached at the pain in his voice. How quickly anger could fall into sorrow. "No doubt you'd done it dozens of times before," she said. "You could not have expected that day to be any different."

"His seizures had been getting worse, striking without warning. And I should have known he'd grown far too weak to swim."

"You were only a child yourself. Children don't think of such things."

But he seemed lost in the memory of it. She wasn't even certain he heard her. "We'd stopped in the middle of the lake when he started shaking violently. His body lurched towards the oars, smashing one into my head, knocking me into the water. For several moments, I was too disoriented to see anything."

All this time, to have felt the burden of those lost moments.

"When I'd gone over, the boat had flipped. I could hear Aiden—such terrible gurgling sounds—but my head was gashed open, and every time I dipped below the surface, I became more lightheaded. I swam the wrong way."

An error for which he'd obviously never forgiven himself. A simple mistake with horrific consequences.

"And then I saw our butler swimming towards me. I could hear Father shouting as he raced towards the shore, ordering Maybanks to save his heir, that he would find Aiden."

"He must have been in a panic." Clearly, Aiden, in the midst of a seizure, would have been the child in greater danger.

"No," Benjamin said, dropping his head into his hands. "He simply chose me."

"I don't understand." Because the implications of what he'd said couldn't possibly be true.

"Father all but admitted it to me on his deathbed," he said, looking up, his face tortured. "He'd loved Aiden, of course, and wanted to save him. But Aiden wasn't in line for the title, and he wasn't nearly as perfect as me. And in that one moment, it had seemed vital I be saved, no matter the consequences."

"Your father wanted your forgiveness before meeting his Maker," she said softly. "And you could not give it."

"Aiden should have been the one to live." His mouth was set in a determined line, his eyes fierce. "So the Alden family name will die with me. I can't kill off the Marworth title, but Painshill Park, his pride and joy, is unentailed. Everything my father built there will rot right along with me."

The words left unspoken were the hardest ones. Benjamin would never allow himself to love or to marry. And that was why he had come to apologize today.

Any woman raised in Society would have had expectations following last night's passionate interlude. Privately, and against his repeated warnings to the contrary, she might have secretly hoped for the same. An admission that she was more than a desire. That she might be someone he could grow to love. But she'd promised she'd not hold him to anything but the memory of their time together. He was taking her up on that promise.

"I am so sorry. Sorry for the pain you bear, for the guilt that follows you still. But you are the one serving your father's punishment. I can't pretend to understand that." She reached out to caress his cheek, startling him. "If we are nothing else, I hope we are friends, so I must be honest. I can respect your decision. But I can't deny my heart is breaking for you."

And with that, she stood and fled the room.

Chapter 25

Dressing up beauty continuously wears it out.
—Fordyce's Sermons to Young Women

Jane stiffened her spine against a strong case of nerves as Sophia's butler announced her to the crowd. Since the moment she'd first been spotted, whispers had followed her progress towards the candlelit ballroom. If the men watched her with undisguised interest, many of the women blanched and fanned themselves, as if a specter walked in their mist. She'd known most of them, after all, in her former life, and it had required all her composure to remember her role on that long walk down the stairs. To be a woman of experience and confidence. Because she'd not felt so alone since that day at the graveyard, when she'd buried her father.

Word had obviously gotten out that Jane Fitzsimmons's French cousin was being celebrated tonight. A throng of Londoners had been gathering outside the mansion since midday, many of them wearing bright red bows of support on their coats and lapels. Reporters had also collected, pencils in hand. No doubt, Lillianne, as a stranger to English Society, would revel in such a welcome. And thus so would Jane. She'd worked too hard at this to disappoint Benjamin, who would join them later in the evening. Would she be able to disguise her imprudent feelings? They'd had only the most stilted interactions since that conversation in the family parlor. They were united in their quest for the missing dossiers, and nothing more.

With a bright smile on her face, one she hoped was suitably mysterious, she crossed into the ballroom, which was festooned with late summer flowers. She approached Sophia, who was beaming encouragement, as the whispers swelled around her.

"Lord above, she might be her twin!"

"But so much more sophisticated, don't you think?" said another.

"Look at that dress! How shocking but utterly delicious! Our Miss Fitzsimmons was a brave one but never so fascinating."

A rather bald observation, that. She nearly lost her footing.

"Madame Fauchon," Sophia said, regal in a gold evening dress with an embroidered overlay. "How proud I am to have you as a guest of honor in my home. So many here are eager to make your acquaintance. Do come and stand beside me, so you may greet your admirers personally."

No sooner had Jane taken her place than a line formed, snaking through the room, people pushing for a place near the front. For a moment, mayhem reigned. One matron actually shoved another out of the way to secure a more advantageous position. To think she'd once measured her worth by her place among them, these so-called doyennes of Society. Their strict rules and codes of conduct had been instituted for one reason and one alone: to prove themselves superior. They didn't judge a person's suitability by intellect, achievement, or even kindness.

Their standards were far more rigorous.

Did one have the necessary bloodlines, for instance, to merit inclusion? Because the marriage mart was a bit like being at Tattersalls during the Thoroughbred sale. You had better know what you were buying.

Did one understand that behavior must be dictated, not by personality, but by convention? Because nothing was more unpleasant than a challenging opinion or thought. Hadn't *Fordyce's Sermons to Young Women* said so?

Did one know the precise angle at which to bend for a court curtsey? Because even though a war was being fought and lives were being lost and thieves worked in their midst, a ball was underway, and there was always the slim chance a member of the royal family might drop by. Society proved its worth by behaving as if the world beyond it did not exist.

But she must set aside her heretical ruminations. All of her lessons at Painshill had been working towards this moment. Even now, the person who'd taken the dossiers might be standing in the line before her, waiting to determine where her allegiances lay. She needed to be alert to every nuance of behavior, every shaded innuendo. All while masking the nature of her true purpose here. At least figuratively, it was time to take her place in this war, to do her part, because Benjamin believed she could. Assuming her brightest smile, she nodded at Sophia, who would perform each of the introductions, and snapped open her fan. It was the only real weapon she had. Thank goodness she'd learned how to use it.

• • •

"You've met Lord Winchester, of course," Sophia said, as he bowed over Jane's hand, lingering longer than he should have.

"You are lovely, *madame*, whether drenched in the beauty of a summer's evening or a summer's storm."

She nodded, fighting a small smile. "You are too kind, *monsieur le marquise*."

"Mr. Frederick Byng and … " Sophia hesitated only slightly. "Miss Petunia Byng."

The dog leapt from his arms at the sight of Jane, barking and pawing at her skirts. "Petunia!" Byng was clearly horrified. "She is generally so well-behaved."

"*Bonsoir, ma belle petit chien*," she cooed, picking the dog up, laughing as it squirmed closer, eager to lick her face. "Such a noble poodle, and what a charming little cape you are wearing."

"She's very picky about whom she likes," Byng said, obviously relieved. "All the best ones are."

"Lord Melbourne." On the committee and here without his wife, Caroline. According to Sophia, she'd been in hiding since that incident at Lady Heathcote's recent ball. Distraught over the end of her affair with Lord Byron, she'd broken a wine glass in front of him and slashed her wrists.

"Welcome to London, Madame Fauchon. Wouldn't it be marvelous if your visit managed to spark a peace between our countries? My brother-in-law, Frederick, is fighting on the frontlines, and I am eager for his safe return."

"I know you must be," she said. "I, too, pray for peace." Would such a man risk the life of a family member in order to sell secrets to the enemy? It hardly seemed likely. But she must not make assumptions.

"Lord Brougham." Another member of the committee, whom she'd met in Hyde Park.

"What a pleasure to see you again, *madame*." It was obvious he wasn't at all pleased. His eyes were already searching the crowd, looking for someone. A contact, perhaps? She needed to see if she could spark a response.

"*Merci, monsieur le baron.* You are a passionate advocate for reform, no? In France, the emperor has a campaign to improve education and health care. I could share the details if you'd like."

That caught his attention. "I would find it fascinating. I will seek you out once the receiving line is done."

"And you've met Sir Aldus Rempley," Sophia said, stiffening visibly. Lord Brougham turned at the name, sniffing with disdain before he swept into the crowd, Rempley obviously disconcerted by the slight. But while part of her reveled in his sudden fall from grace, another wondered why he would venture out to face such contempt. Surely, he'd expected it.

"Madame Fauchon, may I request a dance and a moment in private as soon as one presents itself?"

"Of course, I say yes to the dance, *monsieur le baron*. But to a private moment, we shall have to see." She'd hardly agree to be alone in his company.

She greeted the next person and then the next, on and on. Such a strange experience, being introduced to so many people she already knew.

"Lord Alvanley." A famed wit, the man liked gambling almost as much as her father.

"The Duke of Devonshire." His title newly inherited, he was a cousin to Caroline, Lady Melbourne.

"Lord Byron." Lady Melbourne's much lamented lover.

"Mr. George Brummel." Looking through his quizzing glass, he'd deemed her gown "extraordinary" and "a triumph."

"Lord and Lady Liverpool." England's prime minister, elevated to the position just last year, after the shocking assassination of Spencer Perceval inside the House of Commons. Even though his greeting was gracious, he eyed her with suspicion. Hadn't Benjamin mentioned her role in this? She knew they all worked under his direction.

But a buzz had started in the crowd, at first hushed and then louder as people stepped back, parting to reveal a half dozen attendants in matching livery, their movements fluid as they bowed their heads and swept their arms to the floor.

Canby's voice rang throughout the ballroom. "His Royal Highness, the Prince Regent of England."

Dear Lord above. Thank goodness she knew a court curtsey, after all. She sank into her deepest one, eyes fixed to the floor, inhaling sharply.

"Please rise, our dearest Madame Fauchon. We are so pleased to meet you personally."

"It is too great an honor, Your Majesty," she said as he came into view, inch by inch, during her slow ascent. Jewel-encrusted shoes with a low heel. Silk stockings. Pearl-colored trousers with banded ties at the knees. A red military jacket with epaulettes at the shoulders and gold braiding at the high neck; a profusion of medals and ribbons set on a deep blue sash. Chestnut hair, fashioned in careful curls. A fleshy face with bright, blue eyes. He looked … pained. Could that be right?

Apparently so, because he promptly pulled a handkerchief from his waistcoat and burst into tears. Long, gasping sobs, nearly theatrical, his lower lip quivering. She looked about in a panic, unsure of what to do or say. He had a reputation for tears and an excess of emotion, but this was startling.

"You are a vision from the murky depths, *madame*," he replied, once he'd regained some semblance of control. "Had we not ourselves seen poor Miss Fitzsimmons lost to the Thames, we would vow she'd been returned to us, in the form of her lovely cousin."

"I understand the resemblance is considerable. I am so aggrieved it has caused you pain." If she gave herself away, she'd be shackled in leg irons and sent off to the Old Bailey. Or worse.

"No, it is a blessing. You serve as a reminder of her beauty and nobility. Even though you are French by birth, we claim you for Britain. We say you are English in your heart."

She bowed her head. "I believe you must be right."

• • •

As the orchestra sounded the first strains of the opening quadrille, the prince himself led her out onto the floor, a distinct honor, even if the steps of the dance quickly proved too taxing for his sizable frame. After a few minutes, he decided they were both in need of a restorative, demanding champagne, not just for the two of them, but for all.

Luckily, Sophia's staff had prepared for such a possibility, because flutes were soon being passed throughout the crowd as the prince's own servants poured bottles brought from Carlton House, his London residence. "French champagne, of course," he whispered in a conspiratorial tone. "We can't abide anything else."

"A toast," he declared to the assembled guests, standing at rapt attention. "May we always honor Miss Fitzsimmons and cherish Madame Fauchon."

To emulate the prince, even the most staid matrons downed their glasses in a gulp as giddy laughter swept through the crowd, the atmosphere suddenly festive. "Another, our dear *madame*?"

"How can I say no to such a generous offer, Your Majesty?"

Very soon, he was ordering her a third, threatening her with public intoxication, which would never do. How to deny a prince seemingly bent on her inebriation? How to gracefully decline? As a fourth glass was poured, Benjamin suddenly appeared at her side. It didn't matter that they were only friends and nothing more. How dashing he looked in his severe evening attire, bowing first to the prince and then to her. And how delicious he smelled. Bergamot oil and lemon and something else she couldn't quite define. Something mouthwatering.

"Your Majesty," he said, his voice soft as swan's down on her skin. "May I compliment you on the excellent vintage?"

"Ah, Marworth. How thankful we are for your connections on the coast." The prince swayed towards her, smiling broadly. "Were he not already ennobled, we should knight Lord Marworth for his contributions to our gustatory delight."

"I would knight him for the scent of his cologne." Dear Lord. The prince's booming laughter meant she'd voiced the thought aloud.

"You are a flirt, Madame Fauchon! And the reason, we suspect, for Marworth's approach. Are you angling for a dance then?"

"I'll admit nothing would bring me more pleasure. May I ask for the company of your lovely companion?"

"It's a request best made to *madame, n'est cue pas*?" the prince asked, chortling again at the eagerness with which she agreed, his booming voice following them through the crowd. "A warning to the eligible men assembled here. Lord Marworth has just deflated your ambitions."

Even in her befuddled state, she was tempted to tell the prince that the only thing deflating was her own heart. But she'd never let Benjamin know it.

• • •

When Benjamin saw her with the prince, it had been all he could do not to race to her side. The so-called first gentleman of England had a notorious appetite, and he'd been eyeing Jane like a multi-coursed meal, her dress alone a feast.

Diaphanous crimson gauze had been fitted over pearlescent taffeta, giving the illusion of dewy pink skin wrapped up in transparent tissue, with soft petals of fabric framing her shoulders and dancing with the slightest movement. The gauze then tucked beneath those incredible breasts, outlining their shape. A diamantine brooch, glittering in the candlelight, was nestled between them, seemingly the only thing securing the gauze to her dress, as a wash of crimson color flared over her hips, exposing the creamy underskirt.

"Such a lovely treat, champagne," she said, diverting his thoughts with a wide grin, her feet a touch unsteady. "It makes an occasion so cheerful, do you not think so, *monsieur*?"

"It's your presence that cheers me, Madame Fauchon." It felt unnatural, pretending to this distance between them. Already, his lips were twitching as they took their places on the floor. A Scottish reel had been scheduled, but when a waltz began instead—ordered no doubt by the prince—excited whispers rippled through the crowd, and several couples stepped forward to join in the dance, still considered too fast in certain circles.

He grasped her right hand with his left, placing the other hand at the small of her back, careful to keep their bodies from touching too closely. But he could still feel the warmth of her, the smooth movement of her lithe frame as they twirled about the floor, hips and legs swaying towards each other. So he concentrated on the enemy who might be in their midst and looked over her shoulder, rather than into those shining eyes.

"I might surprise you with the things I know about champagne."

"Might you now?" he asked, unable to resist the challenge.

"I wonder if you can tell me who authored this quote," she said. "'In victory, you deserve champagne. In defeat, you need it.'"

"A man with unrestricted access to generous reserves."

"Excellent guess. I have it on good authority champagne is Napoleon's favorite beverage. Now another. 'Champagne is the only wine that leaves a woman beautiful after drinking it.'"

"Now on that point, I disagree." A woman tipsy on cognac sprang to mind. She was beautiful to him in any guise, in any state, awake or asleep. Especially now, so close in his arms. But he could not focus on such things.

"Sadly, you can no longer take la Marquise de Pompadour to task. She has taken her strong opinions to the grave. She was a dear friend to *ma grand-mere*."

"Your grandmother kept fascinating company."

"Oh, she did," Jane said, nodding emphatically. "Do you know she claimed the coupe goblet for champagne was modeled after Marie Antoinette's décolletage?"

He stumbled, earning several surprised glances. He was not given to social missteps of any kind. Then again, he'd not spent much time in Society in the company of Jane Fitzsimmons, or Madame Fauchon, or whomever she might choose to be. But

God, he wanted to. There was no joy in the realization he was completely besotted.

No sooner had the waltz ended than Jane was besieged. He was glad to see her refuse another glass of champagne from one eager swain but hated that Winchester led her in the next dance. At least the steps of the cotillion would keep them more often apart than together. By all appearances, Winchester wanted Jane for himself. And wouldn't that be a hideous thing to stand by and see? Winchester as prime minister, Jane as Lillianne by his side, forced to live a lie for the rest of her life.

The thought of it struck uncomfortably close. Benjamin had not assumed an identity, of course, but he'd taken on a persona that no longer fit. One motivated by equal parts revenge and remorse, but as much a trap as the one into which Jane had fallen.

How could he have done it? Those long weeks ago—an eternity now—when he'd so easily convinced himself that manipulations served a better purpose. That escaping untenable circumstances was ample justification. That compensation would soothe any regrets. Because little in life was fair.

Torrington's words still echoed ...

"Why would she be willing to sacrifice so much, when this will likely end with her father being exposed as a traitor?"

How had Benjamin so twisted a vow to honor his brother and avenge his untimely death into a perversion of everything Aiden would have stood for? He'd pulled Jane into his own world, one that suffocated, when she deserved every happiness and the love of a worthy man.

Somehow, she'd become the only thing in his life with any true resonance. And he was very afraid the feeling he'd mistaken for a temporary obsession would be far more lasting.

He now knew the true nature of his penance. The treasure she was had not been earned. He was not worthy of her. He had been guided by the selfish need for her company, for her attention, when what she'd deserved all along was his honesty. It had been given too little and too late.

"You're looking so serious, Benjamin." Lady Caroline Melbourne, her voice thin and treacle sweet. Evidently, Sophia's ball had tempted her out of hiding after all, despite her recent disgrace. "Why don't we slip out onto the patio? I can think of a number of ways to cheer you up, all of them mutually pleasurable."

He stifled a sigh, because he was in no mood for her antics. Still, her husband was a suspect, no matter how unlikely, and he was here with a job to do. He gave her a heavy-lidded smile, the one women always mistook for sincere interest. "You were made for pleasure, Caroline, but a trip outside would hardly serve your interests."

She cocked her head, her eyes narrowed. "And why is that?" She did not suffer disappointment well.

"Because Byron can't see you out there, my dear. And we both know you've come to me in order to antagonize him. Shall we dance and put on an appropriately engaging show?"

"I'm the one accused of outrageous behavior," she replied, trailing a finger down his lapel. "And yet you're the one who plays on people's passions. Lead away, then. Let's give the gossips something to talk about."

As he led her out onto the dance floor, he could already hear the whispers starting.

Chapter 26

But tell me, my lovely friends, when the heart overflows with gaiety, is there not a danger of it bursting the proper bounds?
—Fordyce's Sermons to Young Women

The champagne's heady glow had long since faded. Her feet were sore in shoes just the slightest bit too tight, and the boisterous enthusiasm of her last dance partner had been fatiguing. Usually, she loved to dance, but tonight she'd not sat out for a single set. And when breaks had been called, she'd been swarmed by the crowd, feted and fawned over by everyone who'd ostracized her after Father's disgrace.

None of those things, however, could account for the loneliness she felt. A strange sensation, when one was surrounded by so many people. But Benjamin, after their dance, had kept his distance, when he was the only person she wanted to be with. And he was currently waltzing with the awful Caroline Melbourne. Their eyes were fixed on each other, as if no one else was in the room, and his hand had drifted scandalously close to her derriere. Lady Melbourne wouldn't hesitate to take up where Claudette had left off.

"Don't you agree, Madame Fauchon?"

Oh dear. She was still engaged in a conversation with Lord Brougham. "*Mais, oui,*" she said, hoping to disguise her inattention by agreeing to whatever he'd been saying.

"If Wellington can continue his recent string of victories and make incursions into France itself—begging your pardon, but it must be done—the war will be concluded, and we can get on to the important business of reforming our legal system." As Brougham continued speaking, at length and with great passion, she knew at least one certainty. He'd nothing to do with the dossiers.

"It's good to know you will lead the fight, *monsieur*, to make things more just." With a flutter of her fan, because the room suddenly felt too close, she took a step back. "I must beg your pardon. I've just noticed Lady Marchmain motioning for me."

Lady Marchmain was nowhere in sight. But if she heard Lady Melbourne's shrill laughter one more time, she might scream.

"Of course. I will look forward to continuing our discussion later."

Bobbing a quick curtsey, she turned and sped towards the relative quiet of the patio, desperate for a moment's peace as she swept through the doors opening onto it and into the cooler night air.

"How eager you are to join me, Madame Fauchon."

What was Sir Aldus doing on the patio, not a dozen feet away, when it was the last place she wanted him to be?

"*Pardonnez moi.* I did not know you were here." She looked about quickly, her heart sinking as two couples close by rushed into the ballroom for the next dance, leaving them alone.

"Don't be coy," he said, starting towards her. "You saw me come out here. I'd hoped you would follow."

"I did not."

"You are so beautiful tonight, Lillianne."

She stiffened. "You are too familiar, *monsieur*." And coming too close. She backed into an alcove, only to realize she could no longer be seen from the doors.

"There is such a powerful attraction between us." His eyes were dark, his smile unnerving. "And you are so like her."

"I don't know what you are talking about." Her back was flat against the wall of the house, her breath speeding. "And I want you to stay where you are."

To her surprise, he did stop, but only to get a better view of her breasts in the moonlight. He was ogling them, his mouth gone slack. "You have her fire, too, don't you? My lovely Jeannette, who clawed and railed against me. She didn't understand we were meant to be together."

Jeannette. God above. Her mother.

How can you be so cruel? To not even acknowledge me when you know how I feel?

Sir Aldus had been the one. And he'd taken what he wanted by force.

"I knew I must come here tonight, no matter the censure." He was just a few feet away now. "They blame me for something I didn't do, but none of it matters now. You have everything I need."

Fear bubbled up as he reached for her bodice. But so did the darkest fury she'd ever known. The thought of what her mother must have endured at his hands. The thought of her friend, Annabelle, who had nearly fallen victim to a beast much like Sir Aldus. The look in Oakley's eyes when she'd admitted the devastating abuse that had led to Arthur's birth. The scar Banning wore, evidence far too many men thought they could force the weaker sex into submission.

Like them, she would not give up without a fight.

She launched herself at Sir Aldus, screaming like a Valkyrie, knowing a fleeting satisfaction when his hands dropped in surprise, leaving his face exposed. She slammed a rounded fist into one eye and beat the side of his head with the other, relishing his sharp grunt, even as pain shot through her arm. He was every loathsome thing personified.

He was also a man, though, stronger than she, and after his momentary shock, he quickly recovered, his hands biting into her arms, bruising as he pushed her back into the wall. Her shoulders scraped against the stone as he pinned her, his face red from the exertion but with a smile that terrified her. She screamed again, kicking at his knees, his thighs, any place her slippers could make contact. How could this happen, when hundreds of guests were on the other side of that wall?

Suddenly, though, they were no longer alone. Having heard her screams, perhaps, people had started streaming onto the patio, Benjamin at the forefront, every step towards them one of deadly intent.

"Let her go," he said, "or I will kill you where you stand."

Sir Aldus immediately stepped back, as gasps of outrage ran through the growing throng. "It's not what it looks like," he stammered. "She came out to meet me. She wanted this."

Even she was caught off guard by the speed with which Benjamin struck, a single blow to Sir Aldus's jaw, knocking him unconscious to the hard stone floor.

She would never forget the sight as footmen dragged Sir Aldus from the scene. Someone threw wine in his face to rouse him, and his eyes wobbled, one of them blackened, his jaw swollen and likely broken, as blood dribbled down his chin.

And the look in Benjamin's eyes. So many emotions, warring with each other. Anguish. Regret. And above all else, a lethal fury, because she'd instinctively grabbed hold of his arm, making the bruises darkening her skin all too apparent. At the sight of them, he'd made a move towards Sir Aldus's insensate body, nearly pulling her with him, but when she stiffened—her arms throbbing with the pain of the blows they'd inflicted—he stopped immediately, turning towards her with a long pause before he spoke. "I was nearly too late. I am so sorry, Jane."

Shock fisted through her, because others had heard him as well, and a hundred eyes suddenly snapped to them. Benjamin paled uncharacteristically, his mouth a tight line, his face shuttered.

"Why does he call you Jane?" It was Caroline Melbourne, pushing her way through the crowd, looking like a cat cornering something small and furry and helpless.

But she was not helpless. "*Pauvre monsieur* Marworth. I think my errant knight was trying once more to rescue the girl he lost to the Thames."

She could hear sympathetic murmuring, but Lady Melbourne was undeterred. "You are very like Miss Fitzsimmons, aren't you? Shockingly similar."

"So I am told. Did you know my cousin well, *madame*?"

Caroline gave a tinny laugh. "We hardly ran in the same circles. Jane was … What is the word … ?" The woman looked directly at Jane then, eyes unblinking. "She was far too haughty for my tastes."

The crowd shifted uncomfortably, but Jane lifted her chin and nodded. It had been a direct hit and very close to the truth. "That *is* unfortunate. I find I'm far more worried about my own flaws than the ones in others."

Lady Melbourne paused, quietly assessing. "Then you are not so similar after all." She spun on her heel then, returning to ballroom, people edging away, as if she were some sort of contagion. How well Jane knew the feeling.

Chapter 27

The situations of men leave them open to a variety of temptations that lay out their road. Their passions are daily subject to be heated. How hard it is for them to avoid being importuned by excess.
—Fordyce's Sermons to Young Women

Yet another night with very little rest. Over and over, Benjamin had replayed his actions at the ball. How close he'd come to costing them the whole of it.

When he'd seen Rempley abusing Jane, though, something had snapped inside him. The last tethers of his restraint, perhaps, the bonds that had kept his persona in place for so long. In that moment, he'd wanted nothing more than to kill the man.

Which would have meant a complete loss of control. His misstep with Jane's identity proved how close he was skating to the edges of it. In her presence, would he ever again be able to remain separate and apart, casually aloof? When all he wanted to do was keep her close to him and safe?

"Lord Marworth," his butler said, interrupting his thoughts. "There's an urgent note for you. A footman from Sir Aldus Rempley's house is waiting for a reply."

He stood and took hold of the missive, scanning it quickly. It was from Montford, requesting his presence at Rempley's with all due haste. "Let the man know I'll follow momentarily."

He'd relish the opportunity to smash his fists into Rempley once more.

The house was near enough that a carriage wasn't needed on a warm day. As soon as a horse could be saddled, he was off. Within a quarter hour, he was tossing a crown and the horse's reins to a street lad and rushing up the stairs. Several knocks sounded before a harried butler answered the door.

"Lord Marworth to see Lord Fitzsimmons," he said, proffering a card to the man, who stared at it dumbly. "Lord Fitzsimmons," he prompted. "Or Sir Aldus? My presence was requested."

"Of course, my lord. If you would give me but a moment to see who might be available."

Long minutes passed before the butler reappeared, ashen-faced. "Lord Fitzsimmons will meet you in Sir Aldus's study."

It was just a short walk down the hall and then a turn towards an oak door hanging loosely on its hinges. Inside the room several things, all at once, assaulted his senses.

Montford huddled in front of a bare fireplace, a nearly empty bottle of claret in hand, eyes frenetic.

A plain, wooden chair, broken into pieces.

Tall French doors, shut fast on this steamy day, despite the dank, metallic odor in the air.

An imposing mahogany desk, centered in the room, topped with three pieces of paper, neatly ordered.

Puddled around one side of the desk, a dark substance dried onto the floor. A splatter of the same extended beyond it.

Every nerve was heightened now. He'd seen similar things in dark and violent places.

"What happened here?"

"Something unspeakable." Montford's voice was hollow, the claret shaking in his hand.

"Where is Sir Aldus?"

Montford's head tilted towards the desk, so Benjamin took several steps forward, until he was close enough to peer over its edge. A pistol nestled in a lifeless hand. A wide pool of blood. And Sir Aldus Rempley, clearly dead.

"I came here not an hour ago to visit with him, as I try to do each week." Montford's words fell one past the next, careening and off-center. "I found the butler in a panic. He'd heard a gunshot, but the door to the study was barricaded. It took us several attempts to break it open. God in heaven, I'll never recover from the sight."

"Have you called for a runner?"

"I can't involve Bow Street! They'll see this for what it is. He'll be buried at a crossroads, a stake through his heart. Charlotte won't survive it." Montford stood, his movements unsteady. "That's why I asked for you. The servants will swear it was an accident, that he was cleaning his gun. And you are so well-connected. Will you help me spread the story? No one will doubt you."

Benjamin looked over the scene, scrutinizing each detail. "A pistol makes quick work of things. Why did he need to barricade the door?"

"Who can know? Perhaps he didn't want to be interrupted or dissuaded from his path. His humiliation last night must have proved unbearable … "

"Did the butler say if anyone else saw Sir Aldus this morning?"

"A doctor came to see about his jaw, and a messenger came by with a note revoking a club membership. Charlotte meant to visit with me, but Violet isn't well, so she stayed at home. Thank God."

"Have you tried the French doors?" Framed by tall, velvet curtains, they opened onto a private courtyard, not far removed from the street. "Are they locked?"

"I went no farther than the desk." Montford's voice had lowered to a whisper now as he glanced over his shoulder towards the hall door, still slightly ajar. "When I saw him and the papers there, I panicked."

Given the nature of his wound, Rempley would have died instantly. "Did he leave a note?"

"He left behind something even more damning." Montford sloshed the remaining claret into his mouth, spilling it onto his loosened cravat. "Anyone can see they are documents of a sensitive nature. I wondered if you might know what's to be done."

Benjamin turned to the papers then, set one beside the next. The first two were decoded missives, the sort sent over from the War Office to keep Whitehall abreast of frontline developments. But several words immediately caught his attention.

Le Grande Chiffre.

An invaluable breakthrough.

George Scovell, a gifted linguist, deserves the credit.

On the quartermaster's staff, he travels with Wellington.

The missing dossiers. Rempley had hidden them here all along? But why leave them on the desk for anyone finding his body to see, an admission of guilt and pointless scheming? After all, if he'd meant to destroy Fitzsimmons's reputation, the job had already been done. Benjamin looked to the next piece of paper. The note, which bore no signature, was just a few short lines. He focused on the last.

It fills me with unspeakable joy. That the babe might be mine.

The very note stolen from Grillion's. He wanted to crush it in his hands, because Rempley, lying there in his own blood, had gotten off too lightly. He stared down at the body, grey and stiff. Could the man's intent all along have been to so debase Jane's prospects that she'd be forced to act his mistress? She'd already refused his proposals of marriage, the rejections no doubt humbling. Had that been sufficient motivation for a man who had stopped at nothing to get what he wanted?

"Do you think they could be the papers we searched for at Fitzsimmons House? Could Uncle Aldus have unfairly accused a friend? I had no idea what he was capable of."

He didn't answer Montford's question. He was too caught up in a sudden whorl of gratitude. The papers were here; Lord

Fitzsimmons had not been a traitor after all. Jane need never know her father had been the likely suspect.

And something else for which to be thankful, a relief darker and more perverse. She need never know the depths of his own involvement. Was it too great a weakness to be glad for that? That she would see him as a better man than he was?

"I will never understand this," Montford said, shaking his head. "And I can't tell Charlotte the truth. I just can't."

"You were right to send for me," he said, collecting the papers and tucking them into his breast pocket. "Accidents occur with guns all the time. It's terribly unfortunate Sir Aldus was not more careful."

And he did feel it, a suddenly acute regret, not for Rempley's passing but for the reality his death had revealed. With the return of the papers to Whitehall, there was no longer any need for Lillianne Fauchon.

Jane now had the rest of her life to lead. And Benjamin had no part in it.

Chapter 28

An enlightened mind is seldom wrought up in ecstasy, and seldom overwhelmed by terror.
—Fordyce's Sermons to Young Women

"Can that really be the end of it?" Jane asked. After sending a note to the others at Whitehall, he'd driven straight to Lady Marchmain's to share the news of Rempley's death.

"It seems so," he admitted. "He claimed the documents had been stolen, and yet they were found with his body. He'd taken the letter from Grillion's as well."

"To rifle through my mother's things with such utter disregard," she said, shaking her head. "Even so long after her death, he could not let her be."

"Rempley was a predator, a man beyond redemption. In the end, at the center of a spiraling scandal, he took the coward's way out."

"So what does all of this mean?" She'd paled suddenly, making her eyes look enormous in contrast.

"That Madame Fauchon has served her purpose. That she lured the culprit out into the open, just as we'd always hoped." He swallowed against a wave of remorse. "That you are free, when you wish, to begin anew. To find your place."

"Oh," she said softly. How he ached to sweep her into his arms. But he could not do it. People were wrong about a hunger. You didn't feed it. You starved it.

"I'm not quite sure what to do next," she said. "But I should be relieved, shouldn't I? I've a whole new world that awaits me. New experiences. New friends."

"Of course you do," he said with false cheer. "Where will you go?"

"Perhaps the continent," she said, her eyes sparking. "I shall hire myself a dependable guide and travel to the places I've read about, like Rome, and the water city of Venice. Or Switzerland and the towns along the Alps. I should love to see Greece, though that might be too much of an adventure. And of course Paris, when the wars are done."

All he could see were the dangers in such a far-flung journey. "You can't travel anywhere until I've hired guards to keep you safe. I shall interview them personally."

She gave him an uneven smile. "Perhaps I'll disguise myself as a man and hire a bear-leader to go with me. I'll embark on my own version of the Grand Tour."

Surely, she was joking. "Don't let your success as Madame Fauchon turn your head." He glanced furtively at her breasts, though hopefully, she hadn't noticed. "No one will believe you are a man."

With a sigh, she turned towards the window and the darkening sky. Rain threatened. "Perhaps Scotland, then. A house on the coast. I've not been since I was a child."

How hollow he felt. If he shook himself and closed his eyes, could he pretend they were at the beginning of their time together instead of near the end?

"But I do have one great regret … "

He had several. Each of them crushing. "I will change it if I can."

"I wish we'd been able to learn more about my father and the reason why he died. Did you see anything in his papers to offer a clue?"

"Possibly. But it will require a trip to Luton."

Benjamin should never have kept the truth of it from her.

• • •

The thatched-roof cottage was a tidy one, set in the shade of a large poplar tree on the outskirts of Luton. Its whitewashed walls served as a pretty backdrop for window boxes in full bloom, and its neat picket fence was freshly painted. He'd sent a note ahead to Althea Mortimer, asking for permission to visit, and as they disembarked from his carriage, the front door opened. A petite woman near Jane in age swept forward, clad in a black mourning dress with a pleated apron. "Lord Marworth, Madame Fauchon. Won't you please come in?"

"May I offer my condolences on the recent passing of your mother?" he asked. "I was sorry to hear of it in your reply."

"She'd been sick for some time. I'm happy to say she's in a better place now, and that his lordship's visit allowed her to make her peace. I was shocked to hear of his death so soon afterwards."

They were ushered into a front parlor, comfortable with cushioned chairs and needlepoint lace, a tea service at the ready on a table beneath one of the windows. "Was your mother always from Luton, Miss Mortimer?" he asked as they took seats. In the English countryside, an ongoing tryst with an aristocrat from London would not have gone unnoticed.

"Yes, my lord. We've lived here all our lives, though we occasionally traveled into the City before Father died."

Could an affair with Fitzsimmons have begun after a chance encounter? It seemed unlikely with a small child in tow. Not to mention a husband. Had he leapt to a logical conclusion, only to overlook another?

"You are so kind to meet with us," Jane said as she accepted a cup of tea. "*Monsieur le baron* and myself, we are trying to learn why Lord Fitzsimmons came here. Did he know your mother well?"

"Not at all. They'd only met once, before the marriage ceremony," Miss Mortimer replied. "She was helping to ready Miss Charlotte, the poor girl. The whole situation broke Mother's heart."

"Miss Charlotte?" Jane asked, her cup of tea paused in midair.

"Sir Aldus Rempley's ward. My mother was her governess at his country home, not far from here. Loved her like a daughter, she did. Cried until her dying day that she'd never guessed it. That she hadn't kept her safe."

Suspicion trickled through his veins, clenching in his gut. He hesitated, not wanting to ask the question but knowing he must. "Nearly ten years ago, your mother paid a visit to a shop in London. One that specialized in relieving women of an unwanted pregnancy." Jane's head swiveled towards him, her eyes wide. "She purchased several potions. Who were they for?"

Miss Mortimer pulled a handkerchief from her apron pocket. "Miss Charlotte, I'm afraid. But Mother couldn't go through with it. She'd recognized the signs, but the poor girl didn't even know she was with child. And her so young, just sixteen."

"Was it a boy from the village?" Jane asked, clearly shocked.

Miss Mortimer shook her head, her eyes welling with tears.

"Gerard Montford then?"

Taking refuge behind her handkerchief, she shook her head once more, apparently unable to utter the name.

There were long moments of silence before Jane's teacup fell from her limp fingers and smashed on the floor. "Before the wedding, did my … " She gasped, her hands curled around her midsection, as if defending herself from a body blow. "Had Lord Fitzsimmons been told?"

"He knew she was pregnant. Everything had been hastily arranged with Montford. But he didn't know who the father was. Not until he came here, just days before his death."

• • •

That evening, Jane went alone to Fitzsimmons House. The front door was already draped in mourning, and black cloth covered the mirrors in the hall. A waste, when the man's death should instead be celebrated, like a national holiday, his likeness burned in effigy while children danced in the streets.

Was it a sin to hope that at his judgment, Sir Aldus had met not with God's forgiveness but His fury? His death had been too quick. The man should have been roasted on a spit and then drawn and quartered while his heart still beat.

On the long ride back to London, she'd not been able to stop the words from raining down. Shock. Horror. Revulsion. Hatred. They'd spewed like a vein sliced open, while Benjamin sat quiet, listening to her, his fists clenched for the whole of the journey. And yet Charlotte's pain at Sir Aldus's passing was obvious as they sat together in the family parlor.

"I don't know what to say," she hiccupped. "It was so sudden, without warning. It was not like Uncle Aldus to be so careless."

That she would grieve for him, when he'd abused her so terribly. And the awful truth was, even now, as a woman grown, she didn't seem to understand the crime he'd committed against her. After all, she'd been just a small child when she'd fallen into his clutches.

"I feel such pain for you, *ma pauvre*. And who can ever explain why such things happen? Perhaps God was eager for his return home." So He could cast him into the depths of hell. Jane hoped the devil had lit a very special bonfire in Sir Aldus's honor. "Your husband will see you through this, and your darling daughter, too."

"Poor Violet. How he doted on her."

Was that how she'd survived it and stayed sane? By pretending to a world in which the man had doted on her child? One in which he'd been an avuncular guardian instead of a loathsome creature?

"Would it be wrong, do you think, if I don't dress my daughter in blacks? The color makes me so sad."

"Of course not. You shouldn't wear it either." Society be damned.

"It reminds me of such dark days," Charlotte continued. "My parents … both so young."

"I'd heard of it. I am sorry."

"Mother and I used to spend hours together, playing with my dolls. It's one of the reasons I still like them so much."

"And no doubt why Violet does, as well. I envy you the gift of your child." But not the way in which she'd been conceived.

"You'd make a wonderful mother," Charlotte sniffed. "You'd love your children. You'd never leave them alone, would you?"

She wanted to weep. "Your parents didn't want to leave you. They'd come back from the dead if they could."

"Oh, I know that now. Although when I was younger, I sometimes blamed them for it." Charlotte was fiddling with her skirts, smoothing the fabric with her hands. "Blamed them for giving me to a person who didn't want me. Although he did take an interest once I began to mature, and it made me so happy, to be noticed at last. Uncle Aldus admired my beauty."

Her stomach roiled. "You have more value than your beauty, Charlotte. Never forget it."

"And he was such a help when it came to understanding how things would be later, when I married. Although the lessons were terribly awkward … "

Jane fought the urge to fly screaming from the room. She wasn't sure she could hear this without becoming violently ill.

"I don't know how I would have survived that first night, Gerard and I so newly met, without knowing what to expect. That there would be pain. And tears."

An arranged marriage forced upon her to disguise the depths of Sir Aldus's depravity. And Jane's own father, unintentionally complicit.

How earnest Charlotte looked, like a child hoping she'd not admitted to a sin, not really knowing the crime. Jane swallowed against a rush of bile, forcing her voice to be calm. "How young were you when his lessons began, *ma chère*?"

"Fifteen years, six months, and twenty days. Isn't it strange? How some dates stick in one's memory?"

Dear God in heaven, how had she ever mourned her own state? How had she ever believed she'd earned the right to feel aggrieved, or discomforted, or disgraced?

"Does your husband know about your lessons?" she asked. But she already knew the answer.

"Oh no," Charlotte replied. "Uncle Aldus said it must be our secret."

"Of course," she said. "Of course he did."

She would not cry.

Gerard entered the room moments later, a bottle of spirits clutched in his hand, his feet unsteady. Very likely drunk, given what he'd witnessed just three days ago. If Gerard had known what Jane now knew, he'd have done the deed himself.

"Lord Fitz—Simmons," she said, her tongue faltering over the appellation, so long her father's. "My sympathies for the accident claiming Sir Aldus." Lies heaped upon lies.

"Such a string of tragedies." How flat his tone was as he spoke. "First, the other Lord Fitzsimmons, the one who was Jane's father. And then Jane's loss, so unexpected. And now this. Charlotte's dear guardian, so like an uncle, dead without issue. Never knowing the pleasures of a family. The joys of a child."

For some reason, the words sent a shiver through her.

"I tried to see you today," he admitted, falling into a chair across from her, reeking of gin. "But you'd gone missing. I wanted to ask you about the papers. Do you remember I asked to look at them first? They're quite private, after all. Jane should have left them to me."

"I shall send them tomorrow," she said slowly, as hairs rose on the back of her neck. "I haven't reviewed them personally, but I agree, *monsieur*. Jane must not have realized their sensitive nature."

The letter, for instance, leading to Althea Mortimer.

The note Benjamin had shared on their return from Luton. The one from a Madame La Farge. Had he shied away from revealing it earlier because the nature of her business was so dark?

Apart, the letters were nothing of import. Together, though, they were so very damning.

Not just to Rempley. But to Gerard.

Though his head had lolled to the side of his chair, his eyes were steady upon her, unblinking. "Charlotte, my dearest, I've a few words to say to Madame Fauchon in private."

She should leave this very instant. Every instinct screamed it. But she must maintain her façade. When Charlotte kissed him on the forehead and turned from the room, she nearly begged her to stay.

But Charlotte was gone too quickly, and just as suddenly, she was alone in the room with Gerard.

Chapter 29

Our first mother was betrayed by the pride of knowing.
—Fordyce's Sermons to Young Women

"What a nasty business," Greystoke said, tossing back a stiff brandy. "Who could have guessed at Rempley's true nature?"

Winchester, too, seemed shaken. "I defended the man in front of you. In front of the prime minister. To think of the secrets he had access to, someone so unsteady … "

"It's all too convenient, don't you think?" Benjamin asked, unable to forget the horror on Jane's face. "Everything has been wrapped up with such a tidy little bow."

"We have our villain in the piece, cold as a block of ice." Torrington was absently tracing an abstract shape on the table. "The documents back, no harm and no foul. No evidence, really, that Rempley ever intended to sell them. So why take them to begin with? Why blame Fitzsimmons?"

At that, Benjamin set aside his own brandy. Because something unsettling had just occurred to him, his mind still grappling with its implications. "What if he didn't take them?"

"What do you mean?"

"The dossiers were laid out on his desk, neat as a pin. So was the letter from Grillion's. What man, on the verge of suicide, is so tidy?"

"Would you describe the scene again?" Greystoke asked.

"Rempley was dead on the floor, a pistol in his left hand, his eyes still open. His face was bruised, but that would have been attributable to the scene at Lady Marchmain's. His jaw was wrapped in a cloth that went round his head, set by a doctor that morning."

"A man planning to kill himself called for a doctor about his jaw?" This from Torrington.

"And Rempley was right-handed," Winchester said. "I watched him sign any number of documents during our meetings."

No man, having plotted such a demise, would aim the pistol with his weaker hand.

"Montford and the butler found him?" Torrington asked. "He read the notes on the desk and panicked, sending for you?"

"Yes." Keeping those papers neat and orderly, when Montford had barely been able to function.

Benjamin leapt to his feet, his chair clattering on the floor behind him.

"Where are you going?" Greystoke leaned in to the table to make room as he ran past.

"It was Montford all along," he cried over his shoulder. "I have to find Jane."

• • •

Montford's mouth had twitched into something like a smile. "So have you come to judge me, Jane?"

She stilled, hoping she'd misheard him. "*Je m'excuse, monsieur.* You are distraught, your thoughts clouded. I am not Jane, but Lillianne."

He speared a finger in the air, wagging it unsteadily. "For shame. I'm not so easily fooled. Not anymore."

"I'm sorry, *monsieur.* I don't understand you." But she did. And this was a Gerard she'd never seen before. A dangerous one.

"I'll not deny you've done an excellent job of it, the accent, the manners, all that. But when on the fringes of Society, trying to fit in, I made quite a study of people. The so proper Jane Fitzsimmons. The so perfect Lord Marworth."

"Perhaps I should leave, *monsieur*." There was a wildness to him, unpredictable and quite possibly unhinged.

"Carry on with your pretense, if you like. But you're not going anywhere. Do you know why?"

She shook her head, trying not to panic.

His face was devoid now of expression, the effect terrifying. "Because I am vengeance. Like the Archangel Michael, I have weighed the sinners' souls on my scales and condemned them."

Dear God. Definitely unhinged. What had he done?

"But now I must myself be judged. Isn't it the way of things?" He took a long draught of gin. "You must decide, Jane."

"I think you must rest. You are not yourself."

"I will never be myself again," he bit out. "Have you any idea how happy I was, the day I married my Charlotte?"

She swallowed, willing herself to stay calm. "Would you like to tell me?"

"The speed of the arrangement didn't bother me. She was so pretty. Such an innocent and far above me in every way. I leapt at the chance. And when she conceived so quickly, I could not have been more proud. Violet was born too early, of course, but how blessed we were. There were no complications."

"She is a beautiful child." All this time, he'd believed the girl was his own.

"So imagine my dismay when your father paid me a visit. He'd learned something of interest. Something I'd not want to be made known."

"Blackmail," she whispered, as the last of her illusions were shattered, broken into thousands of splinters. Had it been caused by a disease, the corrosion of Father's soul? She struggled for breath, because her lungs had been clamped in a vise.

"You always were clever, Jane. In exchange for my money, he'd not tell the world. And in exchange for dear Uncle Aldus's money, he'd not tell me. Aldus didn't know it was already too late. That his fate had been sealed. Just like your father's."

She gripped the arm of her chair, worried her nails would stab through her gloves and into the wood. "I've heard enough, *monsieur*." How laughable, that she still held on to her disguise. But she didn't want to be Jane Fitzsimmons anymore. Not after this.

"Oh no, my dear. You cannot judge without all of the facts." He offered a swig from the bottle, which she denied, shaking her head violently. "You're quite sure? It helps numb things. No? Very well.

"In disreputable establishments, the sort your father frequented near the end, people up to any task can always be found. I don't have all the details, of course, but I paid to make sure it was done quickly."

How could she sit there while the man calmly discussed her father's murder?

"And I am sorry for it. But you do see, don't you, that he had to pay for his sin? He let me believe things I should never have believed." His voice cracked at that, a hint the telling of this was not so easy.

"But dear, avuncular Aldus. For him, I cannot be sorry. Nor could it be done quickly. He needed to suffer for his transgressions. To lose his position and be utterly humiliated before he paid his price. So I took documents I knew would be missed," he said with a contorted smile. "He'd left them out one night instead of locking them away for safekeeping. So secure he was in his position. So careless."

"Documents of a sensitive nature?" She could not help the question. "Were they related to the war?"

He cocked his head. "So that's what you are about! The tempting French widow, meant to draw out secrets. It's quite clever, but at a terrible cost, don't you think?"

She said nothing.

"I also took the letter from your hotel room. It's not what I'd gone looking for, of course, but I recognized his handwriting, remembered the scandal, and realized Aldus had been at this before."

With that, his odd smile faded.

"I knew just how I would do it. He was quite predictable in his schedule, after all. I would slip into his study from the patio, hide behind a curtain. Wait until he was seated at his desk. Pull the trigger myself, just for the pleasure of it. He didn't even know I was there."

Despite the grim satisfaction in his voice, he was obviously shaken. "Perhaps it would have been better if I'd seen the fear in his face. The surprise. Instead, there was only a gunshot and a terrible thud as he fell to the floor. So much blood and muck. I propped a chair against the hallway door to keep the butler from coming through, laid out the letters, and slipped back outside. Just in time to help discover that Rempley had taken his own life, a coward to the end."

Vengeance indeed. And she was shocked. Horrified. She'd never particularly liked Gerard, but to imagine him capable of this? If the crime was terrible enough, could any punishment be justified?

"No matter what becomes of me, I will always see him lying there," he said, his voice low. "And I'll remember how many years Charlotte and I have wanted a sibling for Violet. To no avail, when that bastard seemed able to procreate at will."

He turned then, curling into his chair and in upon himself, the room silent until his shoulders started shaking with sobs, and the bottle slipped from his hand, its remaining gin soaking into the carpet.

• • •

Benjamin was tearing through the streets of London at a breakneck pace. He'd gone first to Sophia's house, praying Jane was safely there, but she'd left more than an hour before, her destination a mystery. If not for Dobbins, still keeping watch, he'd not have known which way she'd gone. But Dobbins had also offered alarming news. Both yesterday and today, a man fitting Montford's description had been spotted outside Lady Marchmain's house. The same man Dobbins had seen at Sharpe's several weeks ago, hinting that a man needed to be punished, the promise of cash to anyone who could ensure it.

Benjamin had never felt this kind of fear, not knowing what Montford might do to Jane, only that he'd likely killed two people and would hardly balk at a third if it kept his crimes hidden.

How methodically he'd gone about his revenge, the sign of a truly disturbed mind. Fitzsimmons murdered in a setting that would discourage investigation. Their fruitless search of Jane's house, while Montford had the documents all along, stolen to humiliate Charlotte's former guardian. And then Rempley's satisfying disgrace, his death reportedly an accident, though a shameful suicide was already assumed.

Montford had managed to protect his wife throughout, the pregnant albeit blameless girl he'd married. But those sharing blame had been ruthlessly dealt with.

Benjamin's horse was frothing when they reached Fitzsimmons House. Jumping from the saddle, he sped up the stairs, his fists slamming on the front door for an eternity before it was opened.

"Lord Marworth … " Thompson's voice rang out as he raced past, throwing open each door in the hall, his search frantic. Not in the drawing room, the dining room, nor the study. The family parlor lay just ahead on the left. He nearly slid past it, grabbing hold of the knob, hitting his body against the door, forcing it open.

His breath was coming in pants, sweat stinging his eyes as he took in the scene.

Montford sobbing in a chair, Jane's arm patting his shoulder in an effort to soothe him.

"Get away! You don't know what he's done." He flung himself at Montford, grabbing him by the lapels, throwing him against the nearest wall.

The man didn't even put up a fight. He merely slumped to the floor, his expression dazed. Inebriated, the evil sot.

"Benjamin, *ma chère*. You are overwrought."

God, she was magnificent. To remember her role at a time like this, when all he could think of was bleeding the life out of Montford's body. She'd laid her soft hand on the man's shoulders when he deserved no pity.

"This will come as a terrible shock," he said. There was no way to soften the blow. "Montford is responsible for the deaths of both Reginald Fitzsimmons and Aldus Rempley."

How stiffly she was standing, as if the slightest movement would set her off balance. Fists clenching her gown, her face was tortured. "Yes, I know."

Could she be in shock? Had she even heard him? She was pale as a piece of milk glass. "Do you understand what I'm saying?"

She nodded, eyes filling with tears. "He told me the whole of it. I'm to act as his judge and jury."

"He needs to be thrown into a goal, or transported in the hulks, or hung from a tree."

She shook her head, grief widening the space between them. "He needs to go away with his wife and his daughter."

How could she say that? "Surely, you don't forgive him?"

The first of her tears had slipped down her cheeks, silver trails in the candlelight. "I don't think I can. But so many sins are born of passion, don't you think?"

"You don't want this known? Montford punished?"

"It would harm the two people who are most helpless in this. And I can't destroy their lives for a chance at revenge." Montford groaned from his heap. "No doubt God will call him to task for his sins. I think he already suffers for them. But living the lie that I do, I'm in no position to pass judgment."

He wanted to argue with her. They lived in a society where the guilty paid a price for their crimes. But he suddenly found he had nothing he could say.

Chapter 30

Most of our pleasures are prized in proportion to the difficulty in which they are attained.
—Fordyce's Sermons to Young Women

Sophia's carriage had waited for Jane all this time, so he followed behind on horseback, the evening late now, his mind in turmoil. He couldn't understand why she'd walked away from Montford.

Charlotte, hearing the commotion, had come down the stairs in a frilly nightdress, her face creased with concern, her mouth a round circle of surprise. In some ways, she was childlike, and maybe that was a blessing, given what she'd suffered. Jane, as Lillianne, had made all of the appropriate remarks, blaming the pressures of the day, the recent shock they'd suffered. Gerard would be much improved after a strong coffee and a night's rest in the arms of the woman he loved.

Would that he might be so lucky. If this evening had convinced him of anything, it had been the need for complete honesty. She'd all but forgiven her cousin, impossible though it might seem. Perhaps her heart could forgive him, too?

They arrived at Lady Marchmain's, and he asked for a moment alone. Every movement bore the weight of her decision as she agreed, looking as delicate as spun sugar. He should wait but found he couldn't. It felt as if the rest of his life depended on her answer. So, once tucked into a small room off the parlor for privacy, he told her his role in all of it.

And waited, counting out each heartbeat.

• • •

"My father was a suspect in the theft of the dossiers? In fact, the likely culprit?" Jane's mind struggled to comprehend it.

He stared at the wall behind her, though he'd taken an audible breath. "Yes."

"And you've known this from the very beginning?" It couldn't be true.

He cleared his throat before his reply. "Yes."

"You came to my father's funeral, not out of sympathy, but to ingratiate yourself." Her mind was racing. "To charm me into telling you what I knew."

She sensed the tension in him, the stiff resolve. "Yes."

Dear God, the horrible implications of that single word. "My elaborate death and rebirth ... It was all to further your plan. You didn't actually believe I might prove useful. That I might lure the real villain out into the open."

"No, Jane, that's not true," he said, reaching a hand towards her. She recoiled from it, just as she would from anything poisonous. "I thought there was a chance," he said, as his arm fell back to his side. "And it was a way to keep you safe from Rempley. It offered a fresh start."

Her body trembled as she shook her head. "That's what you told yourself, to ease your conscience."

Several moments ticked by on the mantle clock, sounding like an anvil in the silence of the room. "Perhaps," he admitted at last.

She grabbed hold of a nearby chair to steady herself. "Tell me, do you make a habit of upending people's lives on a whim?" Her breath rasped in and out. "Was it easier to justify because I all but leapt at the opportunity? I hadn't realized it was a false one, you see. Father always did say I was too naïve."

"I am sorrier than I can say. You must believe it. I will do everything I can to atone."

"You've already done enough," she said, dropping her head into her hands, hating this small show of weakness. She straightened almost immediately. The weight of his deception had shattered her, but she would not weep. He did not deserve the satisfaction.

That long-ago day, she'd watched the undertaker take the bodies of her mother and brother away, his carriage and cart leaving tracks in the snow. She'd stayed outside in the bitter cold, chilled all the way through, until the wind swept the tracks clean. Odd, to remember it now, to relive the numbness that had invaded first her fingers and toes, then her limbs, and then her heart.

Benjamin had used her. Every promise a lie. Each look and touch and kiss the meanest sort of coercion. She'd blindly believed him. Desperate and pathetic, she'd been caught up in his illusion, for he was nothing more than that. A pretender. A fraud. Hiding behind a tragic history and sad excuses.

How readily he'd admitted his sins, as if he'd expected their revelation to merit her forgiveness. Not unreasonable, perhaps, since not an hour ago, she'd given it to Gerard, who'd killed two men, including her father. Benjamin's actions paled by comparison.

But she'd never been so hurt, nor had her trust been so abused. And suddenly, with bittersweet satisfaction, she knew how to strike back. Because she'd forgiven enough sins for one day.

"So you did this and justified it with the belief your brother, Aiden, would have done the same? Well and whole, he'd have found out the truth, by any means necessary?"

He was looking down now, studying his hands. "No."

"But you solved the crime in the end. Only a few bloodied bodies and perhaps my heart along the way. Aiden would've been immeasurably proud of what you've done."

"No," he said, stiffening. "He'd be shocked by my justifications."

"I find it a bit sad, in truth," she said, hesitating over the words, because one should never be eager to inflict pain. "You've tried so hard to live the life he lost, to be the man he might have been.

And yet, everything you've told me indicates he'd have been more honorable. More noble. Your version is a cheap imitation."

The tight clench of his jaw told her the words had stung. "Don't you think I know that?"

"Then when will you start living your own life? When will you hold yourself accountable for your own actions, instead of hiding behind your father's?"

She'd gone too far. His gaze had turned glacial. "My father did a terrible thing."

"Yes, I know, and all this time, you've blamed him for saving your life instead of your brother's. You've concocted a childish revenge that harms no one besides yourself."

"That's enough, I think."

"You will listen to what I have to say." Her voice had gone shamelessly loud. "I've earned that right, because I hardly even exist anymore. You've made me accountable to no one."

He said nothing. He simply looked past her, as if she'd been dismissed.

"The truth is your father saved you because he loved you. In that instant, the thought of life without you was too terrifying."

"He should have saved Aiden," he bit out.

"Of course. But it was hardly the first time in history that love trumped common sense."

With a violent twist of her skirts, she turned and fled from the room, leaving behind the echo of his voice, calling her name.

Chapter 31

Sorrow is better than laughter, for by the sadness of the countenance, the heart is made better.
—Fordyce's Sermons to Young Women

"You're certain you must leave so soon?" Sophia asked, something like pity in her voice as they walked together towards the door, alone in the hall. "You don't look up to the journey, I must say."

"You are unfailingly honest, Lady Marchmain," Jane replied, attempting a half smile. She'd barely slept since that awful night more than a week ago, and not in her bed, either. The memory of Benjamin, his body wrapped up in hers there, was far too painful. Nor had she been able to stomach much in the way of food. It had all tasted too bitter. "But I am eager to get underway. I'm excited to see Scotland again." She could only hope she sounded convincing.

"Other than the opportunity to watch handsome men hiking in their kilts," Sophia replied, "I can think of little else to draw me there this time of year. And you haven't yet worn all of those beautiful dresses. How can you leave them behind?"

"They might look a bit out of place on the coast, especially since I've no wish to call attention to myself." She would order new clothes once she was free of London, free of Lillianne Fauchon. She certainly had the means to do so. A shocking amount of money had been delivered via messenger from Whitehall, an all too generous payment for her deceit. Another messenger had brought a note from Benjamin, but she'd not bothered to read it, nor the dozens of others he'd sent, along with flowers and extravagant gifts. Forgiveness could not be purchased. She'd returned them all.

"Come now, my dear. You're far too intelligent to hide yourself away in the dreary northern climes. Why not travel? I'll come with you, and we'll make merry together. We'll behave disgracefully in as many countries as possible."

She was tempted to smile, but that would be woefully at odds with her mood. Because she was heartbroken. How could he have done it? Inveigled his way into her heart, knowing all along she'd feel betrayed in the end? How he'd wounded her. The only way to heal was to leave him behind and never look back.

For now, there was only one last scene. The house staff had assembled on the stairs to see her off, a rented carriage fully loaded at the curb and ready for her departure, the horses straining on their leads.

"I cannot thank you enough, *madame*, for all you've done. Such an adventure it has been. I take you with me in my heart." Embracing Sophia tightly, she whispered in her ear. "Please don't tell him where to find me. I plan on forgetting he even exists."

"I can't think whom you're speaking of, my dear."

With a relieved smile and a final *au revoir*, Lillianne Fauchon climbed into the carriage, blinking at the dark interior, which suited her perfectly. And then she was off.

• • •

Everything was a bit unsteady. The sharp pain in Benjamin's knee told him he'd probably knocked into something, and with force, too. Not that he remembered. He was trying very hard not to remember anything and had chosen the most effective and least responsible means of achieving it. Sadly, though, the cognac was done. He knew this for a certainty, because he'd upended the bottle and was currently staring down the neck of it. Not even a drop was left. A tragedy of terrible proportions but not as epic as the greatest tragedy of all.

Madame Jane Lillianne Fitzsimmons Fauchon had left London this morning for parts unknown. Not a note, not a word, not a glance. Oh, she'd whispered something to Sophia Middleton, but the countess would never tell. Damn spies and their secrecy.

What a wreck he'd made of everything.

He quite liked being drunk. Perhaps he should make a habit of it. It numbed his feelings, fostering a heady state of unreality, in which it was likely—nay, certain—that Jane would soon rush back through that door to forgive him. To never leave.

God, he was a fool.

Thus the downside of drunkenness. Generally, he excelled at self-flagellation, but in this state, his thoughts had teeth. What was the point, after all, of sparing oneself? A mind so self-absorbed should also be unflinching when it disappointed. It was an immensely logical observation, of which he was especially proud.

Or he would be, if he didn't feel like flinging himself down the stairs in order to break an appendage, so he could suffer for his sins long past tomorrow, when he would likely be incapacitated.

He missed her desperately. He had the awful premonition he always would. That he'd lost the one opportunity he'd ever had to feel whole and worthwhile. That Jane alone might have made him a better man. Certainly, she was the only person brave enough to call him out for his own stupidity. Because what was his so-called revenge against his father, if not that? He knew now what the bitter pain of living without forgiveness was like. His father had lost two sons on the day Aiden died, though one had still lived.

Somewhere down the hall, there was noise at the front door. Whomever it was, they could go away. Benjamin, Lord Marworth, was hardly at his best. His cravat was askew, his hair a tangled mess, his vaunted wit indubitably soaked in spirits. If he closed his eyes and wished very hard, perhaps he'd be spared.

The knock on the library door, not ten feet away, told him otherwise. Even worse, a moment later, the door swept open to usher in Winchester, resplendent in evening finery.

"You're looking quite disreputable," the earl observed, his mouth curving. "If the ladies of the ton could see you now, I'd not have to fight so hard for their affections."

The urge to mount a spirited defense of his charms died when he saw the reflection in his glass. He looked like hell.

"Bullocks."

It was the best he could manage.

"Bullocks? That is your best retort? You're far worse off than I thought."

Winchester shouldn't cast stones. He was hardly sober himself. Benjamin could tell.

"You persist in imagining a friendship between us," he said, even though it sounded churlish and he'd slurred his way through it. "I don't like you, Winchester. I never have."

The bastard chuckled. "Probably because we're mirror images of each other. I want power and prestige while you can't wait to rid yourself of both."

"Hardly likely," he mumbled.

"I will spare you because you are not yourself. What I do want to know, however, is what you intend to do about Miss Fitzsimmons."

He stilled, even though his head persisted in spinning. "Why do you care?"

"I'll admit she might have feelings for you, which she does not yet have for me." He hated the way Winchester had emphasized the word yet. "And your feelings are obvious to everyone except yourself. So I would like to know your intentions. If you don't want her, I do."

"Of course I want her. She just doesn't want me," he said morosely. "That's the problem. She's left, and no one will tell me where she's gone."

"Given our line of work, I hardly think it would be too difficult to find out." Winchester had thrown his ungainly frame into the nearest armchair when Benjamin hadn't offered the seat. But he was too depressed to protest.

"So if you don't plan on going after her," Winchester continued, "I will. She'd be an excellent asset in my political career."

"She is far more than an asset," he said indignantly. "Besides, you are forgetting something. Jane Fitzsimmons no longer exists. And as Britain's next prime minister—self-proclaimed, mind you—you can hardly marry a Frenchwoman."

Winchester waved the point away like the merest trifle. "If she wants to return to London as Jane, I'll simply invent a story. It couldn't be any more outrageous than the one you concocted. I'll say she drifted downstream but was saved by … an illiterate washerwoman. Yes, that would work quite well."

"You are being absurd."

"Not at all," Winchester insisted, clearly warming to the idea. "Jane knocked her head against a rock and developed amnesia. It took weeks for her to come back to her senses."

Benjamin snorted with disdain. "Obviously, you've been reading too many gothic novels." Had the man blushed, or were Benjamin's eyes playing tricks?

"They're marvelously entertaining," Winchester finally admitted. "But back to Jane. She could also continue as Lillianne, if she wishes. The war is nearly done. Who better to negotiate a final peace than an Englishman with a French wife?"

"She is not allowed to be your wife," he said, an edge to his voice now. Winchester could fantasize all he liked, but Jane would never be his.

"You're not in any position to dictate her future. Not when you've already let her go."

Let her go. Such finality the words had, when he'd never had her to begin with. When he'd done everything he could to push her away, until it was too late. Idiot fool. And for what? To harm whom? Besides himself, the only person he'd hurt in the end was the one he cared most about.

"I didn't have a choice," he said. The reality of it felt like bathing in ice.

"Yes, you did. You just weren't willing to give up enough to keep her. Starting with your pride."

He stared again at the morose reflection in his glass. "I'd give up anything and everything to make her mine."

Winchester sighed. "I suspected as much. So as long as you will admit I am the better man, I will cede defeat and retire from the field."

He swallowed. "If you are willing to give Jane up, then you are the better man. I just can't think of a path that will bring her back to me."

"Oh, if we put our minds together, I'm sure we can think of something."

Chapter 32

Honorable love converts the savage into a man,
and lifts the man into a hero.
—Fordyce's Sermons to Young Women

The weather along the Solvay coast had grown cold, the late October wind carrying a hint of the coming frost, but Jane would not be dissuaded from her morning walk. It had become a refuge of sorts. Climbing along the rocky shorelines, assaulted by the bracing salt air, she had little time for memories. Little time for Benjamin Marworth. She was quite close to forgetting him already. She didn't think of him more than a dozen times per day, if one only counted the hours between the sun's rise and set.

And if she did happen to think of him, caught off guard in a moment unawares, she had only to remember that every good thing in his character had a correspondingly bad aspect. His beauty hid an ugly core. Even though it was also a tortured one. His compassion for others was easily explained. Wasn't it? Every action had been measured by what it could net him, in terms of trust earned and secrets gained.

She shook her head disdainfully, stomping her boots along the path she'd worn through the brush these past several months, wincing at the pebble now stuck in the pad of one sole. Tortured compassion indeed. She gave him far too much credit.

Rain clouds threatened in the distance. She'd become quite good at predicting the weather here, though she didn't yet know many of her neighbors.

Perhaps because there weren't any.

The closest town, Loch Maben, was not three miles distant, but it was a small one. A church, an inn, and a pub completed the necessary triumvirate of country life. There was also a dressmaker's shop and a tiny post station that doubled as a stopping point for the mail coach. A blacksmith's shop. A local purveyor selling the barest essentials. As a fishing community, rumor had it smugglers abounded here, but it suited her quite well. In this remote outpost, she was known as Jane Fitzsimmons Martine, her name a nod to her past and hopefully her future, no matter how bleak it currently seemed.

Best to move quickly then. Being soaked to the skin only recalled days she'd rather forget. Turning back from the shore, she hiked towards her small stone house, leased for now. It represented safety and security. And if there was loneliness, too, she had only herself to blame. Jessica Oakley had surprised her by showing up on her doorstep, not two weeks after she'd arrived. She'd left Painshill Park because she'd been worried for Jane. God bless her and her son, Arthur, who loved the wide open vistas of the coast. The three of them had made quite a happy little place for themselves, even if she envied the bond Jessica had with her son. Jane would never feel that now. She knew it with a certainty that would curl her to a crisp, like a note tossed into a fire, if she let it.

There was a black coach in the drive, a surprise since they'd not been expecting anyone. Yesterday's post had brought a letter from Sophia Middleton, but she'd not yet opened it. She'd worried it might mention Benjamin, coward that she was.

Rushing now to reach the house, she made it through the front door just as the first fat raindrops fell. Shaking them from her hat and cloak, she hung each on wall pegs and walked into the front parlor to find a man seated there, stiff-necked and attired in unrelieved black. Jessica was there as well, stiff-necked, too, her face leached of color, as Arthur cheerfully rolled marbles on the floor in front of them.

"I made it in just before a storm," Jane said, wanting to startle the unsettling quiet.

The man in black stood, as if at attention. "Miss Martine," he said. "I'm sorry to importune your household. My name is Bentley Wiggins, Esquire. I'm here on a matter of sad business."

She immediately turned to Jessica, heart sore when she saw her expression. Whatever news the lawyer had brought, it wasn't good. And Jessica had had too much of grief. "I'll retreat to another room to offer you privacy."

"This also concerns you, Miss Martine."

There was a twitch in her jaw that would not be quieted. A strain in her neck. "Very well," she said, straightening her shoulders as she settled upon an embroidered settee.

Mr. Wiggins cleared his throat. "I apologize in advance for the shock of this. I've a will to read."

"A will?"

Jessica's hands were clutching the arms of her chair. Just as Jane's were.

"The last will and testament of Benjamin Alden, the Right Honorable Lord Marworth."

A hand flew to her mouth as she doubled over. Surely, she'd been sliced in half. How blood and entrails hadn't spilled onto the rag carpet, she couldn't fathom. Hadn't anyone else heard that tearing sound? The sound of a heart ripped in two?

"Are you quite all right?" the lawyer asked solicitously. Had she groaned aloud? Of course she had. The anguish she felt, the clawing heat of it, was excruciating. If she started screaming, she would never stop.

But there was a child here. A child who'd loved Benjamin, too. And he'd no idea that the world had just imploded, turning in upon itself in its grief. She would not frighten him.

"I'm fine. Go on," she replied, sweat beading along her upper lip and brow. She would never be fine again.

"Very well," he said, clearing his throat once more, as if this was a casual oration on any given Sunday. Or the recitation of a shop list passed between a matron and her housekeeper. "Heretofore, and in the king's name, and so on and so forth. The will is newly inked, by the way. Just a month past. Wasn't that good luck?"

There must be something sharp hidden in the room. Something that could separate his head from his neck with a minimum of bloodshed. Or was she imagining all of this? Please, let her be in the throes of a night terror. She was so dizzy she couldn't be sure what was real and what was not.

"To Mistress Oakley and the honorable Arthur Oakley, Lord Marworth has left the property known as Painshill Park, with the proviso they offer it as a shelter, as they see fit, to those who have suffered depredations and disgrace, etcetera, etcetera. Several other people currently employed there are also included in the proviso, with absurdly generous settlements, if I may voice my objections at this sensitive time. One never wants to give those of a certain station the means to put on airs. By the by, the Park is fully funded, so you certainly won't lack for money, Mistress Oakley. No, indeed."

At that, Jessica burst into tears, Arthur rushing forward to offer a pudgy-armed embrace.

"You'll know just what to do, Jessica," Jane said, her voice wavering. "And it means security for you, for Arthur, and the others."

Not an hour ago, she'd doubted Benjamin's compassion.

"As for Miss Martine," Mr. Wiggins said, pausing over the text. "This I'm to read directly to you, my lady."

He cleared his throat yet again. Did several vocal exercises, or so it seemed, many keening notes among them. Took a long pause once more, and spoke.

To Jane, my eternal love …

Her breath stilled with the very sincere hope she would never breathe again.

> I never thought to find you. You have been both my undoing and my savior. When you left, I wanted to flay myself for every hurt ever inflicted upon you. Every disservice and dishonesty. That you suffered many of them at my hands tears me apart, and I will take that sorrow to my grave. If only I could begin anew and work to make myself a better man, one worthy of you. If only I could still earn your forgiveness. Know that with my dying breath, I will dream of seeing you once more and folding you into my arms.

"How tragic," Jessica whispered.

Jane could only nod mutely. The room had gone indistinct.

"You've been given the majority of his unencumbered assets," Mr. Wiggins continued. "Investments spread far and wide, 'round the world really. You're quite the heiress, with enough funds to settle anywhere you wish."

Did he think it mattered? That she cared in the least about money, when a hole had opened up inside her? A chasm, growing wider as pieces of herself fell through it and away. Soon, there would be nothing left except the pain, which she feared would last through this last life and into the next.

"Mr. Wiggins, if you would," Jessica sniffed. "When did it happen? How did it happen?"

"Oddly coincidental, it was," the lawyer mused. "The day after this new will was drawn up and signed, a friend, a Lord Winchester, saw Lord Marworth walking near the Vauxhall Gardens. Seems he slipped and fell into the Thames. His body was never recovered."

She gasped, as hope speared her. Hadn't that ruse already been played? Dear God, let Benjamin's death be the least original thing he'd ever done.

• • •

She raced from the room, flying into her chamber to search frantically for Sophia's letter. Wouldn't Sophia tell her the truth? That his death was a lie, an elaborate hoax, just as hers had been? That he'd seen a chance to begin again, to leave regrets and revenge behind so he could forge a new path leading to her? The past didn't matter anymore, nor did her future if it was not spent with him. She could forgive him anything. How indulgent to think she could not. She loved him. She always would.

The letter was right where she'd left it, of course, on top of the small, white escritoire. Just a simple piece of vellum, folded in thirds, with the power to dictate whether or not she died inside.

She fell to her knees and prayed. Prayed as she never had before, with a desperation that left her shaking. And then she reached for the note and sat upon the floor, bracing herself against the foot of her canopied bed. One heartbeat. And then ten, each accompanied by a sawing breath, making her lightheaded. On the twentieth, she unfolded the letter.

Dearest Miss Martine,

How do you find the Solvay climate? A friend not far from you says the weather is turning colder. He's made a stop in his travels, near Annan, having taken a temporary lease at Caerlaverock Castle. A beautiful place, but most assuredly lonely, which I do worry about. He's not been well of late. Something to do with a broken heart and an ill-advised swim during an intemperate time of the year.

Could you put my mind at ease and pay him a visit? You may find you have much in common. And in any case, cold fall evenings are best spent in the company of someone handsome, don't you think?

If you cannot, I will understand, but I do so hope he will find the area both restorative and hospitable. He will be leaving in November for climes unknown.

With deep affection,

Sophia Middleton

Post script: Have you heard the unfortunate news about Lord Marworth? The ton has lost its shining light, and once more, that tiresome Caroline, the Lady Melbourne, is threatening to slash her wrists because of his sudden disappearance into the depths.

The note floated from Jane's fingertips as a bubble of laughter escaped. It was soon joined by another, and then several more, until she was laughing uncontrollably, tears streaming down her cheeks. She was behaving hysterically, but she could not help it. She could hear Mr. Wiggins, clucking sympathetically out in the hall.

"Poor Miss Martine. She's gone quite mad with grief, hasn't she?"

Chapter 33

How much nobler, the power to save rather than destroy.
—Fordyce's Sermons to Young Women

From a distance, Caerlaverock Castle looked like the loneliest place on earth. Faced with red sandstone and set amidst acres of rocky pastureland, it was more a fortress, complete with a moat, than a place spun from fairy tales. A good portion appeared to be in ruins, its south wall crumbling into brackish waters.

The east side of the structure, however, appeared to be more recently built—from the seventeenth century at least—and as she approached, leaning out the window of the carriage she'd hired, she thought she saw lights twinkling. Not many, but signs of life in an otherwise barren expanse.

She'd not brought Jessica. In truth, she'd wanted to be alone when she saw Benjamin again. No filter for his actions. No sounding board for her thoughts. It wasn't as if she had a reputation to protect.

However, when the carriage clambered across the drive, stopping at the entrance to the castle, she knew a moment's hesitation. Although it was romantic in its benign neglect, this did not look like a place suitable for Benjamin Alden, Lord Marworth. Caerlaverock, in this condition, was better suited to a crofter. Perhaps Sophia had misunderstood the direction? No one had emerged to greet the carriage. There was only a profound sense of emptiness.

Still, she disembarked. As a sharp wind off the lochs gained strength, she knocked on the door. And waited. Apparently, there was no one to answer it. However, she did hear a chopping sound, evidence someone was nearby. She followed it, walking along the castle face and past one rounded corner. She could see a makeshift shed nestled against one of the walls and a man within, shirtsleeves rolled up despite the chill, slamming an ax into a wood log, cleaving it in two.

At the sight, her heart cleaved as well. His hair had grown longer, curling almost to his shoulders, and his jawline was shadowed, several days unshaven. Once-elegant clothes—trousers and a linen shirt—had been sacrificed to the task at hand and would never again be presentable.

But he had never been more beautiful to her. He was alive, and he was here, not thirty feet away.

"Benjamin."

She'd whispered his name, but it must have carried on the wind, because he looked up, his expression inscrutable, as the ax slipped from his hands, forgotten.

"Jane?" He blinked, pushing hair back from his eyes, standing rooted to his spot. "What are you doing here?"

Not exactly the reception for which she'd hoped. "I might ask you the same. Why have you moved into a Scottish castle with winter on the way?" How thin his face was.

"I'm setting a new fashion, of course." At the corner of his mouth, she saw the first hint of a smile. "All the best people will soon be doing the same."

She looked at the turrets silhouetted against the sky, several stones missing from each. "Why a decrepit castle, then? Not to mention one appearing woefully understaffed?"

"Well that, I'll admit, I'd not anticipated." He'd taken a hesitant step forward. "I'm traveling incognito, you see. Mr. Alden does not impress a booking agent in the same way Lord Marworth does."

A reminder of the enormous step he'd taken. "Why did you do it? Why did you abandon your title and give away your property?"

He stilled. "Wiggins has been to see you?"

She nodded.

"He moves quickly then. Another thing I'd not foreseen." He studied his hands for a moment, rubbing his thumbs and forefingers together. "The honest answer is I'd seen another person pull it off, and thought I'd give it a go." His feet shifted in the barren soil. "It seemed an appropriate penance."

To that, she did not quite know what to say. Had he really done it because of her? Because of what she'd done? "It sounds like a lonely existence."

His eyes, when they met hers, were as blue as she'd ever seen them. "I've gotten quite used to loneliness these past few months. I've never been so lonely in my life."

"Lady Marchmain sent a note and said you might have need of company." With nervous fingers, she tucked a wayward strand of hair behind her ear. "How lucky to find you were so close, not an hour's ride away."

He took another step forward. "Quite a coincidence, that. I can't imagine how it happened." He touched her cheek, the lightest caress, before stuffing both hands into his pockets. "May I invite you inside? There's not much to it, but I've collected a few rudimentary supplies. I'm even capable of a moderately decent tea."

"That is precisely the reason I've come," she said, willing away her sudden blush. "To judge you for your tea."

• • •

His heart was beating ferociously, his breath uneven as he led her back to the castle. What did it mean that she was here? Had she come out of pity because Sophia had told her his woeful state?

He'd convinced himself she would never willingly see him again. It was why he'd followed her here. Why he'd leapt at the opportunity to lease this ramshackle castle, the closest available property.

He'd wanted something far closer. Something close enough to chance a glimpse of her in town. Close enough to follow her home from a distance for her safety. Close enough to watch her walk along the path she'd worn near her small stone house.

He'd spent a lot of time on horseback lately.

And it had been an exquisite torture. The best he could have devised. To be able to see her from afar, as he hid in the shadows, close enough to see but never to touch. He'd meant only to ensure she was well. To be certain she'd found her footing. And of course she had. He was the one floundering. How he dreaded the approach of November, when he'd told himself he must leave her behind. Because no matter what he and Winchester had imagined, he could not trail after her forever. If she couldn't forgive him—and it was hard to see why she would—he must accept it and say a final goodbye.

And yet she was here.

Through the front door, and into the great hall, a cavernous space with high, coffered ceilings and stone floors and walls. The moth-eaten carpet did little to quiet the echo of their footsteps towards the enormous center table, stained and scarred. He took an oil lamp he'd left upon it, anxious now, and escorted her through a labyrinth of dark corridors.

"However do you know your way?" she asked behind him. It was nearly as cold within as the outside, as he'd learned through a month's worth of endless nights.

"Trial and error. And lots of practice."

"Are you not frightened you'll take a wrong turn and never find your way back out?"

"And admit to fear?" he asked, glancing over his shoulder. "Even if only to myself? Never."

A final turn and the corridor ended at a heavy oak door with an ancient iron latch. With a quick movement, he had it open.

"How pretty," she said, perhaps surprised by the cheerful room. They were in the newer wing of the castle. A pair of tall windows looked out on hills in the distance, a fireplace faced with blue and white delft tiles nestled between them. There was a settee with rounded bolsters, along with a pair of upholstered Chippendale chairs and several small tables. Earlier, he'd lit oil lamps along the walls and left a fire burning in the grate, the stacks of wood he'd cut corded beside it.

"You've been awfully productive with that ax," she said.

"I've been trying to keep myself busy." He turned to face her. "Apparently, I'm quite good at smashing things."

"A man of many talents. Even more than I'd suspected." She undid her cloak, setting it beside her on the settee, as he committed every moment to memory. No matter what happened between them, he'd been given this one day.

"Is it a worthy talent, do you think?" He approached her cautiously. "The ability to take something whole, knock it from its foundations, and break it apart?" He wasn't speaking about firewood anymore.

"I suppose it depends," she said, "on whether or not the pieces can be put back together."

Her words hung in the air, as the tea he'd promised was forgotten. Jane looked as vulnerable and uncertain as he'd ever seen her.

He knelt on the floor at her feet. "I'm afraid I don't know the answer to that. I'm terrified, actually, even though I said I'd not admit to fear." He reached up, folding her hands into his, his touch as gentle as he could make it. "I would give everything I have left, everything I am, to know the answer."

When she withdrew her hands, his head bowed. "I understand," he said quietly, looking away as he began to pull back. But her hand on his chin stilled him.

"No, you do not," she said, raising his eyes to hers. "That tree you struck down? I think for the whole of its life, from sapling to maturity, it has longed for this moment and the chance to warm you. And if there was pain as it was broken apart, so be it." She touched her fingers to his brow then, tracing down the curve of his whiskered cheek. "Its sacrifice was willingly made."

He caught her hand, pressing it to his lips. "I hope to God that tree is a metaphorical one. Because I can't keep you out of my heart. You are rooted there. And if I lose you, the pain will never leave. I'll spend the rest of my days wishing I'd had the courage to tell you."

"To tell me what, Benjamin?"

He took a deep breath, because once it was said, he would no longer be able to pretend otherwise. "That I love you. That your honesty and bravery made me want to stop living a lie. That without you, I will never be whole."

Her head tilted to the side, her eyes soft, but for several long moments, she said nothing. And it was agony, the waiting, not knowing if her next words would destroy him. With each beat of his heart, he became more certain they would.

"When Mr. Wiggins came to my house today," she said, her voice hesitant, "I thought I'd lost you forever. And it was the greatest pain I've ever felt. That I'd left you without saying goodbye."

Her words felt like hammer blows. "You've been given this chance then," he said, his voice hoarse. "I've known all along that I don't deserve you." And it was true. It was right and just that his sins not be forgiven.

"No, you don't understand," she said, clasping his hands. "I love you desperately. And I don't care if either of us deserves anything. I want to be with you, no matter the circumstances. If that can't happen, you must tell me. So I can run back through that maze of corridors, find my coachman, and escape into the night."

"You do realize your coachman has long since left and that you're stuck here until morning?" His heart was pounding wildly. Love. She'd said the word and could not take it back. "Not that I plan on letting you out of my sight, ever again."

Her smile seemed to light her from within. "That would lead to shocking improprieties."

"One can only hope." His tone was teasing, but he had never been more serious. "We are two people without a past. But together, we can start again. If you will let me, I promise to love you, every day, for the rest of my life, with all that I have."

"You've already willed me most of your possessions," she said, one finger tracing his lips, sending a shaft of heat through him. "Have you forgotten it already?"

"Then take my heart … "

Chapter 34

Discreet reserve in a woman, like the distance kept by royal personages, contributes to maintain the proper reverence.
—Fordyce's Sermons to Young Women

"Does your heart come with the rest of you?" she asked, staring up at him through her lashes. "Not that it isn't a lovely organ, beating so constantly. But I think I would miss your eyes. Not to mention the wonderful things you can do with your lips and your tongue."

Surely, she'd not meant that the way it sounded. "I do have a well-deserved reputation for wit."

"And modesty, too." She smoothed a strand of his hair. "But I was thinking of another skill set entirely."

At that, his thoughts scrambled. Because she'd just moved closer, pressing against him.

"It's really quite unfair, how you've kept those skills to yourself," she continued, trailing her finger along his cheek. "When I would be your most attentive student … "

His body all but begged for her touch. "I'll tell you anything you want to know."

"Will you?" Her hands were at his shirt, unhooking the buttons, slowly slipping it from his shoulders, until his chest lay bare. "Tell me then, how does this feel?" She leaned over, kissing down the length of his neck as he gasped.

"Like heaven."

"And this?" She flicked her tongue along the nub of one nipple, teasing it, pulling it into the heat of her mouth as he shuddered with desire. It was raging through him, tensing every muscle.

"Like I've never wanted anything more."

"Perhaps we shouldn't talk each thing through," she whispered, eyes sparking. "I find I learn things best when I'm shown them."

His heart skittered, as if loosened from its moorings, free from tethers. The two of them were alone together. No one else for miles.

"Then let me show you what you do to me." He grasped one of her hands, flattening it against his heart. "Do you feel that?" She nodded mutely. He trailed her hand across his chest, her fingers leaving a trail of goose bumps in their wake. "Do you see what your touch does?" How seductive her smile was, not a hint of shyness, her mouth a revelation of enticement. He placed her forefinger on the pulse at the base of his neck. "Watch how my body responds to you."

Moving slowly, his eyes never leaving hers, he began unbuttoning the neck of her traveling gown. So prim it was—high-necked and starched, almost severe in its styling—so very different from the clothes she'd worn as Lillianne. But devastating all the same, especially as her throat came into view, and then the edge of her chemise, and then the curve of her breasts.

"I think you should move faster," she said, her voice catching. "Your pulse is beating so quickly, but your hands are taking an eternity."

He'd have laughed if he weren't so caught up in the beauty opening up before his eyes. The oil lamps flickered, casting a wash of gold against her skin, bared now to the light. Her breasts exposed to his gaze.

His undoing.

"Jane … do you know what will happen if I touch you further? I will strip all your clothes away, mine as well. And I will drive my body inside you, as hard and as far as I can, until I drive my way into your heart. I won't be able to stop."

Her eyes met his, naked with longing. "Don't you know you're already in my heart? And that I don't want you to stop?"

He swept her up in his arms then and moved to his bedroom, kicking open the door, laying her on the soft coverlet set over a bed of down. The fire he'd stoked earlier was still burning, but it was nothing compared to the heat coursing through him. Because she was stripping off her gown and chemise, shimmying out of her stockings and slippers too. And then she was bare, all creamy skin and soul-shattering curves.

God above. "You are a masterpiece. I … " He stumbled over the words. "Are you certain?"

She merely nodded, her teeth biting into her lower lip.

Slowly then, so as not to scare her, he stepped out of his clothes, peeling away each layer, until he, too, was naked before her.

Her eyes had gone wide at the sight of his arousal, just the slightest hint of fear. And it was crushing to think he could frighten her. "Shhh, don't be scared," he soothed, as he lay over her, flesh upon flesh, the sensation so incomparable he laid his head into her shoulder, just for the chance to breathe her in.

"You are the beautiful one," she said, her voice threaded with need. "And I'm not frightened. I'm anxious."

He smiled against her skin. "They are not the same thing?"

"Not at all. Not to my mind."

"Tell me the difference then."

"I have been frightened I would never see you like this," she said, the blush across her chest unmistakable, for all her bold words. "But I've been waiting to feel you like this for so long, it has made me anxious."

Her hands were pulling at his hair, lifting his head to center it over her own. Her eyes were eager, her lips soft as she joined their mouths. She was heat and need and pulsing desire. Suddenly, he could not get enough. Her breasts rounded against his chest. His legs tucked between her hips. His hand sought the nub at her core, rubbing along it, tentatively sliding a finger into her, then two, as her body began to writhe.

Each sensation stole his breath, magnified by emotion in a way he'd never known. As he kissed her, mouths melding, he pulled his fingers away from the heat of her, easing the tip of himself into her slick folds, shuddering with the need for restraint. It had never been more important that a woman find pleasure in his arms.

He'd made only the slightest movement when she thrust her hips against him, breath hissing from her lips, a moan caught in his mouth. He could feel the tension in her, a coiling of pain. But when he tried to pull away, to protect her from it, she held him fast, hands at his hips, pulling him against her once more, forcing him into a slow, pulsing rhythm.

And he was powerless against it. He wanted her so badly, had from the moment that began all of this. So he moved against her again, groaning at her heat, her scent, at the way her body clung to him. Marveling as her own breath became more fevered, her excitement palpable, rising with his. Their bodies moved in tandem, sweat between them, each thrust closer to the crest. Only when she cried out did he allow himself to do the same, throbbing into her, shuddering with his release.

• • •

Much later, Jane was still nestled in his arms.

"You're marvelously creative," she said, her voice drowsy, her head upon his shoulder as she burrowed closer.

"That's because I have you as my source of inspiration," he said, trailing his hand along her side, exploring each curve and hollow. He couldn't seem to stop touching her. He wanted to learn every inch.

"Do you know, I've just remembered something."

"What's that, my love?" Another thing he couldn't seem to stop doing. Saying that word. It was such a miracle. He'd bared his soul, and she'd not run screaming into the night.

"You never did make me your tea."

He smiled up at the ceiling, the room gone dark now. "I didn't want to overwhelm you with too many talents at once."

"Such conceit," she said, yawning. "It's a good thing certain parts of you recommend themselves."

"I don't suppose you'd be willing to tell me which ones?" But as he peered down, he noticed her eyelids were slipping, her lashes crescent shadows against her cheeks. "No, I can see that will have to wait until morning. The list will be far too long."

"It might even take a lifetime," she sighed. "You can't ever leave me if you want to hear them all … " She nuzzled closer, her voice fading now. "Remind me to tell you about the grapes … " And with that, she was asleep.

"Don't you realize I can't leave you?" he whispered, so as not to wake her. "You hold my heart in your hands, remember?"

Chapter 35

April, 1816
Valladolid near Castile-León

Enjoying her breakfast out of doors at half past two in the afternoon, Sophia Middleton turned her face towards the sky, basking in the warm Spanish sunlight. For too long, she'd been kept from this, her magical estate set amidst olive trees, high in the hills above Castile-León. She and Stephano, her second husband, had been blissfully happy here before the wars began and death tore them apart.

But the wars were done now. After the second treaty of Paris, Louis of France was back on his throne. Napoleon had been exiled to the remote island of St. Helena, and English Society was once more spreading its wings, flying off by land and sea to climes denied them for the better part of a decade.

Calling for a snifter of brandy—it was the afternoon, after all—she settled into the tiresome correspondence she'd done her best to ignore, piled high on a silver salver. Why did people persist in writing her when she didn't like the majority of them?

Still, one letter, more than two months old, earned a smile. It was from Lady Tremayne, usually based in London but traveling now in Greece.

> You will not believe the rumors flying, Sophia. There was that flurry of gossip, back in '13, that Benjamin, Lord Marworth, and Jane Fitzsimmons had been spotted exchanging vows at Gretna Green. As if Marworth would ever be so déclassé. Jumping the anvil indeed, not to mention the fact we all know they're both dead, and his title's gone anyway. What people won't do to stir embers long since cold.

And yet, since my arrival here, I'll admit to having been inundated with shocking, firsthand accounts. The young Duke of Devonshire insists that not two years ago, he saw them in Rome, laughing uproariously as they drank wine beside the Trevi Fountain.

Since Miss Fitzsimmons would never have tolerated such a public spectacle, I immediately dismissed his account.

Until I heard Mr. Byng had spotted them, as well. Traveling with his dog, Petunia, in Venice, he swears he saw them pass by on a gondola in the Grand Canal, Marworth himself at the helm, punting stick in hand! Supposedly, Petunia made a great fuss at the sight of her patroness, drawing their attention. When both smiled in her direction and waved, Byng saw something shocking. Miss Fitzsimmons was enceinte!

And now, there is evidence once more that a great conspiracy is afoot, although one of a most romantic nature. With my own eyes, I saw a young family admiring the Parthenon not one week past. The mother, so like Miss Fitzsimmons, was whispering about Greek gods and fables to an adorable little boy, while the father, a less civilized version of Marworth himself, looked on with eyes to make your heart quicken. What to think of it all? Are we such desperate souls, to imagine that ghosts from the past are in love and happy still?

As to that, Sophia couldn't say. Nor did she have the time to bother. In just a few days, she was expecting visitors from the sunny isle of Greece. A stunningly happy young family, where there was laughter in abundance, and expectations for the future hinged only on the sun's rise.

More from This Author (From *Once Upon a Wager* by Julie LeMense)

Praise for *Once Upon a Wager*:

"A beautifully written tale of a bet gone horribly wrong and a couple struggling to overcome his past mistakes. I *j'adore* a reunion story, and this one is truly captivating."—*Valerie Bowman, award-winning author of Regency romance*

"Julie LeMense strapped me in, spun me around, and sent me on a dizzying roller coaster of loge, anger, honor, passion and everything else in between."—A Novel Thought with Jess

"Ms. LeMense has penned a nearly flawless debut Regency romance that will have fans of the genre begging for more."—5 stars, *Chanticleer Book Reviews*

"Compelling and heartwarming without being overly sentimental. A refreshingly different historical romance. In short, I loved this book!"—*5 stars, Lil Miss Vix Reads*

July 1808
St. James Street, London

Alec Carstairs, heir to the eighth Earl of Dorset, looked down at the letter on his desk, torn between feelings of frustration and something else he refused to acknowledge. Her handwriting was as awful as ever—undisciplined, like the young woman herself—but he knew better than to blame any long-suffering governess.

Annabelle Layton did as she pleased. She always had, regardless of the consequences.

> Alec,
>
> I am sorry, as you well know. Two years is past time to forgive me, don't you think? The whole episode is best forgotten. You needn't miss Gareth's party again. I do not, I believe, have a sickness that is catching.
>
> Please say you will come.
>
> Your erstwhile friend,
>
> Annabelle Layton

A ragged sigh escaped him, the force of it sending the missive skittering across his desk, a Tudor-era monstrosity sent over from his family's London town home. Of course he'd forgiven her, if that was even the right word. She'd been so young then—just sixteen—uninhibited and free, with little thought for propriety or decorum. Forgetting the incident, however, was another matter entirely. It had irrevocably changed the way he saw her … to his everlasting shame.

"My sister insisted I hand deliver it," Gareth said, dropping himself into a tufted armchair across from the desk, startling Alec from his thoughts. He'd all but forgotten Layton's presence in the room, an unintended slight that had thankfully gone unnoticed. Alec's distraction would only have piqued Gareth's curiosity. After all, Gareth, like Annabelle, wasn't easily ignored. Both were golden haired and blue-eyed—a gift from the stunning Lady Layton. They'd been the boon companions of his otherwise lonely childhood. But none of them was a child anymore.

"Say yes, Carstairs. If you are any kind of friend, you'll not make me go back to Astley Castle by myself. God knows I'd rather stay in London."

So would Alec, but he undoubtedly had different reasons for that sentiment. "My schedule is very full, Gareth. My father has secured a new seat for me in the House of Commons, and I must memorize the current legislation. It sounds like another excuse, but it is not." And it wasn't. Not really. Alec felt the press of his new position closing in all around him: the impressive bachelor lodgings, the tailored wardrobe from Weston, the stacks of leather-bound folios packed with Parliamentary proposals. The eighth earl insisted that his son's surroundings reflect his recently elevated status.

"Have I ever told you your father frightens me? I swear his face would split down the center if he attempted a smile."

"He is stern," Alec admitted, "but only because he takes his responsibilities so seriously." As a child, he'd been frightened of his father, as well.

"Well, he is a spoilsport all the same. You're only twenty-five. Why must you bother with the Commons?"

"I'd rather talk about the party, Gareth. I should think you'd be eager to attend. It will celebrate *your* birthday, after all."

"Yes, but who knows what they've planned? Last year, the order of precedence going into dinner was decided not by titles, mind you, but by the high scores from an archery contest Annabelle organized out on the lawn."

Alec refused to smile, despite the temptation. "Surely she didn't lead the way into dinner? She hasn't even made her debut." To do so would have been highly improper. But not atypical.

"How did you know Annabelle won?"

"Of course she did. You're forgetting we taught her the finer points of the game." Just as they'd taught her to shoot pistols, bet on cards, and ride bareback. He'd had a hand, he supposed, in making her into the hoyden she'd become.

"Annabelle will always play to her interests," Gareth admitted. "Which means that this year, there will be lots of dancing at the party. She's mad for it, all of that spinning and skipping about. I ask you, who wants a Scottish reel back home when I can dance with the high-flyers in Covent Garden? Now there's a dance I don't mind doing."

An inappropriate image of Annabelle came to mind, but Alec forced it aside, turning his focus on her brother. "You look as colorful as any bird-of-paradise in the Garden, Gareth. That satin waistcoat is nearly blinding in the afternoon light. My eyesight may not recover."

"Just because Brummell dresses like an undertaker doesn't mean that I have to be similarly sepulchral. Especially when there is a party I must attend. Say you will come. I don't know the reason behind your estrangement with Annabelle—and do not deny there is one—but I'm certain that she's to blame. She can be a maddening creature. Still, she misses your friendship. She said … let me think … that it 'had more value than you have lately accorded it.' I had to promise to say exactly those words."

Ah, their friendship. Old and inviolable once. Annabelle's barbs, like her arrows, were always well aimed.

With a deep breath, and before he could stop himself, Alec took a sheet of parchment and scribbled a few words upon it. He then folded it upon itself. He extracted a stick of sealing wax from a side drawer, heating it briefly above the beeswax oil lamp on his desk. He dripped a small puddle of wax where the folds met, and pressed it with his signet ring. Satisfied the seal would hold fast against Gareth's attempts to loosen it, Alec handed him the note. "I will be there," he said. "But I have little doubt I will regret it."

Gareth merely chuckled. "If you're going to regret something, make the pain of it worthwhile. Come join me at The Anchor on Park Street. I plan on getting well and truly drunk before I meet up with Digby to play cards. It will lessen the sting of my certain defeat."

"Damien Digby is an ass. He makes you risk too much."

"I can only stand one respectable friend, Alec. And that would be you," Gareth added, "in case you're wondering."

"You say 'respectable' instead of 'boring' to spare my feelings, I know. Go on without me. If I'm to travel to Nuneaton for your birthday, there are things I must do." Like memorizing names, organizing arguments, and—above all else—practicing a brotherly smile.

After Gareth departed, Alec pushed away from his desk, and walked over to the study's large bay window, which looked out upon St. James Street below. Bracing his hands against the sun-warmed panes, he watched carriages and pedestrians move down the cobble-stoned thoroughfare, regretting his impulsiveness. Undoubtedly, his decision was a poor one. What would Annabelle read into his reply?

Annabelle,

I've missed our friendship, too. I will see you at Gareth's party. But you must promise to keep your clothes on.

• • •

As he waited for his father to join him in the library at Dorset House, Alec took a brief glance at its worn leather tomes, all lined up in an orderly fashion along dozens of age-darkened wood shelves. This was Henry Carstairs's domain, the inner sanctum where he built his political coalitions, and entertained allies with brandy after dinner. On the rare occasions Alec had been in London as a child, it had also been the room where Father meted out his punishments. Perhaps that was why Edmunds, their butler, had seated him here, rather than in the family drawing room. The earl's note had hinted at his strong displeasure, though Alec was long past the age of birch rods and bloodied hands.

As if summoned by his thoughts, the earl strode into the room, a sheaf of papers tucked under his arm, his reading spectacles perched on the edge of his nose, making his eyes seem owlish. Trim and fighting-fit, Father would make for a very intimidating owl indeed, though Alec now bested him in height by two inches. He was no longer the small, sickly boy who had so often been ignored, along with his mother. He'd finally earned his father's attention, even his respect, despite their high price. Standing quickly, he offered a quick bow. "Good morning, Father. You wished to see me."

"Take your seat," the earl said, settling into the large baronial chair behind his desk. "I was not happy to learn that you are going to Nuneaton for the Layton boy's fete, when you should be here preparing for the Commons."

"Even allowing for travel there and back, I will only be gone three days. I'll be bringing along the summaries prepared for me, and I've memorized the names of all the members, as well as their political positions."

His father shifted in the chair, displeasure obvious in the tight set of his jaw. "I expected you to join us for dinner tomorrow. Lord Fitzsimmons and his daughter, Jane, will be in attendance. He's proven a useful ally in Parliament, and the girl is a reliable and sober sort. She'd make a good wife for you."

Of late, Father had mentioned marriage repeatedly, and Miss Fitzsimmons in particular. "I'm sorry I was not informed of your plans," Alec replied. "I cannot attend. I've already accepted the invitation to Astley Castle."

"To travel there for a such a short trip, when our Arbury Hall will have to be readied. I think it an imposition."

The Hall, which bordered the Layton estate, was kept in a constant state of readiness, because Father expected nothing less. It wouldn't be wise, though, to point that out. "I won't be staying at the Hall. I'll stop by to have the carriage checked and to greet the servants, but I will sleep at the castle. They'll have a number of overnight guests."

"Those guests won't be from the best families, I can assure you. And the Layton boy is drinking and gambling himself into the grave. I don't like that you associate with him."

"I don't share his vices, Father."

"No, but never underestimate the allure of recklessness. The boy is shockingly irresponsible, and the girl is at an age now when your childhood friendship might be mistaken for something more."

"I am well aware of that."

"Annabelle Layton is the sort that invites scandal. The whole family is, which is something we can't afford, not if all my plans for you are to be realized."

"They are good people who mean no harm."

"They are remarkably odd. Lady Charlotte is weak-minded, and Sir Frederick … I've rarely met a more compulsive man. Nervous and awkward, but mention some sort of flying insect, and he'll prattle on for hours. Lepidopterology is all the rage, but I can't abide butterflies."

When Alec was a child, quiet in a lonely household, the Laytons had seemed exuberant, exotic even. They'd lived and loved with abandon, while he and his own mother had been starved of affection. Alec couldn't fight back a flash of anger at the memory. But those days were past. With hard work and dedication, he'd found a way to earn his father's love. And not just for himself.

But it was true that Gareth was increasingly a victim of his weaknesses. Just yesterday, he'd tried to talk Alec into a large wager. Lord Chetwiggin's grays were racing against Lord Sherford's blacks in a torchlit sprint on Hampstead Heath. Alec and Gareth would leave for Nuneaton beforehand, but Digby was placing a bet in Gareth's stead. Undoubtedly, it would be made for far more than he could afford.

"I'll not return with a passion for lepidopterology, Father. I can withstand a brief exposure to their family." And to Annabelle.

Those owlish eyes were fixed upon him, their expression severe.

"You mean to disagree with me on this?"

"Shall I break my word, then? That is not the man you've raised me to be. This will be a party in the country with old friends, and nothing more."

The room was ominously quiet.

"If you must go, then go," his father said at last. "But remember who you are, and what I expect. Don't do anything that will have unfortunate repercussions. And stay away from Annabelle Layton."

• • •

Annabelle was thrilled to see the familiar handwriting on the back of her note, but she was less thrilled reading it. In fact, only the most rigid self-control kept her from stomping one of her darling green half boots on the stone floor of the terrace. Could he not be done with it? Did he not remember the heat of that morning? The very air had simmered, like a pot set to boil. She'd been unable to sleep. Astley Castle's fountain, hidden from view in the formal gardens, had beckoned like the wellspring of salvation.

She'd known full well that her behavior was scandalous. Ladies did not swim in fountains after all, but the water had felt so wonderful. And she *had* been wearing clothes: a linen shift, even though the water made it rather revealing. Certainly, she'd not expected Alec to be out wandering the castle grounds at dawn, a witness to her shameless display. He had gone utterly still at the sight of her, like a pillar of salt caught between Sodom and Gomorrah.

Even now, she could remember his eyes. Something had burned in them, and she'd hoped, despite her embarrassment, that he'd finally understood she was no longer a child. That she could be more to him than a friend. But the past two years had laid waste to those notions. The only thing burning that day had been his indignation.

Later—after she'd been trussed back up in a suffocating corset and a long-sleeved gown—he'd warned her about the dangers a young woman could face, sounding just like Parson Withersby at a Sunday service. Not that the parson had ever been so breathtakingly handsome.

Since then, however, Alec had come up with an astonishing array of excuses to avoid her. The amusing letters they'd once exchanged with great regularity were now limited, on his part, to polite inquiries about her well being. He was too busy in London being molded into the man his father thought he should be. A man who was hidebound and self-important.

Startled from her pique by the sound of laughter, Annabelle leaned over the terrace balustrade, looking out onto the back lawn. Her parents were chasing butterflies—her mother's hair unbound and floating behind her, her father's shirttails flying like flags in the breeze, both of them swinging their nets with wild abandon. Their plan was to catch dozens of the colorful insects, so they could be released in the Great Hall during Gareth's party. However, she'd have to speak with Mother about that. Those plans had to be changed. Annabelle wanted this party to be remembered for its decorum. If only to shock Alec.

• • •

"Gareth, that is the largest trunk I've ever seen," she said the next morning as her brother burst into the hall in blur of color. "I hope it means you will be staying for a while. It would do both you and your purse some good."

"I can't be poorly dressed at my own birthday party," Gareth said, wrapping her in a quick hug after instructing the footmen to take his belongings to his room. He was wearing a bright green jacket over a puce-striped vest and fawn trousers—obviously a statement of high, if unfortunate, style. "Besides, there's nothing wrong with my purse. I've had a rush of luck at the tables lately, and I'm expecting to hear the news of my biggest win yet once Digby arrives."

"Who is this Digby? You've not mentioned him before."

"Damien Digby. I met him a few months back. He has got a gift for picking winners. I think you'll like him."

She doubted it. She didn't like anyone who indulged her brother's gambling habit. He regularly exceeded his allowance. Whenever he came home from London, he and Father closeted themselves in the study, arguing about money in angry whispers.

Of course, he invariably returned to the city with an additional bank draft. Her parents liked to joke that Gareth could charm the stripes off the famous zebra at Astley's Amphitheater. With a ready smile, he was so undeniably good-looking that most of her friends were madly in love with him. He got whatever he wanted. They both did.

Which is what made the matter of Alec Carstairs so infuriating.

"You shouldn't be spending so much of Father's money, Gareth. Have you forgotten that I'll be going to London for the Little Season in September?"

"How could I? You prattle on about it in every letter. I've warned all of my friends. We're going to decamp en masse to Brighton."

"I will ignore your insults," she said, fighting back a grin. "Tell me, what does Alec think about this Mr. Digby?"

"You can guess the answer to that, Annabelle. Honestly, Carstairs has forgotten how to have fun. Any day now, I expect to find he's gone old and arthritic."

Even so, he was still the most handsome man she'd ever seen. And tonight, she would not be ignored. Mrs. Markum from the village had made up the most beautiful dress for her. It was the palest of cream silks, shot through with silver thread, and delicately embroidered with tiny flowers. Her hair would be pulled back with the clips Father had given to Mother on their wedding day. They were shaped like butterflies, the wings sparkling with dozens of small diamonds.

Tonight, she would dare him to find a trace of the girl he pretended her to be.

• • •

Just as evening fell, Alec walked up the crushed stone drive to Astley Castle. Despite its rather grandiose name, it was more accurately a fortified manor house, although it did have a moat. Briefly the home of Lady Jane Grey, England's unfortunate Nine Days Queen, it had also served as a garrison for Cromwell's forces during the Civil War before passing into the Layton family. Tonight, however, the house gave no hint of its troubled history. Japanese lanterns were strung, not only in the trees leading up the drive, but also in those surrounding the house, and the effect was magical. In the early dusk, a gentle light bathed the grounds, softening the lines of the old home, coloring it with pale pinks and darker purples. Alec heard strains of music and conversation. In fact, it appeared to be a remarkably conventional party, which was something of a surprise. Surely, circus animals were lurking somewhere.

The oversized front door was open to the evening air, and dozens of people were assembled in the Great Hall, which was brightly lit with wall lanterns. Chandeliers decked with wax candles flickered high above as Gareth's parents received their guests. Sir Frederick, who often panicked in crowds, was hiding his misgivings well, and Lady Layton was radiant beside him. Gareth stood next to her, dressed in a colorful approximation of evening attire, but he seemed distracted. His eyes were darting the crowd and looking for someone. A footman with the champagne tray, no doubt. Alec did not see Annabelle.

But then familiar, melodious laughter washed over him, and he turned. A willowy, honey-tressed blonde stood at the center of a crowd of adoring men. Her face was hidden from view, but her gown—the color of moonlight—caressed her curves like a lover. Alec braced himself, every nerve taut. As if sensing his presence, she looked over her shoulder and smiled.

God in Heaven, he should never have come here tonight.

Annabelle had been only four years old the first time he saw her. He'd joined his mother on a neighborly visit to Astley Castle, and the little girl had utterly charmed him, struggling to sit still while Lady Layton served tea to her guests. Delicate, soft, and pink, like a rosy-cheeked doll, she'd roused all his protective instincts before kicking him in the shins to gain his attention.

If only he could see the girl she'd once been in the woman standing before him. Even two years ago, there had been hints of her, hiding in the body of a goddess. But there was nothing childlike about Annabelle now. She was spectacularly lovely, with arched brows, high cheekbones, and cornflower blue eyes that took his breath away.

Excusing herself from her admirers, she walked toward him with a slow smile. Then again, walking was not the right word. Swaying was the better choice, and all he could do was stand there, heart slamming in his chest as she approached, the gossamer silk gown caressing her curves. Were it dampened—as was the fashion with London's faster set—it would be almost transparent. Just like that morning when she had gone swimming in the fountain, casting a spell over him like a sorceress.

"Alec, how nice you could join us this evening. I worried that in the end, something pressing would keep you in London. So often in these past two years, that has been the case." Once, she'd have embraced him impulsively, laughing all the while. Now, she gave a surprisingly ladylike curtsey, extending one gloved hand. He leaned down to press a kiss upon it, and if his lips lingered a moment too long, he was rather proud of his self-control. It had been just enough to breathe in the scent of her—a familiar mix of honeysuckle soap and the lemon drops she loved. But there was also something new. Something dangerous.

"I wrote that I would be here, Annabelle. I am man who honors my obligations."

She tilted her head, angling it up toward him, her eyes bewitching beneath half-lowered lashes. "Is that what I am now? An obligation?"

She would scramble his wits if he wasn't careful.

"Of course not. We're old friends, despite the distance between us."

He'd been referring to the distance between London and Nuneaton, but he was certain she had leaned closer. His body all but screamed it.

"Perhaps we can ease that distance tonight."

God above. Did she have any idea how that might be interpreted? He managed a self-conscious pat on her shoulder before stepping back, hoping he appeared collected and calm, instead of dizzy with the nearness of her.

"You are looking very well," he said after a long pause. "How … big you have become."

And with that asinine statement, he turned on his heels, vanishing into the crowd.

• • •

Why must Alec be indifferent to her, when so many other men were eager to gain her attention? There was Horace Briarly, the squire's son from the village. He'd vowed his eternal love these past three years or more. Lord Percival Spencer, the rather rakish heir to a viscountcy in Warwickshire, made every excuse to visit her father with lepidopterological concerns—though it was obvious he had no interest in the hobby. And then there was the widower, Sir Boniface, an amateur artist. He'd already presented her with a number of lovely paintings, although it was embarrassing to have six portraits of oneself. Wherever Annabelle went, men seemed to sprout up like spring flowers.

But none of them was as endlessly *fascinating* as Alec Carstairs. So noble and decent. So restrained and responsible. The one reliable constant of her childhood, he'd become the man against whom she measured all others.

Not to mention the beauty of him. Wide shoulders, narrow hips, and long legs, all encased in immaculately tailored clothing. Dark brown hair, still wavy but shorter now than she remembered. Beautiful lips, wide and generous. Prominent cheekbones and a straight nose that flared slightly. Those toffee-colored eyes that always reminded her of Cook's caramels, still warm from the stove.

Gaining his attention this evening required a new strategy. But she couldn't plot effectively if she was caught up in a conversation with Horace, who was heading her way like a hound on a scent. She quickly blessed the wall of potted palms beside the door. With a quick movement, she slipped behind them, escaping out onto the drive.

As escapes went, it was poorly planned. It was a party, after all. Guests were getting out of their carriages and walking up the meandering stone pathway to the castle entrance. Distracted by thoughts of Alec, she walked directly into a small group of men who were newly arrived. One of them caught her with his arms, steadying her before she could knock both of them down. Glancing up at the blunt-featured man, she offered a hasty apology and spun away. He called after her, but she was in no mood to speak with strangers. She headed into the castle's elaborate gardens and the swiftly descending darkness.

Passing clipped boxwoods and yews set in a pattern dating to Elizabethan times, she followed a gravel path into the heart of the gardens where a Roman folly stood, reflected in a semicircular ornamental pond, her fountain at its center. The pond was filled with gold and silver fish, and as a child, she'd loved watching sunlight shimmer on their scales through the water. Several bubbled to the surface at her approach, hopeful and expectant, but tonight, she had nothing to offer but a half smile.

There was a bench hidden behind the folly, and she took a seat there. Her collision had wreaked havoc with the elaborate coiffure her maid, Mary, had created. Annabelle fumbled with an errant clip, but that sent another wave of heavy hair tumbling over her shoulders. It wouldn't do to be seen in this state. She could only imagine what Alec would think. At least, the new Alec. The one who was so stuffy. Thankfully, though, she was alone.

Until quite suddenly, she was not.

"I was sure my eyes had deceived me, but they did not. You are exquisite."

The voice belonged to a strange man, his approach almost silent in the soft grass. Annabelle merely edged further into the shadows. "Sir, I don't wish to be rude, but I would prefer to be alone."

"But your beauty holds me spellbound," he said easily, as if he'd practiced the line.

She looked up. It was the blunt-featured man. He had light brown hair and pale gray eyes, and while she could not guess at his age, he was far older than she. "This is hardly the time for false flattery. And the party is that way." She pointed needlessly toward the house.

He moved slowly toward her. "What is your name?"

"As you well know, it would hardly be proper for me to say. We've not been introduced." Nor should she be alone with him here in the dark.

"Such becoming modesty." He smiled, flashing uneven teeth. "But I insist on knowing who you are." He took another step closer as he slowly withdrew the glove covering his left hand. "Tell me, my dear, if I trailed my fingers down your cheek, would your skin be as soft as it appears?"

So he was that sort of man. "You should know that I always carry a small pistol on my person," she said, her voice impressively calm. "Just in case an unfortunate situation like this one should arise."

"Really?" His eyes gleamed in the darkness. "Why don't I feel my hands along your body, and see if I can discover the place where you've hidden it?"

"Touch her," another voice ground out, "and I will break both of your arms."

Alec. He'd followed her, after all. He was suddenly towering over the stranger.

"Carstairs, what an unpleasant surprise. The lady and I are having a private discussion."

Ignoring him, Alec turned to face her. "Are you all right?" Taking in her disheveled appearance, he added tersely, "Has he hurt you in any way?"

"No, I am fine," Annabelle replied, masking her relief. "I merely needed some fresh air."

"I meant no harm," the man said, raising his hands in mock surrender. "I was merely engaging in an innocent flirtation with a desirable woman."

"She's little more than a child," Alec bit out. And as offended as she was by his comment, this didn't seem like a time to argue.

"She is hardly a child, Carstairs," the man drawled. "If she were, I doubt you'd be treating me to such a manly display."

She could sense the tension in Alec. He was keeping his temper in check, but just barely.

"Who are you?" Annabelle asked. "Why are you here in my home?"

"Your home?" His eyes widened with surprise. "You must be Miss Layton, Gareth's sister. He and I are very close friends."

"Of late," she said, "he has been less particular in his friendships."

The stranger darkened at that. "As it turns out, we are business partners of a sort. I am Damien Digby, at your service."

Gareth had been wrong. She could not like Mr. Digby.

"How utterly perfect you are, Miss Layton. When your brother spoke of your beauty, I thought he exaggerated. I can see now he was being coy. I will look forward to seeing you inside."

With a cold look at Alec, he turned and strode purposefully toward the house.

• • •

"Don't you know enough not to run off without a proper escort, Annabelle?" Alec demanded, anger sharpening his voice.

At his tone, her own temper flared. "I was more than fine, Alec. I've grown … what was the word you used? Oh yes, big. I'm big now, like a sturdy tree out in the lawn. Perhaps if you think on it, you can come up with an even more unflattering term. In the meantime, I will take care of myself."

"Don't be foolish. You don't know what a man like that is capable of."

"You heard him say he meant no harm." Even as she spoke the words, she knew they were false. She'd seen the look in Digby's eyes.

"He is a cad, the very worst sort." Alec put a hand to the edge of his cravat, as if it were suddenly too tight. "And much as it pains me to say so, you are at an age when such men will seek you out."

"I cannot help the fact that I've grown up, Alec. I'm sorry the end result of it has been so unfortunate."

He met that statement with a long moment of silence, merely watching her in the moonlight, a muscle twitching in his jaw. "I don't think that is the right word."

She didn't want to find out which word he would choose instead. Her confidence had been battered enough for one evening. "I have to return to the party." She started to move away, but he put his hands on her shoulders to still her.

"Have you really taken to carrying around pistols, Annabelle?"

"Of course not. I was bluffing. I would never ruin the line of this lovely dress."

His eyes sparked briefly with amusement, and perhaps admiration. "Lovely as your dress is, you can't return to the party looking as you do. Let me help you."

He reached down to loosen one of the diamond clips tangled in her hair, and slowly worked it free, standing so close she had to remind herself to breathe. He smelled of sandalwood and crisp, clean linen. "This one will also have to be reset," he said, moving to the other clip, his amusement fading. In moments, the rest of her hair tumbled down to her waist, and he ran his fingers through its long length in an effort to smooth it. Then he cleared his throat, dropping his hands to his sides.

"I'm not much of a lady's maid." He tucked the clips into her gloved hands and stepped back.

"People will wonder what we've been doing out here in the dark," she said, daring him to think of her that way. But his face was inscrutable, and she fought back a stab of frustration. "Of course, no one would suspect you of misbehaving. You are far too honorable. You're practically my brother."

"I am not your brother, Annabelle. And I'm not as honorable as you think." Abruptly, he turned toward the castle. "Follow me to the servants' entrance, and go up to your room from there."

She hurried to keep up with his long strides. "Go straight to your maid," he called over his shoulder. "Dinner will be served soon. Your absence will be noticed if you don't hurry."

He was dismissing her, because she was a foolish girl he neither wanted nor needed. It was evident in every terse, clipped word.

When they reached the house, she passed quietly through the doorway leading into the kitchen. In the confusion, as the staff prepared trays of food to be brought up for dinner, she was able to slip by unnoticed. In moments, she was up the stairs.

• • •

Only when she'd vanished from sight did Alec allow his careful control to slip. The ghosts of his past were all around him. He and Gareth and Annabelle, rolling down the hillside over there on that warm spring day, laughing aloud as governesses and tutors ran after them, bemoaning grass stains and inappropriate behavior. That long ago summer night, sitting with Annabelle on the bench behind the folly, her hand in his, because while she loved to look up at the stars, she was frightened of the dark. That afternoon when he'd come down from Oxford for a visit, and she leapt into his arms. His only searing thought had been, "how beautiful you've become." That morning two years ago, when everything changed.

He hadn't been able to sleep. It had been intensely hot, even at that early hour of the morning, so he'd gone for a walk, hoping for a breeze. Hearing her laughter, he'd been drawn to it, never expecting to find Annabelle dancing in the fountain, a pagan goddess of the dawn, water coursing over every nearly naked curve. The pink tips of her breasts had been visible through her wet shift, and he'd felt like the worst sort of lecher for wanting her. Even now, he hardened at the memory, his mouth dry as dust.

Annabelle was free in a way he'd never been, full of life and laughter. She was warm, vital, and sparkling, like flames in the night. But never had someone been more unsuited to the path that he must follow. His happiness was not his own. It did not matter that he wanted her, that he could no longer deny his desire. How shocked she'd be to know that while he had been untangling her hair, he'd been imagining it wound around him, her body naked beneath his own.

Printed in Great Britain
by Amazon

46261298R00179